'Some books just demand the adjective "wonderful". This is one of them.' *The Times*

'Itani's evocation of Grania's world of silence, and the myriad ways we communicate with those we love, is masterly, as is her rendition of hell in the Flanders mud. Despite the dark subject matter, this is a book filled with light.' *Guardian*

'*Deafening* has a very particular grace and eloquence, and the spareness of the writing beautifully complements the power of the emotions which Frances Itani describes.' Helen Dunmore

'There's not a single false gesture in Frances Itani's *Deafening*. Despite its subjects – war, romance, disability – it's a story of careful, measured emotion, bleached of all sentimentality . . . every page of this story betrays the hands of a mature writer who knows exactly what she's doing.' *Christian Science Monitor*

'*Deafening* is a remarkable and absorbing first novel. Itani's writing is clear-headed and sure-handed; her strong characters will not leave you.' Charles Frazier

'The book is a meditation on silence and communication, where the alienation and confusion of war become metaphors for the way in which language can be a minefield for the deaf. In a world filled with sound, Grania's story is a stirring reminder that human engagement occurs on various levels.' *Literary Review*

'*Deafening* is a slow and graceful read, richly textured, keenly felt and witnessed and at times almost unbearably moving.' *Quill & Quire*

'A tender tale of love against the odds.' *Company*

'Exceptional novel . . . a remarkable accomplishment.' Alistair Macleod

'A lovely novel about a woman's deafness and the horror of war.'
Daily Mirror

'Itani takes a subject that could have been treacly and sentimental but makes it into something admirably understated, touching and restrained. She writes lyrically about the magical, mysterious way that language, intimacy and trust enable a deaf woman to hear the sounds of the sea and of music – and of how cataclysmic historical events can touch, shatter and ultimately strengthen even the most interior life.' *People*

'The subtlety of Itani's writing is nothing short of remarkable . . . her voice is pitch perfect . . . Itani is unquestionably a prodigious talent.' *Toronto Star*

'War and deafness are the twin themes of this psychologically rich, impeccably crafted debut novel set during WWI . . . remarkably vivid, unflinching descriptions of his ordeal . . . eloquently expresses Itani's evident, pervasive faith in the unexpected power of story to not only represent life but to enact itself within lives. Her wonderfully felt novel is a timely reminder of war's cost, told from an unexpected perspective.' *Publisher's Weekly*

'I found this an exquisite novel that gave me some understanding of the isolation and frustration for living in silence and a new respect for language.' *Manly Daily*, Australia

'An impressively daring first novel from Canada immerses us in both the world of the deaf and the world of WWI trench warfare . . . Husband and wife embody Itani's theme: the power and reach of love – love that falters only in the face of the unknowable. Itani never loses control of her tricky material: the result is an artistic triumph.' *Kirkus Reviews*

'A superb novel' *Winnipeg Free Press*

'Less a love story than an inventive fusion of a deaf woman's narrative and a soldier's tale, Itani's American debut unfolds with slow, deliberate eloquence and brilliantly described sights and sounds. Jim and Grania pine as wartime separated lovers do, but their story's real strength is their separate, if parallel, struggles to deal with their unforgiving surroundings. Her original treatment of classic wartime romance will make Itani's readers want more.' *Booklist*

'The novel is studded with haunting perceptions of soundlessness.' *Independent*

'It reminds me of that quiet authority I saw in *Cold Mountain*. I had the same feeling in the pit of my stomach. It's the sort of book that you read and want to ask the author where she learned all this . . . She's writing about language from the point of view of a deaf woman and she did something the best I've ever seen done anywhere besides James Joyce's *Portrait of the Artist as a Young Man*. She starts out with a very simplistic, naive youthful point of view and it matures with the character. That is so hard to pull off.' Kaye Gibbons, *Atlanta Journal Constitution*

'This is a psychologically rich deeply atmospheric and exquisitely told story.' *Woman & Home*

'Itani has the power not only to make us see and hear, but to believe.' *Hamilton Spectator*

Frances Itani is the award-winning author of four acclaimed short story collections including *Leaning, Leaning Over Water* and three poetry collections. She has also written a children's book, and was poetry editor of *Canadian Forum* for several years. She grew up in Quebec, has travelled extensively, and now divides her time between Ottawa and Geneva. *Deafening* is her first novel.

Frances Itani

Deafening

SCEPTRE

Copyright © 2003 by Writes Inc. Itani

First published in Canada in 2003 by HarperCollins Canada
First published in Great Britain in 2004 by Hodder and Stoughton
A division of Hodder Headline

A Sceptre Paperback

1 3 5 7 9 10 8 6 4 2

A CIP catalogue record for this title is available from the British Library

ISBN 0340 82893 5

Printed and bound in Great Britain by
Clays Ltd, St Ives plc

Hodder Headline's policy is to use papers that are natural, renewable
and recyclable products and made from wood grown in sustainable
forests. The logging and manufacturing processes are expected to
conform to the environmental regulations of the country of origin.

Hodder and Stoughton Ltd
A division of Hodder Headline
338 Euston Road
London NW1 3BH

The Artificial Method is a system founded by one Heinicke, a Saxon, who pursued successfully the occupations of farmer, soldier, schoolmaster, and chanter. . . . This system aims at developing, by unnatural processes, the power of speech, and the educating of the ear. It takes a much longer time to educate the pupils by this system than by other methods, and more painful efforts on the part of the pupil. Indeed in many cases it is so painful to the poor deaf-mute as to cause blood to issue from the mouth.

Canadian Illustrated News, August 1, 1874

Magic Lantern Views:

At first I saw the picture of Hon. R. L. Borden and our teacher told us that he is the Premier of Canada. The next picture I saw was King Albert I of Belgium. Then another one was King George V. He looks like the Czar of Russia. I saw the pictures of some German buildings. One of them was a Cathedral on which the English soldiers had dropped bombs. They did right, as many Germans dropped bombs in England. They were doing just the same, and not unjustly. I saw Germans riding in carriages through Belgium. They were boastful as they did not ask the people's permission. Many soldiers marched on the road.

Gertie Freeman
The Canadian, May 1, 1915
Belleville, The Ontario School for the Deaf

1902

"Your name," Mamo says. "This is the important word. If you can say your name, you can tell the world who you are."

"Graw . . ."

"Sounds like claw. Like the claw on the cat that prowls at the back. The one your father won't allow in the hotel—or in the house either, for that matter."

Grania has been watching closely but she's not certain what her grandmother has just said.

"Claw," Mamo says again. "Watch my throat, watch my lips."

"Claw."

Mamo nods. "Good. I believe this is coming from your memory. 'Graw' is the part that means love. Now, say Graw-nee-ya." Mamo bares her teeth. Her lips shape the child's name in separate parts. The way Grania sections an orange and puts the segments back together again to make the orange whole.

"Graw-nee-ya." Grania bares her teeth and Mamo laughs.

"Is that what I look like? Don't try so hard. Say it easily. Graw-nya. Over and over. Clearly and well."

But her older brother, Bernard, calls her Grainy. Has done since the week she was born, and won't stop now just because the scarlet fever she had last winter made her deaf. Bernard's lips smile when he says the end of her name.

With her sister, Tress, it's different again. When Tress calls her Graw, her jaw drops. Tress and Grania have already begun to make up their own language, with their hands.

Mother's lips make a straight line. She does not smile or laugh when she says that Grania must pay attention every second, every minute. If she doesn't, people will think she's stupid. She has to be ready all the time.

Ready? For what?

To break through the silence.

But the silence also protects. Grania knows. Being inside the silence is like being under water. Only when she wants to surface, only then does she come to the top.

Mamo calls the family together: Mother, Father, Bernard, Tress, even Patrick, who has only recently begun to speak himself.

"Don't treat her differently," Mamo tells them. "Talk to her the way you did before she was sick. Include her in everything. Don't leave her out. She may be only five years old but never stop speaking to her, whether she understands or not. Encourage her to talk back. In a month, she'll be six and she is going to need schooling."

Mother has not made up her mind about schooling. Twice a week, she goes to the Catholic church and prays that Grania's hearing will come back. Even though the priest shakes his head, Mother has not given up hope.

Father looks at his third child, his red-haired daughter, her brows scrunched, eyes intent, her glance flitting from one pair of lips to another. Father tries to keep his sorrow at bay. He knows that the child will never hear. Dr. Clark's diagnosis has been emphatically clear.

Patrick, the baby, walks from one pair of knees to another, balancing as he goes. "Talk," he says, imitating Mamo. "Talk, talk."

I

1903–1905

Chapter 1

A deaf child will learn 300 to 500 words in a year if at all intelligent. First, the child is taught the sounds and then how to combine them.

Lecture, The Toronto Fair

Deseronto, Ontario

"Go to my room." Mamo is pointing to the floor above. "Bring the package on my bureau."

Grania watches her grandmother's lips. She understands, pushes aside the heavy tapestry curtain that keeps the draught from blowing up the stairs, and runs up to the landing. She pauses long enough to glance through the only window in the house that is shaped like a porthole, even though it's at the back of the house and looks over land, not water. She peers down into the backyard, sees the leaning fence, the paddock and, over to the right, the drive sheds behind Father's hotel. Far to the left, over the top of the houses on Mill Street, she can see a rectangle of field that stretches in the opposite direction, towards the western edge of town. A forked tree casts a long double shadow that has begun its corner-to-corner afternoon slide across the field. Remembering her errand, Grania pulls back, runs to Mamo's room, finds the package tied up in a square of blue cloth and carries it, wrapped, to the parlour. Mamo pulls a low chair over beside her rocker. Her rocker moves with her, out to the veranda, back to the parlour, out to the veranda again.

"Sit here," her lips say.

Grania watches. Her fingers have already probed the package on the way down the stairs, and she knows it is a book. At a nod from Mamo she unties the knot and folds back the cloth. The first thing she sees on the cover is a word, a word picture. The word is made of yellow rope and twines its way across the deck of a ship where a bearded captain steers and a barefoot boy sits on a rough bench beside him. The boy is reading a book that is identical to the one in Grania's hands—it has the same cover. The sea and sky and sails in the background are soft blues and creams and browns.

Grania knows the rope letters because, after the scarlet fever, she relearned the alphabet with Mamo. The yellow letters curve and twist in a six-letter shape.

"*Sunday*," Mamo says. "The title of the book is *Sunday*, but you may keep the book in your room and look at it any time you want. Every day, we will choose a page and you will learn the words under the picture. Yes?" Eyebrows up. A question.

The book is for her. This she understands. *Yes*. Her fingers roam the cover but she has to be still or she will give Mamo the fidgets.

"There are many words in the book," Mamo says. "So many words." She taps her fingertips against the cover. "Some day, you will know them all." She mutters to herself, "If you can say a word, you can use it," not knowing how much Grania has understood. "We will do this, word by word—until your parents make up their minds to do something about your schooling. You've already lost one year, and a valuable part of another."

Mamo's finger points at the book and her eyes give the go-ahead flicker. Grania opens the stiff cover and turns the blank sheet that follows. The word *Sunday* is on the inside, too, but this time its letters are dark and made of twigs instead of yellow rope. The page that follows the twigs is in colour.

A brown-and-white calf has stopped on a grassy path and is staring at a girl. The girl is approaching from the opposite direction. She seems to be the same size and age as Grania; she might be seven or eight. Only the back of her can be seen—blue dress, black stockings, black shoes. Her hat, daisies tumbling from the crown, droops from one hand. A doll wearing a red dress dangles limply from the other. The doll's hair is as red as Grania's. No one in the picture is moving. The calf looks too startled to lift a hoof.

Grania points to two words beneath the picture and looks at Mamo's mouth.

"'BOTH AFRAID,'" Mamo reads.

The first sound erupts from Grania's lips. "BO," she says. "BO."

Mamo makes the *TH* shape with her tongue. "BO-TH."

Grania tries over and over, watching Mamo's lips. *TH* is not so easy. She already knows *AFRAID*. Afraid is what she is every night in the dark.

"Practise," Mamo tells her. She lifts herself out of the rocker, leaving behind the scent of Canada Bouquet, the perfume she chose because of its name and because she chose this country and because of the stench of the ship she left behind many years ago, and because Mr. Eaton sends the perfume from his mail-order catalogue in tiny bottles that cost forty-one cents. The air flutters like a rag as she walks away.

Grania breathes deeply, inhaling the scent. She sniffs the closed book and squeezes it to her as if it might get away. *Both* and *afraid* roll together, thick and half-new on her tongue. She runs upstairs to the room she shares with her older sister. Tress is stretched out reading her own book, *The Faeries*. Sometimes, Mamo and Tress read aloud to each other, after Tress walks home from school. Grania watches their lips, but she doesn't know the stories.

"Say," Grania says to Tress. She points to the words beneath the picture. "Say in my ear."

Tress's glance takes in the new book. She knows it is a gift from Mamo. "What's the use?" she says. "You won't hear." She shakes her head, *No*.

"Shout," says Grania.

"You still won't hear."

"Shout in my ear." She narrows her voice so that Tress will understand that she is not going to go away. She turns her head to the side and feels Tress's cupped hands and two explosive puffs of air.

Tress listens as Grania practises, "BOTHAFRAID BOTH-AFRAID BOTHAFRAID."

"Pretty good," her mouth says. She shrugs and goes back to *The Faeries*.

*

Supper, like all meals, is eaten at the big oval table—the family-only table—in the private corner of the hotel dining room, next door. All through the meal Grania thinks of the brown-and-white calf and the girl in the blue dress. She sees them in her head when she walks along Main Street with Mamo in the early evening, and when she lies in her bed later, eyes open in the dark.

"Bothafraid," her voice says softly. She doesn't want Tress, across the room, to hear. A breeze wisps through the window sash above her sister's bed.

Tress's window faces the slope of roof that tilts towards the upper balcony of the hotel. From up here, house and hotel appear to be joined, though they are not; there is a roofed, open passage-way between. A second bedroom window looks over Main Street and the Bay of Quinte, a large bay that slips in from the great Lake Ontario, which is part of the border between Canada and United States. A single maple tree grows up past this front window of the girls' room.

Almost every family activity takes place on the short stretch of road that is the Main Street of town. To the east, not far past Naylor's Theatre, Main Street ends where land meets bay. The western end of Main, where Grania lives, tips up to join the old York Road, now Dundas Street, which leads west through Mohawk Indian lands and on to the city of Belleville, twenty miles farther along the bay. To the east, the same road passes through the northern part of town and leads to Napanee, Kingston and the St. Lawrence River. Much of the town of Deseronto lies below this road, on the edge of the bay.

The town is like an overgrown village, really, but the Rathbun industries have been here for years and have made it a company town that boasts a railway, and steamers, and numerous enterprises sprawled along the waterfront. Many of the factories and stacks of lumber, the mill, the coal sheds, the railway-car shops, the tracks and the turntable for the engines lie between Main Street and the shore. On both sides of Main there is a mixture of houses and places of business: telegraph office, confectioner, baker, grocer around the corner, Chinese laundry with steam-covered windows, gentlemen's tailor, general store, *Tribune* printing office, post office with its high clock tower, barber on the other side of the street, Naylor's Theatre towards the end, harness shop, fire hall and hardware. On the back streets are the undertaker, more grocers and bakeries, police and library in one building—library is where Aunt Maggie works—community halls and churches, and the billiard hall. Mamo names the buildings when she walks with Grania through the town, but Grania knows that she is permitted to visit only grocer, butcher and post office when she is on her own.

Father's hotel is always busy because it is on the corner of Mill Street and Main, directly across from the railway station and the wharf, where the steamers dock.

In the girls' upstairs room in the house beside the hotel, there is no window over Grania's bed. Her side is wall. Wall on the right, windows front and left. She has learned right and left from Mamo. She thinks of the *Sunday* book and the new words beneath the picture. Neither calf nor girl will ever move towards each other. They will be waiting for her when she wakes in the morning and opens the cover. She will stare at them and there they will be, face to face, looking at each other on the page.

*

"You're smart," Mamo tells her. They are on the veranda and Mamo has brought the rocker outside. Mamo is relentless. She articulates firmly and carefully into the air, and Grania is expected to keep up. "You could read lips before you were deaf. When your parents wanted to talk—grownup talk—they had to turn their backs to whisper because you were so nosy. Do what you've always done. Before you were sick. You're the one in the family who sees."

Grania watches Mamo point to her own eyes. "Since you were a tiny baby, you've seen what's around you. As soon as you could raise your head, you peered up over the side of your cradle." She laughs, thinking of this.

Grania knows when Mamo is talking about baby times. She can tell from the softening in Mamo's face.

"Did I have thick sense?"

"Thick what?"

"When I was a baby. Aunt Maggie says I have thick sense. I know what she will do before she knows."

Mamo smiles. When she smiles there is an up-and-down line between her eyebrows. "I see." She holds her arms open, and Grania walks into them and waits while Mamo smacks a kiss onto her forehead.

Mamo turns sideways from the waist and draws a six in the air with her index finger. Grania watches the number assume its invisible shape.

"Six. Six-TH sense, not thick. If you have it, you shouldn't be talking about it."

Now Mamo's pointing finger makes a circle. "I'm going to turn you around—keep your eyes open, wide open. When you stop, tell me what you see. Understand?"

A game. Grania understands. She feels Mamo's hands on her shoulders and allows herself to be turned. Once. Twice. When she stops she is facing the end of her own veranda, looking between the pillars that support the hotel balcony, a dozen feet away.

She turns back to Mamo.

"Now look at me," Mamo says. "Use voice, no hand signals. Keep the language you already have. What do you see?"

"Wood post." This comes out high.

"Bring your voice down." Mamo lowers her palm through the air. *She's* using hand signals. "Colour?"

"White. Uncle Am and boys painted." Two of her cousins had come to town from a farm near Bompa Jack's, to help paint. That night, they were allowed to sleep in an upstairs room of Father's hotel.

"*The* boys painted."

"Not Bernard. He worked in dining room on paint day."

"What else?"

"Man."

"*A* man. Who?"

"Mr. Conlin. Beside telegraph office." She has also seen the Telegraph sign nailed between two poles, but she doesn't mention this.

"Wearing?"

Grania shrugs.

"Look again."

One more look. She tries to focus, remember. Turns back.

"Funny hat. He wears *the* hat inside *the* post office where he works."

"Good girl. Colour?"

"Like coal bin. The coal bin."

"What else?"

"Hat is round like Uncle Am's but with a hole punched in."

"I know," Mamo says, to herself this time—she's forgetting the game. "He won't replace it. He's too proud." She sits forward. "The fight was a few years back and he won't buy a new hat."

"Fight?"

"Ah, you read my lips even when I talk to myself. He helped your father get some rowdies out. They came in on the steamer. They weren't Irish, those rowdies. Well, they did manage to get them out, sure enough." She leans back again in the rocker. "Someone must have spilled salt that day."

"Salt?"

"Means a fight. Never mind. Look again. Is there a band on the hat?" Mamo's fingers curl to create the width of a band. *More hand signals.*

"Dark." Grania's hands instinctively cross in front of her face, semaphore flags. She cannot know that two years later she will be taught the same sign.

"What is Mr. Conlin doing?"

This time, Grania doesn't need a second look. "Wait for Cora to pass because Cora is nosy. Then chew tobacco and go back to post office. The post office."

"You're the one who's the Nosy Parker."

Jack Conlin turns in their direction, and waves.

*

At night, Grania tiptoes across the rag rug, counting six steps between beds. She crouches by her sister's bed, waiting. Tress has told her that the springs creak and will give them both away if Grania climbs in beside her. Mother and Father sleep in the next room and Mother will be listening.

"No talking," Mother has warned. "Grania is not to leave her bed." It was to Tress that she said this when she came to say good night, but Grania saw the frown on Mother's face and read her lips before she finished speaking.

There is something else Grania has to consider in the darkness— the walls. Aunt Maggie, who lives with Uncle Am in the tower apartment above the post office, told Grania that the walls have ears. Mamo agreed that this was true, and she and Aunt Maggie smiled while Grania weighed the information. Every night now when Grania goes to bed, she scrunches as far away from the wall as she can because she does not want the wall to hear. She does not want to fall into the place where the wall swallows sound.

A shadow appears at the front window where the branches of the maple stretch up. *Things that move, things that don't move.* The shadow slides across the oval mirror with the reed trim, and across the framed picture of daffodils. It slides past the washstand and jug, and above the bureau and over the sampler Mother stitched when she was fourteen years old, lines from "The Breastplate of Saint Patrick." *God's eye for my seeing, God's ear for my hearing.*

The shadow slips out of the room. "Watch for things that move," Mamo has taught Grania. "Watching will keep you safe."

Shadows sometimes take Grania by surprise. Under the moon there are shadows. There are times when she walks outside with Mamo or Bernard in the evening, and electric lights shine out of a window and make not one but two shadows that glide beside her. She is startled by this, and keeps a close watch until the shadows merge again into one.

From her crouched position on the floor she allows herself to sink to the rag rug. In the same movement—holding back, even as her body leans forward—her shoulder nudges the edge of her sister's bed. Tress's hand slides out from beneath the sheets and slips into her own. Tress shifts some of the blankets over the side and bunches them to cover Grania's shoulders. The two hold hands and sleep, one on, one off the bed, all through the night.

*

Mamo takes her by the hand and leads her to the clock in the front hall, the one that was carried in the burlap bag with the wide shoulder strap, the bag stitched by Grandfather O'Shaughnessy himself. He carried the clock all the way from the beautiful land called Ireland, where he and Mamo were born in the same town, and grew up and loved each other and married. When Grandfather died on the ship and was buried at sea near the coast of their new country, it had fallen to Mamo to carry the clock. When they reached Quebec, she and her four children, two daughters and two sons—Grania's mother, Agnes, the eldest—hoisted the O'Shaughnessy trunk, the bundles, the clock in the burlap bag, and left the ship. They staggered to shore while their legs gave out beneath them. As weak as they were, they were glad to have their feet on land, even though they were facing a second journey. They travelled overland to Mystic, Quebec, where Mamo had a cousin, the only person she knew from the old country. Later, when Mamo's sons were old enough to work and her daughters to marry, they moved to Deseronto on Lake Ontario. All of this happened before Grania was born.

Mamo gave the O'Shaughnessy clock to Mother and Father when they were married. The clock is as tall as Grania's arm is long, fingertip to shoulder, and stands on the pine table in the front hall. It has two short posts that come out at the top, posts that did not snap off during the long sea journey. Mamo gave away the clock but not the burlap bag, which is stored in the trunk along with the small wooden cross she placed there the day her husband was buried at sea.

Mamo stops the clock and turns it towards her, so that only she can see its face. She places Grania's hand against its side. The hand accepts smoothness, cool and polished wood.

"I want you to *feel* time," Mamo tells her. "If my hand can feel the chimes and the ticking, so can yours."

Grania watches Mamo's lips and stares into the shadowy end of the hall while her hand accepts the pulse of the clock. She feels the ticking against the base of her fingers and into the joints where fingers meet palm. Mamo stops the pendulum. The pulse stops and Grania looks up to Mamo's face, and Mamo resets the hands of the clock.

"Ready? Count. How many chimes?"

New sensation. *Th-th-th*—a determined message, arriving through the skin. It stops.

Grania has been counting. "Five. Five o'clock."

"Clever girl. Try again."

Mamo signals.

"Not," says Grania. "Not sounding."

"Good. Now?"

"Three." Each chime pushes into her hand more strongly than the chime before.

Mamo puts a key into the face of the clock and sets it for the last time. She signals, eyes laughing.

"Twelve," says Grania, without using her hand.

"Monkey," says Mamo. "Now you're guessing. But you're right. And being right has nothing to do with your thick sense."

*

Father stays in his hotel office most of the time, because he has business things to do. It is hard work to own a hotel, he says. Everything must run smoothly and the guests have to be satisfied and the food must be good. Mother and her helper, Mrs. Brant, cook the food. Father sits at the head of the family table in the hotel dining room during dinner and supper but he is never there for breakfast. Father calls himself a wine merchant and sometimes he smells like wine, or damp fruit. His smells are different from everyone else's. He has a moustache that curls at each end and smells like tobacco mixed with wax. He wears a ribbed vest with six buttons that Grania has counted, and a watch on a chain that is hooked through number five buttonhole on the vest. Father has broad thick hands, Irish hands that know how to work, he says. He has wavy hair and he wears a silver ring on the little finger of his right hand. One eyelid droops and he says that it is lazy. He has a brother in town—Uncle Am, the caretaker of the big post office building halfway along Main Street. Father's town friends are Uncle Am and Jack Conlin, the postmaster.

Father wears a bow tie, like his own father, Bompa Jack, when Bompa Jack gets dressed up. Father has a new puppy, Carlow, who is allowed to sleep in Father's office. Carlow has a brown patch that circles his left eye. His legs are white, and his back is brown. Grania is permitted to take Carlow outside at the back of the house, as long as they stay inside the fenced area. Carlow is never permitted upstairs in the bedrooms.

Grania shouts commands to Carlow. She makes up sounds and he obeys. But he does not obey Tress or Bernard or Patrick. It is Grania's voice that Carlow understands. Grania protects Carlow from the cat that prowls at the back. The cat that lives in the drive sheds.

Sometimes, when Grania is in the yard, Mrs. Brant opens the loading window at the back of the hotel where she works in the kitchen. If she sees Grania, she slides two raisin cookies across the flat ledge, one for Grania and one for Carlow. Mrs. Brant is a Mohawk woman and she has dark hair and dark eyes and a kind round face. She puts a finger to her lips when she slides the cookies across, and Grania knows that this is a secret between them. Grania loves Mrs. Brant.

Father makes certain that his children don't make a ruckus when they are playing, and that they know their manners at the table. "Use your knife and fork," he tells them. "Don't chew with your mouth open. It's rude."

"What?"

"Not what, Grania, pardon." Grania turns away, her timing split-second. What she can't see she can't be expected to understand.

Father's moustache hangs over his upper lip, and sometimes Grania doesn't know what he is saying. She peers and strains to see, but when his words are hidden she has to ask Tress what he has said. Father doesn't like being asked to repeat his words. On certain days, he goes to Grew the barber on the other side of Main Street and along the boardwalk to have his moustache trimmed. On those days Grania understands. But soon, the moustache grows thick and covers his lip again. Even so, Father sometimes says to Grania, "You don't miss much, my darling." And that she understands.

Grania dreams about Father standing in the doorway of his office. One of his large Irish hands, the hand with the ring, rests against his watch. Father talks to her in the dream and his face is troubled because he thinks Grania is lost. She sees *him* but he can't see her. His lips are moving but the moustache hangs over them and she does not understand. She is clenched with fear and runs towards him but he still doesn't see her. His lips stretch and distort. He gives up on the speaking language and tries to signal with his hands. But he does not know the hand language—not the one invented by Grania and Tress. And though he looks everywhere, he still can't see her.

Father loves Grania. She knows this in the dream. But because he is so sure that she is lost, he turns away and goes back inside his office. Grania is desperate now. She shouts after him, the way she shouts at Carlow, but Father does not turn around. Carlow bounds out through the office door and leaps at her, wagging his tail. Carlow always understands Grania's voice.

*

A warm night. A soft breeze lifts in from the bay. Hotel guests, the women, are seated on the upstairs veranda only a few feet across the roof from where the sisters lie in their beds. It is long past the supper hour and the women occupy the row of rattan chairs that face the water. Directly below, on the street-level veranda, their husbands keep their own company, drinks in hand, spittoons at their feet. Bernard, the only one of the children old enough to help in the hotel in the evenings, is working at the desk in the lobby.

As soon as Mother says good night and shuts the bedroom door, the hand signal comes from Tress, palm held high for silence. The moment the hand comes down Grania slips off the mattress, all the while watching Tress for a sign that will warn her if she is making noise. She tiptoes across the rag rug, sits down and tucks her feet beneath her gown. Father will not return to the house until the last hotel guest is settled for the night. Mother's whereabouts are not so easy to predict. Sometimes she stays in the downstairs kitchen or parlour; sometimes she is next door in the hotel kitchen, planning or preparing meals for the next day. Mother's cooking is so good, people come to stay just because of the food.

Tress pulls herself up inch by inch until she is kneeling on the mattress and can peer through the zigzag tear in the blind. Light from the hotel veranda filters through, enough to illuminate her face. Her dark hair is pulled back, tucked behind her ears. Grania wags her hand, showing her sister which way to shift, *this way*, *that way*, until the zigzag of light falls across Tress's lips. She watches the words spill out while a spying Tress describes the row of women known to them only as the *travelling ladies*. Tress elaborates the pleats and folds of a muslin dress, the laced leather boots, the pearl moon brooch, the buckled belt, the cameo, the style and curl of hair. In childish hand language, with words formed by Tress, and with stifled laughter that threatens to expose them, they create fantasy lives for the women they spy upon. Women who have means and leisure. Unsuspecting ladies who do not know themselves to be observed.

Grania, as she watches Tress report on the ladies, is not afraid. Not as long as she can keep her eyes open, not as long as Tress stays awake, not while words spill their shapes into the zigzag of light across her sister's lips. Not as long as the two of them keep watch side by side against the dark.

*

Mamo holds the book while Grania inspects the picture. There are four words on this page. A curly-haired boy is straddling the corner of a wooden chair that is too high and too big for him. The curly hair makes her think of long-legged Kenan, their friend who is in Tress's class at school and who lives with his uncle on Mill Street. Kenan has no mother or father. The boy in the picture wears a sailor suit, wide collar, short pants, two buttons on the side of each pantleg. In his left hand he holds an open book that is propped tightly against his chest. In his right hand he holds a partly eaten apple. His eyes are dark and he looks out of the picture and past Grania. The picture and the words are black and white.

"'HE TAKES A BITE.'"

Mamo points as she pronounces, pausing so that Grania can examine each word and recognize the separations between. "He - takes - a - bite." Mamo snaps her teeth after the word bite, and laughs at herself.

The boy in the picture is thinking. Maybe he would rather be reading instead of eating. Maybe he should put the book away before he starts to eat. Maybe he is hanging on to the book for dear life so that no one will yank it away. Maybe, like Grania, it is the only book he has.

"Say the words," Mamo says. "Watch my lips, watch my throat."

In her excitement, Grania's voice runs high. The words dissolve into one another and she feels them drift away.

"Slowly." Mamo frowns and flaps her fingers in front of her lips. "You're like a house on fire. Try again but keep your voice close." Mamo's palms press against her chest. *Close. Keep the words close.*

"House on fire?"

"Means hurry too much. Now try again and then practise upstairs or outside. 'HE TAKES A BITE.'"

Grania takes the book to Tress, who reads the words silently before she shouts them down the canal of Grania's ear. "He takes a bite, he takes a bite, this won't do any good!"

But nothing will stop Grania. When she is alone she stands on tiptoe on the stoop at the back, behind the laundry, and she watches her reflected mouth in the narrow window. *Hetakesabite.* She studies each word separately. She holds her voice as close to herself as she can. It is like pressing a pillow against her chest, the way the boy in the picture presses the book to his sailor suit. Grania keeps her voice close to the front of her body and makes it stay in that one held place.

*

Night after night, she tiptoes across the rag rug. The rug feels as if it is moving beneath her feet. Something taps at her from behind. She crouches low and wonders if her breathing is loud. Does she dare nudge Tress to inch over? No, Mother will hear, Mother will be angry. Grania waits for a signal from Tress but nothing comes. She sinks all the way to the floor. She falls asleep, shivering, while trying to keep her eyes open to ward off the dark.

Tress finds her in the early morning and heaps blankets on top of her. When it is time to get dressed for breakfast, she shakes Grania awake. It is Saturday. They fold down the covers and the ribbed spreads, and they air out their beds the way Mamo has taught them. After that, Tress beckons Grania, first to the bureau and then to their shared narrow closet with its rack of wooden pegs. From hooks and shelves Tress pulls stockings, soft belts, under-drawers, scarves. Anything long that can be tied. She puts a finger to her lips, leaves the room and returns with two of Bernard's old neckties. Grania does not see what all of this will add up to but she helps Tress as she ties together a long and variegated rope. Tress nods, holds it at arm's length for inspection, and tests the knots. She shoves her dark hair behind her ears while she concentrates. She loops the rope several times between hand and elbow—the way she's seen Mamo wind her yarn—and hides it at the bottom of her bed, under the covers. She pats the bedspread, and the two go downstairs and through the passageway to the hotel, and into the dining room. Mother is in the hotel kitchen. Father is always in his office by the time the girls come to breakfast.

But Mamo is here. Drinking tea from her china cup and saucer, and teaching the word *Pekoe* to Patrick. Mamo always leaves a little tea in her cup before she gets up from the table; it is bad luck to drink the last half inch from a cold cup.

Patrick pulls at Grania's sleeve when she sits beside him. He reaches up with small insistent hands and turns her face, forcing her to look at him, to focus on what he wants to say.

Grania reads his lips. "P-Ko," she says. She likes the word that is Mamo's tea. Patrick laughs, and Mamo reaches over to stroke Grania's cheek, and Grania, thinking of the rope upstairs, exchanges looks with Tress.

"Haven't you two swallowed the canary," Mamo says. She looks from one to the other.

Grania looks to Tress's face for information, but Tress is not going to tell. Grania knows this won't matter to Mamo anyway. Grania and Mamo have secrets of their own. Doesn't Mamo sometimes take the burlap bag out of the O'Shaughnessy trunk, and sling it over her shoulder when she takes Grania for a walk?

When things get bad.

*

All day, Grania wonders.

In the evening she goes upstairs while there is still light in the sky. She pauses at the porthole on the landing and looks far to the left, to the field at the northwest edge of town. The forked tree casts out its quivering shadow. She goes to her room and climbs into bed. She stares at the carefully stitched words in Mother's sampler. The words say something about God's eye and God's ear, and she wonders if Mother learned the words at church. She stares at the yellow daffodils in the frame. She raises a finger in the air and traces the outline of the jug on top of the washstand. She waits and waits and tells her body to be still but it won't be still. To make the time go faster she pounds her heels into the mattress as fast and hard as she can, but the covers become untucked. Tress comes in and puts her hands on her hips when she sees the mess at the foot of Grania's bed. She closes the bedroom door and makes the sign for quiet while she tidies Grania's covers. She slips into her nightgown, kneels to say her prayers, and turns out the light. She reaches under the blankets and pulls out the homemade rope, tosses a looped end to Grania, loops her own end and ties it firmly around one ankle. Grania watches through the shadows and does the same. The rope drops between them, over the side of Tress's bed, across the oval rug, up and over the end of Grania's mattress. It disappears between her sheets. From separate beds they kick and move their feet and legs until they are satisfied with the rope's position.

Now Grania lies stiffly on her back, waiting. But Tress doesn't move. Grania tries shifting her tied foot and pulls. She feels resistance. Then, two tugs back. She tugs again to be sure.

She is one tug, Tress is two.

She rolls on her side and stretches the rope until it is barely taut, just enough so that she can feel Tress at the other end. Now the rope name-signs are clear. Now the two create tug patterns, back and forth—patterns that are meaningless, that make them laugh silently to themselves in the dark.

Grania does not think about falling into sound. She dreams the softness of rope secured around an ankle—a scarf, a sock, a tie. She is bound to shore, no longer adrift in the dark. She is not afraid. She sleeps a deep and restful sleep.

*

Between breakfast and lunch, when the hotel dining room is quiet, Mother walks through the passageway and brings Grania to the kitchen at the back of the house. Mother pours a cup of tea for herself and sets it on the table. There are suds in the cup. Grania wants to tell Mother that suds are lucky. But Mother has heard every one of Mamo's sayings and will not want to hear them again. Isn't Mamo Mother's own mother? This is complicated to think about because it means believing that Mother was once a small girl named Agnes, and she has no picture in her head for that.

"Watch what I'm saying. It is dangerous not to hear," Mother says. "Especially when you are outside, away from the house. You can be hurt. I want you to listen." She cups a hand behind her right ear. *Listen.*

She has placed a scarf on the kitchen table, and a wide lid that is used to cover the fry pan.

"Stand here." She positions Grania in the middle of the kitchen and picks up the lid and the scarf. "Listen hard. Do you understand? I am going to cover your eyes. I am going to drop this on the floor." She feigns dropping the lid but does not release it. "Try to hear. Point where you think it lands—front, behind, this side, that side."

Grania watches with interest. Mother's lips are tight, her eyes dark with intent while she folds the scarf to make a narrow band. She has not removed her apron, which is wrapped over her dress like a vest and tied in the middle. The stripes of the apron are as blue as the inside of the speckled pot hanging from a wall hook behind.

Grania nods. She breathes through her mouth while Mother places the scarf over her eyes and partly over her nose and knots it at the back of her head. She feels hands on her shoulders and she is turned, once, twice, and firmly stopped. Mother's hands let her know that she is to remain still.

The floor is covered with spider-cracked linoleum. Grania is wearing long white stockings and lace-up shoes. A quiver of vibration enters the right side of her body. She points right. Mother removes the blindfold.

"No," she says. "But it's not your fault. Bernard came in and slammed the door. You heard the door, that's good."

Bernard looks back as he walks through to the hall. He heads for the heavy curtain draped across the bottom of the stairs. He rolls his eyes and shakes his head, enough so that Grania can see but Mother cannot. He bolts for the stairs and disappears, the movement of the curtain settling behind him. Grania knows that because of Bernard's bad lung he will be short of breath before he reaches the top. She has seen him upstairs, one hand pressed against his chest, his shoulders rising and falling as he breathes.

The scarf covers her eyes again, more tightly this time. She tries to open her eyes under the cloth, hating the darkness. Her body sways and recovers. Shoulder blades are poised. There is tingling in her hands, her fingers, her calves. Her feet want to jump. Is Mother in front or beside or behind? Something shudders through her. She points to the left, behind.

Mother tugs down the blindfold. She is not smiling. "Two times," she says and holds up two fingers. "I dropped it two times. Back there, and close behind." She walks to the end of the kitchen and demonstrates where she first dropped the lid. Grania watches it wobble-wobble and settle to stillness on the floor.

"The second time was good," Mother's lips say. "Before that, the noise was too far away. Next time, I'll use a bigger lid."

Mamo walks into the kitchen, one eyebrow raised. The scent of

Canada Bouquet sweeps in with her. "What in Sam Sorrow is all the noise?" In the same split second she sees the blindfold around Grania's neck.

Mother unties the scarf and waves Grania away. She will not continue while Mamo is in the room. "Find Tress and go outside," she says. "Go and find Kenan and Orryn, and play."

Grania moves towards the screen door but turns and stands in the doorway, trying to see the words that fall from Mamo's lips.

"You're wasting your time, Agnes. If you want to help her, take off her shoes. Let her feel the vibrations through her feet. Send her to special school. Belleville isn't that far away. It's small, but it's a railroad city. It will be easy to get her there and back. The school has been there for more than thirty years—though God knows I'll miss her if she goes."

Mamo does not add that she has been making inquiries, asking around. "She needs to learn to read and write," she says. "To speak with some of the hand language they teach there. She already uses her hands—her whole body—when she talks to us. She won't be held back. She'll learn quickly—you know there's no one quicker in this family."

Mamo's voice softens as she lays her hand on her daughter's arm. "Accept her as she is, Aggie. Stop feeling guilty. It isn't your fault. No matter how hard you try, no matter how much you want to, you'll never be able to make the child hear."

But Mother has turned away. She bangs the lid back onto the fry pan and twists the scarf between her hands. Mother will make her own decisions about what Grania will hear and where she will go. Mother has been the cause of Grania's deafness, and she will be the one to help her get some of her hearing back.

*

Grania and Tress walk through town, away from the bay. Their friends Kenan and Orryn are not around. When the girls come to the schoolyard they head for the edge of a cluster of maples, where there are two swings. Grania stares at the summer-empty school-house, the one Bernard used to attend, the one Tress goes to now. The one Patrick will attend when he is older. The one Grania would be allowed to go to if the scarlet fever hadn't stopped her ears from hearing.

She climbs onto the swing and pumps her feet. If she swings high enough, the leaves of the tree brush her shoulders just before her body sinks down and up again.

Two boys Grania has never seen before run into the schoolyard and over to the swings; they push at each other while they wait their turn. Tress knows one boy; his father works behind the desk at the hotel called Deseronto House, which is also on Main Street. The boys look up while Grania swings. They shout a word and then they point and run, looking back, laughing as they pelt across the open schoolyard. Grania laughs too, but she is puzzled. She looks to Tress, who has slowed her own swing and now jumps off. Tress is not laughing. Her lips make three words.

"Run, Graw! Skunk!"

Grania leaps. The girls run across the yard and collapse beside the boys. Skunk stink is in the air.

"Skunk!" Grania yells at the boys, but the skunk has already hurried along the edge of the trees and disappeared.

"Skunk!" she yells again. But she sees that the word has come out wrong. The boys are laughing at her now.

"Dummy!" the taller boy yells. "Listen to her. She's a dummy!"

Grania reads the word from his lips and sees a shout from Tress. The boys run off.

Tress places her hands on Grania's shoulders and makes her look at her lips.

"Skunk."

"Skunk!"

"No."

Why is it wrong? She is saying what she sees. She yanks away from Tress's grip.

"Don't give up," Tress says. "It won't work if you give up. *Sk! Sk!*" Tress is scowling.

"Skunk."

"Better." Tress shrugs. She points after the boys, who are far away now. To make Grania feel better she points to the boys again and makes the crazy sign beside her ear—*fingers bent, wrist waggling.* She heads back towards the swings.

But Grania wants to stay where she is. She wants to lie on the grass and sleep a long sleep. She has slipped back. She has used what Mamo calls her "weary speech" but she doesn't care. Not one bit. She feels like yelling out the worst sounds, the difficult, impossible sounds, *sk* and *ch* and *sh*. She feels like mixing them up on purpose. Let Tress be as grumpy as she wants to be. Grania will invent her own language, and no one, not even Tress, will be able to understand or interfere.

But she needs Tress. Without her, she won't know what is going on.

She follows her sister back to the swings and climbs on and pumps her feet. Her shadow swings beneath her, *fat-thin, fat-thin,* and every word she knows drops away. She allows the words to fall, one by one, and pulls into the place where her silence lies, the place where she is safe. She kicks her feet at the sky.

*

"THEN BEGAN A TERRIBLE FIGHT." Three children at a fence are watching a cowboy who is trying to stay on a bucking horse. The horse's body makes an arc; its back legs kick straight out behind.

Grania knows the word *fight*. A short word that spills into the air with one lip movement. Mamo tells her she pronounces it only too well. They practise the caption until Grania is able to repeat every word correctly.

Mamo closes the *Sunday* book for the day. "When the children taunt, fight back," she says and puts an arm around Grania.

But what Grania reads from Mamo's lips is *taught*.
When the children taught, fight back.

Grania can make meaning from any word, right or wrong. Sometimes she carries a sentence in her head for years before she understands her mistake.

When the children *taught*, she is going to be ready to fight.

*

When Mr. Eaton's new catalogue arrives by mail from Toronto, the old one may be pillaged for play. Grania and Tress sit on the rag rug, each with a pair of Mamo's sewing scissors. Carefully, they separate whole pages from the binding. They begin to cut out their family, trimming carefully and closely around necks and chins, elbows and toes. The ladies they prefer are the ones wearing drawers and chemises, or long walking skirts. On these models, other clothing can be fastened once the ladies have been pasted to cardboard. The ladies have tiny waists and bountiful hips that tilt back curvaceously, and this makes them look as if they will fall forward on their correct and smiling faces. The ladies have to be propped, to stand.

The sisters make tiny nicks in the ladies' hands. They give them mirrors to gaze into, and broad hats with turned-up rims and feathers that sweep to the side. They dress the ladies in gowns that spill regally around the floor at their feet. If the ladies are travelling ladies, they are draped with opossum capes and fox muffs. Or marten collars that have heads and claws that meet backs and tails when a slit is made in the centre and a lady's head popped through.

They give their ladies camisoles with widely cut paper tabs to fit over delicate shoulders; they give them lace trimmings and bows. They provide boots for their feet, tea sets to pour, feather dusters to swish, fans to flutter, and mangles with three rollers so they can wash the family clothes. Because the ladies are forced to stretch out straight, they are tilted onto davenports and given the longest beds to lie upon. They sleep in fits and starts because their eyes are always open wide.

The ladies are given whole families, unearned and complete. First, there is a baby, tied up in a barrowcoat. Tress says that when she grows up, she plans to have two babies, a boy named Pritchett and a girl named Jane. Next, they cut around girls who wear white underwear and have wardrobes of petticoats, wide-collared dresses and pointed shoes. The girls' feet are always about to step somewhere. "They are stepping out," Tress tells Grania.

In the expanding cutout family, there is sometimes a brother and always a man. The man is chosen from the underwear page, which makes the sisters laugh and laugh. The men on this page look like strongmen from the circus. The stoutest man is buttoned to the chin; he wears long drawers and stands on black pointy toes. The toes are so small and pointy they look as if they won't hold his weight. But he is easy to dress, in top hat and ample suits. They give him a pipe for his hand, a trunk for a voyage, a long beaver coat, and a ladder to climb should he desire to work outside. They hold the man's face close to the lady's, and they make them kiss, a rapid cardboard peck. They lift the tabs and remove the clothes and let the man and lady stare at each other in their underwear. The man is always known as Oscar. The lady is never given a name.

Sometimes Oscar doesn't listen to his lady. To teach Oscar a lesson, the lady goes travelling by herself. She is given a Saratoga trunk and a cabin bag for her trip. When Oscar speaks to the children, it is to tell them to eat with their mouths closed and to have good manners. The children, especially the girls, pay attention but they never have ears. Nor do the ladies. Not Grania's ladies. Tress doesn't care if an ear is showing but Grania chooses girls and ladies whose rolls or puffs of hair cover their ears. If their hair is swept high, or bunched on top so that tiny bits of earlobe are showing, Grania rejects them. Her girls and ladies do not need ears. They can manage perfectly well without.

*

"Mother," she calls softly. "Mother."

She repeats the word in a flattened way, hoping that the voice coming out of her is not too urgent, hoping that it will bring Mother, without anger or impatience, to her side.

Grania is hot; her hair is stuck to her temples. Her limbs ache; her throat hurts.

"Mother." A staccato call, a persistent code telegraphed through the dark.

Tress appears by the side of the bed. "What's the matter?" She makes their private sign, *palms up*. She's squinting through the shadows. "It's late."

"I'm sick. I want Mother."

"You're not calling loud enough. She'll never hear." Tress opens her mouth and hollers, "Mo-ther! Graw needs you!"

But it is not Mother who comes, but Mamo. Mother is at the hotel, making dough for tomorrow's chicken pot pies. Work at the hotel is never finished. It is Mamo who hears the call.

Mamo removes the gown from Grania's body. Washes and soothes; brings down the fever; tucks back the red hair and blows warm breath into Grania's ear. She crosses the room and holds a hand to Tress's forehead, but Tress is cool and fast asleep. It is Grania who succumbs to colds or *La Grippe* when the germs are going around. The scarlet fever that made her deaf seems to have weakened her, made her vulnerable to illness. Grania and Bernard are the two to be watched. Bernard, seventeen now, was born with the bad lung. The other two, Tress and Patrick—their father says— are as strong as two oxen in a yoke. Tress, now nine, inherited the high forehead, the dark eyes and dark brown hair of her mother, along with her mother's strength.

Mamo thinks of Agnes as a young girl—a dark-eyed girl who ran on her toes before she walked, who delighted in play and expressed herself in laughter. Her father's girl. His child of joy, their first-born. But weeks after the family sailed away from Ireland, Agnes was forced to watch her father's wrapped body slide into the sea. Strong and healthy when they left Ireland, he succumbed to fever on the ship, a fever that hopped like a deathly flea from one sleeping person to the next in the open quarters below. The sheet was wrapped round and round him; the crew stood in silence to one side of his body and remained there while a group of women Mamo scarcely knew wailed and prayed on the other. They faced the silent men as if wailing would hold the crew responsible for the poor food and the lack of fresh air below, and the shortage of water.

Mamo and Agnes stood together, and the sea mist wet their hair, and neither uttered a sound. Their hands rested on the damp shoulders of the three younger children. Mamo clutched the small wooden cross that had belonged to her husband, and after the body disappeared beneath the waves of the dark sea, she went below and placed the cross in the O'Shaughnessy trunk, and there it has stayed ever since.

She had drawn strength from her eldest daughter that day. And after that, responsibility fell to Agnes, more responsibility than should ever have been pressed on a young girl. Mamo knew this, but had little choice when she needed help with the younger three. There was another journey to face over land, after they left the ship, and few prospects at the end of it—except for a cousin Mamo had in Mystic. Any hope they were able to muster had been tied up in the existence of that one cousin.

But Agnes had missed her father. Mamo could scarcely grieve, herself, because she was always aware of the wretched, unuttered sorrow of her eldest daughter. Agnes had begged a scrap of black material from a widow on the ship and she stretched and flattened it and tied it around her neck, a ragged band that she refused to remove. Her eyes dulled; her face became set in some fixed memory or promise of her own. If she wept, she wept away from Mamo's view. And then, one year later to the day, she untied the black rag from her neck and burned it, and ended the mourning for her father. But she was no longer given to laughter. Never the way she had been, as a child.

It was Mamo's ability to tailor a man's suit that had kept the family alive. Eventually, she made the decision to move to Ontario, to the rapidly growing one-company town on the Bay of Quinte. Later, when Agnes undertook to marry Dermot O'Neill in Deseronto, Mamo watched her daughter take on even more responsibility. First, with the birth of Bernard and his poor lung; the loss of a baby girl in childbirth after that; and finally, with the births of the other three. It was during the time between Grania's and Patrick's births that Dermot purchased the house and hotel. Agnes has never had a chance to pause. If the opportunity were given to her, she would probably not be able to stop. Mamo cannot even imagine Agnes looking around and saying, "Now, I will have a short rest."

Mamo knows that Agnes has not forgiven herself for Grania's deafness, that she will always blame herself for the high fever. For taking five-year-old Grania, the night she was so ill, through the open passageway in winter so that she could keep her close, keep her on a cot in the hotel kitchen and watch over her while she worked. But the scarlet fever had been relentless. Grania's temperature had risen higher and higher. Dr. Clark was called and gave instructions to sponge the child, to rotate wet cloths from groin to underarms to abdomen to forehead to chest. Wringing the cool cloths from the basin of water, lifting one and laying another, Agnes' hands moved round the child's body as if it were a clock face, second by second, minute by minute, hour by hour. But the fever did not come down.

Agnes has been hard on herself ever since, but what she does not recognize is that she is also hard on the child.

These are the thoughts that Mamo sifts and sorts through her mind as she sits and dozes by Grania's bed. She has not changed from her long grey skirt, the knitted vest fastened over her high-necked blouse. Tied over both is a grey-blue apron with a wide band that buttons at the back of the waist. Mamo never wears yellow.

Yellow is the colour of marigolds, the flower of death. She holds Grania's hand and stays all night beside the child's bed. She dreams of Agnes and the black rag around her neck. She is surprised when Agnes, the child she once was, stands beside her chair and laughs her lighthearted laugh. Mamo reaches out but she is not quick enough, and when she wakes, it is Grania's hand she is holding.

Now, another voice enters her dreamlike memory. It is a voice she overheard a few days ago, after she took Grania shopping and left Meagher's store hand in hand with the child. The door made a clean slap behind them and a woman's voice trailed through the screen and out into the summer air. "Did you see the way she looked at that child?" said the voice. "Oh, the love on her face when she looked at that poor deaf-dumb child."

*

"Tell me the fire story. The name story. Please."

She is sitting with Mamo on the back stoop outside the laundry. Beyond the stoop is a small bit of yard and after that, the paddock. To the right are the drive sheds. Above and behind is the porthole window, upstairs.

Mamo likes the name story, too. The story of Grania's birth and how she came to be named, the day of the town fire, the Great Fire, 1896, Monday the twenty-fifth of May, the end of the holiday weekend that celebrated Queen Victoria's birthday.

Mamo doesn't know how much Grania remembers from before the scarlet fever or how much she has read from lips with repeated tellings. When the scarlet fever took away the child's hearing, whole chunks of language disappeared. On the other hand, small but surprising remnants have stayed. Her ability to memorize is extraordinary, but her memory of the spoken past is unpredictable in the patterns and combinations it releases. Part of what she retains seems to be by chance. It's as if some words have been stowed with care, while others have been wiped away. All this time has gone by and she has not started school. But now that she is working at the

Sunday book, a page every day, she is recognizing single words. She is, in fact, beginning to read.

"The story, Mamo."

"I'm dreaming—daydreaming. Do you remember what that is?"

Grania reads Mamo's lips and nods. It means surprise words stuck together, like *day* and *dream*. Like *apple* and *eye*, which she finds very funny. "You're the apple of my eye," Bompa Jack, her grandfather, tells her every time he visits from the farm on the Ninth Concession. He has also taught her "hold your horses" and "kick the bucket," which is more hilarious than *apple* and *eye*.

"When we first came to Deseronto in 1880," Mamo says, starting the story, forming the words with care, "it was still called Mill Point. A year after that, its name became Deseronto. A long time before we arrived, almost a hundred years before, Chief John Deserontyon and his Mohawk men paddled here in fifteen canoes. They left their homes along the Mohawk River in New York and made the long journey because they had been promised land by the British king. The Mohawks were rewarded because they were loyal to King George the Third during the American war that was called the War of Independence. Later, the Mohawk chief's grandson requested extra land near the point, not so far from here, and the village began. After that, the village became a town, and because Chief Deserontyon had been a great warrior, the town was named after him."

Mamo does not know how much Grania understands, but she continues. Grania is silent, her eyes watching for the parts of the story she knows.

"I was told by a man after I left the ship from Ireland that when my sons were older, there would be work for them in this place. I met the man on the road to Mystic and he told us about Mill Point. He said it was already on its way to being an important company town—a Rathbun town. The Rathbun men were from New York, and they were powerful and wealthy and they were clever. They knew that a good town needed good workers. When it was time for us to move, I brought my children here. I did not want to go to a place where there were tramps and burglars and clothesline thieves.

"They built a railway here, the Rathbuns. And a roundhouse. And a railway-car factory, and mills and the steamboat dock, and they brought coal all the way from the Pennsylvania mines, across Lake Ontario, from Oswego in New York. The coal arrived on barges and ships that took lumber back to New York.

"Many people moved to the town—more than five thousand. The Rathbuns brought electricity to the town, and they had the first two telephones. That was the same year we moved here, in 1880. Imagine!" She pauses to consider shouts into boxes nailed to walls, mix-ups that ensued. One of her own sons had been required to answer the phone when he worked as a shipper. Now he was an inspector for the railway, and lived in Toronto. Her other son had worked at the coal chutes until his lungs began to suffer from the black dust. After the Great Fire, he looked for another job and left to keep the books at the new mill built in Tweed. It was said that the Purdy family might be interested in buying the mill.

Grania is watching Mamo's lips for words she knows. "The flour, Mamo." The word *flour* comes out high, as if she is singing.

"The mill burned." Mamo's fingers become flames.

"Because the spark . . ."

"You're getting ahead. It was the day you decided to be born. The steamer called—"

"*Reindeer!*"

"Yes, its name was *Reindeer*. It was close to the long shingle dock and a man said that it threw a spark and the cedar shingles caught fire and the fire began to spread. But the next day, the captain of the *Reindeer* said the spark did not come from his steamer at all."

Whatever the cause, there had been stacks of wood everywhere the eye could see—hardwood lumber and shingles and railway ties. And the wind was fierce, blowing from the southwest, when at three-twenty in the afternoon, the whistle sounded the alarm. That was when the cricketers stopped their game and made a rush towards the cedar mill.

Mamo's flame fingers waggle forward now, and side to side. The flames crossed the railway tracks and Water Street, and after that many buildings burned, more than a hundred, including the beautiful Catholic church that was built on the hill three years after she moved to the town. A man climbed up into the spire when a burning cinder lodged on the outside and took hold. He tried to smother the fire from inside but could not, and he had to get out. Within hours, only the spine of the building was left to show that it had been there at all. Father Hogan was the priest at the time, and he had been out of town that day. When he returned on the four-o'clock train there was nothing he could do but witness the burning. Prayer would not stop the flames. Mamo, remembering, crosses herself and then she makes a steeple with her fingers.

"The church burned, the lumber burned, all that good lumber out on the docks." Grania cannot hear the sorrow that is overflowing, now, from Mamo's voice. There had been other fires in the town, earlier and later, oh yes. But that day, even some of the refuse burners had burned.

"Our house didn't burn, Mamo."

"Not ours. We lived in another corner of town then, back from the bay. That was before your father bought this house and the hotel. Before he moved the family to Main Street—and I moved with you. But your mother, she was bothered by the smoke that night, and that's when you made up your mind to be born."

Mamo falls silent and contemplates the miracle of new life in the midst of destruction. Not only the mill—she considers the waste of flour, Crown Jewel flour, the unbaked bread, cakes and pies—but also the bran house, the cedar mill, the wheat-filled elevator, they too yielded to the flames. The winds were fierce; the air crackled with flying debris and chunks of cinder and shingle and wood. The docks burned to the water's edge. High menacing flames were seen for miles. Black smoke whistled upward and there was a vast red glow across the sky. The Rathbun fire hoses were used for thirty hours without a single section bursting. Napanee sent a fire engine and men; Belleville sent members of its fire brigade; Kingston sent men and a Chatham engine. But with all of this help, with streams of water directed on the mill and the boilers and the chemical works, with men and women of the town using buckets of water in attempts to contain the fire, it was only when a heavy rain began that some of the larger fires were put out. Even so, piles of cordwood burned all night, illuminating the sky. And sodden, black wheat smouldered for days inside the ruins of the elevator.

The rain began at nine-thirty Monday night, a downpour as violent as the fire itself. Lightning and thunder added to the chaos and increased the misery of the families who sought shelter. Water soaked furniture and clothing that were heaped in the streets and in passageways between buildings and outside burning homes. If the gale-force winds had changed direction, the rest of the town would have burned, too. But as it turned out, the citizens managed to confine the fire to the eastern section of town.

There was no loss of human life; that was the miracle. As for the animals, horses were led away as fast as men could remove them. Later in the week the *Tribune* reported that a bantam hen and five chicks escaped the inferno and were found in Deseronto Junction, north of the town, where they were recognized and claimed by their owner. The editor fancied the story, but Mamo, who had seen other things, had not noticed any bantam hen or chicks.

Perhaps it was a blessing that so many people had left town to celebrate the holiday. At eight in the morning, the Citizens' Band played a rousing march as it paraded to the railway station to accompany a trainload of passengers on a thirty-mile excursion to the "Limestone City" of Kingston. Others took the hour-and-a-half steamer trip south across the Bay of Quinte, down the body of water called Long Reach and into Picton's harbour to celebrate in Prince Edward County.

Grania's father was one of those who had left. But he had gone north with horse and wagon to the Ninth Concession in Tyendinaga Township, to visit his father's farm. He'd taken Bernard with him, and two-year-old Tress, and some store-bought groceries for his father and his father's sister Martha. Bompa Jack was a widower and Martha a widow, and she had returned to the pioneer farm to live with her brother. Mamo and Agnes had stayed behind in Deseronto because of Agnes' condition. And heat and flame had levelled almost everything east of Fourth and south of Dundas, that furnace day in May.

Agnes, awkward at the end of her pregnancy, had moved methodically from window to window, closing shutters, tamping wet towels on the floor to block spaces beneath the doors. As soon as she took to her bed, her labour began. Dr. Clark and his wife, Mildred, could not be found in all the need and confusion, and there was no time to send for anyone else, so it was Mamo herself who delivered Agnes' third baby. Mamo was no midwife but she'd been at birthings often enough, including seven of her own in Ireland, with four survivals, and she had listened and she had watched, and she knew what to do. Even so, she was concerned because, the last time, after Tress's birth, Agnes had suffered a dangerous loss of blood.

Agnes was no longer able to see her, Mamo knew that. Not while she was lying in bed in the state of her own fear, perspiring and ranting, terrified of her own blood gushing forth, terrified of being unable to stop the flow. At the same time she knew she had to push forth the life that was about to begin outside herself. Her labour was mercifully short. But her skin became pale and colourless, and Mamo was shocked by the contrast when the red-faced infant, held upside down, wailed its short and sharp new breaths. The baby settled and breathed quietly, and her skin pinkened to a more natural colour. Mamo cut the cord and tied it with a clean white strip of bandage. She wrapped the smooth-skinned baby with the tiny feet and pale lashes and the thickness of red hair—as thick as the hair of a six-month-old child and as red as her own when she'd been a young woman—and it was then that she felt the child move towards her. Felt the strength of this miniature being move towards her like a wedge of falling timber aimed at her heart. Agnes, exhausted, lay on the bed coughing, her lungs irritated by the smoke that hovered over the town. The baby's lungs did not seem bothered at all. The afterbirth slipped into the basin Mamo held for it, and it was then that Mamo began to pray. She prayed silently that Agnes' life would not be taken away by the bleeding. Her warmed hands felt the ridge of fundus high up through the softness of Agnes' abdomen. She waited, and checked again, trying not to show fear on her face. When she felt the ridge come down, felt it harden a little, she prayed again that her daughter's life would not be taken. The baby made a small noise in her throat, as if to remind them that she was there.

"You name her, Mother," Agnes said. "You helped her into life. You name her."

Mamo thought for only a second. *Gráinne.* But unless people were Irish they wouldn't know how to pronounce the name when they saw it written. "We'll spell it the English, the Canadian way," she told Agnes. "Grania." As she spoke, she saw Agnes' colour come back. She saw the flush through her cheeks and she felt the sense of well-being in the room. Agnes dropped into a heavy sleep.

"Mamo?" Grania's fingers were tapping at her sleeve.

"I named you because your name means love. I felt the love coming right at me. From you to me and back again." Mamo made her sign for baby, rocking her arms. She wiggled her fingers to show the love that moved into her heart and went back and forth between them.

"Did my ears hear when I was a baby?" Grania knows the answer to this.

"Your ears heard every sound. I sang to you that first night and many nights after. You liked me to sing 'I don't want to play in your yard.' That was the song you liked best." Mamo sings the title to herself as she speaks, and nods, remembering, *Yes.*

Grania likes this part best, the naming, and the ears hearing, and the song, and especially the love wiggling like fingers, back and forth between them.

"Graw-nee-ya!" she shouts, louder than she should have. Mother comes to the door of the laundry and stands looking at the two of them. Mamo knows she is there because she has heard the steps behind her back. Grania knows Mother is there because she can tell from Mamo's face. Neither turns around to look.

"I'm telling the story of her name," Mamo says to her own back. "Again."

And Agnes, who knows the story well because it is her story, too, has her own rush of remembering while she stands behind them at the laundry door. Her memory is of the long, deep fear during gestation that ended in the unexpected wave of strength and happiness that washed through her after the child was born. It was the night of the Great Fire and she remembers having difficulty breathing, and then joy at seeing her red-haired child. Her husband was away, not even in the house when Grania was born. An emptiness there. And after that, milk fever, which kept her low for weeks; and then, work, the move to the hotel, three children to care for—despite the help from Mamo—fatigue, more fear with another pregnancy, her survival of the birth of Patrick, and then Grania's illness, the cold open passageway in winter, the scarlet fever that robbed the child's hearing. Grania's deafness was Agnes' fault. She could do nothing but throw herself into work; there was always work. All of this, in seconds, sweeps the initial flush of happiness away.

Mamo hears her daughter's footsteps recede.

"More," Grania says. "More fire story, Mamo."

But that is as far as Mamo will travel into memory today. Instead, her lips say, "Monday's child."

"Fair of face," Grania blurts—a verse she once knew by heart.

Mamo looks at her and smiles but she is not surprised. She says only, "Ah, it's still there."

What she does not describe to Grania is the flood of images that comes to her now. Before Agnes' labour had begun, Mamo threw a shawl over her shoulders and walked rapidly through wind and dusty streets to the eastern section of town, thinking she might be of help. An unnatural darkness hovered like a low cloud as she walked. Smokestacks were down near the waterfront; wires were tangled; a chaos of trunks and chairs and mattresses and paraphernalia clogged the streets. She saw a chamber pot, a brass candlestick stuck inside. She remembers women in skirts who climbed the roofs with men, all pouring buckets of water handed up from below, losing the battle as they fought. A man brushed by with a bedraggled rooster tucked under his arm, the rooster beady-eyed in stillness, its feathers singed and black. When Mamo reached Second Street she saw a man she knew from church, Mr. O'Reilly, his mouth a perfect *O*, running from his flaming house with a china plate that held three boiled potatoes. She reached for him but he pulled away and balanced the plate as he passed and continued up the hill. It was the only item he'd taken from his house. When she turned back to look, she saw him sitting on the ground at the top of the hill, hunched over the plate of potatoes as if this were the most precious treasure saved from the conflagration that day.

On Thomas Street, Scottish Mrs. Hunter, her face and arms black with soot, was being kept forcibly from her burning house behind neighbours who stood in a line while men and women tried in vain to get the flames under control. Mrs. Hunter, who had been running back and forth behind the line of neighbours, began to wail in despair when popping noises were suddenly heard from inside her burning pantry. The first pop and the series of loud pops that followed came from jars of preserves, each adding its own sound to the bizarre rhythm. On the fringes of a tiny corner of an inferno that threatened half the town, Mrs. Hunter wept with fresh cries at every new explosion from her pantry shelf. "Oh, my chili sauce!" she cried. "Oh, my plum preserves!" With every pop she moved more deeply to the centre of hysteria. The fact that she had managed to evacuate her seven children to safety before her husband raced up from the waterfront was not mentioned. Nor was the fact that walls had collapsed, that every stick of furniture was gone, that the babies' beds had burned to ashes. As each jar of preserves was heard to explode, Mrs. Hunter could only moan, "Oh, my goose-berry jam!" Perhaps, Mamo thought at the time, Mrs. Hunter's body was remembering the back-breaking work of the previous autumn. Bending over the wood stove, lifting heavy sealers with tongs, up and out of the bubble and steam of the speckled, now melted, pot.

But the worst of the images that comes to Mamo now is the one of the horses. Three drunken men—it was easy to see that they were drunk—were crammed into a wide rig and, with horrible cruelty, they were whipping and forcing a pair of horses down a narrow street between rows of burning houses. The fear of the animals was terrible to see, and men and women shouted, trying to stop the drunken men. This happened quickly—the roar of flames, the clack-eting of the rig, the heavy horses whipped to a lather through their fear, the wooden wheels bumping and veering between flames—but, quick as it was, Mamo never forgot. On her way home, retrac-ing her steps through the streets, she was not surprised to come upon one of the horses, dead. The massive bulk of its lustreless coat rose up like a sudden dark hill between road and boardwalk. Dead from fear, probably. Its heart stopped. She never forgot the sight, or the cruelty of the men.

That night, after Grania's birth, while the town breathed drifted particles in the wake of the fire, while beds were found for those seeking shelter, while thieves robbed purses right out of victims' trunks in the street, while farmers came from miles around to help, there had been no need to call in Uncle Am, who always came in after every birth to puff a cigar around the rooms, upstairs and down, to rid the house of birth odour and the scent of blood. Nor was it neces-sary to burn cloth on top of the wood stove as the midwives did dur-ing their cleanup—not with half the town smouldering.

As Agnes' husband, Dermot, approached during his return jour-ney with Bernard and Tress, his lungs inhaled smoke and fine parti-cles of ash and he watched an unnatural glow in the sky from miles away as he urged his horses forward. His heart tightened. He took shelter under the roof of an abandoned shed on the outskirts of town during the storm, and after that the wheels of the wagon churned through heavy mud. He would not force the horses. When he finally brought his children home it was to a newly arrived, newly named daughter, and a town half-gone. The smell of cinder and ash was to penetrate his and everyone else's nostrils for days and weeks to come.

Strangers travelled from far away to murmur and stare at the ruins and debris: five hundred people arrived from Napanee; a special steamer excursion came from Picton; seventy bicyclists from Kingston rode into town one day, and three hundred the day after that. On Friday, the fourth day after the fire, a dwarf arrived by train and strutted on his short thick legs down the centre of Main Street to see the devastation. He was followed by crowds of children who shouted out to anyone passing that he'd come from Toronto, that he was an Englishman by birth. After the spectacle of the strutting dwarf, more people continued to come, and they gawked, and some helped as residents cleared and constructed and tried to renew their businesses and homes. But even with all the cleaning up, later in the summer—especially after rain—the oppressive charred-timber odour was still settling heavily into the earth beneath the town.

Chapter 2

If your friend says "pea" and you think it "bee" or "me," you are perfectly correct, for you have seen the right movements. Do not worry that you cannot tell the difference.

Lessons in Lip-Reading

Grania steps out of her house, runs down the wooden ramp of sidewalk, crosses the dry road beside Tress and steps up to the boards on the other side. When the boards dwindle, she continues along the edge of the road where the dirt is packed and grooved. Watching her sister closely, she imitates every move: the way Tress carries her wide-strapped satchel, the way she positions her arms.

"Stop," Tress says. "Don't be a copycat."

But Grania can't stop. She has to know what Tress knows. Tress is her interpreter, her safety net. Tress will fill in the blanks when messages come at her from the frightening world they are headed for, called *School*.

Tress shrugs and keeps walking but this time she half-faces Grania. Her upper body turns to the side so her face can be seen and her lips can be read. Using their private language and adding mime, she reviews the rules—though the rules have been told countless times at home.

"Line up, first bell. Girls on one side, boys on the other."

"I won't hear the bell."

"The monitor holds the bell. Watch her hand. Run to the doors." Tress's fingers, despite holding the satchel, run up and down her opposite arm. "Hang your coat on a hook in the cloakroom. Watch the others. Do what they do. Watch the teacher. When she calls your name say 'Here.'"

"I won't know when."

"Watch my face. I'll nod, and you can say 'Here,' fast fast."

"Herehere," Grania says, practising. "What if *you're* not here?"

"Watch the person ahead of you on the list. I'll tell you who."

There is more. "No whispering or talking."

"I talk to you."

"I'll be with the older girls. You won't be allowed. We can talk at recess. Kenan will be there, in my class. And Orryn will be there. He might be in your row."

Grania isn't thinking about Kenan and Orryn, their friends who live in side-by-side houses on Mill Street. She knows they'll be there. What she wants is to go over the list one more time—what is forbidden, what is not.

Tress hasn't finished. "In arithmetic don't count on your fingers. Teacher hates finger-counting. She carries a yardstick but she doesn't whack."

Grania has missed most of this except *whack*. She has not considered *whack*. She hasn't thought about arithmetic either, although Bernard helps her to count coins when Father is sometimes out of the hotel. Grania sneaks around the corner and into the closed bar and Bernard stops his work and opens the cash register drawer and lets her count coppers, five-cent pieces, tens and twenty-fives. Sometimes he gives her a five-cent piece for herself. One that she can take to Meagher's store to spend.

"If you need a drink,"—Tress makes their private sign for water, tapping at her lips—"there's a cooler."

Grania's head is going to burst. Tress knows all of these things that she herself will never know.

"If you're called to the chalkboard, the chalk is on the ledge."

Is this, then, familiar ground? Will there be a chalkboard like the one she carries in her head? Every word she has learned with Mamo is coiled against the white and shining surface of her imagination. She has never told Mamo about this. Or Tress. Nor has she told them that every word she sees on this surface is made of rope letters—twisted yellow rope.

The chalkboard at school, she quickly sees on her first day, is not white but black. It stretches across the front of the room and along the wall on one side. It holds numbers and sums and words and lines, and at the end of the day it is wet and slick and dries unevenly after the monitor washes it down. A cardboard alphabet in its proper order marches along the upper edge of the board. Grania knows the letters perfectly because long ago, after the scarlet fever, she and Mamo printed and cut out their own alphabet at home. Now, Mamo prints in the air, her index finger forming words beside her as if the air is a sheet of paper that Grania is supposed to see. The words are invisible but Grania sees them. Mamo used to print in capitals, but during the past weeks the printing has become writing. Air writing, she and Grania call it. Mamo twists her upper body to the side when she writes the message in the air, so it won't be mirror-reading for Grania.

A chart of vowels is on the classroom wall. On the first day, the children mouth the sounds: A - EE - EYE - O - YEW. Grania follows their lip and throat movements as they chant. But vowels, she quickly learns, are unpredictable. Once they move inside words, they can't be trusted because the way they are said is forever changing.

Grania is never called to the board. She sits in her desk, one of twenty-nine children in a room that holds a wood stove enclosed by a wooden barrier on four sides. The other twenty-eight students are paired, two to a desk. Grania sits alone and watches moving mouths and lips and tongues. Her teacher, a plump young woman with a round face and small pointed teeth, smiles at her the first day and takes her by the hand to her seat but, after that, she has no extra time to look in Grania's direction. Words fly through the air and fall, static and dead.

Only the captions Grania has learned at home with Mamo take turns shifting and sliding in her head. This is what Mamo has given her, the gift of pictures and words, learned and remembered and stored. On the board, she recognizes words she already knows, but she learns few new ones. Instead, she sits in her seat and amuses herself silently by reviewing in her memory the captions in the *Sunday* book, the ones she practises in the evenings with Mamo. She twists and turns each letter, stringing words together with yellow rope.

Bless them both, said Granny Moore.

Give the password, was the next demand.

Go at once for the nearest doctor.

What is to become of us? asked Dulcie.

*

There is a dictionary at the back of the schoolroom, on a shelf above the water cooler. Weeks after she starts school, Grania works up enough courage during recess to stand on tiptoe and lift the book down. It is heavier than she has imagined. Her arms sink as she places it on a lower shelf and props it open. She finds the pages with the letter G—the letter that starts her name. Column after column and page after page are filled with G words, hundreds more than she knows how to count. Her finger slides from one to the next, down and up and down again.

Grania has questions about all of these words. She is brimming with questions but there is no one to ask. When the bell rings again, the plump teacher with the pointed teeth gives a lesson about nouns. She prints a list of nouns on the board and points to each word with her yardstick: *desk, tree, horse, rain*. She turns to survey the children's faces and smiles as if these four nouns hold remarkable secrets. Every word contains a vowel. Teacher turns her back again. Grania watches as more and more words are added to the list, but she knows nothing of their sounds.

After school, Grania fetches Carlow and takes him around the back of the house, where she sits on the stoop. Carlow is getting big now. Grania shouts commands so that he will understand her and obey.

"AY," she shouts, and Carlow wags his tail.

"EE," she shouts, and Carlow sits.

"EYE," and Carlow leaps towards her and licks her hand.

Grania mixes up the sounds: YEW and O and EYE and AY and she throws in *sk* and *ch* and Carlow knows what to do. Carlow understands Grania's voice.

In the evenings, Mamo helps. Her long index finger moves in slow vertical strokes; her wrist bobs to fill the space. "Knee," she says. "Sounds like tree." She points to her knee and writes through the air, *k-n-e-e*, to show how the *k* slips in like a trick. The *k* hangs in the air after Mamo's finger finishes writing. The *k* has to be ignored when Grania speaks *knee* with her voice. It is one more thing she is supposed to know.

"Look for a little word inside a big one," Mamo says. She reaches for the *Sunday* book and chooses a page that has one word beneath the picture.

"Seashore." Mamo's finger points beneath the picture of two children playing on a beach. "Break the word in two. The first part is like the letter *C*. Now, add it to shore. *C-shore.*" Mamo makes *shore* with her lips.

Grania is intimately aware of Mamo's lips—soft and careful but never slowed. She studies the word as it falls. She says *C* and *shore* over and over again. She twists the word into yellow rope and stows it in her memory. *This is how it sounds.*

Now she studies the picture on the page. Sea is where she would like to go some day. Sea is different from bay. She can look at the Bay of Quinte from her bedroom window any day. But the C-shore she has in mind is not the one Mamo's finger points to now; it is another that Grania has found at the end of the book.

In the end picture, a girl in a dress and sash and stylish hat is caught in waves that have swept up past her knees. She is falling sideways, but just before she goes under, she is saved by a fisherman. Or perhaps he is a lighthouse keeper—a light is blinking from a tower on a cliff above the scene. The man has a beard and wears a seaman's hat, not unlike the one worn by the bearded captain on the cover of the book. It is clear that the man is taking long strides through the water and that he has every intention of rescuing the girl. He reaches out his arms and props her as she falls. For reasons Grania cannot see, the girl—her eyes bright with fear—does not seem to be able to help herself. Grania studies the girl and wonders.

Mamo helps with the caption: "DAN CAUGHT THE CHILD IN HIS ARMS."

If Dan hadn't reached out, would the girl keep sinking through the waves? Would she fight her way back to the surface? Grandfather O'Shaughnessy is under the sea, but that is different. Mamo told her the story of Grandfather dying on the ship after they left the beautiful land called Ireland. That is when Mamo became a widow. A sheet was wrapped around Grandfather's body—around and around. Prayers were said and he was dropped over the side of the ship and buried at sea. Women were wailing, but not Mamo, not Mother. Their grief was silent. "Some grief is so big, it has to be held in," Mamo has told her. Grandfather is under water now, somewhere in the big ocean.

When Grania is alone, she goes to the drawer in her closet that holds her cutouts, and she brings out an earless girl who looks the same age as herself. She unfastens the shoulder tabs of the girl's automobile coat and the waist tabs of a long skirt with large buttons. After that, she finds the remnants of Mr. Eaton's bruised and cut-up catalogue and searches until she finds a picture she knows is there. It is the only bathing suit for girls or ladies in the entire catalogue. At first, it is hard to tell that it is a bathing suit at all, except for the scene that has been drawn behind the girl who wears it on the page. There are wiggly waves for water, and sand, and tiny figures sitting or playing in front of a sharply drawn horizon.

Grania cuts off the girl's head because part of an ear is showing.

She trims around the neck, the sailor collar, the short puffed sleeves, the narrow waist. She needs only the bathing suit itself. The bathing skirt reaches down to the knees where it meets the girl's high black stockings. Grania ignores the stockings and cuts off the girl's legs. She leaves enough space for tabs at the shoulders, lifts out the suit and fits it perfectly to her own cutout girl.

Her girl will go to the C-shore. Her girl, without ears. She will play all day if she wants to; she will kneel in the sand and let it run through her fingers; she will wade into the wiggly waves and hold her breath and duck under; she will open her eyes and feel water pressing from above. No one will see her or know where she is. When she wishes to surface, up she will come, popping into sight between waves the way the ladies' cardboard heads pop through their marten collars.

Grania moves the girl about and practises the C-word by singing it into the side of the earless cardboard head. After she puts the girl and the bathing suit away in the drawer, she sits on the side of the bed and sings the sea word into the roof of her own mouth. She shapes her cheeks around it. Some day she will be able to say all of the words in the *Sunday* book. She will learn the breath and movement of each. If she makes a mistake, she will try again. She will try until she knows every sound.

But words *have* no sound. Not for Grania. Only feeling, as they form inside her mouth and vibrate against the lining of her throat.

*

"You should be at a proper school for deaf children," Mamo tells her. "You're losing time. You would learn new things. There is a special school in Belleville."

Belleville is the city that is farther west along the bay. Grania travelled there on the steamer last fall when Mother took her and Tress shopping for winter clothes. The steamer left Deseronto in the morning and stopped at Northport and carried on to Belleville. They were on the steamer for two hours.

"Would I have to sit still? Like in Deseronto school? At my desk?"

"I don't suppose your feet will get pins and needles."

Did she see the lips correctly? *Pins and needles?*

If at special school they put pins and needles in the children's feet, she will never go. She will run away instead. Like the girl in the *Sunday* book.

"Goodness," said Mother. "Dulcie seems to have run off."

*

Grania is playing on the veranda with Patrick and Tress. They have invented a game. They are supposed to shout out a sound and bounce from chair to veranda railing and back to chair. They have to touch the railing; they have to be quick. If they aren't quick, they're *out*. The last one to reach the chair is *out*. Grania must watch closely. So far, she has not been *out*.

Two children come out of the hotel dining room with their parents and hop down the steps. The family is staying in an upstairs room of the hotel. The children stare over at the house veranda, a few feet away. They would like to join the game. They hear Grania's shout. It is not like the shout of the others.

The children's mother steps forward. "What's the matter with your sister?" she asks Tress. She sees that Tress is the eldest.

Tress steps in front of Grania. The game stops.

"There's nothing wrong with my sister," she says. "She's my sister, that's all."

Patrick shouts and leaps to the chair. Tress and Grania go back to the game. They are making a ruckus. Grania has still not been *out*.

*

There is no one in the kitchen and no one upstairs. Grania goes to the parlour to see who is in the house. The sun is down, the parlour curtains closed. It is only after she is inside the room that she realizes she is alone.

Darkness has fallen abruptly. She turns to face the hall, but now the hall is dark. Mamo is not in her rocker, though someone has brought the rocker in from the veranda. Grania stands behind it, her heart pounding wildly. She inches back and flattens against the corner wall. She wants to move forward to get to the doorway, but she can't; she is pinned by the dark. Someone will have to come and turn on a lamp. She calls out—she does not know what noise she has made. She calls out again. Where are Mamo, Tress, Patrick, Bernard, Mother, Father? Where is Carlow? They have left her alone. Shadows press around her. Her feet lock to the boards of the floor. When Mamo comes in and switches on a lamp, she is startled by a young body propelled forward off the wall like a stone from a sling. Grania rushes into her arms. Mamo comforts and soothes until the child is no longer afraid.

*

After school, Mother gives Grania a folded note. She is to carry it to Mr. Whyte at the butcher shop on Main Street.

Grania doesn't want to go. She wants to slip away to the dugout, the new place where she plays with Kenan and Orryn and Tress. She turns away and pretends not to see, but Mother forces her attention back. "Give the note. Wait for the meat. Come straight home."

Mother's face is dark; her lips are tight because she has been extra busy all day. Mamo has been in the hotel kitchen helping Mrs. Brant, but there is more work to do. Mamo is tired now; her arthritis bothers her. She is back in the house, upstairs in her room, lying down.

Grania walks along Main Street. It is late October, a sunny afternoon. She is wearing her white blouse and her navy skirt. Every time her foot presses down on a cedar board in the sidewalk, a trill enters her foot. Music, she thinks. My feet are making music.

Mr. Whyte takes the note from her hand and she stands to one side while he waits on two women who were in the shop before her. The soles of Grania's shoes are buried in sawdust that is strewn over the oiled floor. She shuffles her feet. The room is filled with choking odours. Mr. Whyte is wearing his blood apron; she has never seen him without it. Behind the counter, close to his hands, the scaly feet of a dead hen, stiff as yellow twigs, point to the ceiling.

He finishes wrapping a string of blotchy sausages and wipes his hands, adding more specks of blood to the apron. He turns to Grania to speak but the voice part of him cannot be seen. She looks out through the screen door because the light in the shop is dull and because Mr. Whyte keeps turning his head, right and left, before he finishes saying his words. He shrugs to himself and checks the note and picks out a heavy cut of raw meat and slaps it onto waxed brown paper. Now Grania watches again. His hands weigh the meat on the scale. He lifts the edges of the paper and his fingers tie the package with long string that dangles near his face from a roll above his head. The roll is stuck on a hook in the ceiling; every part of it is splattered with dots of dried blood. He picks up a knife—there is blood on that, too—and he cuts the string and knots it outside the package.

Grania accepts the parcel of meat. "Thank you," she says, but the words stick in her throat and come out wrong. *Keep the voice close.* It's good that Mamo isn't here. *Here to hear.* Grania smiles, immensely pleased with herself because she knows the difference. Like see and sea. *I see the sea in the picture.* She thinks of the earless cutout girl, and the C-shore, and Grandfather O'Shaughnessy at the bottom of the ocean, and Mamo telling her that he is at peace. Mamo says that in the beautiful land called Ireland, fresh breezes blow in every day from the sea.

Mr. Whyte looks at her again and smiles because he thinks she is smiling at him. He picks up a pencil and enters the cost of the meat in the ledger. He bows formally as if he is part of a picture in her *Sunday* book. Grania wants to get away from the odours in his shop. *Dulcie grabbed the package and ran.* Unless she can get outside this minute, the smell of animal blood will never come off her clothes. She shoves the push-bar that is nailed diagonally across the screen door, runs down the short ramp to the boardwalk, and keeps running until she reaches the next block.

She slows to look around, lifts the package to her chest and presses tightly. Soon the workers will be spilling out of the factories and mills and will be heading home for their supper. She sees Kay, a girl who sits beside Tress at school. Kay smiles and her hand makes a small wave. Kay has a kind face that seems to hold a secret. Her cheeks look as if they are hiding acorns inside. Grania likes Kay, and waves back.

She reaches the post office corner and is about to step down to the ridges and grooves of dried mud before she crosses the street, but she feels something wet against her skin. She looks down and sees, with horror, that a crimson stain has seeped across the front of her white blouse.

Trouble. She runs around to the side door of the post office and up the wide staircase, up another flight, up and up, and she bangs on Aunt Maggie's door. Sometimes when she visits, Uncle Am lets her climb to the clock tower above the apartment, but not today. Uncle Am will be working somewhere in the building.

Aunt Maggie opens the door, sees the red splotch, sees the package, sees the tears and pulls Grania in by the hand. She sets the meat on the table, unbuttons Grania's blouse and helps her off with it, her lips making the shape *tst-tst* as she shakes her head.

"We'll have to fix this. Your mother . . ."

She wraps Grania in a dressing gown and goes to work, soaking and rinsing the blouse in a bucket of cold water. With each quick rinse and dip, the water becomes red and then pink and pale and finally clear.

"We'll have to be quick," Aunt Maggie says. "Before your mother sends out a posse." She lifts the irons that are always at the ready on the back of the stove, and exchanges them one by one, pressing the blouse against a towel that she has folded onto a corner of the kitchen table.

"No time flat," she says, but Grania misses the words. The blouse is crisp and dry, except for the seams.

"Can't be helped," Aunt Maggie says. She holds it out for Grania to slip into. The blouse sticks to Grania's skin but the stain is no longer there.

Grania runs for the door and down the stairs, runs back up again because she's forgotten the package, holds it away from her blouse and runs the rest of the way home.

Mother is busy in the dining room when Grania slips through the passageway and into the hotel kitchen. Mrs. Brant is there; she holds a finger to her lips. Grania slides the package onto the pull-out metal surface of the cupboard, and Mrs. Brant slips her a raisin cookie and shoos her back to the house. Mother does not even know that Grania is late.

*

The following afternoon, Grania brings a new word to Mamo. A word she has taken from Aunt Maggie's lips. *Paw-C*. A little word inside a big one?

"Who said it? When?" Mamo is interested, perks up, sits straight in the rocker that has been carried out to the veranda. She tightens her fringed shawl around her shoulders.

"Aunt Maggie. She said Mother will send out a Paw-C."

Mamo thinks for a moment.

"A cowboy word," she says. "In America. Though we were not unfamiliar with the word in Ireland. *The sheriff and his posse chase a bad person.*"

"Oh," Grania says, not understanding. She has seen the last two words on Mamo's lips—*bad person*.

It will be her secret, then. Hers and Aunt Maggie's. She will never tell anyone, not even Tress, about the *Paw-C* or about being a bad person or about the blood.

"Did you choose a picture?" Mamo says, opening the *Sunday* book.

She did, but now her fingers turn to a different page, not the one she'd chosen for today.

A boy in a wide-brimmed hat is about to leave a campfire, and he is looking back. He has a sad face. A short rope dangles from his hands. A cowboy, seated on the ground beside the fire, threatens the boy with his fist. Another cowboy is rolled up inside a blanket, asleep. DON'T COME BACK WITHOUT THE HORSE.

Mamo reads the words beneath the picture. She nods her head. "Well. You picked a hard one. This may take a few days but we'll work on it as long as it takes. One word at a time. Watch carefully. If you can say a word, you can use it. Don't ever forget."

*

Friday afternoon, Grania and Tress run out of the girls' entrance, Orryn and Kenan from the boys'. For hours, Grania has done nothing but sit. Every time she tries to read Teacher's lips, Teacher moves her head or turns her body away. After lunch, Grania was given a picture book to look through but she rested her head on its cover and fell asleep. Orryn poked her in the back to wake her, and Teacher didn't even notice.

She doesn't want to be bothered with me, Grania tells herself. She slows to a walk. Agitated, one hand taps the side of her skirt to make a rhythm. *Can't be - baw-thered. Tea-cher - can't be - baw-thered.*

Kenan, who has the longest legs, is the first of the four friends to run down towards the water, east along Main Street, past the post office, past Naylor's Theatre, across the road and through the hidden path to the edge of the old Rathbun pier. Grania, sluggish today, is last; the other three have disappeared inside the dugout. She scuffs along shore, checks in all directions to be certain no one is around, ducks under the widest board and enters the tiny room that has been scraped from the earth. Above the dirt ceiling, planks of the rotting pier extend a few feet over water. The pier was abandoned long ago, long before the children took it over. The dugout beneath is carefully boarded on the sides—work done by Kenan and

Orryn. Only the four of them know about this secret place and where to raise the widest board that allows them to slip inside.

The room is large enough to hold them if they scrunch and face each other, two and two. Narrow boards have been nailed together to make a small bench on one side. On the other side are a milking stool and a driftwood stump. Grania, last in, sits on the stump and tucks her skirt around her so it won't drag the ground. Sometimes baby frogs hop along the floor. The dugout is dry but holds the odours of dampness and old fire, the fire that swept through the town the day Grania was born. The earth floor is hard and smooth, like Bompa Jack's root cellar at the farm. Light filters down, seeping through an opening between boards—streamers of afternoon sun.

"Password?" This, from Orryn, half-heartedly.

"Wooms."

Grania makes the wiggly worm sign with her index finger and they all laugh, Grania too, because the worm password always makes them laugh. It is Grania's word and they say it Grania's way, *Wooms*.

Grania looks to Tress to see what the others have been talking about. Tress's face is self-important, as if she is about to make an announcement. Her dark hair has been braided and pinned up by Mother, which makes her look older. She raises her shoulders, lifts her chin and glances around at the other three.

"I'm going to marry Kenan," she says. "When I grow up." She half-turns and her finger writes *marry* in the air beside her. Grania reads the spacious letters that link up before they disappear.

Orryn, whose hair is so black it looks as if he has slapped water on it to flatten it down, laughs as if this is preposterous. Orryn likes to laugh and joke. "Is it true?" He wants to hear from Kenan himself.

Kenan smiles his sweet smile. His curly hair flops over his forehead. "It's true. But we aren't going to tell my uncle or Tress's parents until we grow up."

Grania looks from one face to another and wonders if this is something all children decide when they are ten years old.

*

When Cora's daughter, Jewel, marries Mr. Whyte's son, Tress and Grania walk up St. George Street to the Presbyterian church and lean into the fence and watch the wedding guests spill out and down the steps. This church, with its stone tower, is not like the new Catholic church that was built after the fire. The Catholic church, where Mother prays twice a week and where Grania is taken with the family every Sunday, has a square tower and two sets of double doors. Grania has never been inside the Presbyterian church.

The guests at the wedding are dressed in fancy clothes and hats; some of the women wear short capes with ruffles around their necks. Mrs. Whyte's flounced skirt has rows of dark silk banded around the bottom. Grania stows the information to tell Mamo. She and Tress try to get a close-up look at Jewel in her wedding dress. Jewel and Mr. Whyte's son will be moving to Ottawa, the capital of Canada, after the wedding. A gust of wind catches Jewel as she reaches for the arm of her new husband, and she grimaces as the folds of her dress flap against her hidden legs.

Cora looks towards the street and, seeing Grania with Tress, says to her husband, "Who will marry that pitiful child when she grows up? She may have a sweet little voice, but no one except her family can understand a word she says. If they don't find someone deaf and dumb, she'll end up living with her mother the rest of her days."

Grania grabs Tress's arm and yanks her away from the fence. "That's what she thinks," she shouts.

Tress runs along sideways, trying to keep up. "What? Did you read Cora's lips? Did she say something mean?"

Yes, and yes. It is easy to read Cora's lips. But Grania will not tell.

Later, she goes to Mamo. "Why does Cora hold her mouth so tight?"

"That's the way she is," says Mamo.

Mamo continues, this time talking to herself. It's the way Grania picks up information, watching Mamo's lips spill extra words into the air. "It's part of the general burden that must be borne. Cora's self-righteous ways."

"Burden?"

"Did you see that? Heavy load. Cora is one of the town's heavy loads."

Grania does not understand. "She looks like a crabface to me." Grania thinks of Cora's narrow chin, her pointed noise, her thin ankles and feet.

"You'd better not be saying that in front of Cora."

Mother has something else to say. Grania watches Mother's lips. "I've known Cora since before I was married," she says. "Cora was unlucky enough to grow up without brothers or sisters. If you grow up in a house full of people, you have more than yourself to think about. Cora had only herself and she became selfish. That's what happens to an only child. That's all there is to it. She was an only child."

Grania is more confused than ever.

What does Mother mean, "a lonely child"? How does being lonely make Cora selfish?

Grania does not ask. But she does know that when she grows up, she is not going to live the rest of her days with her mother.

*

"Don't let deafness hold you back," Mamo tells her. "Don't let it defeat you."

Defeat?

In the Deseronto school, she doesn't want to be separate from the hearing children but she is always separate. She sits at the edge of the room, alone in a double seat. At morning recess, the children tease. Not every day, but some days they tell her that the way she talks sounds funny.

"Say *spit*."

"Thpit."

"Ha Ha. You said *thpit*."

Grania makes the crazy sign at them, her cupped hand waggling beside her ear.

Long-legged Kenan comes to her rescue in the schoolyard. Some-day, Kenan will marry Tress. He will be part of the family and he will keep Grania strong. Mamo says that Kenan is a good boy. Kenan is Grania's bully.

After Kenan sends the others packing, Grania goes to the edge of the schoolyard and lies back against a stump. She looks up at stump's neighbour, tall tree, and she watches leaves and branches flicker and sway at the top. If she stays here with stump and tree, she is safe. The teasing children can do what they want. For her, alone is best.

By noon, she has forgotten morning recess. The children shout and play, run and holler. They pair off and grip each other's wrists and swing in fast circles until they spin and spin and fall to the ground. Grania joins in. Plants her feet against the earth, turns and turns until she is reeling with dizziness. She drops, breathless, to the grass and stays there, cross-legged, tucking her skirt beneath. The others sit, and make a sudden circle with Grania at its centre.

A new game begins, unfolding as it is imagined. Is that a word? A sound? Grania watches one mouth move, then another, and laughter on the faces around. She is caught up by this and she laughs, too. Someone at her side says something; other faces are watching. She turns her head but misses the sound, the word. Whatever it is bounces from one child to another, erupting the way mayflies erupt on the surface of the water, quick, impossible to catch. A word hopping, one pair of lips to another. Excited, she reaches for but can't see the sound. The children keep it in front, overhead, behind, to the side.

But behind does not exist. Not for her. Behind is the darkness outside of thought. It's the place where sound gathers, sound that she is not meant to hear.

"What?" she cries to the circle of children, but her voice only makes them laugh. *"When the children taught, fight back,"* Mamo *has told her.*

"Tell!" Her voice soars.

They are jeering now. They will never tell. "Dummy!" they cry. "Dummy!"

Grania pushes herself up, looks around wildly, and they back away. She makes fists but the tears are welling up. *Fight back.* She charges into one girl but the girl runs away. The children scatter and Grania is suddenly alone. She goes to find Tress. Tress puts both hands on her shoulders and makes her look. "Don't give up," her lips say. "Don't give up."

But Grania's shoulders sag with defeat. She scuffs towards the girls' entrance and stands there by herself. She waits and watches until the monitor's wrist swings the bell, *up down, up down.*

*

In their room at home, she refuses to leave Tress alone until Tress shouts in her ear. "SPIT SPIT SPIT." What does it matter that Grania hears nothing? Some part of her head will hear, even if her ears do not.

Now it is her turn. "Listen," she says. "Tell when my voice is wrong."

Tell.

Tress listens for a few moments but she is impatient. She has homework to do.

"Watch me, Graw. What am I saying?" She faces Grania, moves her lips and pretends to speak. But Grania can tell that her sister is faking. Her throat, her tongue, her cheeks, her breath are not making real words.

Grania jumps on her, sits on top of her. "You'd better help me," she says. "Helpmehelpme say it right."

But Tress is not in the mood. "Just a minute," she says. "Wait."

She holds up a palm and looks towards the closed door. "Mother is calling. I'm supposed to tell you to go down."

But Mother doesn't want Grania at all. Tress only wanted to get rid of her.

Grania goes outside to the backyard. Carlow looks at her as if he's been waiting. The patch over his eye makes him look like a dog pirate.

"SPIT!" she shouts, and he comes bounding over.

"BAD PERSON!" she shouts, and he sits beside her and thumps his tail.

"GET THE POSSE!" she yells. She climbs the back stoop and he climbs with her. She practises SPIT over and over, and Carlow listens, and stays close, and cocks one ear.

*

After supper, Grania goes to the parlour and finds Mamo there alone. "Will you blow in my ear, Mamo?"

Mamo looks up from her rocker. She doesn't have to ask what's wrong.

"You belong in school," her lips say. "No matter what happens, you do belong."

She pulls Grania to her lap—a big girl now. Doesn't matter. Mamo slips her fingers beneath Grania's hair and blows softly into the child's ear.

Grania has seen the words fall from Mamo's lips. She feels Mamo's soothing breath and chants to herself, *Do be long. I do be long.*

But there is something wrong with this.

Mother says, before she walks down Main Street to shop, "I won't be long."

Then what does Mamo mean? *No matter what happens, you do be long.*

By bedtime, Grania is worn out from thinking. She goes upstairs, ties the rope around her ankle and climbs into bed. Tress comes up soon afterwards. Grania waits. As soon as she is sure that her sister is attached at the other end, she gives her leg a vicious yank. She grins to herself in the dark.

*

Saturday morning, Mamo lifts the burlap bag from the trunk. She reaches down and runs her fingers over the small wooden cross and says a quick prayer before she closes the lid. She slips the strap of the clock bag over her shoulder and signals to Grania that it is time to go for their walk.

"What do you and Mamo do on your walks?" Tress wants to know.

"Pick up stones," says Grania promptly. "On the shore."

And sure enough, she brings back a speckled stone and a piece of coal and sets them on the bedroom sill.

But Tress thinks she saw lumps in the bag *before* Mamo and Grania left the house.

"No," Grania says. "No." She remembers what Mamo has told her. It is their secret.

When things get bad.

*

Saturday. It is July first, the Dominion Day holiday. Father's lazy eye is almost closed against the sun. "Up you go, my darling," he says. His Irish hands lift Grania into the seat in the wagon but not before the black mare rolls its eye sideways to stare. Grania stares back and the mare flicks its head as if to deny her presence. Uncle Am's horses are the finest in town, after Father's. Everyone knows that no one loves horses more than Father. Sometimes Father spends more time with his horses than he does running the hotel. That is what Grania has read from Mother's lips.

Tress climbs up beside Grania; Patrick is plunked down beside Uncle Am. Mother and Father and Mamo and Bernard will stay home to look after the guests. The hotel is fully booked for the holiday weekend and Mrs. Brant will be off, but her daughter will come to help Mother peel and prepare vegetables in the hotel kitchen.

Bernard stands on the steps of the hotel. Bernard has wavy hair, like Father. His mouth shapes "Bye, Grainy," and he waves his hand. Grania doesn't have to hear to know that he is a soft speaker.

She looks at Tress, seated beside her, to make sure she hasn't missed anything. There isn't an emotion she can't read on her sister's face. Tress makes the sign in their homemade language, the sign they've invented for what Mamo calls "no patience at all"— *Let's get going, let's get going.*

Uncle Am tilts his hat forward to shade his eyes. He signals the horses, and the wheels lurch forward. Grania tightens her hat ribbon under her chin.

The wheels bump up, down, forward, all at the same time. Grania closes her eyes against the sun and opens them again, remembering that Mamo has instructed her to pass along her greetings and to report what she sees. "I want to hear about your grandfather and that mixed-up Irish family of his," she said. "Your father must be the only man in the county to have two uncles who are priests and another who rides King Billy's white horse in the Orangeman's Parade." Mamo smiled when she said this, and Grania looked for the up-and-down line between her brows.

The year before, Grania had watched the Orange parade from the post office roof. She was boosted up the ladder that was lowered out of the hall ceiling, just outside Uncle Am's apartment. She climbed through the hatch and found herself staring at the flat part of the roof outside the tower clock. Another ladder, inside the parlour, went up into the tower, but this ladder was different; it took her outside. Uncle Am held her by one wrist and Aunt Maggie by the other, so she wouldn't step too close to the edge and be in danger of falling off the roof. She could see the bunting and the flags waving on the street below. She could not see Tress—who was looking after Patrick—though Tress told her later that they had waved up at her.

This year on the twelfth, Grania will again climb to the roof with Uncle Am and Aunt Maggie. Father's uncle will once more be riding King Billy's white horse. Last year, Bernard stayed close to the hotel, ready to help when the crowds came to the dining room after the parade. Bernard is the home-stayer. That is what Mother calls him. Bernard never likes to be far from home.

Uncle Am's back is responsible and tight as he holds the reins. *Horse, eye, sun, rump, hickory at the side of the road.* Grania lines up the pictures in her memory so she can describe them to Mamo. *Leaves toss inside the maples. The bay is a dark bulge below the town.* When they pass the Catholic church, Tress gives her a poke because they are in the exact spot where Mamo crosses herself every time she goes past in the buggy. The two-storey house beside the church looks stark and bare, with empty verandas upstairs and down. At the top of the church steps, one of the double doors is propped open with a board. Father O'Leary, who has a birthmark shaped like a pipe behind his ear, must be inside, letting in the warm air. Mother calls this the changing time of year, just after summer has begun, when outside is warmer than in. Even though Grania is outside now, she thinks of what the church is like when she is in. Dank and cool, the aroma of burning coals and wax, a solemn heaviness in the air. A place where children have to behave. When everyone else is praying, Grania moves her lips any old way and pretends to know what is going on.

It will take almost three hours to reach her grandfather's farm. Because it is a long trip over bumpy, dried-up roads, they are going to stay overnight. Bompa Jack is Uncle Am's father and Father's father. Grania tries to arrange the line-up of fathers and brothers and uncles and great-uncles in her head. Tress and Patrick sleep part of the way, but Grania stays awake the entire time. She stores pictures of rocks in the fields, and endless trees that throw off shadows. She knows that Bompa Jack calls the trees *bush* and not *woods*. She sees a rabbit hop out of the bush and sit at the edge of the road. The rabbit does not frighten the horses. Uncle Am turns and sees that she is the only one awake and his lips say, "Did you see?" And she nods.

Grandfather stands outside the farm house, suspenders over his shirt, ready to greet them as they arrive. He has a wide build and a stern face and he is not as tall as his own sons. Grania knows that Bompa Jack hides a smile behind his stern face. She can see his laughter before it happens. He removes his hat and squints up at the girls, holding out his arms. Grania jumps down with no shyness at all, but Tress climbs down from the other side before she goes around to be kissed and hugged. Grania looks at the barn, at the split-rail fence, the conical heap of manure past the first gate, the smooth rock surface on the slope behind the house. She sees the open-sided milk house, the place where Bompa Jack keeps a salt shaker so he can rub a fresh tomato against his shirt, take a bite, add a sprinkle of salt and eat the tomato while he stands. *He takes a bite.* Grania thinks of the boy in the *Sunday* book, the partly eaten apple, the open book pressed to his chest. The words of yellow rope are stored in Grania's head.

The farm kitchen is filled with visitors, great-uncles and uncles and aunts, all sitting around the long table. They rise from their chairs when Uncle Am and the children come in and everyone is hugged and squeezed. There is a white-and-gold teapot on a trivet at the far end of the table. One of the great-uncles, a priest from Marysville, is dressed in black. Grania sees a word here and there as her glance flits from face to face. It is too difficult to see where conversations start or where they continue. Words and laughter erupt around her and she tries to follow, but she can't because so many people are talking at once.

Her grandfather beckons her to the end of the table, where he is seated on a wide chair. He looks directly at her and enlarges the words on his lips. Although he is speaking to her, she can tell that he is also speaking to his sons at the table.

"Your mother's memory will always be alive as long as this redhead is around," he tells them. "Every time I see her she is more like my Sarah. Eyes the same brown. Hair the same red. Look at her arms, look at the shape of her hands." He takes one of Grania's hands and stretches her fingers out over his own. "You're the apple of my eye," he says. "Are you going to say my name?"

"Bompa."

"Grampa," he tells her. "Grampa Jack."

She watches the *J* drop from his jaw, the upward clamp of the *K*.

"Jack," she says. "But your real name is John."

"The Irish up here on the Ninth are all Joes, Jims and Johns," he says. "That's why I'm Jack."

"Jack," she says again. "Bompa Jack."

"Good enough for me. You're as quick as you were before the sickness." He doesn't say the word *deaf*.

Bompa Jack's sister, Great-Aunt Martha, is preparing the next meal with the help of the younger aunts. Great-Aunt Martha shares Bompa's house. She is taller than he is, and wears a close-fitting rimless bonnet inside the house. She is the only person Grania knows who does this, but Mother has told her that Aunt Martha likes the old ways. The bonnet is grey and looks severe, but there are rose-coloured ribbons tied under the chin. Grania stows this picture in her head, so she can report to Mamo.

There are rhubarb pies with lattice tops lined up along the counter, and Grania stores this, too. Mamo will be sure to say, "And what did the women serve for your supper?"

The wood stove has been lit and the air in the long kitchen is warm and close with the smell of roasting meat. Bompa is always threatening to find a new husband for Aunt Martha. "There's still a good leg on the cook," he says, pointing to her ankles as she walks across the kitchen. "We'll find her a new husband yet."

Laughter erupts again. "He's an old fool," Martha says to Grania, looking out from inside the bonnet. "That's all he is."

"And still vain," he says. "I would like the camera brought out for this occasion." He looks to Martha as if Martha will know where everything is.

Grania sees the word *camera* and thinks she also sees the word *school*. She looks to Tress to get information, but Tress has turned aside. Sometimes it is not easy to follow Bompa's speech. Like Grew the barber, who trims Father's moustache, Bompa tries to help Grania understand by exaggerating his words. But his lips end up distorting, and Grania loses the wholeness of them, and the words end up running all together.

When the camera is placed in Bompa's hands, he sends for his shirt. His new one. And his bow tie.

The new shirt is eight years old but it looks new because it is worn only twice a year—Christmas Day and the anniversary of the day when Grania's other grandmother died. Grandmother Sarah was burned in the woods in the sugar bush fire, when her long wool skirt caught up some sparks and burst into flames, and no one could save her. Every year in April, on the date of her death, the children tell the story to one another, even though none of them knew her when she was alive. She was burned during what Bompa Jack calls "the maple moon." She ran to the shallow creek with her skirt in flames and broke through the ice and tried to wet her clothes to put out the fire. But the burns were severe. And though the dressings were tended and changed every day, she died before the week was out.

Uncle Am disappears upstairs and comes back with Bompa's crisply ironed shirt and his black bow tie. Bompa slips the suspenders from his shoulders until they droop below his waist. He changes into his new shirt and leaves the shirt-tail hanging over his work pants. He spends a moment knotting the bow tie. He looks like a catalogue version of himself.

"In 1901, I paid twelve and a half cents for the tie," he says, looking around at the others. "It was sent to me by T. Eaton, Esquire, himself." But everyone has heard the story.

He looks to Grania. "Come out," his exaggerated lips say. "I want you to use the camera."

He places it in her hands and everyone goes outside and he shows her how to hold the black box steady against her waist, how to look down and centre him in the tiny square window, how to press the sunken button. He wants head and shoulders only; his hand paints a frame around himself, through the air. The aunts and uncles stand back, frozen in a semicircle, as if by remaining still they will also be part of the composition. Even though he knows the button has clicked, Bompa maintains his pose: shoulders tight, smile hidden, lips closed to present a firm jaw. When he feels it is prudent to move, he unfastens the bow tie, slips off the new eight-year-old shirt, and puts the work shirt back on. This time, he tucks the worn collar down into his neckline. It is warm out here in the sun. He hauls up his suspenders, and now he looks like Bompa Jack again.

Another photograph of Bompa is taken, this time in his ordinary clothes, standing with all of the relatives. Everyone has a serious face for the photograph. Grania takes a long breath and steadies the camera and presses it to her body. Her palm shields the tiny window to keep away the sun.

The last photo is taken by Bompa Jack. It is a photo of Grania and Tress and Patrick, sitting on the rough bench that has been dragged out from under Bompa's favourite tree.

The evening meal is served early because everyone is hungry and because some of the aunts and uncles have to return to their farms and homes before dark. A lamp that sits on the wide window ledge is now lit. Everyone joins hands around the table while the great-uncle who is a priest says grace. The talking stops while food is passed around. There are potatoes that have been browned in the pan alongside the roast beef. Another pan is filled with gravy that is flecked with dark brown bits that have broken away from the roast. Before supper, when Aunt Martha poured the juices from the pan into the gravy, she looked at Grania as if they were conspirators and her lips said, "We always save the goodness in the pan." There are new carrots from the garden, and creamed peas, and a pot of fresh tea for the adults, and milk for the children, carried from the milk house and poured into an enamel jug. There are pickled beets and corn relish and, finally, cooled rhubarb pie served with fresh cream.

After everyone has eaten and beds have been allotted—Tress and Grania will share a narrow room upstairs that has a curtain across the doorway and a pipe hole in the floor—and after the uncles have gone back to their farms with their wives, and after the priest returns to Marysville, Grania sits on the veranda with Bompa Jack and the others. The sun sinks lower and lower until lips can no longer be seen.

She is glad to let go of the conversation. She is worn out from try-ing to store the events of the day, from watching eyes and throats and lips and teeth and tongues. She sinks into the warmth and haze of family that surrounds her and she falls asleep. She is carried by tall Aunt Martha upstairs to bed. Tress and Patrick are right behind. They follow the dense odour of kerosene and the flame that darts and flickers while Bompa holds the lamp high and precedes them up the stairs.

In the early morning, Grania tiptoes down before Tress wakes, and watches Bompa Jack as he stands at the kitchen washstand that has a bucket under its open drain. He lathers his face with his badger-hair shaving brush and shaves his cheeks and throat in long soapy strips. He plunks his hat on his head and sits at the table with Grania, while Great-Aunt Martha makes his tea and prepares breakfast.

When it is time for Uncle Am to go and get the horses ready, Bompa Jack gives each of the children a gift: for Tress, a gold wish-bone pin that belonged to Grandmother Sarah; for Patrick, a small carved horse that he can hold in his palm; for Grania, the camera, which is placed in her hands. She is not sure of all that has been said, but she is certain that the camera is now hers. Goodbyes are said quickly because it is Sunday morning and Uncle Am is going to take them directly to the church in Marysville on the way home. Once again, while the children are being hugged and kissed, Grania thinks she sees the word *school*.

Chapter 3

Vibration plays an important part—the voice, in some instances
in the making of letters, coming from the chest, then from the
throat, the nose, the chin and often times the top of the head.
                                            Lecture, The Toronto Fair

August. The heat soaks into Grania's skin. She and Mother board a
steamer and they cross the bay and then Lake Ontario, a long jour-
ney of almost nine hours before they reach the state of New York.
By the time they are met and reach Aunt Annie's house in
Rochester, it is time for Grania to go to bed. She follows Aunt Annie
up the stairs, through a shadowed hall and into a room where
Grania and Mother will share a narrow bed. Aunt Annie is
Mother's younger sister. She has eyes that look like Mamo's, and
her chin moves the same way Mother's does when she talks. Aunt
Annie and Mother have catching up to do, and it is late when
Mother comes to bed.

In the morning, a taxicab is hired. It has a flat roof and high
wheels and black sides, and Grania steps up behind Mother and sits
as straight as she can, and hangs on to the hardness of the door
while the taxicab lurches and jolts through the streets. They are
driven to a modern office building where, on the second floor, they
find the office of a special doctor who knows about ears. They are
beckoned into the waiting room, and Grania sits on an uncomfort-
able chair that is too high for her, and she tries to look in every
direction at once. When the doctor comes to the doorway, Mother

flutters her hand to show Grania that she is to follow, that she is to sit up on the edge of a padded table inside a smaller room. The doctor helps her up. His skin is mottled; his cheeks are lumpy; his eyes are the brightest blue. Grania is relieved to see that his eyes are kind. While the doctor's face is turned towards Mother, Grania inspects four charts along the nearest wall.

She is astonished to see that every chart contains an ear. A giant, coloured ear. Each huge ear is different from the next, each drawn to reveal a maze of meandering tunnels and shapes. Letters and words and arrows point into and out of the ears. Inside one, a black shape is coiled like a shaded snail. In another, a network of tightly packed tunnels resembles beehives that have been sliced open to reveal the activity inside. The tunnels in this chart shoot off in many directions. In the third ear, there is a shape like a bent wishbone. A green balloon—or is it a pea?—is stuck inside that ear's passageway. The last ear holds the shape of a tiny horseshoe.

Grania has never before seen the inside of ears.

The doctor peers inside her own ears with a light. He taps a smooth stick along a series of bells that are suspended from a wooden frame on his desk. He picks up a small angular hammer like the one Grania has seen in Dr. Clark's office in Deseronto. After that, something two-pronged and silver. The blue-eyed doctor raps this on top of the desk and places it behind Grania's right ear. He taps again and holds it behind the left.

Thud. Thud.

While he is doing this she thinks, *sea*, or is it *C*, the word she sings when she is by herself. The doctor forces her attention back, and signals that she is to close her eyes. He holds something to her head and this time it sends vibrations into her skull.

She opens her eyes. He raises a hand to conceal his lips but she sees that his cheeks are moving. He lowers his hand to his side.

"Did you hear?" his lips ask. "Did you hear the word I made?"

He leans towards her. Mother leans forward in her chair. Four eyes are watching for the answer.

She pauses.

"Grania," Mother's lips say.

"No," she says, with her voice. "No."

But she feels. She feels the sea singing deep inside her head.

She watches Mother's disappointment.

"She blocks us out," Mother tells the doctor. "She keeps her focus away unless it pleases her to pay attention. She turns away from me."

"She picks and chooses?"

"Exactly."

"The girl is totally deaf," he says. "There is nothing I can do. Scarlet fever has done this to thousands. She should be sent to a school with other deaf children. She is nine years old—no longer a little child. You don't want to waste more time before beginning her proper education. She has already lost several years. We have a school here in Rochester—a good school. I could give you a referral, make inquiries on your behalf."

"No." Mother stands and faces Grania. Her lips say that they are returning to Canada. They are going home.

"It would be a simple matter to arrange a meeting," the doctor says.

But Grania sees the set of Mother's chin. Grania is glad they are going home.

They leave the office, but not before Mother pauses and turns back to face the doctor. Mother has remembered her manners. "Thank you for seeing my child," she says. "Thank you for your advice."

*

"What are they saying? Is it about me?"

Father and Mother are in the parlour and Grania has been sent from the room. She and Tress are in the kitchen. Mamo is nowhere to be seen; she might be upstairs in her room or outside on the stoop. Tress lifts her chin, turns her head so that her ear closest to the parlour can hear.

Listen.

"Not loud enough," the lips say. "I can't hear what they're saying."

But Grania sees from Tress's face that this is not true.

"Tell."

"There's nothing to tell."

"Are they sending me away?"

Tress's hand makes the signal for quiet.

"Tell," Grania says again. She tries to make her voice whisper. "Are they sending me to deaf school?" Between her and Tress hangs a tiny puff of air. Now her voice changes.

"Tell."

She feels her hands being lifted by Tress. There is a look on her sister's face—what is it? Something that has not been there before. What? Something twisted, her mouth. Tress is looking far far back. Or maybe far far ahead.

"They're sending you away to live at the school," she says. Grania is frightened when she sees that Tress is crying and she, too, begins to cry. Her whole body is shaking. "The school in Belleville," Tress says now. "The one for the deaf and dumb."

*

It is Grania's last day at home. After a special supper at the corner table in the hotel dining room, she and Mamo walk along the shore of the bay, hand in hand, heading towards the rocky place near the edge of the woods. Mamo carries the lumpy clock bag, its strap slung over her shoulder. When they return home, Mamo pulls Grania to her lap in the rocking chair and they rock together for a while, and Mamo blows into her ear.

Father comes to the house to get her and takes her to his office in the hotel and sits her on his knee. She knows that he has been outside this evening, because his sleeves smell like stable and horse. He gives her a hug and a kiss and they sit quietly together. Carlow is on the floor and puts one paw over his pirate eye and Grania says "YEW," to make him feel better. Father's moustache has been trimmed by Grew and, when he begins to talk to her, Grania understands most of what he says. He tells her that if she is afraid of the dark at school, she should say her fears out loud. She should send them out into the dark.

Grania is surprised. How does Father know that she is afraid of the dark? Maybe Father knows about the ankle rope, too.

"Say your fears into the dark, my darling, and they will go away," his lips tell her.

Grania tries to understand and she nods and smells Father's tobacco smell and he takes her by the hand through the passageway, back to the house.

Now Grania is in her own bed, tucked in by Mother. It is late and she thinks about Patrick and Bernard in their beds in their shared room at the end of the hall. She thinks of Mamo in her room, of her parents on the other side of the bedroom wall. Do they have fears? She thinks of everyone in the family sending their thoughts out into the dark. Does everyone want her to go away?

She pulls hard at the ankle rope, her lifeline, the ribbon of night language she will no longer have with Tress. She senses stillness across the room. She moves her foot. No response. She tugs the rope again. Tress is suddenly beside her, standing at the edge of the bed, leaning over and pointing to her own lips.

"Stop," she says. "I have to sleep, Graw. I'm tired."

Grania closes her eyes and commands her body to be still. If she moves too much, Tress will detach herself and slip the end of the rope over her foot and off. If that happens, Grania will be cut adrift, cast out into the floating dark.

Her leg tenses while Tress returns to her bed on the other side of the rag rug. The pattern of leaves outside the window flutters against the shade. She has to keep Tress attached but she also has to fall asleep. She tries to dull her brain but she can't turn off the pictures in her head.

She gets up, risking Tress's anger.

Tress is still awake. "What's the matter now?" Instinctively she raises her head so that Grania can see her lips in the zigzag of light.

"I can't sleep. It's too dark."

"Tell your brain to stop thinking."

"What?"

"That's what I do. It's easy. I tell my brain to stop thinking and then I go to sleep."

Grania returns to her bed, but her brain won't stop thinking. The more she tries, the more her brain creates pictures. She drifts in and out of half sleep. She finds herself inside a sea of tunnels. She follows hand signals and painted arrows and the sluggish movement of snails. Her ears are below water but she fights against going completely under. The seashore girl at the end of the *Sunday* book drifts by, lifting her head off the page to look at Grania as she passes. She is wearing her hat and sash and dress, and she is still waiting to be rescued. A flotilla of earless ladies with willowy waists and trailing skirts sails by. Oscar, the cutout man with the black pointy toes, floats past in his catalogue underwear. Despite his stout belly, he does not seem in danger of sinking. Grandfather O'Shaughnessy's body surfaces, turning over and over in the rolled-up sheet. The cutout girl in her new bathing suit dips down and pops up through the waves, but she is alone and makes no sign that she has seen the others.

Grania thrashes soundlessly in her bed as she feels the press of water from above. She forces her arms and legs to move. She rises to the surface. In the morning she wakes and finds herself in bed with her sister, snuggled close. Warm and covered, safely tucked, deep down inside the blankets of Tress's bed.

*

Mamo sits in her rocker in the parlour, alone in the house. She has slept poorly, the night before. Bernard is next door at the hotel, Patrick with Mrs. Brant in the hotel kitchen; Tress is at school. It is a fine September day but Mamo does not go out to the veranda. Even so, with the windows open, she is alert to a change in the air. Autumn has begun. In the early morning, she placed her gift inside the child's new canvas trunk before the trunk was loaded onto the back of the wagon. Agnes and Dermot have not yet returned from Belleville.

Mamo feels as if the creases in her face won't yield, as if her lips won't speak. She can do nothing but sit by herself with the school newspaper, *The Canadian Mute*, on her lap, and think of the child during each step of her journey.

The child, the child. She looks down at the paper and reads: "Every child should get a letter from home at least every two weeks. Some pupils seldom, if ever, hear from home and this is shameful. On the other hand, it is better for parents not to write too often, as it keeps the mind of the pupil from its work."

Mamo's stationery is ready in the drawer of her bureau, upstairs. Wearily, she turns the newsprint page.

"Every year we are sent an exceptionally bright lot of lads and lasses and, if their parents will give us time, we hope to make manly men and noble women of them."

Mamo sighs. She reaches for and unfolds a separate sheet, the official instructions sent from the school. For the third time, she examines this as if it is a document from a foreign land:

The Ontario Institution for the Deaf and Dumb
All deaf mutes between the age of seven and twenty, not being deficient in intellect, and free from contagious diseases, who are bona fide residents of the Province of Ontario, will be admitted as pupils. Length of schooling is seven years, or in the case of a late arrival, until the student reaches the age of twenty. There will be a vacation of nearly three months during

the summer of each year. Parents, guardians or friends who are able to pay will be charged the sum of $50 per year for board. Tuition, books and medical attendance will be furnished free. A qualified physician visits the Institution every day and a trained nurse is always in attendance. There is a well-equipped hospital where every sick child is given the best of treatment.

Deaf mutes whose parents, guardians or friends are unable to pay the amount charged for board will be admitted free, but clothing must be furnished by parents or friends.

At the present time the trades of Printing, Carpentering, Shoemaking and Baking are taught to boys. Female pupils are instructed in General Domestic Work, Tailoring, Dressmaking, Sewing, Knitting, the use of Sewing Machines and such Ornamental and Fancy Work as may be desirable. Manual Training in woodwork for boys, and Domestic Science for girls have been introduced.

Good, says Mamo to herself, thinking of her own skills and how she learned them in the old country, taught by the generations before her. Good. All of this will help Grania in her future.

Most pupils receive training in the sign language every afternoon. Articulation classes are held between 11 a.m. and 1 p.m.

When pupils assemble in the classrooms each morning, the teachers will open by prayer. At one o'clock, the pupils assemble in the chapel. After prayers, they will be dismissed in a quiet and orderly manner and they will again proceed to their regular classes. Prayers are those prescribed for use in the Public Schools of Ontario. Methodist, Anglican and Catholic pupils will be taken to the appropriate church in the city every Sunday morning. Catholic pupils also receive religious instruction Friday afternoons from 2 to 2:30 p.m.

The next is difficult to read and more difficult to know. Mamo has read this part twice and has discussed it with Agnes and Dermot. She knows it is a rule that must be complied with, but it bangs in discord inside her head as she forces herself to read again:

> Pupils will not be permitted to go home for Christmas. If chil-
> dren are taken away at that time they will not be permitted to
> return until next fall. There is a good reason for this rule. It is
> impossible for a majority of the pupils to go home for Christ-
> mas—the distances are too great and the cost too much. If
> some went home, others would be rendered discontented and
> unhappy. Moreover, the work in the classroom would be
> greatly interfered with. If all or a large number went home,
> some would be almost sure to bring back contagious diseases,
> as frequently did happen in years gone by before this rule was
> made. Of course it is a great deprivation for you not to have
> your child with you at Christmas but this is one of the sacri-
> fices love must make.

It is enough. An institution of rules and more rules. Mamo lets the papers slide to the floor. How can she not see the child for nine full months? And Christmas away! She herself has pushed the parents to send the child to school. She closes her eyes and makes no attempt to stop the tears from pouring freely down her cheeks.

Chapter 4

*A number of years ago I visited a large school for the deaf, and
taught all the pupils to use their voices. In a few cases the effect
was decidedly unpleasant, the voice resembling somewhat the
cry of a peacock.*

Alexander Graham Bell

Belleville, Ontario

After the heavy doors close behind her, she is taken to the dormitory and shown to her bed. It is the second Wednesday of September. At the residential school that houses 271 students, Grania O'Neill is last to be admitted, last to arrive. She looks around her and begins to cry, and she cries for the next two weeks. "Don't cry," say the adult lips around her. "Be a good girl and don't cry."

No one but the hearing staff has to listen to the outflow of wails and miserable snufflings that escape her body. During the last three days of this period, she cries without sound. Her classmates see but do not interfere, remembering their own arrivals. There have been other new students and other tears, but Grania is the only child who cries without let-up for two weeks.

On September twenty-seventh the house mother pulls down the covers to wake Grania as she does every morning, and continues on to the other beds. Ceiling lights are on. It is five-fifteen. Grania has been dreaming that Father is in the doorway of his office. His lips distort as he calls out, "Where are you, my darling?" He turns away as Grania wakes, even though Grania shouts after him and tries to make him see that she is not lost.

She sits up, leans against the metal bed frame and decides that she is finished with crying. She flattens her unhappiness the way she and Tress once pressed leaves inside Tress's book *The Faeries* and placed it high on the closet shelf. She gets up and follows the other girls to the hall and to the bathroom. She never sheds another tear at the institution, not during all the years she is a student. The whites of her eyes redden severely from time to time, but never again is Grania known to cry.

What she does not see is the bound ledger, the *Descriptive Register* of the institution, where several facts were recorded the day of her admission.

Date of Birth: May 25, 1896
Birthplace: Deseronto, Ontario
Cause of deafness: Scarlet fever, age five
Hearing loss: Total

She was vaccinated against the smallpox in 1903, has no offensive disease, and there are no other cases of deafness in the family. Her father, last name O'Neill, is the owner of a Deseronto hotel.

The final questions on the left side of the ledger are:

What are the number and names of other children in the family, including the mute?

What is the child's natural capacity? Bright, dull, stupid or idiotic?

Beside the last question, written with a fine nib in black ink, is the single word: *Bright.*

An extra note added later, in blue ink, states that the child has spent one year at a Regular Hearing School and that she has received some home schooling. "She seems particularly adept," the note continues, "at lip reading."

A four digit ledger number, which will be her number throughout the remaining years of her childhood, is entered beside Grania's name.

*

Grania tries to read the unfamiliar lips of strangers but sees only faces, moving cheeks and bobbing chins. This is so frightening, she pulls farther inside herself and does not attempt to use her voice. Not in the way she is used to speaking to her family. At home, she can say anything and be understood.

On a Thursday evening, after the second week of tears and surrounded by a sea of faces and a whirr of hands, she follows the other children to the dining hall. She sits at the table, takes two bites of meat from her plate and finds the meat to have a strange taste. What she reads from lips around her, lips trying to be helpful, is that she is eating something called *Swit steak*—pounded beef cooked in broth and catsup. She has never eaten beef prepared this way at home. In the hotel dining room there is catsup at every table, but Mother never mixes it with meat in the cooking. It was Grania's job to fill the catsup containers. She thinks of Tress helping her tilt the big jar to fill the small ones, and when she thinks of Tress she lays her head on the cloth-covered table. She knows instinctively that if she stays awake she will cry. But she has made up her mind not to cry again. *Some grief is so big, it has to be held in, Mamo has told her.* She falls asleep beneath the conical rays of light reflected from the lamps that hang from the ceiling. One of the older girls at the table wakes her and signs, using the hand language. Grania has learned some signs from the girls in her dormitory—it has been necessary to learn quickly—but she has no idea what is being communicated now.

She looks around in panic, and what she sees is a large vast room filled with strangers. It strikes her at this moment that she might as well be in an orphanage, her abandonment is so complete. There is no Tress to be her go-between, no older brother, no smaller brother, no Father, no Mother, no Mamo to be her comfort. Mother kept her at home, and now that she is nine years old, she has been sent away. Mamo is part of the conspiracy that has brought her here. Mamo *wants* Grania to be away at school. "You need the schooling," she told Grania when she held her tightly on her lap before she left home. "You need to learn what other deaf children are learning."

Grania thinks of the heavy closed doors at the entrance of the school, the marble staircase that leads to a wider landing. She will never escape through the big doors by herself. She stares at her plate until the girls are dismissed from the table and she follows them out of the room and outside and across the path to her dorm. While the others prepare for evening study, the quiet period before lights out, she sits on the edge of her bed and calls up every detail of her arrival two weeks earlier, and of her parents' simultaneous departure.

*

When Father's horses had pulled up to the main entrance, Grania was helped from her seat and waited while the new canvas trunk was hoisted down behind her. A group of curious girls stood in a clump at one side of the heavy double doors and stared. Each girl had a flat bow in her hair, pinned butterfly fashion at the back of her head. Grania did not want to look at the staring girls, and she turned away. The sun glared like a yellow eye. The horse nearest Grania looked on in sympathy. *Horse, eye, sun,* she said to herself, storing the pictures. *Father, Mother, doors, dark.* But she would not be going home to report to Mamo. Mamo was in Deseronto. Grania took in a long slow breath. The scent of the air had changed. Without warning, autumn was moving in to take summer's place.

What happened next, Grania is no longer sure of. She and her parents might have walked through the big doors. Or an adult from the school might have been standing outside the building to greet them. Did the doors bang shut behind her? Did Father and Mother say goodbye beside the wagon—or inside, near the marble staircase? The doors had made a sound. She was startled. Or has she imagined the sound?

What she remembers is that Mother leaned over to kiss her goodbye. Mother's dark eyes showed something new, and Grania had hoped, for a moment, that Mother would grab her by the wrist and take her home again. Then, Father was hugging Grania and his lips were saying "Goodbye, my darling."

She has no picture in her mind of her parents stepping back up into the wagon.

One thing she does know for certain. Although the distance by horse and wagon—or steamer, or train, or even automobile if her family were to own one—was just over twenty miles, she might as well be two hundred miles from the family she would not see again until summer of the following year.

Her trunk was not taken to the girls' residence where, within moments of her parents' departure, she was led by the tall and gaunt house mother, Miss O'Shaughnessy, who has the same name as Mamo. Instead, the trunk was taken to a lower room, where its contents were fumigated. Later the same evening, her clothes, reeking of fumigant, were brought to the dorm. Along with these, she unpacked her horn comb—a gift from Patrick; an olive-wood hairbrush from Bernard; a matching hand mirror from Tress; the black box camera from Bompa Jack, and one precious roll of film. Her parents had given her a small purse containing two shining fifty-cent pieces. The King, wearing his crown, was on one side of each coin, a wreath of leaves on the other. The spending money was turned over to the house mother, to be administered by the school.

A posed photograph of Mamo in its own cardboard frame, taken in Deseronto's Fairbairn Studio, was tucked inside Grania's *Sunday* book and signed with x's and o's, which Grania knew to be kisses and hugs. The photograph was new, a surprise. In it, Mamo was seated on a chair with a tall back. She was wearing her high-necked blouse and her knitted vest. The white strands of her hair were pinned with long hairpins that Grania knew to be there but that were invisible in the photograph. Grania stared at Mamo's hands as if seeing them for the first time. The raised veins, the lumps and arthritic nodes on her fingers, were all captured within the frame.

But Mamo's face was the same. Her eyes looked directly at Grania. If Grania moved, the eyes followed. On Mamo's face was *love*. The same love that had moved back and forth between them the night of the Great Fire. Grania wiggled her fingers to herself the way Mamo did when she told the name story, the story of the fire.

Mamo had been careful to tuck the photo of herself beside a page of the *Sunday* book that Grania knew well. In the picture, a girl of Grania's age was wearing a dress and buckled shoes. She held in her hand a triangular sailor's hat that had been folded from newspaper, and she was perched on a wide plank stretched across the mouths of two open barrels. A boy, holding a cardboard sword and wearing an eye patch, was standing on the grass nearby. The girl was staring with a fierce look out of the page and did not seem in the least to be afraid. Grania knew the caption by heart: *Dulcie is a very brave girl, said the pirate.*

Grania thinks of the walk she and Mamo had taken the evening before she left home. They'd walked along the shore of the bay to the rocky place near the edge of the woods. The place where they carried the burlap bag from the O'Shaughnessy trunk. *When things get bad.*

Grania, sitting on the edge of her narrow school bed, commands herself to remember.

*

She soon learns that even though she is encouraged every day to use her voice with her teacher, she is barely understood. She resolves to keep her voice inside, not to let it out. But her teacher, Miss Amos, won't settle for that. She taps Grania on the shoulder, watches her lips, brings Grania's attention back to her own lips to see the shapes of the words she is trying to say. Grania has been put into a mid-level group because she is quick to lip read, and because of the home schooling with Mamo. It has been decided that she will be taught a mixture of oral and manual training.

Miss Amos instructs her in the single-hand alphabet, which Grania, already knowing her printed letters, has no trouble learning. She also learns to use the signing space in front of her neck and upper chest. Signs made at the lower chest and waist are harder to see. She tries to watch faces, as well as hands that are in motion around her. "Keep eye contact," her teacher insists. If Grania looks away, once again Miss Amos brings her attention back.

Miss Amos, in her twenties, has dark brown hair in a style rolled back from her forehead. Every day she wears an ankle-length pan-elled skirt, a long-sleeved blouse, and a narrow tie that hangs from neckline to waist. Every day, the necktie is a different colour: Kelly green, old rose, heliotrope, fawn, cerise. Miss Amos is eager to teach, eager to have the children learn. Sometimes she rolls the sleeves of her blouse right up her thin arms and past her angular elbows, as if she is digging in to teach the children one more impor-tant thing. She delights in their accomplishments. She is as proud as they are, when the children achieve.

Along with Grania, there are eleven other children in the room. Eight of these know the sign language. They signal to one another with animation; they prance like mimes. Grania watches the expres-sions on their faces change as rapidly as the messages on their light-ning fingers and hands. She begins to learn signs for food: her small closed fist raps her temple for cabbage; knuckles rub an imaginary tear from the corner of her eye for onion; two fingers tap-tap the back of her hand for potato. She learns to cut a hand wedge for Sun-day pie; she grinds her palms together for cheese. During a meal in the dining hall, when she sees a spider on the wall, she crosses one wrist over the other and sends her fingers scurrying through the air before her, delighting the others at the table.

She begins to send signals out slowly from her body, but she is frustrated by the flap and flurry of hands that face her when signals try to come back in. At times she sees nothing more than a rapid blur and cannot differentiate even one sign from another. Her eye movements are not quick enough to catch up to the speed of the hands and fingers around her.

Instead, she pays attention to lips as she has done at home. But in the classroom, Miss Amos wants more: she wants Grania to anticipate, to see a signal that a word is about to form, to guess what it will mean as a whole. This works in slow motion with Miss Amos, whom Grania now tries to please, but away from the classroom the other children expect her to understand not lips but hands, and at their speed. If Grania does not understand, she is left out.

The only place where she can move lips and hands freely, in any way she wishes, is in the chapel. During daily prayers, surrounded by other deaf children, there is no one to hear or notice the babble of nonsense words that Grania's voice speaks, or the meaningless signs her hands create. She begins to look forward to the regular time when she can stand in the chapel and blather anything at all. Every day, she comes away from the chapel feeling refreshed.

And then, unexpectedly, one Saturday as she walks through the dark panelled corridor on her way into the dining hall, she watches spelling fingers that face her on the way out. The fingers spell C-E-D-R-I-C. Cedric is on duty, an older student warns. Which means: *Behave during the meal.*

Mr. Cedric is a teacher as well as the editor of the school paper, *The Canadian Mute.* He is not unfair, but he expects good behaviour when he is in charge. It is only when Grania finishes eating and leaves the table that she feels a delayed rush of triumph. She realizes that when she walked through the doorway on her way in, she understood the finger-spelled name.

The next day, missives that once tumbled incomprehensibly through air become single words strung together, sentences she can understand. A language is taking shape, one in which, haltingly, she is beginning to take part. She misses and misunderstands, but puts meaning—right or wrong—to words that come at her in sign. Her hands, to her surprise, and jerkily at first, begin to send ideas out. Her face and body punctuate; her eyes receive. She is falling into, she is entering a new world. She is joining the larger conversation of hands.

Grania now knows that her deafness will always have more significance at school than it ever did at home. The teachers are constantly bringing the fact of it to her attention. It is their mission to try to fix the damage deafness has inflicted upon her speech; relentlessly, they try to remedy and repair. She is marched back and forth between classes. She is taught by one teacher with signing hands and other teachers who know only how to speak. The new matron of the school, who arrived shortly after Grania, knows no more of the sign language than she does. The children watch and laugh and give encouragement while Matron also attempts to learn.

Grania sees hands that are open and relaxed, and fingers that are stiff and stuck as tightly together as if they are glued. In class with Miss Amos, she tries to train herself to feel her voice, to keep the measure of its volume. As all but one of her teachers are hearing, she has to take care that her voice does not blurt out and make a hard noise, a bad noise.

Through all of this, and knowing that her Deseronto home has been stored in a private place buried inside herself along with her tears, she slowly begins to feel that she has sisters and brothers, more than she could ever have imagined. The difference is that these children, almost three hundred of them, are like herself. Sisters and brothers who are not afraid to raise a hand and ask a question of a teacher like Miss Amos, with her Kelly green tie and her rolled-back hair.

*

Grania creates words silently inside her mouth. Her teacher is telling the story of Sammy and the monkey and turning over cards that hold pictures of a monkey dressed in a waistcoat and a flat round hat. Miss Amos writes on lines ruled across the chalkboard.

     Sammy bought a monkey.
     He sold the poor monkey because it was sick.

When the story is over, she taps her hand rhythmically against her side while Grania and eleven other pupils in the room try to chant

> p as in pie and
> b as in buy
> and m as in my.

And Grania slaps the side of her own dress.

In the afternoons, they take turns sitting in pairs on side-by-side chairs that are pulled up to a low table that has a rectangular tilting mirror attached to the back. Grania's partner is Nola, who is also nine years old and who has been deaf from meningitis since she was two. The girls pucker their lips, leaving a small opening between; they growl at the mirror, showing teeth; they open and shut their mouths. When they finish their turn at the table, they return to the front of the class and stand at Miss Amos' desk and blow out candles for *P* as fast as the teacher can relight them. More drill, day in, day out, week after week, the class recites

> oo
> as in boo
> as in boom
> as in whom.

Wooms, Grania thinks. *The password.*
Poom, she thinks.

Her private word from the dugout under the wharf. Someone made a stink, but who? She thinks of Kenan who is going to marry Tress some day, and Tress herself, and their joking friend Orryn, and how they all laughed inside the hideout and tried to teach her to say the forbidden word *fart*, but Grania refused and made her own word: *Poom*.

Where did the word come from? She laughs to herself.

Did she laugh out loud? Miss Amos is frowning.

> The tongue draws back inside the mouth
> ah, bah

> and bow-wow
> and huff muff.

And she is so tired.

The days run together and she is instructed to use more voice, more breath, not so much breath. She holds fingers to her teacher's lips and feels the puff of air with *beat* and *peat*. And places a hand on her teacher's throat for *fox* and *flax*.

"Lightly, now," her teacher tells her. "Feel the word. Now to my throat, back to my lips. Let the shape of the word fall into your fingers. Scoop it up with your hand."

> I for ice
> See the rice.
> See the mice.

"Voice, use voice." Miss Amos' lips shape the instruction, again and again. "Work at control. You must control your voice."

The children print careful words across their slates. They learn to pass sound from one pair of lips to another. They shout into the air, test their own throats, lips and tongues. They roar out of the silence inside them.

*

On Sunday afternoon, Grania accompanies the other children to the assembly hall to see the magic lantern views of "The Life of Christ." Most of what is signed by Mr. Norris, the teacher who shows the views, is understood. Grania sits in the partially lighted room and is amazed to see each of the stories of Jesus presented in a picture. She thinks of the sampler on her wall at home: *God's eye for my seeing, God's ear for my hearing,* and wonders if Saint Patrick might have been deaf and used God's ear to hear.

After supper, when she is back in her dormitory, Grania organizes and reorganizes every item she owns. At the bottom of her drawer are two letters she has received from home, one from Mamo and one from Tress. Each is a page long and has been unfolded and read and folded again. Mother will be writing next, Tress told her in the last letter. Grania checks the contents of her shared cupboard, and her shelf in the communal bathroom down the hall. She has a hook for her towel, her own cup, a place for toothbrush and soap. In her room, she arranges and rearranges stockings and underwear, two nightgowns, an extra pair of boot-laces, handkerchiefs, and wide ribbons for her hair. The ribbons are a gift from Aunt Maggie, who brought them to the house and buffed them over a lightbulb on one of the parlour lamps to get the store wrinkles out.

She folds and pats two sets of long woollen drawers for winter, and one Swiss-ribbed top. In Payson's Indelible Ink, her name is printed inside each item of clothing. She inspects her horn comb, her olive-wood brush, the photo of Mamo lying flat in her drawer— she does not want anyone but herself to look at Mamo. She holds the hand mirror given to her by Tress and stares into it and says words of her oral homework. She fastens a nib to her pen and dips the nib in ink and writes out her letters. She makes neat words and sentences and reads what she has copied from lines Miss Amos wrote across the board during Friday's class. She sits on the edge of her bed and lifts her *Sunday* book to her lap and turns the pages. She invents her own caption: *Dulcie was an orphan who lived at the school the rest of her days.*

After supper, when it is time for lights out, she lies stiffly on her back and keeps her eyes wide open in the dark. When her eyes adjust to the beam of light that slides under the door, she turns on her side and looks around. Some of the girls are older, twelve and thirteen. Each is aware of the word *quiet,* the word used by hearing teachers and staff, but never by the children.

Who cares? Nola once signed to Grania. *Who cares about quiet?* Noise is something that is present during the hours of light. It is the quiet of hearing persons that rules the dark. Every girl in the dorm has learned *quiet* through warnings, in the same way that Grania learned *quiet* at home when she tiptoed across the rag rug.

Nola stirs from her bed in the corner. Every night after the house mother shuts the door, she slides out from beneath the covers, kneels on the floor and prays. Grania can see her lips in the dim streak of light. Nola always says the same prayer: *Please God, don't let me wake up blind.*

Nola has told Grania that at home, after she became deaf, her mother wakened her every morning and asked, "Can you see?" Every morning, a different object was held up for Nola to identify— a thimble, a spoon, a doily, a cup. Nola has been asked so many times if she can see, she is now terrified that she will go blind.

Across from Nola is Bridie with the heart-shaped face. She wears her hair loosely pulled back and held in place with hairpins that she is forever losing. During the day, she is the liveliest of all the girls, but at night she pulls the covers over her head and refuses to look out again until morning. And Erma is there. Erma who never stops talk-ing—with voice—to herself and to everyone else who cannot hear.

Grace is not totally deaf; she has a low level of hearing. But Grace's biggest wish is to have no hearing at all. She tells the others that in articulation class, her teacher nags her: "Blow your nose, clear the passages. Feel the pressure in your ear canals. Listen to your sounds." She is supposed to find the place in her ears where she is deaf.

"How do I know where I'm deaf?" her hands ask Grania. "Teacher says: *Swallow, listen, blow your nose.* That's supposed to tell me where I'm deaf in my ears. But if there is other noise in the room, I don't hear anything. And there is always noise in the room."

But Grace knows how to use her voice. The others watch and know that she is the best speaker of them all. She arrived at school when she was eleven and tried to leave the same day she arrived. As she wasn't allowed to leave, she learned what she had to do, and this is the part of the story Grania likes best.

Grace taught herself to turn off sound. Listening with a tiny bit of hearing makes her so tired, she has taught herself, instead, to be deaf. She has learned to fall into her own silence—the place where Grania and the others live without choice. And Grace knows how to stay there. While she was learning to be deaf, she stuffed cotton down her ear canals and then braided her hair and pinned a circle of braid over each ear so the teachers wouldn't see. She has tried everything she can think of to block the entry of sound.

Celia is a long-necked girl who pretends to be fearless, but Grania knows—as do the others in the dorm—that every morning at the same time, eleven-thirty, just before dinner, Celia walks into the girls' washroom to have a cry behind the door. After three or four minutes, she wipes her eyes, comes out and catches up to her class in the dining hall, where she can be seen laughing and using the sign language with her friends. But first, she has to have her daily cry. It is Celia who complains to Grania that no one checks their dormitory at night. Miss O'Shaughnessy sleeps in her own room down the hall. "Everyone thinks we are sleeping, but we could be dead," Celia says, flipping a palm to make the sign for dead.

But Grania is not worried about being dead. Grania is worried about the dark. She hates the dark. She keeps her eyes open as long as she can. She thinks of what Tress told her at home. *I tell my brain to stop thinking, and then I go to sleep.* She tries not to miss Tress. But she can't help herself; she misses her every moment. She misses Tress telling her what is going on. She misses the language of the ankle rope and the gentle tugs that anchor her to her sister's bed. Grania remembers her talk with Father and, from the unfamiliar mattress, she begins to list her fears aloud.

> Don't let me live here forever.
> Don't let them lock the big doors.

Don't let me be an orphan.
Let me go home again.
Don't let me live here forever.
Don't let me be an orphan.
Let me go home again.

She chants to herself, her fingertips tapping the side of her leg as she throws her fears out into the dark. She inches her body down into the bed and even deeper into the place where her silence lies, the place where she is safe.

*

In the middle of winter, Fry—her real name Freda—is led to the dormitory. Pupil number 272, Fry attended school earlier in the United States and has now moved to Ontario with her parents, Canadians returning to Toronto, where they were born. During their trip back, they have dropped Fry off in Belleville, along the way. Fry, deaf from meningitis since age four, lost her hearing and her spoken language as well. She has had difficulty using her voice ever since. She was a good student at the American school and there is little she cannot communicate in the sign language. But her old school began to shift exclusively to the Oral Method, and it is for this reason that her parents have moved her back to Canada.

The house mother pushes and shoves and rearranges beds in the dorm and, for reasons of her own, assigns the tall girl to the now-empty bed beside Grania. When Grania walks into the room, Fry looks up and smiles. She has green eyes that stare into Grania's, and straight-cut bangs. Her arms are covered with more freckles than Grania has ever seen on one person. A small round depression is visible in each cheek, whether she is smiling or not. There is a scent of lavender coming from the clothes she is wearing. She and Grania become instant friends.

Fry is able to use the language of hands more rapidly than anyone

Grania has ever seen, but she is self-conscious about her voice. "My voice is broken," she tells Grania that first day when they sit on the edge of their beds and face each other. She makes the sign for break with her hands, and snaps the invisible voice that falls between them. "My voice is broken broken broken."

*

"Tell me," Grania's hands say. Since Fry has moved to the dorm, Grania's own sign language has improved. "What was it like when you lost your hearing?"

Fry replies in a beat as one hand bats the air over her shoulder. "Long time past. Five years now. I was sick—weeks in bed, not much remembering now. But I remember my heart pounding so hard I thought it would explode. First time I went outside, I felt my own footsteps walking through me. Like being trapped in a drum. I believed I was hearing. Maybe it was before the sickness. Maybe it was the last bit of hearing I had." She looks away, then back. "What do you remember?"

"Sounds. I think there are sounds in my head."

"Which sounds?" Fry leans forward.

"Doors closing." The edges of Grania's palms slam together, facing out. "Big doors. By the office, at the entrance. First day here, I heard them shut behind me." She stops.

"You felt the doors," says Fry. She makes a face. "The way we feel thunder."

"No, I heard them." Grania is insistent. "I heard the doors. Sometimes I dream about them banging." She pauses. "I had a dream last night. Father brought me to his office to tell me I was going away—to a school where children's ears do not hear. I was brought here, and then—my parents were outside the doors and I was in. I banged at the wood, and the house mother came." She makes the O near her cheek, the name-sign for Miss O'Shaughnessy.

Grania recalls, in the dream, looking up to a row of teeth, a wrinkling of skin, a face not unkind, wreathed by greying hair. She also remembers that in the dream, when Miss O'Shaughnessy's mouth moved, she was babbling. She raised her index finger, the other three fingers joining the thumb. Her hand slid back from the side of her lips and made the tiniest bounce along the line of her jaw. The babbling continued, but Grania understood. It was her first formal word in the sign language—*dormitory*. The word that led her to the building where she slept her first night away from family and home.

"It's the sad place," says Fry. "The big doors. Where we all cry when our parents leave us."

"I cried," says Grania. "Every day for two weeks." She hasn't talked to anyone else about this. But now it is part of her history in the place. And she has a friend to tell.

*

On the third Wednesday of June at the end of her first year, after nine long months of school, Grania lifts the soft-sided bag with the wooden handles that Father has brought with him so that she can carry her own small things on the steamer. Father has already arranged for her trunk to follow them to Deseronto. Grania sniffs carbolic when she thinks of the trunk; her own and everyone else's will be fumigated, clothes and all, when they return in the fall.

She isn't going to think about the fall. She steps out through the big doors at the entrance. Today, a wedge of wood keeps each of the heavy panelled doors open so that people can come and go, in and out. Grania crosses the lawn two steps behind Father. When they reach the dusty road in front of the gates, she turns. The weathervane on top of the roof, the steps, the buildings, all pull firmly together as if to say, "We'll still be here in September."

She turns her back.

From the road, the waves of the Bay of Quinte appear soft and grey. It is almost one o'clock in the afternoon. By four, every student will be gone, the little in care of the big, the big in care of teachers or supervisors who will deliver them to collecting points or appointed meeting places along the railway lines—west and east and north and south. Since early morning, horse and rig, express wagon and flat-roofed taxi-buses with open sides have been hauling away trunks and luggage and every trace of the students and the school year. After final assembly, even motor cars have arrived at the main entrance to collect the few children who are to be driven home in private vehicles.

Grania and Fry hug each other and tears spill down Fry's cheeks. Both girls know that when they return in September, Grania will be placed entirely with the Oral students, Fry with the Manual. No matter what, they vow, they will always be best friends.

Miss Amos is wearing a cheerful strawberry red necktie on the final day of school, and a jacket over her long-sleeved blouse. She is busy coralling a group of children in her care, but she looks up as Grania leaves and she waves. Several of the older students, the seniors, are putting on their serious faces. The moment they walk or are driven through the gates, or step onto a railway platform, or wait on a wharf—the moment they leave the school grounds—they know they are entering a world fraught with the unannounced and the sudden. They have to blend in, they have to look normal. They are about to rejoin the hearing world.

As Grania walks behind Father, the fingers of her free hand make *T* for Tress as she taps the letter against the side of her dress. She is travelling towards the sister she has not seen since the previous September. She wants to run, but Father walks steadily towards the dock and she catches up to him and keeps his pace. She glances at him sideways as the steamer approaches. His moustache needs a trim but she doesn't care. She stays close to his side, and thinks of Grew the barber, and Main Street, and Father's hotel, and the tower apartment, and Carlow, and her friends Orryn and Kenan, and the dugout. She thinks of her brothers, and Mother, and Mamo. She thinks of the journey ahead, the journey of just over two hours that will take the steamer to Northport for a brief stop and, finally, to the Deseronto wharf and home.

*

After laughing and being hugged by Mamo and Mother and Bernard, and Patrick who has grown so much, and after touching everything she can see to make sure it is all as she left it—rocker, woodbin, mantel, clock—and after sniffing Mamo's Canada Bouquet, and after shouting a vowel at Carlow, after all of this, she and Tress run upstairs and shut the door to their room. The beds are in the same place, the rag rug between. The framed daffodils, the oval mirror, the sampler about God's eye and ear hang from their hooks on the wall. The maple outside the window is in full leaf.

And now, the boundaries of their old private language explode as they begin to add in the new hand language that Grania has brought home. She teaches Tress with patience and expertise, positioning and repositioning her sister's fingers, palms and thumbs.

This is the sign for girl—she draws her thumb along her jawbone as if to tie a bonnet ribbon under her chin. *This is the sign for play*— she makes the Y sign and shakes out both hands. When the deaf boys' team played hockey against the speaking boys in Belleville, her class was taken to a game. *This is the sign for race, for running.* She tells Tress about Victoria Day: how the children were taken for a picnic in a clearing in the woods by the bay. The senior girls gave a demonstration of fancy club swinging, and she was fascinated with the precision of the drill. She does not want to swing Indian clubs herself, but she might learn the scarf drill when she is older. Tress has never seen Indian club swinging or the scarf drill, and Grania stands on the rag rug and flings her arms about, trying to transfer the picture of tumbling clubs.

What Grania remembers most about the Victoria Day celebrations is that she wanted nothing more than to enjoy herself and to run races with Fry. They came second in the three-legged and first in the boot race, and won an orange each and two candies. At the end of the afternoon, she and Fry helped with the smaller children, getting them back to the dorms, walking slowly up the low incline. Miss Amos tried to keep up the spirits of the little ones in the younger classes, and led them in the signed chant:

The twenty-fourth of May,
The Queen's birthday,
If we don't get a holiday,
We'll all run away.

That same evening, they ate prunes and bread and butter and milk for their supper, and later, after dark, they were taken outside again to watch a display of Roman candles, fire balloons and sky-rockets, pin-wheels and fountain wheels. The night exploded silently before their eyes while, tired and excited, they leaned into each other's warmth, their skirts tucked beneath them as they sat on the grass of the school lawns that were lighted all around with electric lights hidden inside Japanese lanterns. All of this, she tries to convey to Tress.

*

It is years later, after Grania learns to *own* the sign language by tak-ing it inside herself—though the hearing teachers will eventually forbid its use while she struggles to please them with her voice—it is years later when she realizes how close to the visual-gestural lan-guage she and Tress actually were with the childhood signs they once invented for themselves. *Follow,* one thumb tracking the other; *want* and *eat* and *smile* and *water* and *fly.*

For her part, the first summer Grania comes home, Tress attempts to gather up and tell all of the remembered events that happened within house and hotel since Grania left. They communi-cate with excitement, Grania reading her sister's lips as easily as she had before she left—the invisible air writing, too. Tress's index fin-ger writes C-o-r-a while she brings up the old complaints. Cora meddled in Aunt Maggie's job at the library, and Aunt Maggie would not put up with it and gave Cora a piece of her mind. Grania tries to slow her sister's story, tries to put the meaning of things together. A piece of mind, she quickly realizes—and makes the adjustment to understanding—is an expression like kick the bucket, or apple of my eye.

The sisters pause and sink back on their beds. They realize almost at the same instant that it is impossible—the catching up. Too much has happened. Three seasons have passed. They will have to live inside short moments of the present, like travellers who shed parts of their lives, like the travelling ladies upon whom they used to spy across the roof. Like wisps of cloud that vanish inside a summer wind.

After Grania has been home for three days, Mamo sends her to get the *Sunday* book. Apart from the pictures and their captions, there are stories, too—hundreds of words in stories that Grania still does not know. When they put the book down, Grania begins to teach Mamo the hand alphabet—which the old arthritic hands delight in learning. M-a-m-o, Grania spells, and she creates a name-sign, tapping a three-fingered *M* against her cheek.

Father has Grania's roll of film developed, and Grania arranges her photos on the black pages of the new album that is waiting at home, a present from Bompa Jack. There are photos of Fry, and Fry and Grania together, and Nola, and Miss Amos, and Bridie and Erma and Celia and Grace. And there is one of the editor, Mr. Cedric, with the older boys in the print shop, all wearing their striped aprons, a kind boy named Charles holding up a copy of *The Canadian Mute*. There is a photo of the large rink in winter, and another of a group of boys standing beside a deep puddle outside the steps of Gibson Hospital, which Grania labels in her neat handwriting: *Boys at school*.

When Father is not around, Mother prays for a miracle, and before Grania returns to school, she and Mother make the long trip east, first by train and then by steamer, down the St. Lawrence River, to the shrine of Ste. Anne de Beaupré in the province of Quebec. Grania stares up at huge wooden chandeliers and a towering crucifix, and sees men and women around her standing, sitting, standing. She feels Mother's hands, one on each side of her head. Mother prays, and crosses herself, and Grania goes still and waits to see what will happen, but nothing changes inside her ears. She moves her lips in babbling prayers of her own when Mother tells her to pray to Ste. Anne, but she does not let Mother hear. Mother understands her voice and will know that she is making up the words. She watches to see what Mother will do next, and she follows as they walk between church and Cyclorama on their way back to the wharf. They are admitted inside and climb high steps to see the depiction of Jerusalem, and Grania, holding the railing, circles the platform and stays close to Mother in case large hands reach out of the giant panorama that surrounds them and pull something from her ears. Something that keeps her from hearing and that Mother wants removed. Mother crosses herself again and prays, and Grania keeps a close watch, and waits, and moves her lips in a babble. But nothing happens inside her ears.

Mother insists, during the trip, that Grania use her voice. Mother has not learned any of the sign language that Grania brought home with her at the beginning of summer. "Too busy," she says whenever Grania tries to teach her. "I have too much work to do."

At the end of summer, despite the trip to the shrine and despite Mother's prayers, Grania is still deaf.

In September, her departure approaching, Grania takes Carlow to the fenced backyard and sits on the stoop beside him and pats him on the back. Her voice makes swooping sounds as she begins to sing. Up and down and out of her head, the words swoop like the flights of swallows. She sings the title, "I don't want to play in your yard," over and over, because that is the only part of the only song she knows. Carlow listens, and understands. And Mamo, standing behind the laundry window inside, also listens and understands.

Grania goes upstairs and folds her clothing into her sturdy canvas trunk. The trunk is sent ahead to Belleville, and she travels—again by steamer, westward along the Bay of Quinte, this time escorted by Aunt Maggie, who has errands to do in the city—to the dock at the bottom of the slope across from the school grounds. The details of Grania's first year away have already become lodged inside a hard casing of her memory. She tries to keep the summer memories of home in front of these, so that she can carry them back with her to the Belleville school.

And there is something else. Something Grania knows. Before she hugs Father and Mother and Mamo and Tress and the boys, and before she boards the steamer at the wharf across from her house on the corner of Mill Street and Main, she looks north, to the town she is leaving for the second time. There is her family home with the veranda and its leaning fence along the Mill Street side; there is the open passageway joining the two buildings, and the columns and steps of Father's hotel. There is Carlow beside the veranda post, staring forlornly after her. She stares back, and waves, and looks hard at the upstairs window of the room she shares with Tress above the street. She does not cry. What she knows in that moment, and what she clearly understands when she looks back, is that there are things she will never be able to impart, things that will never be understood—not even by Tress or Mamo. Things that make up the portion of her life that is now lived, separate and away, at the institution in the land called *School*.

II

1915

II

Chapter 5

The Lusitania, *the largest and fastest passenger ship in the world, was torpedoed and sunk by a German submarine ten miles south of Kinsdale, near Queenstown, Ireland, on Friday, May 7th. The Germans gave the people of the ship no warning and she sank in fifteen minutes. 1150 persons—passengers and crew—were drowned, including 50 babies and 100 other children under 2 years, aged women, and heart-broken wives and mothers going to the bedsides of wounded husbands and sons. The survivors numbered but 767. Some 140 bodies were recovered and buried at Queenstown. To celebrate this murder of 150 babies, the 'Kultured' schoolchildren in Germany were given a half-holiday. By this slaughter of the innocents, is the Kaiser trying to out-Herod Herod?*

The Canadian

Belleville, Ontario

"They tell me, at the school, that you'll be joining up." It was neither question nor statement—perhaps something of both.

Jim nodded. "But not until the fall."

The man between them was stretched out on his back on the long board table in the kitchen, where he'd been carried before their arrival. His face was the colour of pale ash and he was looking up at the two of them. His glance darted from one to the other, as if reading their faces would tell him the sum of what he needed to know. A yellowed scar bulged through the man's eyebrow, which gave his face an expression of calamity already known. His wife had stuffed a bolster under his neck to support his head and, except for not know-ing the fate of his leg, he looked as if he'd be all right for a while longer.

"Will you bring a clean towel?" the doctor asked, and the woman left the room, passing them as she did.

Dr. Whalen's voice was deep and slow. The voice of patience learned. It was the way Jim thought of him, a tired man who had the necessary patience to get through the work that set itself before him from sunrise to sunset. Jim knew that he was called out in the night, too. And he was the regular physician at the Ontario School for the Deaf. He also worked weekends if a baby decided to be born, or if a patient in his practice—or a child at the school hospital—needed attention. The institution on the Trent Road had been part of the landscape on the outskirts of Belleville for forty-five years. A new-comer to the area, Jim now knew that the institution had changed its name a few years earlier, that it was a large school for a small city of ten thousand, and that deaf children were sent from every part of the province and from other provinces, too.

There was a tourniquet of sorts around the man's upper thigh. No, Jim saw now that it was more bandage than tourniquet. It cov-ered rather than constricted. It had been someone's shirt, the cloth a dull moss colour, washed many times. It had been folded flat, and the sleeves were wrapped around and tied. There was surprisingly little blood on the makeshift bandage or on the man's pantleg, which had been slit up the side as far as his waist. The man's boot and stocking had been removed from one foot. Jim's glance took in the scissors on a corner shelf near the single step that led up to the next room, where the man's wife had disappeared. The edge of the step was smooth and worn, leading to a dining room or parlour. Every farmhouse had a parlour. Jim's grandparents in eastern Canada had had one, and so did his uncle in Ontario—Uncle Alex, whose family Jim had stayed with when he'd first arrived.

The injured man's son, who looked about twelve or thirteen, was standing at the far end of the kitchen where Jim and Dr. Whalen had come in. His face was as pale and anxious as his father's but he looked hopeful that he might be asked to do something. Jim could see the side of Dr. Whalen's black Ford over the boy's shoulder, through the window at the end of the room. A rifle hung on a rack above the window frame. There was another window near the stove and water reservoir. There was no electric light, but this was early afternoon, and there was light enough in the room.

Dr. Whalen unwrapped the makeshift bandage and spoke to the man directly for the first time.

"Ah, Herbert." This caused everyone standing—the woman had now returned with three folded towels—and the man lying to look at him, waiting. "I think this is going to be all right. Can you move your foot? Your toes?"

As if encouraged by the doctor's voice, Herbert not only moved his foot and toes but raised his leg, too, which caused him sudden surprising pain. He slid his jaw to the side and gritted his teeth, and his leg slumped back to the table.

"No no, not that," said Dr. Whalen. "Give it a chance." He pressed the leg firmly into its natural position and raised his glance slightly to Jim, who collapsed open the doctor's leather bag. It split lengthwise into halves, and the doctor reached, without looking, for syringe and needle. He sawed at the crease of an ampule with a dull blade and snapped off the glass top. He injected the contents into the man's upper arm. The man closed his eyes.

Dr. Whalen was working swiftly now, cleaning the wound, pouring solution while Jim propped Herbert so that the area could be fully exposed. It was a dangerously wide and uneven tear, six inches or more around the side and back of the thigh. Jim saw the layers of fatty tissue and muscle spilled out on the surface; these had flopped inside out instead of being tucked inside the skin where they belonged. The wound was almost bloodless. Gut had already been threaded through the eye of the curved needle; the suturing was finished in ten minutes.

"If you'd ripped an artery, you'd be a dead man, Herbert. There's not even a broken bone here. You'll have a scar, a thick one, and it's going to be ugly, but it's the best I can do, given the wound. Rest a bit, will you? And try to stay off that jagged tin roof."

Herbert managed a grimace. "I need the leg to work," he said. "Can't be running a farm hopping around on one foot." He spoke sullenly, but his colour was coming back, the scar through the eyebrow less prominent now. Another calamity dealt with.

The leg was washed and properly bandaged. What remained of the trousers was cut the rest of the way through and Herbert was helped off the table, leaving the splayed trousers behind. He hopped on one boot to the kitchen sofa. There was a comic look about the movement, though no one smiled. The boy was outside now, admiring the auto that shone in the sun, circling round, reaching in to touch the steering column. He stood back to admire the pleated seat backs, the diamond-patterned seats. In the kitchen, the woman laid a quilt over Herbert's legs, then saw the men to the door. On the faces of the boy and the woman, there was nothing to be read but relief.

*

"My boy will be leaving in July." Dr. Whalen continued as if forty minutes inside the farmhouse had not interrupted the earlier conversation. "Artillery. He says he wants to be a gunner."

At the word *gunner*, Jim looked down at his own hands. His grandmother, who had raised him, had taught him to play piano with those hands.

Dr. Whalen caught the look. "Have you thought of something on the healing side? Orderly? Field ambulance? Stretcher bearer? You've seen a few things working with me the past winter. There's much you could do to help, Jim. I'd go myself, but I'm too old."

They were following Cannifton Road and the narrow Moira River the short distance back to the city. Belleville, halfway between Montreal to the east and Toronto to the west, rested on the north shore of the Bay of Quinte, the same bay that Grania's town, Deseronto, looked over. The Moira ran south through Belleville and emptied into the bay, just east of the School for the Deaf. The school had been built back from the edge of the bay in 1870; it was there that the two men were headed now.

It had been a cold winter during the months Jim had been working for Dr. Whalen. Two months earlier, in March, men with horses and ploughs had cleared the snow from the bay in front of the school, marked the ice beneath, sawed it into chunks and floated them in the water. The ice, a foot and a half thick, had been pulled out block by block and loaded onto sleighs, individual blocks weighing three hundred pounds. The school had its own ice house. Now, because of the long winter, it was well stocked for the rest of the year.

Despite spring runoff, the water level of the Moira was dropping, though a good current could be seen from the Ford. Even so, there was a mood of stillness as the two men followed the course of the river. Clouds were banking high on the far side of the sky, and dust rolled out behind the motor car as they drove.

"I haven't figured out exactly what to do," Jim said now. "It might be November before I get away. Uncle Alex made me promise that when I finish working for you at the end of the summer, I'll stay for the fall sawing."

"The *Lusitania* helped my son with his decision, Jim. The drowning of those women and babies was a cowardly act. A brutal act by cowardly men."

*

Jim had not mentioned Grania to Dr. Whalen, but it was she he had been thinking about during the conversation with the older man. He had first met the young woman with the red hair the previous fall, when he had been working for Dr. Whalen only three weeks. It was her stillness that compelled him to a halt. He had been humming; he had sprinted in from outside, down the stone steps of the school hospital and into the lower bandage room.

He'd fallen silent because there she was, standing like a small contained island in the middle of the room. Perhaps a gathering moment before she organized the tasks that would move her forward in several directions at once. Despite this being a hospital, he could hear a cacophony of activity from children in the ward upstairs. He had taken three stone steps down and through the shaded passageway, and now he felt the brightness of artificial light in the open room. He had come in at the side, the delivery entrance, where the bricks were coated with a thick display of vines. He thought of the thickness of the vines. He thought, *She hasn't moved, why hasn't she moved?* But he was the one standing there with packages stacked to his chin.

The vine leaves were darkening outside. He wanted to tell her. He wanted to say something about the lime green streaks through the leaves; how they twined—perhaps they'd been cut back intentionally to frame the windows upstairs. But she would know this. She worked here; she would think he was not in his right mind.

The hospital, Gibson Hospital, initially intended as a place to isolate children with infectious diseases, was divided by a hall down the middle, on the first and second floors. Jim guessed that upstairs, beds were assigned to boys on one side, girls on the other. A balcony on each level stretched across the front of the building and the effect of the whole was that of a large and elegant two-storey house. As for the young woman with the smock over her calf-length skirt and her back to him and her bright red hair swept up and pinned—he had never seen her before.

He walked forward and set the packages sent by Dr. Whalen on the shining surface of the countertop. Miss MacKay, the nurse on duty, entered the room from a short corridor, having come down a set of stairs herself. What was surprising when she spoke to him was that the young woman with the red hair—she was facing Miss MacKay—still had not moved. He walked behind her and his arms—as they reached over the counter—flickered, or so he imagined, into her peripheral vision. She showed no sign of being startled. She pulled a list from her pocket, looked it over, and tucked it into her pocket again.

She was deaf. Too late, he was sorry he had approached from behind. Any hearing person would have jumped a foot if he'd moved in from behind like that. No, a hearing person would have been aware of the noise made by his feet, would have been aware of the sound of him running down the steps of the passageway.

He hadn't intended to startle. But she wasn't startled.

"This is Grania," Miss MacKay said, introducing. "Grania O'Neill. She's been working with us for several years, ever since she graduated. She did the Home Nursing course when she was a student, and then she stayed on. We're short-handed these days, we always are. It's been worse since one of our nurses joined up—people at the school seem to be leaving every day."

Grania watched Miss MacKay's lips and Jim watched Grania—a visual triangle. Miss MacKay was explaining. "He helps Dr. Whalen; he works for him. He moved here from the east, from Prince Edward Island, and now he stays in Belleville."

"Jim Lloyd," he said, and held out his hand. He watched Miss MacKay's fingers spell his names into the air, a quick but emphatic pause between the two.

Grania's eyes were on the nurse's right hand, not on Jim's face—or only fleetingly. She looked at him directly then, and returned the greeting. *Her voice. A lilt of song.*

"How do you do." A small soft hand in his. She saw a speaking man, a lean young man with dark brown hair and dark eyes whose arms hung down as if they were loose in their sockets. He had long slender fingers, and he was taller than she, and he had an earnest face. She saw *earnest* in his eyes.

What Jim saw in Grania's face was strength. A strength so still, it was possible she did not know it was there. Her skin was pale and clear, her eyebrows furrowed slightly, giving her face a quizzical expression, as if she were figuring things out. Her eyes were brown, and when he looked at her he felt that she knew something, perhaps something peaceful, or wise, that no one else could possibly know.

Miss MacKay continued. "We've had a card and a letter from our nurse in England. During the crossing no one was allowed to take off their clothes or their boots at night. They had to be ready to get into the small boats quickly in case they were torpedoed by a submarine!" She was breathless using the words *torpedoed* and *submarine*, as if these were threats that were spoken of every day.

Jim turned back to Grania.

But Grania was gone. She had disappeared up the back stairs. He heard light footsteps, a pause at the top. And then, the sound of her was lost in the general inside and outside noise of the place.

Chapter 6

The son of one of our employees, who is at the Front with the first Canadian Contingent, was at the now famous battle of Langemarck where the Canadians so distinguished themselves. He had a very narrow escape when a German bullet, whizzing past his head, cut the lobe of his ear. He dropped to the ground and a Captain fell dead on top of him. Later in the battle, while assisting to move one of the big guns, he had his foot crushed by one of the wheels and is now in a hospital where he is doing well and hopes soon to be "at it" again.

The Canadian

Grania had been dreaming, same old dream. She sat on the edge of her bed and pushed back her long hair. She reached for and expertly slid two curved combs along the sides to hold the hair in place. She pulled up the counterpane and slipped into her dressing gown, and in her rush past the mirror detected movement from the bed on the other side of the room. Fry rolled over and opened one green eye and then the other, and she made a face. One pale arm, blotted with freckles, was outside the covers. She had been rubbing half-lemons on her arms since Grania had first known her, insisting that this diminished the number of freckles, but Grania had never noticed a bit of difference in all the years they'd shared a room.

They were in the new residence now; they had moved a year ago, just before the June visit of the Duke and Duchess of Connaught, their daughter the Princess Patricia, and their entourage. The royal party had arrived in a grand automobile that glided onto the school grounds while the younger children, lining the edges of the walk, waved their small Union Jacks. Grania had taken a photo with her box camera that sunny day but it had come out disappointingly blurred, the faces no more than featureless smudges. All that could be seen were the large-brimmed hats and long dresses of the Duchess and the Princess Patricia, and their closed parasols pointing to the boards of the outdoor platform. The Duke and two other men wore top hats. The bunting, strung between trees behind the platform, had drooped. In the photo, the scene appeared rather sad. But it hadn't been sad at all. There had been huge excitement that day. That was before the start of the war. Now, one of the visiting party in the photograph was dead: Colonel Farquhar, Commanding Officer of the Princess Patricia's Canadian Light Infantry, had already been killed in action at the Front.

The official opening of the girls' new residence had actually happened after the royal visit, in October, the day before the children's Hallowe'en party. Premier Hearst had visited to do the honours that day, but the girls had moved in long before that.

Grania now held up a palm to Fry. *Sunday*, she signed. *Church. Don't go back to sleep.* Fry was off duty but in charge of getting the younger girls to breakfast. After that, she was responsible for taking the older Catholic children to St. Michael's before seven. Like Grania, Fry was one of a few students who had stayed on at the institution to work after graduation. Fry worked in the big kitchen from which meals were served, nine months of the year, to more than three hundred children and staff. Towards the end of June, Fry and Colin would be married. Tall blond Colin had been in the Manual class with Fry when they were students, and now worked as Mr. Cedric's assistant in the print shop.

The rest of Fry and Colin's class had long since dispersed, as had Grania's schoolmates from the Oral class. Many had returned to their parents' homes to live. Some young men had left for type-

setting jobs in other cities. One boy, a good friend to Colin, worked
in Pittsburgh and wrote to Colin frequently. In July, Colin and Fry
would be moving to the upstairs of a house within walking distance
of the school, where they had found three rooms to rent. In September, Fry would return to work in the kitchen, and Colin to the
print shop.

Grania thought about Jim. He had been part of her life for more
than eight months now, and he had managed this by appearing
from a far-off place she knew nothing about—Prince Edward Island,
by the sea. After her first meeting with him at the school hospital
last fall, he'd persisted in returning to speak to her; he'd come back
on the pretext of doing an errand for Dr. Whalen, even when there
was no errand to invent. In the winter, with her parents' permission, he had taken her to meet his Uncle Alex and Aunt Jean at their
farm in the country, not far from Read. At Easter, he'd travelled by
train with Grania to Deseronto for the day to meet her family. Tress
and Kenan, who'd married the year before and now lived in rented
rooms in a house on Dundas Street, had come to the hotel to join
the rest of the family for dinner. Everyone had greeted Jim with
enthusiasm except Grania's parents, who had been courteous but
cautious. "Bring him home," Mother had written to Grania in
advance of the visit. "But make no announcements."

Were her parents worried about him going off to war, worried
that Grania would be left alone? Kenan would be leaving soon, and
Tress would be alone. Or were they concerned because Jim was a
hearing man? In any case, there was no announcement to make.
Not yet. But Grania knew it would come.

At home, Patrick had questioned Jim relentlessly when he discovered that he would be joining up in the fall. Patrick wanted to talk
about nothing but the war. Bernard had greeted Jim warmly and
quietly. Mamo declared to everyone, when Jim was not in the room,
that it was plain to see that he cared very much for their Grania.

To Grania, Jim was a persistent and earnest young man who was
full of hope. Being with him gave her hope—if anyone could dare to

hope during a war. Jim often hummed, his lips moving in some private song of his own. She said his name aloud, and smiled to herself. He had told her that when she spoke his name, it came out sounding like *Chim*.

Grania did not know how events would unfold, any more than anyone did, heading into the summer months of 1915. She felt the tension underlying all talk of war; she saw the anxiety of families when a loved one in uniform said goodbye. She tried not to think about Jim joining up in the fall. Newspapers were predicting, as they had the previous autumn, that this time the war really would be over by Christmas. But a steady flow of young men continued to leave the country. More and more had signed up since the sinking of the *Lusitania*. And Grania knew, and Jim knew, that within months he would be leaving for *over there*.

*

The previous fall, moments after Miss MacKay had introduced Grania to Jim in the bandage room, Miss Marks, Grania's former teacher from her senior years, and now her friend, had come down the steps from outside, leading a long line of students who were arriving to have their measurements taken. Every fall, heights and weights were recorded and hair checked for nits. One by one, the numbers were entered in the student pages of the ledger called *Medical Records*, along with head, arm and leg measurements. These would be repeated in June, for comparison, at the end of the school year.

Miss Marks had left the pupils with Miss MacKay below, and followed Grania up the stairs. She fluttered her hand to get Grania's attention.

"You've forgotten," her lips said. She was smiling. "There's a trick." She swiped her hand across her own forehead, *forget*. Miss Marks had learned the sign language and always signed and spoke at the same time.

Grania frowned. *Trick?*

"When you meet someone. I saw the young man downstairs. There are always tricks."

Grania's eyes, intent, watched the familiar lips.

"Tricks the deaf children have been teaching me ever since I first came here. I may be able to hear, but I'm always learning, too."

"You're the teacher who sees as much as we see."

"Never so fast."

"What trick?"

"If you're worried about not being understood, get the person to talk. You take charge. We used to go over this in class. Ask questions while you're watching lips, tongue, mannerisms—all the cues you need to give yourself time. You can lip read every person in this place, Grania. But the hearing world is out there beyond the gates."

"I go back to it every summer."

"Back to your family. Protection."

"True." Grania's index finger arced forward off her chin, *true.* "You want me to *ingade* in conversation."

They both laughed at their private joke. For years, Grania had understood one of the instructions in Articulation class to be *ingade in conversation*. Miss Marks had caught and corrected that, but only by chance, and long after Grania had finished school.

"Next time a young man arrives at the door . . ."

But Grania was already arguing with herself.

I could have stayed downstairs. I could have "engaged" in conversation. I could have said more. I know the words. I could have joined in. But she had not. Jim Lloyd was a hearing man and she had run away. She had escaped to safety up the stairs.

*

At this moment, she was wishing that she had wakened earlier. She hurried around the corner of the main building, alert to aromas wafting from the kitchen. Cook would be preparing pancakes for hungry children who were being roused—older helping younger— and making their way through the halls to stand before rows of sinks. As milking had to be done before breakfast, the farm boys were already up and out at the barns. On the dining tables there would be maple syrup in plenty this morning. Sugar snow had come and gone, farmers' trees were tapped, the new syrup was in, the old no longer rationed. The children loved their syrup, and their Saturday-night candies, too, if they had a copper to spend when the basket was passed around.

Grania felt unevenness beneath her shoes as she almost stumbled over a clump of earth. New shoots had shoved up through last year's old grass and the surface was damp with dew. Every year, the older boys pushed the heavy roller over the lawns to flatten the lumps. She looked back to see if her feet had left an imprint. She had been counting under her breath—316 steps from dorm to hospital door, part of her internal knowledge of the place. As she approached, she saw movement and looked up. Miss MacKay was on the upper veranda, shaking a blanket over the railing. She waved, and made the sign for *La Grippe*. Like most of the staff she was a hearing person, but she knew more of the sign language than most. She held her nose and, with one hand, flung out her fingers: *La Grippe, almost gone*.

Grania signed back, *We hope*. She laughed, a muffled sound coming from her throat. *La Grippe* had raced through the dorms, tiring everyone out. Only a month before, the children had been quarantined for another reason: there had been so many measles cases in Belleville, no one was permitted walks or excursions into the city.

Grania glanced to the right as she rounded the building and paused when she saw soldiers marching on the road past the school. Reminders of war were everywhere; she was surrounded. Soldiers were frequently seen near the Armouries, and at the Belleville station where they said their farewells and joined eastbound trainloads of other soldiers passing through. Uniformed men in brown were also seen on Zwick Island, where they sometimes did their drill, and on Front Street and along Cannifton Road.

When word of the *Lusitania* had first arrived at the school, Cedric

had stopped everything to pen his editorial, and Colin and the boys
in the print shop had had to work extra hours to reset type. Grania
had been frightened by the news. She remembered a small boy who
had drowned in the Bay of Quinte one summer when she'd been
home for the holidays, and she recalled the sorrow on the faces of
his parents. After the funeral, Mamo had shaken her head grimly
and said that the boy's family had been known to grow marigolds,
the flower of death, in their garden. Now, it was impossible for
Grania to expand the image of one dead boy to encompass the picture of 150 dead babies floating in the sea off the coast of Ireland.

The beautiful land called Ireland. It wasn't so easy to conjure that,
either. The picture she had always had in her head was the one her
grandmother had given her through story. With the sinking of the
Lusitania, Mamo's word picture was being replaced by another, one
that held murky waters and dark sea and drowning babies washing
up through waves. It was this picture that lurked in her mind, the
one that erupted no matter where Grania was during the day.

As she ran down the steps and into the bandage room, she
checked the clock. She was not late. She was wearing her knitted
sweater coat, a gift from Mamo that kept out the chill at this time of
year, and she braced herself before she pulled it off. Sometimes, in
the early morning, every building on the hundred-acre grounds was
bleak with cold. But the sun was up. A warm day was promised.

Grania had been invited to work at Gibson Hospital the year she
graduated, because she had the aptitude—or so the charge nurse had
told her. "The aptitude for putting those animated hands of yours
into the fray." She did not have a delicate stomach. She could clean
up after a child who had thrown up without throwing up herself.
She could change a dressing and compress a stye. She could smooth
a counterpane with forty-five-degree corners. She could make a bed,
with and without a child between the sheets, and had done both
hundreds of times. She worked six days a week and occasionally had
two days off together. The infirmary never closed while school was
in session—except on "Miracle" Christmas Day the previous year,

when not a single child had suffered from indigestion or an infected throat.

Today, once the sick children were washed and bathed, it would be her job to prepare the ledger for tomorrow morning before Dr. Whalen visited. Mrs. Sutton, the charge nurse, would be back Monday as well. The charge nurse never worked weekends except in times of epidemic, and there hadn't been one of those since early winter, when the thirty beds had been filled with children spotted with chicken pox. The sign had been common enough in the school halls—two fingers plucking at the cheek—as students searched one another's faces for telltale spots.

Grania thought of Fry and hoped her friend had managed to stay awake; Fry was notorious for sleeping in. After she and Colin married, it would be Colin's responsibility to push her out of bed in the morning. If he stayed. He had invented every trick he could think of to try to join up, even knowing that the army didn't need deaf boys. And Fry didn't want him to go. They had talked about moving to Toronto, where their families lived; Colin was certain he could get a job in a print shop there. But if Fry left her job in the school kitchen, the only hope she would have for work would be as a domestic. Ads from Toronto were frequently placed in the school paper: *Good deaf girl, wanted for domestic work.* If Fry were to leave, Grania would be without her best friend.

*

In the late afternoon, after work, Grania had an hour to fill before she was to meet Fry. They planned to walk up through the orchard after supper, before the evening chill settled over the grounds. She stopped off at the main building to pick up a copy of the school paper to take back with her to the residence, and she leafed through it as she walked.

The school paper, printed twice monthly since 1892, had started out as *The Canadian Mute* but changed its name during the 1913 school year, after the official name of the school changed. The school dropped the word *Dumb*; the paper dropped the word *Mute*. When pupils were enrolled at the school, their parents were sent a copy in hopes that they would subscribe, fifty cents a year. The paper did more than report school news; it shared information with schools for the deaf in many parts of North America and, in some ways, was a wide-reaching community paper. Students continued to subscribe after they left school, and some sent news back. Mr. Cedric had been editor-in-chief and teacher in the print shop for the past fourteen years.

Grania always read Cedric's editorials, as well as articles and stories and "Items of Interest," but her favourite page was the "Locals" because it was here that the children spoke for themselves. Cedric made corrections, repaired grammar and put the children's words into what he called the King's English. Much of the time, he flattened the voices until they merged to become one. But some voices refused to be flattened, and this was what Grania looked for—voices that were too distinct to be made to disappear.

This week, as always, the students were drawn to disaster. Because the *Lusitania* had been torpedoed after the submission deadline, most of the writings were about other forms of disaster. Grania lay back on her bed, propped by pillows, and read what the children had to say.

I received a welcome letter from my mother. My cousin has gone to War. My uncle fell and broke his arm and split his nose in pieces. Another cousin ran a nail through his thumb and blood poisoning set in. They live in England.

My brother wrote that when he was in the trench many bullets went over his head and he heard a noise like bees buzzing.

Yesterday some boys told me that some German soldiers took a Canadian soldier and they hammered the nails into the Canadian's hands. He was very much hurt. They were brutes.

I heard that my Uncle died at the first of the month. He left a widow and seven children. Uncle was sick with heart trouble. He is better off out of this wicked wicked world.

I have an uncle who is doing garrison duty in Bermuda. When he left, he looked such a brave soldier, I could hardly keep my tears inside my little eyes.

Grania smiled at this, written by young Paddy, who was twelve and whose heart melted at every occasion. Another boy, Charles, wrote:

Mr. Sails went to the barn and caught 35 chickens. He chopped off their heads and carried them to the kitchen where the feathers were plucked. The cook put them in the boiler.

Chicken and dumpling day, a Sunday two weeks before. Grania and Fry, who'd been off that day, helped the children, who sat at side-by-side tables. Every child had a plate, knife and fork. Every table had a cloth, five children to a side, enamel serving bowls at both ends. Colin, on the other side of the room, went up and down the rows tucking napkins into the collars of the little boys. Colin would be a good father if he and Fry ever had children. Which, Grania thought, would not make Mr. Bell happy—if he were here to know. Colin, unlike Fry, had been born deaf to deaf parents. Mr. Bell had worried himself over marriages between deaf people, even though he had worked with deaf children in Boston when he was a young man, and had married a deaf woman himself. Now he lived close to the sea in Nova Scotia, not far from the province in which Jim had grown up. Grania turned a page of *The Canadian* and read the notice about Mr. Bell's new book, available from New York. "Professor Alexander Graham Bell has made a profound study of the human voice and, in this work, has actually taken apart the human larynx and all its accessories as if it were merely a telephone. His disclosures are fascinatingly interesting and highly instructive."

Maybe our own students here at school will have a better chance for learning, Grania thought. Better than we had. The schooling had recently been extended to ten years, rather than the seven she had put in before her own graduation. Maybe, she thought, the students will have a real chance, now, to improve reading, writing, spelling, the big problems that are often never overcome.

Fry had struggled with written English all through school, and Grania had worked many long evenings beside her, trying to help, trying to pass on what Mamo had taught.

She turned back to the paper and a change of news.

I received a nice letter from my cousin. She was at a dance in California. She got the first prize for waltzing. She has learned the fox trot and all the new dances.

I am tired of hearing about this war.

And so am I, Grania thought, so am I. It made her body clench to think of it. It was a war Jim would soon be heading into. But she had not given up the hope that it would be over before he would have to leave.

The last two items were written by Cedric.

King George V has forbidden the use of liquor in his household, during the continuance of the war. His Majesty's example has been followed by many prominent people in England, including Lord Kitchener and Premier Asquith.

The children, naturally, have faith and trust in all that comes from home and when they have been taught in school to write 'a pair of boots,' and then read in a letter from home 'a pare of butes,' they are placed, as it were, on the horns of a dilemma.

Grania wondered if the parents who sent the letter would be reading Cedric's high-handed column.

A shadow crossed the doorway; she saw the movement before Fry entered the room.

Fry plunked down on the edge of her bed and stretched out her legs. "Four weeks," her freckled hands signed. "Four more weeks, and Colin and I will be married."

*

"You look so far away," Fry signed to Grania.

They were sitting side by side on a mound in the orchard, up behind the farm buildings. Asparagus grew wild beneath the apple trees, which were in full blossom. Grania marvelled at the rows of trees and their geometric pattern; she could look around her from any spot and no matter in which direction—ahead, behind, diagonally—the lines of trees, like spokes from a hub, were exactly straight, whether the ground beneath them was uneven or flat. Every tree had the same distance between it and the next, on all sides, allowing for sunshine and growth.

The ground was still warm from the day's sun, the air heavy with fragrance. The aroma that enveloped the two friends varied with the shifting breeze—sometimes strong, sometimes faint. It was the strength of this aroma that told Grania when to look up at the leaves to detect the activity of the breeze. The slow, purposeful flights of the bees had diminished in the past few moments; the sun was about to set. Far off, three flattened clouds drifted over the bay. It was a place of such peace, Grania wished she could sit here forever. She inhaled the scent deeply and thought of Mamo and her Canada Bouquet, and she tried not to be homesick. Soon, she would be back with her family in Deseronto for the summer. Jim had promised to visit as often as he could. She missed him now, though it had been only three days since he'd last been at the school hospital with Dr. Whalen. Next weekend, they were to go on a picnic with Colin and

Fry, in Jones Woods near the bay. Grania and Fry had already made plans for the food they would take.

"I am far away," Grania replied to her friend. "But I like coming to the orchard. I never get tired of it." Her right hand was undulating. "You know, when I look at clouds drifting, I think *song*. Or maybe *music*. Problem is, I don't know what goes with the words. Mamo told me she always sang one song that I liked when I was small. Before I was deaf."

"The hearing," Fry said, "when they meet us, they always ask the same. *Do you miss music? Do you miss the songs of the birds?* As if nothing is worse."

"Music and birds are important to the hearing."

"When I'm in a bad mood I say, 'How can I miss what I don't know? So what if I can't hear birds. I can see them.' "

Grania had never tried to explain to Fry that she believed, or imagined she believed, that music and song were everywhere. Not only in clouds but in flights of birds, in oak leaves that brushed the dorm window, in the children's legs as they raced across the lawns. "It's silly, isn't it," she signed. "My memory of sound is gone for all those years—fourteen years—but I feel as if my brain remembers music."

"No, not silly."

"And I still have the same dreams I had when I first came here." She shrugged. "The dreams don't make sense. Everyone babbles with voice, and I understand. No one is deaf, no one is hearing. Songs I don't know, sounds I can't remember. Things are always mixed up."

Fry's hands cracked the egg sign and mimed scramble, and she and Grania looked at each other and started to laugh.

"Do you ever feel sorry for yourself?" Fry asked. Without waiting for a reply she continued. "I do. Sometimes I think hearing people have an easy life even though I know they have problems, too. But hearing people never had to learn to speak all over again. *Your* brain forgot sound; *my* brain forgot language. Even though my mother was right there to defend it. Every day, every day, she tried to make me remember. All the time, she corrected me. *Pronounce. Think before you speak.* I was her burden. That's what she called me. *My heavy burden.*"

Fry's arms and shoulders sagged as she signed *heavy*. Grania had heard the stories before, and she patted her friend's arm. They never got over the old memories.

"Cora was our burden—the town's, Deseronto's." Grania's right hand shaped C-o-r-a, as she finger spelled the name. She had told Fry many stories about Nosy Parker Cora. "Your mother tried to make you remember; my mother hoped to make me hear." Her fingers bobbed slightly, one hand raised as she made half the sign for *hope*. Then, both hands made the word *pray*. "Mother never gave up the guilt. I think she still believes that if she prays enough, some-day I won't be deaf."

She felt the hard wall that was Mother's will, Mother's intent. Three years after she finished school, here in the orchard, she could still feel Mother's will.

Grania remembered the jolt of the steamer as it bumped and shuddered its way to the edge of the St. Lawrence River and against Ste. Anne's wharf. She remembered the procession of men and women—mostly women—as they paraded up the pier in long dresses and dark hats. Eighty pilgrims trekked past the lone tree, between two lanterns, beyond the first doorway with its massive sign: *Magasin de CYCLORAMA*. From the deck railing, Grania had watched the sign grow larger and larger from far off, before she and Mother disembarked. As they walked up the pier, her fingers spelled C-Y-C-L-O-R-A-M-A against her dress. She made the word on the side that was away from Mother, so her fingers would not be seen.

Three flags—one was the American Stars and Stripes—hung sideways over the tall panels of the circular building. After they passed the store entrance, Grania lost sight of her mother and became squeezed between two stout women who had their heads down and whose lips were moving like mourners'. She thought she was going to smother but squirmed away and found her mother again. A thin man, his cheekbones and finger bones showing under his skin, was standing by the railing outside the store, a straw boater in his hand, and he led the crowd forward at a faster pace. Grania was amazed that such a rickety-looking man could move so quickly. He led them first to the big church, Ste. Anne's, up the slope. After that, at the Cyclorama, Grania remembered how small she had felt next to the massive panels that encircled her.

Later that summer, Mother wanted to take her to Montreal, to the little chapel on the mountain where there was a statue of Saint Joseph. Mother's sister Annie had travelled from Rochester to Montreal one summer and had written to Mother about her pilgrimage. She had prayed to Saint Joseph and had walked up the dirt road to the chapel and she had been spoken to by Brother André himself. Mother was convinced that Brother André could heal Grania's ears. But Father had said, "No." Grania would not be going to Montreal. "No more miracles," he told Mother. Grania had seen the white flush of anger on his face. "No more miracles for Grania."

*

Fry was waggling her fingers to get Grania's attention, to bring her back.

"Even now," Fry signed, "I stumble over words. You've watched me. When I can't find a word, I finger spell under the table like a little child. But some words still look the same to me. When I speak, I find out that the hearing say them differently. *Wind* and *wind*. *Tear* and *tear*. No wonder we get confused. How can I look at a word like c-u-p-b-o-a-r-d and know that its sound is supposed to be *k-u-b b-e-r-d*?" Fry spelled the words expertly, her fingers punctuating the air. "If you hadn't helped me, I wouldn't know any English at all."

"Yes, you would," Grania said. But she knew the problems that Fry still had with grammar and the written word.

In a parallel way, Grania had been encouraged to use voice—all the time, voice. In her senior classes, it was Miss Marks who'd helped her to shorten the time lag, to turn delayed understanding back into spoken response. She'd coaxed Grania and her classmates farther into language than they'd ever imagined they could go. It was Miss Marks, too, who had said, "When you lip read your partner, keep your back towards the light. The light should fall on the speaker's face. Always keep your back towards the light."

Grania had tried to please this teacher she loved. During the years she'd been a student, there had been good teachers and teachers who were not so good. Some bullying took place, and always there was disciplined order to rule every activity. But Grania had struggled to put tongue and throat and breath around each word she uttered. And Miss Marks had listened, and pushed, and listened again.

Now that Grania and Fry were workers at the school, each year at this time they watched the senior students worry about leaving their sheltered surroundings for good. Many had no choice but to return to their parents' homes, something Grania and Fry had vowed they would never do. Grania reminded Fry of this now.

"At least we haven't ended up like old Mr. Wadsworth," she said. "Do you remember how we worried so much?"

Fry nodded. Mr. Wadsworth, a deaf man, lived alone in a one-room shack by a gravel road on a tiny patch of someone else's farm—someone who felt sorry for him. He carried pieces of paper and a pencil with him everywhere, and had done so all his life. When he visited a neighbour, or attended a church supper, or a dance at someone's farm, he sat patiently, waiting for someone to sit with him and write messages on his paper.

Grania had often imagined him going home at night, sitting alone and looking over the scraps of paper, reviewing the day's conversations:

How are you?
Good, good.
Weather fine today?
Oh yes.

She looked at her friend, whom she dearly loved, and again she thought of the evenings and weekends she had tried to help with the written language. Fry still had no use for articles and prepositions— what Grania thought of as *joining words*. Fry had never understood why they were worth the bother.

Grania thought of the *Sunday* book. *Mamo saved me,* she said to herself, but not to Fry. *Mamo saved my life.*

She wondered if Jim understood how important Mamo was to her childhood and to her life now. Jim had lost his parents—they had died of typhoid—and he had been raised by loving grandparents. But they, too, had died. Grania had met only his Uncle Alex and his Aunt Jean. She wondered if Jim would consider her larger family his own after they married. And they would marry. Despite Mother writing to say, "No announcements."

It was possible, through all the years of believing she would somehow make Grania hear, that Mother had never given a thought to the idea that Grania might have a future of her own to consider.

Chapter 7

We are coming, Mother Britain,
we are coming to your aid,
There's a debt we owe our fathers,
and we mean to see it paid.
From the jungles of Rhodesia,
from the snows of Saskatoon,
We are coming, Mother Britain,
and we hope to see you soon.

The Canadian

Deseronto, Ontario

Tress's husband, Kenan, was gone. In two weeks, her own husband, Jim, would leave, along with hundreds of others from the area who had signed up.

Husband. She was not used to shaping the sound. *Chim*, she said, and repeated his name. *Chim*. She moved about Aunt Maggie's kitchen, a large bright room with a high ceiling patterned with swirls. She had known this place since childhood, but now it seemed shadowy and unfamiliar because she was in someone else's home, trying to prepare a supper meal. Before her aunt had left, she'd opened doors to show Grania cupboard shelves and pantry shelves, and told her that she and Jim were to use whatever they wished. They had accepted the offer to stay in the tower apartment because Grania's aunt and uncle had for some time wanted to travel across Lake Ontario to Oswego, to visit Aunt Maggie's sister in the state of New York. Uncle Am had climbed up inside the tower, Jim behind him, on the ladder built into the back wall of the parlour, and showed Jim where to oil the gears of the tower clock. He showed him how to do the checks around the building, the offices below, the security, the jobs that were to be looked after while he was away. For now, the entire top floor, the only apartment in the building, was Jim and Grania's private place.

Grania was living with a man, sharing her sleep with a man. She was lying beside a man at night on the blue blanket spread out over the carpet in the parlour. She thought of the strangeness of this but, along with the strangeness, the love that was natural between them. In the morning they folded the blanket, the padding underneath, the bedding on top, and stashed it out of sight. They did not sleep in Aunt Maggie and Uncle Am's bed. They wanted their own space. And it was not the first time Grania had spent the night sleeping on a rug.

Jim had signed up with the Canadian Army Medical Corps and would go to a field ambulance depot where his training was to begin. He had been granted two weeks to settle his affairs. He was in the city now, for the day, and would be back on the early-evening train. They had been married the twenty-third of October in the church at Marysville, and a celebration had been held afterwards at Bompa Jack's farm. Mamo had been there, Mother and Father, Tress and the boys, Great-Aunt Martha, aunts and uncles and great-uncles, Fry and Colin, and Jim's Uncle Alex and Aunt Jean. Jim had promised his Uncle Alex that he would remain in Canada until the fall sawing was done, and the promise had been kept. Dr. Whalen sent a cheque, with his good wishes, and said that he was pleased that arrangements were being made for Jim to join a field ambulance unit. His own son, now a gunner, had left in July, as planned.

Grania thought of the stillness around her during the wedding ceremony. Or perhaps she had shut out everyone except Jim. She'd had a sense of being cocooned the entire day; she barely remembered details until they reached Bompa's farm. Then, the kitchen furniture was pushed to the end of the long room and there was dancing, and she was hugged, and kissed, and her hand was shaken, and gifts and wishes were pressed upon her. But throughout the afternoon and evening, she was aware of Jim no matter where he was standing—in the kitchen, in the parlour doorway, in the dining room where the buffet feast had been laid out over the rarely used Irish linen and the even less used oval table with a leaf inserted for extra length. Grania knew where he was at every moment. When they looked up and caught each other's glance, they might have been side by side. He was just beginning to realize that he could speak to her silently across a full room; that his lips would be understood no matter how much noise, no matter how many people were between. He had begun to describe his actions, as if she couldn't see for herself. He was laughing. *In a few minutes, I'm going to borrow that mouth organ. I'm going to play, and do a jig to celebrate.* His feet did a little hop. *I'm going to work my way across the room and ask you to dance.* He stopped laughing. *My love,* his lips said, in silence, *My love.*

Grania reached over now to switch on the ceiling light. She had left her job at the school hospital in the middle of October, ten days before she was married. Now she was up over the post office, peeling potatoes in Deseronto. She remembered the buckets of potatoes she and Fry and the older girls had peeled in the sink room at school when they'd helped out in the kitchen every Christmas Day. Fry was still at the school, still working in the big kitchen. Since their marriage, she and Colin had moved into their rented rooms. Now that the fall term was under way, they walked to work together early every morning.

Grania pulled out the shelf of the flour cupboard and did not glance up again until she felt vibrations. Jim was in the doorway between kitchen and hall. He was rapping on the wall, trying not to frighten her by appearing suddenly at her side. If she hadn't been so absorbed, she'd have seen him standing there. His hair was wet, his brown jacket soaked to his arms and chest, and—she saw now—his back was soaked as well.

"Were you frightened? By the storm?"

"Storm?" She read the word from his lips and glanced to her left, to the window that was set at a slant between ceiling and floor. She could see the slopes and angles of the tower roof. Her glance took in the window seat, Aunt Maggie's ivy plant, the menacing sky beyond. It was dark out there, for the hour. She had switched on the light without noticing what was happening outside.

"You didn't know? You didn't feel?"

She crossed the hall to the street side of the apartment and looked down from the dining-room window. The storm that had terrorized the town for the past thirty minutes was over and she hadn't so much as looked up. Branches had been knocked down and were blowing along Main Street. Leaves were flying through the air. There were wide puddles below; the mud was thick and deep, the road messy and grooved. Already, wheels had been trapped: three men were pushing at an auto. A tired-looking horse was being led away from a mired, abandoned buggy.

Jim had taken off his muddy boots on the landing at the top of the stairs, but more mud was spattered up his trouser legs. He removed his jacket and came to stand beside her at the window and looked down and shook his head, and then he reached over and closed the dining-room curtains.

They stood, face to face. He was taller by four inches, and she looked up. As if in a dance, they turned, back to back. He tipped his head to rest against hers and she felt his wet hair. Then, they were face to face again. He placed both hands on her swept-up hair, and he hummed softly. She felt the hum and leaned forward. She put a hand to his throat. His skin was cool. He was always singing or humming. She pulled away to see if he wanted to speak.

*

She had taught him the alphabet and some of the sign language and he could make slow words, but they had also begun to create a language of their own. It arose as naturally as the love between them, an invented code no one would ever break.

The tiniest flicker of her index finger resting against her dress and he moved to her side.

His name-sign, her gift to him—a *C* turning over to become an *H* that tapped once over her heart. *Chim.*

And he, delighting in the new language of hands, returned a *G* close to his own heart.

When they were visiting Tress's town friends in Deseronto, he brushed a fingertip over his lips and signalled across the room. *Now I'm going to take you home.* But it meant something else, too. Grania's cheeks reddened furiously when he made this public-private display, though no one else had noticed.

In the tower apartment they lay on the blue blanket, the parlour curtains pulled back so that they could see the night sky. He lay beside her in the dark and she turned on her right side, where she could tuck in closely.

She wanted to talk. The room was dark unless there was a moon, but she did not need the moon. She closed her eyes and raised the fingers of her left hand to his lips. Though at first he was astonished, he understood and began to speak. His careful words fell into her fingertips and she whispered back and they conversed like this, side by side. She had been well taught; her hands and body remembered the countless times at school when she had sat on a chair facing her teacher.

"Place your fingertips over my mouth. Lightly now. Feel the word. Now to my throat, back to the lips. Let the shape of the word fall into your fingers. Scoop it up with your hand."

He had never known a language that so thoroughly encompassed love.

She had never felt so safe.

*

He had quickly learned that she did not need full sentences in order to understand, that her ability to focus the immediate was extraordinary, that with lightning speed she was able to fill in the gaps. He saw query on her face, her reddish brows forming the barely discernible frown.

He watched her silence.

But Grania knew when she was being watched.

"Tell me," he said. He wanted everything. He watched her brown eyes focus on his face, her glance as it darted to the background, right, left, back to his lips. *What did she see? He wanted to know.* "Tell me, so I'll know. About being deaf. Start with the worst thing." He leaned towards her, listening hard.

They were sitting on the blue blanket where they had brought their trays and eaten their breakfast. They could not be seen from the street below. The late-autumn sun warmed the room and he saw the varying shades of red in her hair as light fell across her.

"The worst thing?" She thought for a moment. "Not having information that everyone else has. No—worse is when information is withheld—the smallest detail—by someone who thinks it isn't important enough to pass on."

"More. Something I can't know."

She did not have to ponder this.

"The way I see the world."

"No one sees so much."

"The way I see is divided. Into things that move and things that don't move."

She saw the surprise on his face, watched him stow the information. This pleased her. "You could not have known that."

"I do now."

"It keeps me alive," she said. "Movement and shadow. I rely on those. Mamo helped me, but I learned by myself, too. Maybe when I was a child—instinct." *A horse moves, a swing, an auto, a gate, a cutter, a door, a branch in the woods, a running child. Wind moves;*

it lifts, even sweeps objects from place to place. She thought of Miss Marks during senior class at school, trying to explain the various meanings of sweep.

"The first time I saw you," he said, "last year, in the bandage room at the hospital, I walked up from behind and didn't realize you were deaf. But you didn't move. No part of your body moved. You should have been surprised when you saw me. Anyone else would have jumped, they would have been startled."

She watched and weighed the words. *Always a time lag.* "I remember. But you were not a threat. Not in that place. From the side, I could see Miss MacKay's eyes flicker. When you approached."

She reached across and touched his shoulder. They were face to face. She slipped her hand into his. "You tell something, something I can't know about you."

Tell.

He laughed. "You'll never know how I sing. Sometimes I wish you could hear me."

"I do know you can sing. You know the words to all the songs. Everyone tells me about your voice. You sing every time you're near a piano. Your Grandfather Lloyd played the fiddle—you told me. Mamo likes to hear you play piano and sing when you are home—parents' home—with me." She corrected herself. *Married woman.* "You sing when you're beside me. You hum most of the time. You think I don't know?"

"You can't know. You'll never hear me sing," he teased. "Did you hear me hum the 'Sparkling Waltzes' when we danced at our wedding at Bompa Jack's?"

"I felt the hum. I watch your words. I see your fingers on the keys. I feel your song. I follow your body when we dance. That's how I listen. I listen to your body."

They did not talk about him leaving. She did not agree to the silence; there was simply nothing to say. He had finished his work with Dr. Whalen; he had stayed to help his uncle; he was going to war. She believed that his Uncle Alex had exacted the promise to delay his departure in hopes that the war would be over by now. But the war was not over.

They did not think beyond the end of their time in the tower. They knew that on departure day, Jim would travel to Belleville and leave by the eastbound train. Eventually, when he reached the coast, he would cross the sea.

What Grania had to do was believe that he would come back. Once he was *over there*, he would write. He would not withhold information. Withholding meant keeping her out and that would be worse than everything else put together. He would keep back only what he would not be permitted to tell. If he wrote enough to enable her to create a picture of him there, she would be able to keep him close. He knew her in her setting, and that was what he would take away with him.

*

He wanted to tell her about sound.

"Ask," he said. "Ask what you want to know."

But she had no questions about sound. She would have to make some up. She knew he wanted to understand. She opened one of the narrow windows and saw that a new wind was blowing in off the bay. The tips of the trees that lined the street were waving in a commotion. A ruckus was like a commotion; Mamo had told her that. Father used to say to Grania and Tress and Patrick, when they were children, "Don't make so much ruckus"—and that meant noise.

"The leaves," she said—she was making the effort, to please him—"do they make a wild noise when they are like this?"

"Not exactly the leaves. The wind howls but not the leaves."

She came back to the blanket and curled her feet under her, and wondered. *The wind howls. How many things did she not know? Many. But she knew that wolves howled along the edge of the woods near her grandfather's farm on the Ninth. Bompa Jack had gone outside and shot one with his rifle during the night because it kept coming too close to the barn. He told her that on a clear night the cry of the wolf was like the crying of a baby.*

"Bompa Jack," she said, "when the wolves howl, he feels their voices up the back of his neck."

"Different kind of howl. The wind howls but it can change its sound. It all depends."

It would, she thought. She rested one index finger over the other, making the sign, and lowered her hands to her lap. *It all depends.* Sound was always more important to the hearing.

*

At night, they lay in each other's arms, a light cover over them. The parlour curtains remained open so that if there was a moon, it could show itself. Grania positioned herself so that she could lie with her head on the soft part of Jim's upper abdomen, just below his chest. For a while he sang softly so that she could feel his song. She knew the spot where it began, the origin of song, the onset of breath. The words circled on a thin column of air but were also connected to the low resonant place where she laid her head.

She was certain that she could identify Jim's heartbeat from all heartbeats. It pulsed to her skin, and the rhythm of their breathing merged. He tucked an arm beneath her shoulders and her hair. It was a wonder to him, the way their bodies curled to each other after lovemaking; the way they fitted perfectly together in deepest sleep.

*

Grania had just returned from her work at the Red Cross office, where she volunteered one afternoon a week. After Jim's departure, she would work two. Jim had been up inside the clock tower and had worked at jobs around the building most of the day. For a brief moment when she came into the apartment, they felt as if they were in their own place. The night before, they had talked about having a home after the war, after he would come back. They would have a baby. Two babies, or three. They had allowed themselves to speak of that. And they both laughed when Grania told Jim that he would have to listen for their sounds, that he would have to describe every noise their babies would make. Even their cries, their early cries.

Jim hung up her coat for her. "Is it good," he said, "to come home? To turn your attention off, relax? So you don't have to be alert to everyone's lips around you?"

"No," she said, but she felt the word rise as she was about to explain. *Control the voice,* said the other voice in her head, the one that slipped in unbidden. "No. Most of the time, I *am* turned off. Only when I want to make the effort, that's when I turn on—that's when I'm most alert."

She unpinned her hat and moved towards him. But she saw his surprise. *Dulcie comes up for air and sees the look on his face.* She thought of the earless cutout girl who wore a bathing suit and used to live in the closet drawer next to the catalogue ladies.

Once again, Jim had misunderstood what he thought he knew. It was a mystery then, the silence where she lived. Somewhere between wilful and involuntary attention. Where, despite frustrations large and small, she pulled into her own space.

She saw his disappointment.

"It's what I learned in childhood," she said. "It's easy to let things fall away. To choose what to attend to and what not."

He saw how comfortable she was in her inner place, how private and peaceful. With him, she allowed this to be seen. When she wanted to focus on the world outside herself, she stopped and made sense of the situation. After that, she let in the extra cues.

The glimpse she allowed was enough. The inner place was one he could never know. It was the source of her strength, her stillness; he saw that. Despite all that she told him, despite all of the questions she tried to answer, he understood that he was outside of that place. But when he was away from her, he felt his own strength move towards her, in the same way that he felt hers moving towards him.

*

"What else?" he said. They were walking along Main Street, arm in arm, in the afternoon sun.

"When there are more than two people in a room, if hearing people are talking and change the subject, the deaf person in the room doesn't know. We are back in the old conversation, left behind."

"Explain." He turned towards her.

"We don't hear the asides, the sudden shifts. We can only watch one pair of lips at a time. If someone speaks when we're not looking, well . . ."

He nodded, taking in what he had never known.

Grania carried her box camera in her free hand. Near the end of town, they passed the side-by-side verandas of the hotel and her parents' home. How strange to be an outsider looking in. Someone of, yet not of, her own family.

No one could be seen inside; the hall and parlour lights were off. From the street she saw only shadows and the dark angle of the piano. One evening, after she and Jim had had supper with the family, everyone—even Father—walked back through the passageway and into the parlour, and Jim sat on the round stool before the piano and played. He did not need sheet music; he could play by ear. His grandmother had taught him the notes when he was a child, and he had learned to chord by himself. His long fingers looked as if they were floating across the keys. Grania had stood beside him and watched song come from his lips. She'd placed one hand on his shoulder and the other on the top panel of the piano. Her body had stilled as she'd allowed his music to enter her.

From the street, it was easy to imagine the rooms inside the house and where everyone would be. She created pictures of Mamo, Mother, Tress, Father, Bernard, Patrick, confident of what each would be doing at four o'clock on a weekday afternoon. She tightened her grip on Jim's arm. She was independent now. *Married woman.* But during the summer, when Jim travelled to Deseronto to speak to her parents, there had been barely restrained conversations that Grania thought of as: *What is going to happen next?*

"Of course you will come home." That was Mother. "You can't live somewhere alone as a married woman while Jim is away at the war. Where would you live? What if a stranger came to your door? What if we had to contact you? What if you were in danger?"

Danger? Grania hadn't given a thought to danger. She had always shared a room with Fry in the residence. She had planned to stay on and work at the school hospital. It was Jim who was heading into danger. She had looked to Mamo for support but, for once, Mamo sided with Mother.

Mamo had different arguments. The hotel needed help. Another of Father's employees had left for the war. Bernard was already working long hours in the afternoons and evenings. Mother and Mrs. Brant needed help in the kitchen and dining room. Mrs. Brant was getting older and didn't move quickly any more. Mamo's arthritis bothered her and she couldn't help out the way she used to. And Mother was tired. Grania knew that Mother had lost weight. Her face was gaunt, her apron tied tighter. She seemed to be worried all the time.

The final argument was that Tress was moving home as soon as Kenan left for the war. Grania and Tress would share their old room again, sleep across from each other in their old single beds, live there as if they had never left. Bernard and Patrick stayed out of the discussions, but everyone wanted Grania to come home.

Grania understood the real reason—the one never stated. No one quite believed that she could take charge of her own life. Mother had finally agreed to the wedding, and Grania had agreed to come home. She refused to delay her marriage until after the war, even though that was what Mother wanted. The price of Grania's refusal was that she would move from one area of protection to another. Even so, Mamo had blessed the marriage. She had made an emphatic announcement to the family when Mother was arguing and Father was silent—but siding, Grania thought, with Mother. "Jim," Mamo said, "is a truly decent man."

Now Grania was to return home as if nothing had changed. But everything had changed. Grania had not lived at home—except during the summer months—since she was nine years old. Tress did not seem to mind moving back; she had never left town. In September, after Kenan left, she had given up their rented rooms and moved home. She was already installed in the old bedroom upstairs.

The married sisters were not so independent now.

Tress had made it clear to their parents that she intended to start looking for a house to rent at the first sign that the war would be over. Grania knew that Father would have her and Tress at home as long as they would stay. Despite spending most of his time in his office, or with his horses, or visiting Bompa Jack on the farm, he wanted his family around him. He wanted to know that his sons and daughters were near. And the truth of Mamo's arguments could not be disputed: it was wartime; people were leaving; the hotel needed help.

No, the sisters were not so independent after all.

Grania glanced up at her old bedroom window above the veranda, half expecting to see Tress's face. Most of the leaves on the tree at the front were down. She looked at Jim, and watched his lips from the side as they passed. He was humming again, she could tell. He, too, wanted her to stay with her parents while he was away. She had left the school, left her work at the hospital and said her goodbyes.

Right now, she didn't want to think about any of this. But she had never been good at pushing things away.

"What else?" she said. "About sound." They were nearing the rocky place at the edge of the woods by the shore. She had never told him about her walks here with Mamo, when Mamo carried the O'Shaughnessy clock bag. She had never told anyone.

He looked around and saw a plump bumblebee hovering against a fall blossom. The bee darted sideways in their direction and disappeared, a zigzag flight she followed with her eyes.

"Bee," he said. "The bumblebee is small and fat but makes a big sound."

"Like?" *Mamo always said,* "Sounds like . . ." *and then explained.*

"Like an *M*."

Grania watched him form an awkward *M* with three fingers of his right hand.

"Like an *M* pushed through paper wrapped around a comb," he said. "When it comes out the other side, it turns to a buzz."

"I know about the buzz through the comb. Tress and I did that when we were children. The buzz felt like fur on my lips."

"You tell me something," he said. "Something I've noticed."

She waited.

"When we are with people, in your parents' home, or Bompa Jack's—or anywhere—if there is a noise inside the house, a loud thump or something that sends out vibrations, you never look in the direction of the noise. You look to someone's face, instead—to see what's happened, to find out what's going on. You don't look for the sound, you look for the information."

"Maybe. I don't think about every single thing I do." She had not considered that.

They entered the path and Jim leaned forward and scooped a handful of red and yellow leaves from the ground and threw them at her. Several landed in her hair.

"Feel them crackle," he said. "Drag your feet. They make an autumn sound like no other."

She didn't tell him that for years she had played in leaves, gathered them, helped the small boys at school as they filled their hand carts on the grounds. Before she left home to live at the school, Mamo had often brought her here. They had scraped their feet through the leaves. But no one had ever told her that leaves made a sound like no other.

Well then, what sound like no other?

"When they first fall, there's a softness. The shoe pushes into them—*shoosh-shoosh*—with each step."

She saw the sound on his lips, was not certain enough to try.

"But when the leaves are brittle and dry and the shoe breaks them into pieces, cracklings can be heard. Many cracklings. All at the same time."

"Cracklings?" She laughed at the word.

It was her laugh he loved the most. The sound of an inward sigh.

And the way she murmured when she was sitting by herself. A murmur that sounded like a softly sung *I see, I see.*

And her hands, the way they shaped language.

And the way she said his name. He sometimes asked her to say it, and he listened, and wanted her to say it again. It came out as a clipped "Ch" that joined the "m" with scarcely a vowel sound between. *Chim.*

He picked at bits of broken leaf and tugged them along the strands of her red hair. He had never known that hair could be so soft and thick at the same time. They continued without speaking and stopped at the far edge of the woods where the path came out on the other side. A split-rail fence began where the path ended. She took his picture there, as he leaned against the fence. When he was permitted to move, he tapped his fingers against the wooden rail. There was more to tell about sound.

But she had pulled inside. Sound was outside of her and all around. She knew that.

"Tell me in words," she said. "That will be enough. I will put the rest together by myself."

*

His arm pressed against hers as they sat in the second row of Naylor's Theatre. He was wearing his uniform. It was a brownish colour, khaki, scratchy and thick. She had seen hundreds like it when she worked in Belleville, when soldiers marched past the school. And on the streets, and at the station when trains went through. She pressed her arm back against his and they held the tension like that, allowing it to flow between them. Their days and nights together kept them close. There was little time left.

She removed her hat as the program requested and placed it on her lap just as the light was dimmed and raised up to the centre dome. The Women's Patriotic League was responsible for Friday-night entertainments. This week there were musical solos, recitations, a speech by a visiting colonel from Belleville, and several tableaus. Jim had bought the tickets and made sure they were seated close to the front so that Grania could see the colour and movement of the performances, the dramatic stillness of the tableaus.

There were four of these: *The Execution of Lady Jane Grey*; *Good-Bye Daddy*—a soldier leaving his daughter and son—a tableau Grania did not like to watch, though the audience around her was enthusiastic. *An Autumn Girl* was the third; and the final was *The Allies*. Grania recognized the town girls, and some of the young men. She studied each extravagant, motionless pose. No lips to read. Women around her clapped their hands fervently. Grania was as motionless as the figures on the stage.

During the mandolin player's performance, she felt nothing, but she watched his strumming hand. It was during the piano solo that music began to enter her feet through the pine floor. She was certain she had the rhythm of the vibrations; she concentrated hard. Jim reached across in the dark and lifted her hand towards him. He traced a fingertip around the edges of her palm for several moments and she sat, motionless, scarcely breathing. She was afraid she would make a noise with her throat. They were surrounded by people on both sides, in front and behind. In that crowded place, every seat taken, Jim rested the back of her hand against one of his, and with the other he silently placed a word in her palm. She felt the flush in her cheeks. She did not see the scene change, not until the lights became brighter and the colonel stood on the stage to give the address.

Everyone knew that the real reason for the concert was to step up the drive for recruitment. When the colonel spoke, Grania could not see his lips. She understood nothing. She knew that the event was the tip of a persuasive wave rolling across the country, gathering available young men and sending them to fight for *Mother England*. She watched people cheer around her.

Kenan was gone. Their childhood friend, Orryn, had left the year before, at the beginning of the war, and was now a lieutenant. Grew's son, Richard, a private, had been one of the first in town to sign up; he, too, had gone the previous year. Grew had apprenticed Richard to be a barber like himself, but Richard had been one of the early soldiers who'd first travelled to Valcartier. After that, he had embarked on one of the thirty-two ships that transported the First Contingent to Plymouth. In the barbershop window on Main Street, Grew proudly displayed a postcard Richard had sent, showing the names of all thirty-two ships. An arrow pointed to "my ship"—the *Royal Edward*, the third ship down the centre column.

Grew had been the piano player tonight. Sometimes he played for the moving pictures, too. His long legs had been tucked awkwardly, his tall body bent to the keys. Grania wondered, with his son in France, what Grew thought of tonight's show of patriotism. Richard had already seen action. Whatever his feelings, Grew did not let anyone know.

When the crowd finally spilled out onto the boardwalk in front of the theatre, Grania put on her hat again, and firmly took Jim's arm. *Husband*, she said to herself. *Husband*. There had been several other uniformed men in the audience. People outside were shaking Jim's hand, wishing him luck. She caught a glimpse of Cora, but quickly turned away from the inquisitive stare. She had thought of Cora not so long ago. The day Jim's uniform was issued, he'd walked away from the tower apartment in the morning wearing his brown trousers—his civilian clothes—for the last time. But the sharp creases in his trousers had been pressed the wrong way, down the sides. Jim had always pressed his own until that one pair. Grania had not been taught that in sewing class at school—not while she was doing fancy work—but she had wanted to surprise him. He'd held up the trousers and laughed and, despite Grania's objections, pulled them on anyway. Her cheeks had burned with humiliation—

what if Cora were to see?—but Jim hadn't minded at all. He walked out the door with the creases down the sides of his pants and, when he'd come back, he was wearing his uniform.

He was humming again as they walked along the street, his fingers tapping against one trouser leg. Grania thought of all the words she had spelled to herself that way, tapping against the side of her skirt. She laughed aloud, thinking of the two of them tapping different messages. Jim's message was always music. Her tapped words were a kind of music, too. Music for the upset or alone.

"What are you humming?" she said. "Which tune?" She watched his lips for the answer. His face looked as though he'd been caught out.

He stopped. "Mandolin solo," he said. "I can't get it out of my mind. I recognized it, but I can't think of the name."

He took her hand and tugged her across the street and they walked back up the east side of the boardwalk, in the direction away from the apartment. She did not know where he was taking her, but she didn't protest. He knew about the path, the one that led to the bay at this end of town, by the old burned-out pier. He laughed and pulled away from her, and stepped off the boardwalk, disappearing into darkness. For a moment she stood still, looking into the black space where he'd vanished. She and Tress had walked here in the early dusk during the summer months, fireflies blinking around them, a galaxy of flitting lanterns forming and reforming the shape of light.

She waited for a flicker of movement from Jim. When it did not come, she stepped down and walked forward, unafraid. She was not afraid of the dark when he was inside it with her.

A low remnant of the abandoned pier jutted harmlessly into the bay, its upright timbers black with age. The dugout where she had once played with Tress and Orryn and Kenan was beneath—collapsed perhaps, or even filled in. Now, there were cement sides, and squared-off timbers with wide spaces between. These led to a slightly lower cement platform at the end of the timbers, and this stopped abruptly over water.

Jim was in the shadows. There was a moon, but it had slipped behind a cloud. He stepped in front of her but she was not startled. This time, she was the one who led the way, walking with surety from the end of the path to the place where there was a toehold in the crumbling cement side. She found the notch easily and, despite the weight of her jacket, despite the skirt, which she tugged up to enable her to climb, she pulled herself up quickly. She was already shifting along the edge of one timber before Jim, behind, had found the notch for his boot. She pointed, and he hoisted himself up. She stayed low, inching her way along the beam. When she reached the end she stepped down to the platform and looked back to see Jim at full height, walking effortlessly along one of the beams. *Foolish*, she thought. A cloud of insects could dart in from the bay and flit into his face and he could lose his balance on the narrow surface. *If he falls, he'll disappear.*

But it was too late in the season for clouds of insects. And he was steady. She sat with her feet dangling over the edge of the platform and watched while he extended his arms to the side and walked back and forth, balancing, testing, as if he were a tightrope walker warming up before a performance. She thought of the strongmen in black slippered toes, the moustachioed men of the underwear page of Mr. Eaton's catalogue, their narrow legs and agile pointed feet. Into and out of darkness, Jim vanished and reappeared. It was the way things had happened between them. He had come from away and had entered her life and now he was in uniform and he would have to leave. But he had promised to return.

He walked out of the dark again and dropped down beside her. A breeze was coming up and she received it against her skin. The moon was uncovered now. She inhaled softly, wondering if her breathing could be heard. She wondered if Jim had ever been so still that he made no noise outside of himself. As if to answer her unspoken thought, he circled her waist with his arm and they sat in perfect stillness. She rested her hand on his thigh, amazed at her own behaviour, the ease of doing this. He lifted her hand and examined it under the moonlight.

She made no sign. She was aware of the water below, of weeds entwined in the beams, of the rotting wood scent of the timbers. Jim was close, fixed and solid beside her. This was the man who loved her. This was the man she loved.

His hair had been cut short and she reached up and rubbed the bristles at the back of his neck. He took her hand again but this time it was she who explored his palm and his long, slender fingers, each one pulsing beneath her own.

"Tell me," she said. *Chim.* Her voice. The breeze was rippling the water below them and she wanted to know what he knew. "Tell me if there is sound when the waves move fast."

His fist knocked forward at the wrist, into the air—the sign she'd taught him for *yes.* He shifted so that he could partly face her, and he moved closer so that she could see his lips in the moonlight. "But waves make a different sound when they roll into shore."

"Tell."

"Not loud. Not in the bay. More like lapping. The way a dog drinks from its dish. Like Carlow."

She laughed, thinking of how she had shouted vowels at Carlow. Now he spent most of his hours in Father's office, lying on an old rug made from rags that Mamo had contributed for his comfort.

"At the sea," Jim said, and she watched for the words, "the waves are bigger."

"Sound?"

"Big sound."

"How big?"

"A steady under-roar."

"Under—?" She thought she saw *underwear* and laughed to herself.

He heard the sound; it was like a sigh, and he laughed, too. "I made up the word. Roar. Under-roar. Second noise under the first.

When the white-tips roll in, they are never alone. They merge and cross"—Jim's hands and arms were fluid, criss-crossing in the air— "and when you think they will crash, they slip up over the beach with no fuss at all."

"No fuss."

"In a north wind, it's different." He knew the sign for different and he made it now, separating his crossed index fingers out into the darkness. "Everything speeds up. And there is wind. Not dangerous—unless there's a storm. If the wind is low, the ocean makes a flat sound, a slap." He slapped one hand against the other. "The biggest noise is the roar. One day I stood on the dunes and the roar was so big I had to adjust to the sound before I could go down to walk on the beach. At first I thought it was from one of the new aeroplanes." He pointed to the sky.

"I stood on dunes," she said. She was straining to see his lips. "At the Sandbanks on Lake Ontario. The year we graduated, we had lunch there—a special school outing. We went in autos and drove through Picton on the way. Fry and I wanted to swim in the big lake but we were dressed up and no one brought bathing suits. If we had been alone we might have gone into the water without them."

But they wouldn't. Not in daytime. Maybe at night. But she and Fry would never have been there at night. Instead, they walked along the dune formations with the other girls, and followed the contours of the lake and the wide beach of sand.

She pulled into silence until Jim nudged her.

"I want to go to the ocean," she said. "To see that big sound."

His fist nodded forward again. His finger pointed to his lips. It was dark; she couldn't keep up; it was impossible to see the words. *Time to go back.* They climbed down and worked their way along the path to Main Street. This time, Jim led the way, one hand behind him so that she could follow by grasping his wrist. They were silent as they crossed the empty street. Naylor's doors were closed now; the theatre was dark. They walked quickly, the rest of the way to the post office. Neither tried to speak or sign. Grania kept her head down.

Jim did not look at her, all the way back to the tower. They went round to the side door and climbed the stairs. When they reached the landing at the top, they let themselves into the apartment, and they stood there, and clung to each other.

*

In the hour before his train departed from Belleville, after the men marched to the station and answered the roll and joined their families to say goodbye, Grania's body began to clench, a knot working its way inside. The band that had marched to the station platform continued to play and she felt the beat of the drums inside her. She looked around at the crowd, at the forced smiles, and felt the excitement of many people pressed together.

Her glance took in the glimmering rails, the string of boxcars diverted to the siding, waiting for the troop train to pass through. Water was dripping through the floor of one of the freight cars as if a block of ice was melting inside, and the dirt below was spotted and dark. Bits of coal were strewn along the edge of the tracks. The troop train seemed unusually large, threateningly close. Grania gave Jim the lunch she had made and he somehow managed to tuck the cloth bag that held it under a strap at the top of his bulging kit. Neither of them spoke. He took her hand and held it firmly inside his own and she felt only the pressure of his skin on hers.

Don't let go. The war is close. The war is closing in.

Against her will, a part of her was shutting down. It was happening to him, too. *He is leaving before it's time to go.* And though she hated what was happening to both of them, she knew that in the same way he was pulling away, she was pulling back, searching for the safe place inside herself. If she could find it, she would stay there until he returned.

But the thrill of being part of this moment could not be denied. Jim and all of these men were leaving to serve their country. Many of the soldiers were laughing, and Grania saw them calling out to one another. Jim was grinning now, and made his way through bodies that were pushing forward. Before he stepped up to the coach, he half-turned on the platform and searched until he saw her in the crowd. Hands and arms were waving all around. People clutched small Union Jacks. Parcels changed hands; photographs were pressed to palms; food was passed through the open windows—box lunches and containers of tea. So many men were leaning from the framed arches of the coach windows, it appeared that they would be squeezed back outside again. Hands and elbows were propped against sills and holding tight. A large number 5 was chalked on the vertical boards of the coach directly in front of Grania, the one into which Jim had disappeared.

He was heading east for more training and was to be attached to a field ambulance unit as a reinforcement. After that he would head for the coast where he would sail. He did not know his destination, the name of his ship, the date it would sail or when it would land.

She was unaware of her fingers tapping against the side of her coat. The crowd was pushing again, and once more she was forced to edge forward. Jim made his way down the aisle to the right; she watched his profile appear and disappear from window to window until he found a seat for himself near the end, on the far side of the coach. He dropped his bag and came back to a centre window, leaning from behind. The men were three and four deep, hanging over the sill. Jim searched the crowd again until he was certain they had eye contact. His right hand reached to the left side of his chest and he made her name-sign, the private G between finger and thumb, plucking at the tunic that covered his heart. He grinned, and dropped his arms to his sides. She thought of the way he had looked when she'd first seen him in the bandage room at school, his arms hanging down as if they were loose in their sockets. She could see the soldiers on both sides of him shouting and calling out. Someone said something to Jim and he looked to the right before replying, but she did not see his words. He looked back to her and this time he did not turn away. The train began to pull out slowly, heading east, and then it picked up speed.

Grania made the *C*, his own name-sign the last thing he saw. She let the *C* fall forward to *H*—*Chim*. Her body stilled.

She stood in the crowd for a long time after the train was out of sight. The band marched away. The sky was pale, subdued in a meagre sun. Winter was about to begin. Small clouds were stuck to the sky like thin balls of cotton, barely stretched or puffed. Children played around the platform. Wives and mothers and fathers and grandparents and friends looked as if they did not know what to do or where to go. The train's departure seemed to signal permission for the release of tears, and women were sobbing outright as the older men beside them held their shoulders tightly and looked away into nothingness.

Grania had no tears. She stayed on with several others after the main crowd drifted away. She took in a long breath and held it, and stared hard at the empty tracks as if hopeful that, unreasonably, a second train would pull in and bring the departed men right back. She turned away and, not knowing where she was going, she began to walk.

III

1916

Chapter 8

Approximately 20,000,000 men are under arms in Europe. Allowing three yards for each man's uniform, the clothing for these men would represent 60,000,000 yards of cloth. Sewed end to end together, this strip of cloth would cover a distance of 34,000 miles or one and one half times the circumference of the earth. The buttons for these uniforms would weigh about 2000 tons and would require 1000 horses to draw them comfortably.

The Canadian

The first man Jim met after he was attached to Number 9 Field Ambulance was named Irish and had been with Number 9 since its formation. He had a long thin face, sandy-coloured hair that was thick and unruly, and a gap between his front teeth. A cigarette dangled between his lips. As they moved forward in the breakfast line, he crushed the lit end between his fingers, flicked the ash and tucked the cigarette into his pocket. Jim, watching, could not believe the size of the man's hands. His wrists and fingers were so large and thick, Jim felt his own hand disappear inside the other when they shook hands.

Within minutes of introducing themselves, they had figured out that Jim's Uncle Alex and Aunt Jean had their farm only four miles from where Irish's family had lived for generations, back home near Read, Ontario. Most of Irish's friends who'd joined up were with the 21st Battalion.

"I've met your Uncle Alex," said Irish. "It's hard to believe that you and I haven't come across each other before."

"I only moved there from the east a little over a year ago. I still don't know that many people."

"Your parents?" said Irish.

"Both dead. My grandparents raised me, but they're gone now, too. My grandmother died just before the war began. I lived with her on the north shore of Prince Edward Island. After she died, I moved to Ontario and helped Uncle Alex on the farm—you'll know that his children are young. After a while, I stayed in Belleville— had a room there, and a job going the rounds with Dr. Whalen. I looked after his horse, loaded supplies, delivered messages, that sort of thing. When the doctor bought an automobile, I learned to drive. Then," he added, "I went back to help my uncle with the fall sawing. I married Grania after that." He said her name softly as if talking to himself, as if he were not sure whether to say her name aloud.

Irish nodded. "I'm not married. But I will be, as soon as I get home. She said she'd wait."

He pulled a photograph from his pocket. It wasn't more than an inch square and had been cut from a larger one. He held it out for inspection, and Jim saw a handsome young woman with pinned-up hair and a look of wariness, as if she hadn't trusted the camera. She was wearing a high collar, and an oval brooch at her throat. The photo was unprotected, creased across the lower corner. Irish smoothed his large thumb over the surface before he put it back in his pocket.

"Clare," he said, and Jim nodded as if he'd been introduced.

Jim offered his own photo of Grania. He had shown it to no one until now. He had taken it himself, with Grania's box camera, shortly after they had made up their minds to be married. They had been on an early-summer picnic with Fry and Colin in Jones Woods, near the bay. The women had brought boiled-egg sandwiches with lettuce, and a marmalade cake. After they ate, Jim and Grania went for a walk and he surprised her by stopping, facing her and making a sign with his hands. He clasped one palm firmly into the other, and then pointed to himself.

"Marry me?" He raised his eyebrows, a question.

"What?" she said. "How did you . . . ?"

"Colin. He made me practise until I got it right." He made the sign again.

She burst out laughing. Her inward laugh. But she had already nodded, *Yes, Yes.*

He had taken the photo after that. Grania's face had a quiet, determined look, her skin pale, even in the photo. She was not used to being in front of her own camera. She had removed her hat, and her long red hair covered her ears and was pinned loosely at the back. He remembered how she had stared unblinking while he'd looked down into the window of the black box.

He buttoned the photo—protected in a tiny cardboard frame—into the lower pocket of his tunic, and patted the outside of the pocket with his hand.

"We were married last October," Jim said. "The party afterwards was at her grandfather's farm up on the Ninth, in Tyendinaga Township. Her family is all Irish. Her grandmother on her mother's side, her Mamo, lives with the family. We had two weeks, Grania and I, before I had to leave, and we spent those in Deseronto, where she was born."

"I've been to Deseronto," Irish said. "I've taken the steamer there."

"Grania's father owns a hotel on Main Street, right across from the wharf and the station."

"I know the one," said Irish. "I've stopped in there for a meal or two. The place is known for its good food."

The line was moving quickly and they loaded fried eggs and bread and potatoes into their mess tins and headed for a long table where they squeezed in at the end and sat side by side.

By one in the afternoon they were paired off because they were the same height, five foot nine. They had worked all morning with two other men Irish already knew, Evan and Stash. Stash had black hair and thick eyebrows and a fierce look about him, but Jim could tell from his voice that he was a gentle man. Evan was Stash's opposite, with fine features and thin, light-coloured hair. He seemed nervous, never staying still. He spoke rapidly.

"It's just his way," Irish told Jim. "But you can rely on him. We've all learned that."

This man Irish is going to be my friend, Jim told himself that night as he lay on his cot in the dark. His legs were aching and his arms were stiff. There had been ten-minute rest periods, more training, a lecture on First Aid, another lecture, more grub, early supper, and Irish had introduced him around. "This is Jimmy boy," he said. "Look at the arms on him. If they don't come loose, they'll be exactly the right length to carry a stretcher." And the others laughed, and made him welcome.

Jim had hoped to walk into town in the evening—the money changers had followed on the heels of the new arrivals when they'd marched into camp—but he was too tired. He had English money, but the only thing he wanted was more food. He was hungry all the time. The hunger had started weeks ago, when he'd boarded the train in Belleville. The box lunch Grania had prepared for him had been devoured shortly after the train pulled out. He'd been hungry as the train headed east, and hungry when it stopped at one small station after another. In some towns, while the bands were playing and the boys were boarding, women, complete strangers, handed up sandwiches and containers of tea through the open windows. Each time this happened, he had been surprised and grateful. He'd been hungry on the ship while crossing the Atlantic and during the train journey through English countryside. He had looked out at passing hedge and winter pasture and when he'd arrived at the camp, he had still been hungry.

Hungry or not, he had kept his eyes open. It was cold and damp outside but he was utterly amazed to be here, to be present. He had solid English soil under his feet—the mother country. *Mother Eng-*

land. He'd heard the words often enough at home. He vowed to start a letter to Grania in the early morning so he could tell her where he was, and what was happening, and all that he had seen.

"My love," he said silently, as if he planned to start a letter that minute, believing that she would somehow receive his thoughts through the dark. But what came out was, "I am so tired." His arms reached out and he fell asleep on the narrow pallet. Words in his dreams were not addressed to Grania at all but were mixed with images from the day's hard training and with stories told and passed around after supper. And it was the voice of Irish that surfaced.

"They were terrible seas, Jimmy. Terrible seas in the crossing. We hit a storm third day out and had to stay below. The boys threw up, vomited right out the side of their hammocks onto the tables, the very tables we ate off in the morning. I've never breathed such foul odour, and I hope I never will again. I had one glimpse outside during the storm and I looked up and all I could see was a solid green wall rising over the ship. I was so terrified I tore back down though I didn't think it mattered much where I was. We were hit so hard I was sure I was done for. One of the boys washed overboard, Jimmy. We were told that some of the boys tried to swing a boat clear to go after him, but there wasn't a hope. He disappeared, swirled away in the dark, and after that the boys were nothing but gloom. There wasn't a soul who wasn't sick at heart, but we were kept busy, and then we stopped thinking about him—as if he hadn't existed. He was taken in an instant. He didn't even get his fair chance at Fritz."

War, Jim thought, wide awake again. So far, it's all words and dreams. We know nothing, really, except that the man overboard could have been me on my ship, or Irish, or any one of us.

He shifted onto his back and stared into the dark and stretched his arms at his sides. His own crossing had consisted of endless physical drill, brisk air, sometimes sunshine, sometimes rain. Lifeboat drills were sprung at irregular times to keep the boys on their toes. Conditions had been crowded and he'd found it hard to sleep. And then, by chance, halfway across, he discovered an empty crate in an alcove at the end of a corridor, and after that he was able to sneak away most nights and be by himself. It was cold in the crate, but being cold was better than breathing the smothering air of a thousand bodies below.

Some evenings, before turning in, he had joined the singsongs. The boys, wearing lifebelts over their uniforms, pressed around one of the four pianos on board. A few times, Jim had been at the keyboard. They started out with lively songs, "Casey Jones" and "Tipperary," and moved on to "Silvery Moon," and ended up downright sentimental with "Love's Old Sweet Song." Jim knew every word to every song. Occasionally, he sang alone.

Later, in the submarine zone, when lifeboats were swung outboard, the men had no trouble keeping up their spirits. They were more worried about not getting to France in time to see action than they were about going down at sea. Their biggest fear was that the war would be over before they could get there in time to take part in the show.

*

For days and weeks in the camp near Hindhead the men of the Ambulance drilled until all arms were reaching out in sleep. Reaching for patients, reaching for stretchers. Booting the hinge, flipping the stretcher, booting the other end, hoisting it over the shoulder. Jim was learning methods of carry: four-handed, two- and three-handed seat, fireman's lift, fore and aft lift. Crossing a ditch, crossing a wall, loading a wagon, unloading a wagon, horse ambulance, motor ambulance. And continuous, never-quite-satisfactory number drill. Two-bearer, three-bearer, four-bearer. Repetition, repetition, bearers falling in and numbering off—march, stoop, lay hold, position, turn about, rejoin squad. They ran around one another, formed up in parallel rows, took turns being the patient, collected the kit of comrades who were the acting wounded, and competed with other squads while the rote sank in. Jim could snap open and kick shut a heavy stretcher with his eyes closed, and did.

When not doing route marches or drill, the men dug drainage ditches, laid pipes, took turns at sanitary fatigues, cleaned equipment, polished buttons, looked after their uniforms and nursed their bruised and blistered feet. They attended lectures addressed to several units merged for training. Many of the lectures were given by medical officers. It was this part of the training that held the most fascination for Jim, because the assembled boys were called upon to do various tasks of first aid. Some of the boys in the larger group were to be attached to hospitals on the French coast. One man, a Prince Edward Islander like himself, but from Charlotte-town, had left for Étaples as a replacement, to work in Number 1 Canadian General Hospital. Most were staying with the Ambulance. Jim and Irish, by now a skilled and reliable team, remained with Number 9.

They applied pressure dressings and mummified limbs; they wrapped gauze over puttees, around each other's legs. Jim found his tongue slipping into a new language of tourniquets and anchoring and figure eights. He bandaged heads and strapped pretend fractures of the upper arm. *Nature has provided a splint that is always available, the side of the chest.* He positioned slings on a grinning, gap-toothed Irish, who prompted him when the knot rested too heavily over a bone. He used the reef knot, never the granny knot. *A reef knot will not slip and yet is easily undone.* And he helped Irish, whose fingers were so large he was awkward tying the knot in the first place.

They learned to handle fractures of the femur. *Machine-gun fire will be directed between hip and knee; most fractures will therefore be in that area and will be compound or open. It may be necessary to treat shock and haemorrhage before transporting.* They were instructed in the use of the "greelie tube" and the administration of morphine. *After morphine is given, the patient's forehead is to be clearly marked with an M.*

They used whatever was at hand to splint and immobilize a limb. When ordered to improvise arm splints, they ran for sticks or roll-ups of old papers, or they twisted items of each other's clothing. As the boys they'd be carrying—if only they could get to them across the Channel—as the boys would have rifles, they were taught to improvise with bayonets, too, if there was time to create a fast splint.

One day they were taught to give an injection of water to an orange. *The orange represents the muscle.* They plunged their first needle into the battered fruit and held their breath. *Every wounded man will receive the anti-tetanic serum.*

Jim took special courses and became aware of what was clean and what was not. If assigned to a field hospital, he would hold his hands in front of him after touching a dirty dressing, and he would consider himself contaminated. He would hold his hands that way until he could get to water and scrub with soap. A new awareness opened in his mind—an awareness of the invisible world. He had never before given any thought to the invisible world, but now he understood it to be swarming with multiplying bacteria. He took pride in his training, and each time he learned one new thing he added it to the count of what he already knew. His store of information was growing. He watched, and listened well.

At night he fell onto his bed, sometimes fully clothed. He and Irish walked into town a couple of times and looked around and walked back. The town people were friendly; everyone wanted to talk. But he had to rise early, there was no thought of staying up late. He lay on his mattress in a fatigue that was absolute, shoulder sockets numb, hands and wrists aching. Sometimes his mind was startled by what he imagined to be the heavy rumble of distant guns. *Over there.* Maybe it was thunder. Terrifying things were happening without him. He was afraid, but he wanted to be in the midst of those terrifying things. The disturbing echo to the south and across the Channel kept him from needed sleep, pried a wide inner eye, an unprotected chamber that refused to shut down.

He wrote a letter to Grania from the camp one evening, after the rumbling had started up again. He knew the rules. No place name could be mentioned, no movement of troops, no brooding thoughts that could harm the war effort.

> *My Love*
>   *I am still training, as before. It is all we do from early morning until we fall into bed at night. It seems as if we will never be ready.*
>   *Sometimes, I hear a sound like thunder. How can I describe this sound? An invasion in the dark, a pulse that grows in the head. It starts as a level throb and, after that, it weaves its way like a thread through every nerve in my body.*
>   *Irish and I are anxious to contribute. We all are—all the boys in the Ambulance. As soon as we have word of departure, I'll try to let you know.*
>   *All my love,*
>   *Chim*

*

On a Wednesday at eight-thirty in the morning he and the boys received their leather identification discs. By ten they were wearing stiff new boots and were part of a muster parade. Jim looked around him in wonder. He was one of ten thousand soldiers from many places anticipating the approval of the bushy-browed, small-eyed Sir Sam Hughes. Some of the boys said that Sir Sam was a powerful and eccentric man. A man, Jim saw, who enjoyed conducting the inspection. After the formalities were over, all pomp and ceremony, Jim was back at stretcher drill. This time, excitement jumped from one man to another. They knew they were leaving soon, but when? The Australians and New Zealanders were beginning to arrive in France from other theatres and from fresh training, and the Canadian boys wanted to get there, too. Any place they would be sent would be better than endless drill on this side of the Channel. So far, the higher authorities had conspired to keep them away from the war, even though their fellow Canadians had been in France and Belgium for over a year.

On Friday they were paraded again and their kits inspected by officers from Headquarters. After that there was Bank Parade and then, free time. Jim had begun to smoke the first day he'd arrived at the camp, and he stopped now to buy a pack at the canteen. He took out a cigarette and stuck the pack in his pocket. He had a few hours off and wanted to be alone. He wanted to get away from the constant noise and activity of the camp. *It might be my last day in England,* he said, beginning a silent letter in his head. *This might be it.*

He listened to the wheeling gulls as he started out. The air was cold. He walked towards the south, imagining coastal sky, the kind of sky he knew and loved. He tried not to think of his childhood on the island. He tried not to think of Grania and what she might be doing at this moment of a Deseronto morning. He could see wisps of grey cloud to the east, and larger, flatter clouds to the south. The road followed a series of low hills for several miles, and after that there was nothing but stubbled field. He came to a wall of low stone and followed it along the edge of an enclosed field. He sat quietly until his hands and feet began to numb.

His life was changing. Events were occurring rapidly, one eclipsing another. He had been caught up in a great, moving, humming machine such as the world had never seen, and he knew and felt this. He stood and stomped his feet and flexed his fingers and once again faced the direction of the coast. There was only silence to be heard. Not a sound. Yes, one—the birds hidden in hedge and scrub around him.

*

On Sunday after Church Parade, after rumour and speculation, after endless preparation, the men of Number 9 were told that they were leaving for France the next day. They were officially part of the Third Canadian Division. From that moment, no one was permitted outside camp lines.

Jim and Irish fought off their usual hunger and fatigue, and hauled beds, straw mattresses and tables to QM Stores. Kit bags and surplus kit were sent to Shorncliffe to await their return. When given these instructions, few remarks were made. None of the boys joked about leaving belongings behind. No one wanted to be the one to jinx what might be set to unfold.

Jim went back to the rapidly emptying canteen and purchased chocolate and biscuits and tinned salmon. He and Irish folded their extra blankets and turned them in. They were permitted to keep and carry one. They went to the writing room provided by a local church and sat with paper, pen and ink and wrote letters to Grania and Clare, and left them for posting. In the morning, after an early breakfast of beans and porridge, they were issued two thick sandwiches of bully beef. By eleven o'clock they had travelled by train to Southampton and were standing next to a cattle boat. The horses were loaded and, after the horses, the men. Number 10 Field Ambulance was also aboard. The boat eased out of its moorings and into the harbour and dropped anchor. It stayed there, no reason given for the delay. No one bothered to explain and, as always, rumour and speculation started up. Awaiting escort? Mines? Submarines? Jim had listened to constant offerings of uninformed opinion back at camp, and he listened to more of the same now. No matter how many times one of the boys said he was certain they were about to depart, the boat remained where it was, anchored fast.

He began a letter to Grania in his head, one of the many that could never be sent.

> Sometimes I can't remember what I have actually written and what I have told you from the mind's eye. We are not allowed to keep diaries. Even if this were permitted, there is so much weight to carry, an extra sheet of paper would be too much to

add. If I could scratch a note to you now, this minute, this is what I would tell: the fear in the eyes of the horses as they were led up the ramp; the darkness of their coats, the warmth of their bodies; the skittishness of some. My own jostling comrades, as tightly packed as the horses. The good humour and bad jokes. The stench of being close together inside heavy clothes and under heavy packs. The feeling of stagnation as we sit, lean, or stand. We are ready to go but we are squashed onto a cattle boat that keeps us in England and brings us no closer to the shores of France.

A monoplane appears out of nowhere. The buzz in the sky hovers overhead like a portent. It is a wonderful machine to see. I try to imagine the thrill of freedom a man unknown to me must feel up there, sailing through the sky, looking down on us, a luckless clump of men trapped within the confines of an old cattle boat.

There was nothing to do but wait. Listen to endless chatter. He found Irish and sat with him, leaning against a stack of wooden crates. Irish was full of stories; he never ran out. "There are stories galore in everyone's family," he'd told Jim shortly after they first met. "Stories just waiting to be told."

"Will we sail or won't we, Jimmy?" he said now, and moved over to make room. "Patience is a virtue according to my late grandmother, though she wasn't a patient woman herself. Did I tell you how good she was with needle and thread? The skill came in handy when my grandfather fell off a rafter in his own barn and scalped himself on a hay knife. There was no doctor in the area at the time, my dear Jimmy, so Grandmother rallied her young sons and together they dragged him into the house and laid him on the kitchen table he himself had built, and she sewed the lifted scalp back on. She never stopped scolding him throughout the procedure. And Grandfather is alive and well today, though Grandmother is not."

Jim wondered, with his new knowledge of bacteria, how Grand-father had managed to escape infection, or even blood poisoning. But Irish, reading his mind, laughed and said, "It would take more than germs to knock over old Grandfather. He's a fit man today."

The boys around them were playing cards in close, small groups. Some at the far end of the boat were singing; a lieutenant held a miniature notepad in his palm and, with a pencil, was sketching nearby ships. The noise level was high because they were still inside the harbour. But a hush fell over everyone at the same moment, and there was a sudden rush to the side.

A large hospital ship had pulled into harbour and now approached, and slid by the cattle boat like the majestic vessel it was. The murmured information that went around said that it was loaded with wounded men from the Eastern theatre, men brought to England from the Mediterranean. The feeling of respect, pride and emptiness that Jim felt as he looked on was mirrored in the faces of the boys around him. He could see stretchers that had been car-ried up from between decks. Uniformed men and nursing sisters moved among them, preparing serious cases to be offloaded to a waiting hospital train and into motor ambulances that could now be seen lining up along the dock.

> The wounded boys on that ship have done everything, and we have done nothing. They have fought and served and have been part of the show and now they are injured, and deserve to be looked after. So far, I have not cared for a single wounded man in flesh and blood. So far, I have not seen the enemy.

In the early evening, after five endless days of lying idle, the cattle boat hauled up anchor and slipped out of the harbour. Lights were extinguished and silence fell over all, broken only at the beginning by the order to put on lifebelts. Jim sucked in his breath. The boat was met by two ominous dark shapes and escorted across the bleak waters of the open Channel. Jim's heart was pounding, his mouth dry. Hours later, on the other side, the cattle boat slid into the dock at Le Havre in the waning part of the night. It was still dark on a Saturday morning. It was April 8, 1916.

*

I have seen a Hun. It was not quite dawn when we left ship and there he was—Fritz, a prisoner—working on the dock alongside the Imperials. I couldn't help but stare, and tried to get a closer look. The Imperials were loading heavy crates but they were the ones who looked glum. The Hun was the happiest of the lot. This surprised me but what was I expecting? A monster, a poster Hun like the ones I've seen back home? Thick neck, square forehead, evil glaring eyes? At the least, I expected a sullen prisoner. But the boys say the German prisoners are happy to be out of it. Their war is over. It was something though, seeing Fritz. He was my height, fair haired, fit and healthy looking. He stared right at me, and he was laughing. An ordinary human being. It is hard to believe that in appearance he is so like us.

Right away I was put to work on guard duty, not guarding Fritz, but our own boys in case they tried to go out of bounds. We've been issued waterproof capes, hat covers, flasks, Red Cross bands, spirits of ammonia, mitts, and gas helmets, which we are required to carry at all times. We'll be given more gas training soon. During my first gas course I spun out of the choking hut, eyes inflamed and so full of tears I was blinded. I stumbled down the outside step and collapsed to my knees and then I caught hell for blocking the exit. The thing to remember is to stop breathing the second the order is shouted. Even half a breath already taken, and you're done for. There were many besides me who suffered that day.

There are things I cannot say in my letters. Things that go through my head. I want to tell you everything, but the cen-

sor's eyes are now inside my own. Every time I sit before a
piece of paper, four eyes instead of two stare at the blank sheet.
I will store what I can in memory.

There had been an early and violent thunderstorm and they
marched in high winds, in its aftermath, away from the busy docks
and away from the houses of the town where women worked in the
streets. They passed an elderly man who was trying to hitch up a
frail and limping horse. A hand plough leaned against an outhouse
wall. Jim glanced over at the tiny patch of wet and soggy earth, and
wondered if the horse could manage at all—or the man, for that
matter. One was caved in, the other stooped over. He'd thought it
too early in the season to work the earth, even though the larch
buds were open all along the way.

A bundled-up young woman, perhaps the elderly man's daughter
or granddaughter, stood in the doorway of a second outbuilding.
Her face was expressionless as the Canadians marched past. A grey-
haired woman was making her way on a bicycle, parallel to the
Ambulance men, on a wet path below the road. A band of headscarf
partly covered her hair; her coat was buttoned to the neck to keep
out the dampness and the cold. She was steering the handlebars
with one hand and held a propped hoe over her shoulder with the
other—the way the boys had been trained to carry their empty
stretchers. She ignored the men's presence, and did not turn her
head as they marched on the road above her.

They marched as they'd trained, 120 paces to the minute. After
fifty minutes they rested for ten, and during the ten they plunked
themselves down and grabbed for their cigarettes.

Jim pulled the smoke into his lungs, savouring the first taste as it
rolled over his tongue. Everything was new, every sight a wonder.
And the stories continued during the break. So many stories, passed
from man to man. Not surprising, with millions of men from the
Empire milling from place to place, picking up stories as they went.
Irish settled beside him on the ground and they were quickly joined

by Evan and Stash. Stash began to tell them about a Canadian he'd been told about who had been issued two left boots and was forced to walk through twenty-two miles of clinging mud. The soldier tried to complain but no one would listen, as there were no extra boots to be had. At destination, when the march was over, he shot himself through the head. Jim could not shake the story from his mind as they got up and continued their own march.

Stash swore that the story was true but it is hard to hear this.
It is one more story of a war we have seen only from the edges.

When they arrived at the overnight camp, no one knew for certain how many nights they would be here. Rumour was circulating again. A stack of printed postcards was distributed, one card to a man. Jim accepted his, looked it over, took a pencil from his pocket and began to stroke lines across the surface.

*

In icy winds, he led an advance party back to Le Havre for rations, a long and bitterly cold walk. While his own feet suffered, he could not stop thinking about the boy who had been forced to wear two left boots. How could the corporal, the sergeant, the officers have allowed this? He thought of the boy all day, and again in the evening when he was squashed into the back of a cattle car next to Irish. Evan and Stash had stayed together but were nearer the door. On the outside, a sign had been fastened—"33 Men to the Car." As there was no space to lie, the men were pressed shoulder to shoulder, body to body, most of them in sitting position, grumbling and cursing throughout the night. One of the boys managed to loosen a board to let in air and there was more grumbling about the cold. In the morning, they got out at Abbéville and stretched, and had their hot tea and bread.

Jim stood shivering in the drizzle, the tea scalding his throat, though he welcomed the liquid sliding down. A French woman approached from behind, selling cakes from a broad flat basket supported by straps looped over her shoulders. She was young and had a small thin face and her hair was covered by a kerchief. Her skirt, too long for her, was frayed along the bottom from brushing the rough ground. She looked into Jim's face and said only, "Monsieur," and he pulled out a few French coins to purchase a square of cake that fit inside his palm. It was yellow and sticky but not sweet, and he bit into it slowly, trying to make it last. The young woman smiled at him from under the kerchief and later, after he climbed back up into the car, he remembered her smile and her small, thin face. Squashed beside Irish, Jim pulled his own silence down around him when the grumbling started up again.

The train pulled forward and paused frequently, chugging slowly through Boulogne and Calais, stopping to take on coal and water. Far off and in no discernible pattern, long, low booming sounds were heard, again and again. The train passed through miles of low country, and it was four-thirty when the men finally detrained at the busy station in Poperinghe, Belgium. Jim and Irish were detailed to help offload ambulances and trucks from the flat cars, and they worked steadily in the rain. By the time they were finished, the station was dark and unlit, and the men were soaked through. From all sides, as they kept their bodies moving to stay warm, they heard about the shelling of the town the night before. Six had been killed. Jim tried not to be dismayed by the matter-of-fact way the news was passed on and received.

His own sense of urgency increased during the march forward to rest camp, where they were to stop overnight. Ammunition carts and trucks and motorcycles were clattering past in both directions, a steady commotion all around. The road was narrow and chaotic, but there was a sense of purpose to all of this movement. At times, traffic was so dense, the road was completely blocked and they were forced to wait along the side. Jim realized only later, much later, as he was shown where to bunk down, that the sound of the big guns had accompanied them all the way.

I wish I could write these things to you. I am close behind the line, and have been assigned to a small hut. It is crowded, but for a change no one is grousing. I think the men are glad to have a place to rest their heads. Irish and I have vowed to stick together. We've known each other only a short time but I feel as if a brother has entered my life after a long separation. I think he feels the same. I was first up this morning and sewed a pocket in my tunic for my gas mask. Irish was still asleep. I'm learning to tell when he is awake and when he is asleep, because he can sleep standing up. In standing sleep he has a puzzled look, as if daring our superiors to question his ability to stay alert. When he is awake, he never stops telling stories. As for today's events, this is what I know so far: we are heading up to Ypres to relieve Number 1 Field Ambulance. No other information is given until the last minute. This is the way things work. We've been told only that four of us will be chosen to go to the trenches, the rest to the dressing station in groups of eight to learn the ropes. We are to start out at a march. No one is to sing. No one is to smoke.

*

He tripped more than once along the road because the footing was uneven and dangerous. No moon, no stars, he walked through a darkness constantly interrupted by fireworks and flashing lights. He was behind Irish, Evan, Stash and the other bearers making their way up the Salient in single file. They had left just before dark, led by a Private Angus, who had been in and out of the line for the past several weeks and whose job it was to guide them to their destination, near St. Eloi. Angus walked briskly, not only because he knew the way but because he was cold. He had nothing to say, and unlike the boys who followed him, he gave off the air of advancing like a veteran. Even so, there were moments when they lost their way and clumped together while he stopped and

reconsidered in the darkness. They moved forward in the corrected direction for another twenty minutes, and Angus stopped
again. The others came to a halt like dominoes about to topple.
Angus ducked out of sight. A whistling was heard overhead, and
then a loud shriek. It was Evan, shouting. He hit the ground hard
and rolled into a ridge of mud. The others remained on their feet.
Angus reappeared out of the dark and offered Evan a hand. He saw
Evan's sheepish look and patted his sleeve. "Don't worry," he said.
"It was a good reaction." It was the kindness in Angus' voice that
surprised Jim.

Explosions had started up around them in earnest. So much noise,
it was impossible to tell whose side was firing the big guns. *Both, it
has to be both,* Jim thought. *I hope most of it is coming from us.* He
followed Angus inside a structure he hadn't seen until he was
directly beside it, and he stepped down suddenly into a room of
wounded men. Most were on stretchers on the floor. Although it was
the Advanced Dressing Station, it was nothing more than a sunken
mud hut, sandbagged on the outside and partly on the inside, too. A
piece of dark rubber sheeting that covered the entrance had been
pushed aside as they entered, and was pulled back again over the
opening. The medical officer—the M.O.—in charge was standing in
the centre of the room. His lips were moving. He was speaking to a
soldier who was lying on one of three raised stretchers that had been
set into parallel trestles pounded into the dirt floor. The raised positions were occupied by severely wounded men. Jim saw the wobbly
M printed on the nearest soldier's forehead. The face below the *M*
was the colour of grey wool; the head—one ear across to the other—
was split open.

Angus had already moved to the back of the hut, ignoring the
activity in the centre of the room. The injured boy's head was an
open dirty mixture of blood and bone. It was so piteous, Jim's eyes
tried to refuse the image, but it was too late. He held his breath, but
stepped forward because the M.O. was signalling to him and Irish.

The M.O. was manoeuvring between more stretchers that had been set every which way around the edges of the dirt floor, and he managed to avoid stepping on a wounded soldier.

"Take him out to the yard." A hand gestured towards the soldier with the split-open head and then towards the back of the hut where Jim now saw that there was another covering of rubber sheeting. The doctor seemed to have spoken in a whisper but Jim realized, in the split-second lull between explosions, that he'd heard what the doctor had said. Even so, the M.O. was motioning again with his hand. *Sign language.* He moved back to the centre of the hut and leaned over the middle stretcher, surprising Jim with the lightness of his movements because his face revealed such obvious fatigue. The torso of the boy he was leaning over was covered in blood. The upper part of the uniform had been violently wrenched off.

Jim bent to lift the stretcher of the boy he'd been ordered to remove and realized that the boy was not dead. Long shuddering sighs were coming out of the extended and exposed throat. The boy's clothing had been opened and his sternum was sucking in hard every time his lungs tried to pull in a breath. There were long intervals between these terrible attempts to get air. Jim gripped the handles and felt or maybe heard Irish signal the lift and they left the trestles behind and carried him out, passing two walking wounded who were entering and who stood aside to let them exit. The sheeting closed behind them and they were in darkness again.

They found themselves in the yard, a spongy area of ground from which stench and moan seemed to rise up out of the earth itself. It was a small, churned rectangle of soil where bodies had been laid, most of them directly on the ground. Others were on stretchers. Someone had tossed straw over the dead boys' faces. A hand, palm up, was sticking out over a blanket that had been pulled up to cover a corpse. The face could not be seen but the hand seemed to expect something to be placed in it. Jim looked down at the boy they had set among the dead and dying, and said a quick prayer. He thought the boy looked at him for a moment but he wasn't certain that the eyes had seen his own.

Other stretcher bearers were carrying loaded stretchers out of the hut now, and they were heading back at a good pace in the direction of the Main Dressing Station. There, the wounded would be treated and sorted again. No one noticed that one more body had been placed outside; no one noticed Jim. The noise around him was relentless. He wanted to stay to help the boy he had abandoned, but what was there to do? His feet followed Irish and he looked at his friend's face and saw that it was completely white and then he saw nothing because they stepped down into the hut again, in darkness. A shout, and a candle was quickly lit; a match flared, another and another—each to a candle stuck in a bottle, or in melted wax, upright in a battered mess tin.

Jim's eyes focussed again on the soldiers lying in the room, the ones who had not yet been attended by the doctor. He began to see individual detail: fragments of uniform, thick muddy cloth driven through skin into muscle and wound, open flesh that oozed dirt and mud. Wounds that were filthy, contaminated. How could the M.O. hope to clean up tissue and bone? Jim thought of the lectures he'd attended during his training in England—he had scrubbed his hands, held them out. Here on the floor of the hut there were two buckets of muddy, bloody water, placed against a corner wall so they wouldn't be kicked over.

"*Infirtaris*," his mouth said. "*Inoaknonis*." He spoke the words knowingly, a chant to himself. No one could have heard him anyway; the din and thunder of the guns had assumed every bit of hearing space. His ears were tunnelled with pain, and he looked down at his hands and saw his own long fingers flexing rapidly as if conducting themselves through a bizarre set of exercises. He stared into a jagged hole that was a man's abdomen. A twist of bowel was lying outside the body, and someone had made a crude attempt to shove the loop back in with two abdominal dressings. The bowel was so pinkish, so clean looking in this shadowy place, the sight of it almost made Jim shout. The fingers of the soldier clenched spasmodically, much the way Jim's fingers had been flexing. Jim could not tell if the man lost consciousness, because the fingers suddenly relaxed and stopped moving. A highlander lay silent, arms folded across his chest as if he'd been readied for placement inside a coffin. He had a leg injury, maybe not so serious. Looking at him, the peace on his face, Jim remembered Herbert's anxiety as he was stretched out on the farm table when Dr. Whalen had sewed up his thigh. Herbert had been a lucky man.

The boys on the stretchers had received anti-tetanus. Some of them, the ones who were not going to the yard outside, were tagged, pieces of rectangular cardboard pinned to their uniforms with safety pins.

There was no time to think. The noise rose to a greater pitch and Jim had a frantic moment when he thought his head would explode. A corporal by the door gestured to him, and Jim understood that he and Irish were to start a carry back to the next station—a PPCLI man with a destroyed femur. Pieces of bone and pinkish-white tendon had been exposed and a layer of heavy dressing slapped on. If they could get him to the Main Station farther back, he would be sorted and treated, along with the others headed there now. After that, he would be moved again, to the Clearing Station, and then the railhead, and on to the coast and then to England—to Blighty.

Jim gathered himself, resolving to be steady as he lifted. There was no chance, no luxury of four bearers being available to do a shoulder lift. Stash and Evan had already left, carrying a patient of their own.

The man was heavy, but not as heavy as some Jim had carried during his training. He glanced over at Irish and saw that he, too, wanted out of this room of pain and death. They stepped up and outside, adjusting hands to the familiar grips of the stretcher. Machine-gun fire rattled close around them, and Jim had to force himself not to duck. He took half a dozen steps and the sky lit up. If he ducked, he'd dump the patient, and if he dumped a man with a shattered femur, the injury would be made worse and the man's pain unbearable. As it was, the soldier was frighteningly silent. Jim saw the outline of two bearers ahead, and two ahead of those. He increased his pace, being in the lead. He and Irish had trained together so thoroughly, so closely, their feet were in step the moment they were under way. They tried to stay in the tracks made by the others, and set out with their first carry across a land that was broad and flat and pocked with holes and mud traps at times as deep as their knees.

Irish and I go back and forth four more times in the night. I force myself to see what must be seen, to do what I have to do. We walk through sound that bears down upon us like an engine on tracks. It is so thunderous, so close, I keep checking the sky for signs of a storm. A storm would be a relief. My skin feels as if it will burst inward, inside the sound that is all around.

When we get back to our billets in the morning we want to collapse but immediately we are ordered to move to new billets again. Mice made a nest in my packsack while I was gone overnight. I dump the sack in a hurry, contents scattering. We eat breakfast. How can we eat after what we have seen? We do, we are famished. Eggs and potatoes, we fill ourselves up. In the few minutes I have before we leave, I pay an old woman for a half bucket of hot water, and I wash. I fill my water bottle. The sun is out. The room of wounded men, the yard of death, are obscene dreams in the morning's brightness. I have begun my work in this war.

Chapter 9

My dad said that if you saw five men talking and a shell exploded nearby, when the smoke had gone they would not be there because they would be blown to pieces. When the Germans first used their gas, Dad was caught and had to go to the hospital. Now, every morning when he gets up he has a bad cough. Dad will stay at Knox College Hospital for about two months.

The Canadian

No matter where she was or what she picked up to read, war news was now pointed directly at her. Town papers, city papers from Toronto or Ottawa or Belleville, or *The Canadian* from the school: there was no possibility of remaining indifferent. She was subject to constant bombardment of unfiltered information, true or false. It did not help matters that shortly after Jim's departure, the government in Ottawa published casualty figures: 539 officers and 13,017 men killed in action so far.

She could scarcely speak Jim's name except to Mamo and Tress. No matter what she was doing, day or night, he was always behind her first layer of thought. After he left on the train, she had stayed overnight in Belleville with Fry and Colin. One day after returning to Deseronto and moving back to her parents' home, she wrote her first letter to him. She sent that, and another and another, but none of the letters reached him before he sailed. When she received a response, it was to tell her that five letters had arrived in England, in a clump together.

The day she mailed her first letter from the town post office, she understood that from that day forward it would be an act of faith to print name, rank, number—all of the unit information she had to include—and expect that her words would actually reach their destination. The address she wrote across the first envelope was so long, it seemed impossible that she could stow it in her memory. At the time, she had thought so.

Now, the newspapers were alerting her to ideas she had never before considered.

Postage need not be paid on letters or parcels addressed to prisoners of war.

She had never given a thought to prisoners of war.

Sugar and chocolate, because of their strength-giving properties, have become part of the daily ration of soldiers in the trenches.

There had been a rush on sugar and chocolate in the stores of the town. Supplies had run out because so much had been sent overseas.

When chocolate is given a soldier, he is better able to fight off fatigue and resist breaking under nervous tension.

She had not known about that.

Before Christmas, six hundred soldiers had arrived in Belleville and had used the canning factory on Pinnacle Street as their barracks. They had probably sailed shortly after Jim; Grania thought that they, too, were probably part of the Third Canadian Division.

When she had worked at the school hospital, she used to see soldiers marching in the direction of the fairgrounds, or to Zwick Island. In good weather, she'd seen them picnicking near the school dock beside the bay, just below the flag station. She wondered, if she and Jim ever had children, if she would tell them that there had been a time when trains stopped, on request, at Mileage 114.9, the Deaf and Dumb stop. Cedric, in the school paper, had an opinion, as always. "Dumb," he once wrote, "has the secondary meaning of dull, stupid, or doltish. The word *mute* brings forth the image of an attendant at a funeral."

Grania missed Fry, who wrote once a week, the letters arriving in Deseronto the day after they were mailed from Belleville. She had just collected this week's letter from the post office and, after taking Father's business mail to his office and a small package to Bernard, Grania went to a quiet corner of the hotel lobby to read what her friend had to say. Fry's news was not surprising.

Colin tried to join up, she wrote. *Third try. But at last minute, he was found out.*

Grania thought of Colin's blue eyes, how they must have burned with intent as he'd tried, once again, to bluff his way through. This time, using his considerable lip-reading skills, he'd managed to get as far as the end of the physical exam.

> *He turned away to pull on his clothes and Doctor spoke. Colin does not know what he said. When Colin did not answer, Doctor was suspicious. Then, special check of hearing was done.*
>
> *I am not sorry. I know it is hard for you, worrying while Jim is over there. Colin volunteers with school cadets. On days they have drill, he helps when he finishes work in print shop.*

Grania knew that Colin was again considering a move to Toronto to work as a typesetter. A deaf man who owned his own business had contacted him twice. It was one of the few ways the boys could get work after they left school. They'd already worked in the print shop; their visual accuracy was exceptional, and they could not possibly be bothered by the noise. There had been an article not long ago in *The Canadian* about printing presses owned and operated by deaf persons—there were five in the west, and two in Toronto. Fry's parents still lived in Toronto and would be happy to have her there, but for Grania it would mean that her friend would be more distant. As it was, they visited back and forth as much as they could. The last time Grania had taken the train to Belleville was to accompany

Mamo, who needed a new coat. She and Mamo had met Fry, and they all had tea together on Front Street.

> *Colin knows former student who did enlist. Last spring, do you remember we were proud when Owen visited school? He wore Red Cross badge on his sleeve. Now he is corporal and we think he left Exhibition Grounds in Toronto to work in diet kitchen in military hospital. Teachers here say he will never be sent overseas. But Owen's success makes Colin hope. And it is not first time Colin is rejected.*
>
> *If we were allowed, we could do more. You and I could work for Empire. With our Home Nursing training we could help look after sick and wounded when boys come back to Canada. Instead, we volunteer, and knit pneumonia jackets and knee caps. I don't think we are welcome in factories, either, where women our age work now, when many speaking boys are overseas. I am not feeling sorry, Grania, but something else happened to Colin and that discouraged me.*

Grania set aside the last page of Fry's letter, feeling discouraged herself. She had not received a letter from Jim for three weeks. The letters from England arrived in clumps on this side of the ocean, too, and not necessarily in order. Everything depended on the ships.

At least Jim was still in England the last time he'd written. He said he was training, and anxious to get across the Channel. It was worse for Tress, whose letters from Kenan were now sent from *Somewhere in France.*

Grania picked up the "Locals" page that Fry had torn from the school newspaper and enclosed with her letter. The paper arrived by mail twice a month, but Fry, knowing how Grania loved to read what the children wrote, always had Colin bring home an early copy. She sent the "Locals" page ahead, even though Grania's subscription copy followed a day or two later.

This week, the children at the school were preoccupied with the fire in Ottawa. Disaster would never stop being a main attraction.

We heard that the Parliament Building in Ottawa was burned last week. It was thought that the Germans set it on fire but we were mistaken. Sir Wilfrid and Lady Laurier had invited some ladies to a party; they heard that the Parliament Building was on fire and Sir Wilfrid got an auto to ride there. When Sir Robert Borden heard of the fire, he ran to see it without his hat and coat, so he lost them.

Some entries were about war.

There are a lot of wounded soldiers. Some men have their legs off, and some have one or two arms which have been blown off by shells or something else.

My Aunt has two sons at the war. They have gone to France and she is alone at home. Poor Aunt! Her sons are feeling fine and not worrying about the future, so my Aunt is trying to look on the bright side and will leave them in her Heavenly Father's hands, knowing that He doeth all things well.

Our principal came to the chapel where we were watching the magic lantern show. He carried an Edison phonograph and played some music but I could not hear it because I am a deaf girl. The hearing people enjoyed the music very much. They looked pleased.

Last month we asked if we could have a carnival. We made funny clothes. I dressed in a plain dress and went as a suffragette—votes for women, you know.

Grania turned the page and read one of Cedric's items.

Deaf and speechless, Jaime, the 6-year-old son of the King and Queen of Spain, finds his greatest pleasure in a moving picture theatre, which has been built in the royal palace for his amusement. Despite his affliction, the 6-year-old princeling is a bright and merry little boy. He is to be taken soon to the French Institute for the Deaf and Dumb at Paris, but the physicians hold out little hope of the restoration of his faculties.

She folded the tear sheet and put it away. She picked up the last page of Fry's letter and read it to the end. It was sometimes like this with Jim's letters. She had to brace herself to get through them at one sitting.

Tuesday after work, Colin walked to city and crossed foot-bridge over Moira. He was going to Front Street on errand for Cedric when two women he never saw before rushed up. They were speaking at same time and he could not lip read more than few words. They pinned white feather to his over-coat and marched off. He came home humiliated. For an hour he was upset and paced up and down before he told me. He said he pulled the feather off and threw it on road and came home. Cedric's errand is still not done. This happened day after Colin tried to join up one more time.

Grania was certain that one of the words Colin had read from the lips of the two women had been *coward*. Her own Aunt Minna, in a letter to Mother, had written from Toronto saying that some women—women who had no sons, or whose husbands were too old to serve—were marching up and down the streets as if they'd been appointed by God, calling out to young men suspected of being indoors and safe behind the walls of their parents' homes: "Come out, young cowards! Come out and sign up!"

She thought about Colin, deaf at birth, born to deaf parents, tall and fit-looking with his strong body, his wavy fair hair parted almost in the middle. He would have looked carefree enough as he walked along the Belleville street. Who could know, or even imagine from outward appearance, how many times he had tried to slip past recruiting officers and medical examiners? Colin, with his hands shoved deep down into his pockets, had always made an effort to fit in. But there was something so deliberate about his stance, it succeeded only in drawing attention. When he was confronted on the street, he must have wondered what was happening, what the two women could want from him. The realization would have come when he had seen the white feather, shame and anger burning his cheeks.

*

Now in their twenties, Fry and Colin had known since their teens that their lives would be joined together. Not the way Tress and Kenan decided, at the age of ten, that they would marry when they were older. Not like that. It was knowledge that asserted itself during the last years they were students at the school. Everyone else knew, and did not question. Colin used to stand to the side at morning recess when the girls danced with one another—and his eyes never left Fry. He didn't care that he was teased by his friends. Two by two, arms around waists, the girls danced. No music needed; there was only the swish of skirts, the scuffling shoes, the rhythm created out of silence. The group broke up suddenly when everyone had to line up for a slice of bread and a spoon of molasses. Grania shuddered when she thought of the thick syrup, how she had choked when she'd tried to make it slide down her throat.

In the afternoons, the girls went back to class to learn sewing while the boys went to the print shop or the shoe shop, or to carpentry. Most afternoons, the girls did fancy work, learning and perfecting stitches. It was difficult to come out of the Belleville school and not sew like an expert. Other days, they mended.

Miss Wyse, the sewing teacher, would reach into the basket of clothes that had been set in the centre of the room, sewing machines along one side, a bolt of cloth spread down the long table nearest the door. Light streamed in from the peaked windows. But there was no fancy stitching on mending day. Once a month the girls mended the boys' clothes, which usually meant patching trousers. Each girl picked up a needle and thread and went to the circle of chairs. Miss Wyse distributed the trousers, a pair to each.

"Why can't the boys sew their own patches?" Fry had signed to Grania.

Miss Wyse signalled her to work. No talking, no signs.

But when the teacher left the room for a few moments, the girls checked the names in the waistbands, jumped up from their chairs, and swapped. Grania was handed Edgar's trousers and shook her head, *No*. Edgar was a boy who tried to trip the girls on the rink during carnival. Edgar was foolish. She settled, instead, for Charlie's. When Colin's trousers were identified, they were quickly passed around the circle. Fry always sewed the patches on Colin's clothes. No one ever disputed her right to mend for Colin.

Now, not so many years later, Colin was doing everything he could to leave Fry and go away to war.

Was it selfish to want the men to stay home? They were sent into danger. Many were killed. It was someone else's war.

Grania knew what Jim would say: *This is our war, too. We are needed.*

One evening, when he'd been singing in Aunt Maggie's kitchen in the tower apartment, she asked what the song was and he told her, "Dear Hame hid awa' in the Glen." He wrote out the title for her; he had learned the words that week. While they put away the dishes after supper, she teased him about singing to the plates and pots and pans. She saw now that every moment they'd shared during the two weeks in the tower had been part of an elaborate farewell. They had shut everything and everyone else out. It was only later, after Jim left, that she understood the true intensity of their time together.

He had leaned over the backs of soldiers at the open window of the train. He had made her name-sign with his hand. She carried the picture in her memory—Jim reaching across his tunic, the coach with the chalked number 5. There were no yellow-rope letters in this picture. Only her husband, searching for her in the crowd.

Now, the same trains that had crossed the country from west to east, collecting cheering boys who kept time to thrilling vibrations of marching bands, were crossing the country in the opposite direction. Pulling the same cars, half-empty, from one coast to the other. Puffs of steam rose into the air and vanished while the walking wounded helped offload the limbless and disabled. Some days, after a train passed through, the platforms in the towns were strewn with an unaligned jumble of vacant, staring, young-old men. Grania had seen them in Deseronto and in Belleville and in Napanee.

Jim had left Canada excitedly, heading for the country of the King, His Most Excellent Majesty of the British Dominions beyond the seas and Defender of the Faith. She thought of the children at school when Cedric had raised his ruler like a baton at the front of the crowded Assembly Room, and taught the motto of the Empire Day Movement. One King, One Flag, One Fleet, One Empire. The children's hands had shaped the signs of loyalty, their earnest young bodies standing smartly to attention. She had been one of those children. And so had Colin. And so had Fry.

*

Grania folded Fry's letter and slipped it into her pocket. She glanced up to see Bernard crossing the lobby. He smiled but did not stop to speak. She thought of Fry and Colin again, and was not surprised that they were both discouraged. Colin had been accused of cowardice. Grania felt her own anger rise on his behalf, but she knew there was nothing she could do. Nothing the three of them could do except continue to try to take charge of their lives.

It had been Miss Marks who had helped the students understand the concept of taking charge, and Grania thought of her now. "You will have to ignore some things outside of yourselves," she'd told them. "But try to be in charge of your own information. If you rely on others to tell you what is going on, then others will be in charge of your life. Some things you can act on, some things you cannot. Try not to be frustrated while you learn what you can do."

Grania hoped that Colin remembered the discussions. He wanted badly to do his bit in the war but that was not going to be allowed. It would take courage to ignore the insults of people who did not know half as much about conducting themselves with dignity as Colin did.

Chapter 10

We left the station and went to a hotel, where we boarded, until Monday. A soldier introduced his mama to my mama, so my mama was not lonesome. The soldier was lame and his right arm was almost dead, but he was cheerful. It all happened one day when they were marching at Camp Borden. Some girls threw cigarettes to them and they all wished to get one, and our friend fell and his comrades fell on top of him. He has two brothers in khaki. One has been returned home crazy, and the other came home at the same time as my dad.

The Canadian

In the late afternoon, on her way home from the store, Grania stopped off at the post office. She reached into the box and there, in her hand, was the first item of mail sent to her from France. Proof that Jim was at the war, in the war, a part of the war. She tried to take in the information at a single glance: the right-slanted handwriting, the texture, the date, *April 8, 1916.* She thought of Jim's long fingers, his gentle hands, one holding the card, the other holding the pencil. She raised the card to her nose but could detect nothing more than the scent of handled paper, of use.

What she held in her hand was a Field Service Postcard, pale and brownish coloured, with pencil lines drawn through print. Apart from the date and a dark amoeba-like smudge beside the year, the only handwritten word on the entire card was a name. He had signed at the bottom, *Chim.*

She stepped back and took a breath and steadied herself against the wall. Why did the card seem more of a threat than a greeting? Jim had held it in his hands. It meant that he was alive—on the eighth of April. Of course he was alive; if he were not, she'd have received a telegram. But now it was the third of June. There must have been delays all along the way; this had taken longer to arrive than his earlier letters from England. She gripped it tightly with both hands and read the lines printed on the card.

> Nothing is to be written on this side except the date and signature of the sender. If anything else is added the post card will be destroyed.

Jim had obeyed instructions and had drawn a line through every sentence on the face of the card except *I am quite well.* Lines had been drawn through:

> I have been admitted into hospital
>> sick
>> wounded
>> and am going on well.
>> and hope to be discharged soon.
> I am being sent down to the base.
> I have received your
>> letter dated _____
>> telegram dated _____
>> parcel dated _____
> Letter follows at first opportunity.
> I have received no letter from you
>> lately
>> for a long time.

Grania now saw that one other word was bare and exposed. This was at the bottom of the card and the word was *lately*. Somehow *lately* seemed more personal than *I am quite well* at the top. But because she had sent a number of letters, she had no way of knowing which had been received and which had not. At the time of writing the card, Jim indicated only that he'd received no letter *lately*.

They had planned to number their letters after his departure, but she had given up on that hopeless system almost immediately. Letters took four weeks, or five, or six—the card had taken almost two months—and it was her belief that anything received at all was entirely by chance. She'd received short letters from Jim telling her that he was safe, that he was learning new things in his training, that the boys wanted to get on with the show and get to France. Sometimes he wrote to her about sound. Or he mentioned his new friend, who turned out to be from a farm not far from Bompa Jack's. From the time Jim had joined the Field Ambulance, he had something to say about his friend Irish.

She looked at the card and again she read *I am quite well* and *lately*, as if these words represented all that was unsaid between them. She rubbed her finger over the smudge at the top. Maybe it contained a truly private message. She smoothed the corners of the card and slipped it carefully into her handbag and went back out to the street.

She knew she could not return home immediately. She saw Grew on one side of the street, and Cora on the other, heading towards her. She ducked around the side of the post office and went in, taking the stairs past the landing and the offices on second floor. She did not, at this or any other moment, want to be told one more time by Cora that she had a sweet little voice. She continued up the stairs, inhaling the scent of oak, aware of the late-spring air, aware of the pulse of her own echo as she followed the curvature of the banister. Her palm brushed against the richly stained wood, her fingers tracing the ridge of pattern as she climbed. When she reached the top, she was not disappointed to find that Aunt Maggie and Uncle Am were out. Quietly, she let herself in.

It was the first time she had been alone in the tower apartment since the day after Jim's departure, when she came to collect her things before she moved home. That same evening, Aunt Maggie and Uncle Am had returned across Lake Ontario from their trip to Oswego.

She glanced left, then right, left, right. Each room opened off the wide main hall. She hung her coat on a hook and walked to the end of the apartment and began to inspect each room as if she were a visiting stranger, someone returning to a place she had known long ago in an intimate, remembered life.

Here is the kitchen, the long room at the end on the left. This is where Aunt Maggie cooks. And where Jim had flipped French toast to perfection in the cast-iron pan, his lips singing as he presented it to Grania for her breakfast. *Across the hall, this is the place one dines.* But she and Jim had never dined here; they had eaten their meals picnic-style in front of the windows of the parlour so they could look out over the bay, setting the trays of food on the carpet between them.

Walk backward now; these are the chambers for sleep. But not where she and Jim had made their bed.

Turn right and enter the parlour. How elegant this room, so seldom used by Aunt Maggie and Uncle Am. The room chosen by Grania and Jim—she glanced at the carpet—*the place where they unfolded the blue blanket and placed the pillows on top, and two blankets on top of those. The place of sleep. The place of love.*

She shut the hall door behind her. Against the back wall of the parlour, a small square window looked down over the inside stairs she had just climbed. The outer windows, the ones that faced the street, stretched up from the baseboard and lined the front of the room. She walked to these and looked over Main Street and the southern edge of town. The tower apartment was the only building on the street to command a view from this height. Even so, she felt the urge to be higher. In the back corner of the room, ladder rungs had been built into the wall in direct vertical ascent to the tower. Mindful of her skirt, she climbed, rung by rung, remembering a day she had come up here with Jim. When she reached the trap door, she pushed it open and latched it back, and stepped up and over to the platform at the top.

As children, she and Tress had been permitted to climb the ladder inside the tower, but only when Uncle Am was behind, ready to catch them if they slipped. He had lifted them, each in turn, to the south face of the clock, the peering-out place, so that they could see past the Rathbun industries along the water's edge and over the arms of the Bay of Quinte beyond. Each time she had looked out, Grania had imagined herself in the lighthouse that blinked from the page of her *Sunday* book. The C-shore page. *Dan caught the child in his arms.* While one part of her never accepted the girl's passive sinking through the waves in the picture, another part of her had. *Under* was the calm beneath the surface. *Above* the surface, mixed-up things could happen, and did.

Now Grania stood inside the four faces of the clock and thought *under*, and *beneath*, and *behind*. She tried to think of places where, for the hearing world, all would be still and silent. Not here, inside a clock.

The only person who climbed the tower these days was Uncle Am. It was his job to oil the gears and wheels, to wipe a thick cloth across the iron structure, to rotate the long jutting rods that attached horizontally to the centre of each clock face so that the outside hands could be corrected. Jim had been up here to oil the clock during Uncle Am's absence. When Grania had climbed up with him, she ·had shown him the peering-out place. Grew had been up here, too, almost two years ago. His son had left on the steamer to report to the barracks in Belleville, and Grew had raced up the stairs to the apartment and asked Uncle Am for permission to climb the tower so he could watch the steamer—and his boy—sail westward down the bay.

She imagined Grew's long legs climbing the ladder, perhaps touching down on every second rung. She thought of how he had stayed in the tower long after the steamer was no more than a speck in the distance. "He stood," Aunt Maggie had said, shaking her head, "even when there was nothing to see but water and sky."

Grania understood why Grew had stayed up here to stare at the horizon. Just as she understood why the few remaining people on the platform of the Belleville station stayed, long after the troop train departed. Jim had been on that train and she'd been among those few. The ones who lingered stared into the vanishing point that had swallowed the train. When, finally, she had turned away, it was to turn towards a change in her life.

Jim had gone to war.

*

She had walked away from the station looking straight ahead, not wanting to see the face of anyone she knew, not wanting to speak or communicate. She did not cry; she never cried. Her feet had kept her moving.

Later that afternoon, she made her way through familiar streets and climbed the outside stairs to the apartment that Fry and Colin were renting in the small house not far from the school. She could not have told anyone where she had been during the intervening hours; to this day she did not know where she had wandered. Fry was home, and when she saw Grania, she did not ask questions. She pulled her in and hugged her tight and headed for the kitchen to put on a pot of tea. If Grania wanted to be alone, Fry would not be offended. If she wanted to stay over, she could sleep on the sofa. There was little extra room, but she was welcome.

But Grania had not wanted to be by herself. She sat in the kitchen and watched while Fry signed the news of their friends at school. Grania did not smile or pretend to be happy. When Colin came home after work he, too, understood. She was content to sit at the supper table and watch him communicate the things that had gone on in the print shop that day. On his way home, he told them, he'd passed two soldiers on outpost duty on the road in front of the school. They had been placed there so that none of the troops in Belleville went out of bounds without permission. Colin had saluted as he'd passed.

Grania had watched the conversation, but had felt no need to nod or join in. What was most dear to her was being held in a tight place high in her chest. She felt as if she would be forced to take shallow breaths for days and weeks and months, until Jim would come home. She remembered Mamo helping her to keep her voice close; she remembered how she'd been trained at school to hold her words before letting them out. But this was different. Something else—not words—was locked inside her. Locked inside that tight closed place.

*

She reached out a hand now and touched the side of the huge tower bell. It was taller than her own height, and suspended over air. A massive, rigid clapper, attached to the workings of the clock, was perched above the outer rim of the bell and ready to strike. In Aunt Maggie's parlour below, a tall mahogany cupboard cleverly disguised the clock's long pendulum cables that stretched down through the tower and were suspended over a deep bed of sand. When Grania had first entered the parlour and walked past the floor-to-ceiling panels of the cupboard, she had not remembered the three-foot depth of sand at the bottom. "If the cables ever come crashing down . . ." Uncle Am once said, but he didn't finish the sentence. The mahogany cupboard had been built upward from below, through the ceiling and into the tower. No one ever suspected that cables were suspended inside.

The inside-out clock faces loomed before her, and Grania turned herself to the south, towards the front, to the giant milk-white face that presided over the bay. She searched for the spot between IIII and V where long ago someone had scraped away the paint and cleared an uneven space—the peering-out place. Up here behind the clock, she was always surprised to see the numeral IIII. She never gave it a thought while she was standing in the middle of Main Street below, looking up. Had she not learned her Roman numerals at school? Wasn't the numeral four supposed to be IV? But clocks were like this. Except the O'Shaughnessy clock, which had numbers.

She pressed her face to the scraped-away portion and stared. As she stared, she relaxed and felt herself become the fixed point. No one knew she was here. Hers was the eye that gazed through and looked down over the town.

It was not washday, but a few bits of laundry were waving from the clothesline in McClellands' backyard a little way along the opposite side of the street. Pillowcases pegged close to the stoop meant that women's undergarments were inside, discreetly hidden. The glass in the side windows of McClellands' house was wavery, distorted in shadows that were altering in the quickly fading sun. As Grania peered through the clock, Mrs. McClelland, a sweater gripped tightly over her shoulders, stepped outside, climbed the stoop, unpegged the pillowcases and their contents and hurried back to the house. Although June had begun, there was still a chill in the evening air.

Patrick walked past, not knowing that he was observed from above. Mildred Clark, too, walked briskly along the street, probably heading home. For years, Dr. Clark and his wife, Mildred, had treated ruptures and dropsy, contusions and boils, women's conditions, men's ailments, broken bones, lumbago and despair. Every death certificate spanning a generation of town history had been signed by Dr. Clark, and most of the town births recorded in the registry also bore his name.

Grania raised her gaze up and over the houses on the south side of the street, over the remnants of industry and the tracks and the station and the wharf, to the sweep of the bay that lay before her like a rumpled sea.

There was Forester Island. There, the pointing finger of Long

Reach and the Bay of Quinte, water slipping around and between the juts of land. Prince Edward County lay beyond, and beyond that, the great body of water that was Lake Ontario. All of this, from here, was imagined in the way she imagined Jim's ocean, which she had never seen. Where passing ships pushed their way through waves that battered at their sides. Where the higher the waves, the louder the sound of their roaring. Had Jim not written about this during his trip across the sea? In letters penned in half darkness while he was suspended over the same beating waves he described? From his private place, inside an empty crate into which he slipped every night after "Last Post," he wrote to her after darkness wrapped itself around crannies and outlines of a blackened ship that was odorous with bodies moaning in cramped sleep below. Below, too, were the horses, their tails wrapped with puttees to protect them from rubbing against the ship's walls. Jim had been discovered by a lieutenant but was told that if he kept quiet and out of trouble, he could stay, the officer being aware of conditions below.

Compared to hammocks strung over tables—the occupants roused before six every morning so that breakfast could be served—the crate was, for Jim, a luxurious and cavernous space. A space in which he created his own warmth, propped paper against his knees and wrote to tell her that he dreamed her face, her long red hair tucked beneath his arm, the smooth skin of her fingertips brushing lightly across his lips. So lightly, in his dreams he could not tell if her fingers were receiving his thoughts in the dark.

*

There is no light, now, in the tower. Grania is still. She focuses until her thoughts are as sharp as she can hone them. She is aware of her heart pushing blood to her head, her torso, her limbs. She gathers her own silence, the comfort, the safety of it, the silence in which she lives. She expands this until it is outside of herself and fills every space around. She slides it past her fears about Jim—has he not promised that he will survive?—and pushes it beyond herself, and

spreads it along the shore of the bay and into the woods at the eastern edge of town, and past the cemetery, and past the end of the great
body of lake water, and east through the forests she has read about,
and down the long waterway of the mighty St. Lawrence River,
towards the sea. The more she is able to focus, the farther her silence
extends, spreading slow and even, like moonlight over water.

It crosses the ocean now. And on the other side, it routes its way
past forests where, for miles, trees are covered with moss on only
one side. It drifts over coastal lowlands, slips in and around high and
narrow houses imploded on themselves, shards of blasted stumps,
chalk pits, slag heaps, collapsed rooftops and shattered brickyards. It
drops, suddenly, into a close-knit maze of saps and trenches,
uprooted trees and snapping branches, parapets and firesteps and
funkholes and odd-shaped patches of sheeting and tin. It searches
for and finds one man. He is with his buddy Irish and more than
twenty-four hours ago they were alerted for duty. Because they are
always hungry, they have been sure to carry extra rations of hardtack and McConachie stew up the line. They have collected their
steel helmets, which they are wearing for the first time. They've
moved forward in small squads while shells explode around them,
first to the Asylum, where the dressing station is in the cellar, and
after that they have moved forward again.

Part of the way, Jim has had to walk doubled over—sometimes at
a run—through a communication trench. He is soaked from perspi-
ration; he is played out when he arrives. There have been moments
when he thought he would fall and block the trench and force others
to step over him so that they could keep moving. The air is heavy
with smoke and fume; damage to the main road is extensive. The
Germans had begun bombarding Canadian positions all along the
front lines of the Third Division, during the morning of the second
of June. Underground mines were exploded after that. Now, there
are more than thirty reinforcements, stretcher bearers from the 9th
brought forward to work alongside bearers from the 8th and the
10th. They are told that many men from the Canadian Mounted

Rifles were killed or taken prisoner early in the day; some were buried when the earth exploded and fell back down upon them. Several who survived were taken out but many remain behind. All of the forward positions in the Canadian area have suffered severely, Mount Sorrel and Sanctuary Wood among them. Men are half-crazed with the whine and burst of shell, the spout of flame, the continuous rattle and boom. The dressing station in Maple Copse took a direct hit and was blown in, and those who were still alive and could be saved were moved farther back again. Wounded men have crawled on their hands and knees or, pitifully, have tried to get back from the line on their bellies, hoping to reach any sort of shelter at all. Some of the evacuated are the ones who were wounded earlier in the copse, but the aid post is abandoned now, and the captain in charge tries to establish order, tries to organize the wounded into small parties, especially the walking wounded, who can be escorted back or who can help someone more seriously injured than themselves. Jim and Irish are put in charge of small parties and they carry the most serious cases for hours, and there are no breaks, and their arms and shoulders have numbed. A gas alarm is given and they pull on the detested masks and breathe hard, and saliva drools down, and the goggles fog over and still they carry the wounded. They are told it has been a false alarm and, relieved, they rip off the masks, though their eyes are pained and smarting. The communication trench they use for several of the carries is partly blown in and clogged with bloody limbs and body parts and dead boys, but there is nothing to be done for the dead. Men who have passed here before them have picked up some of the bodies and tossed them over the side so they could get through themselves, and the ground is covered with more of the dead. The soldier they are carrying now has been shot through the face; half the face is gone; it is just missing. A terrible sound is coming from the place below the hole where his lips and mouth should be. Some of the bearers set down their stretchers along the way and stop to dress the wounds of soldiers who are badly injured, but they themselves are killed. A dead bearer kneels on the earth with an open dressing in his hand, but nothing can be done for the dead.

Jim takes a step and feels an arm roll beneath his foot. He knows it is an arm because in a glance down when the sky is exploding, he sees a fist at the end of a sleeve. He keeps on, trying not to think, trying to get those who are living out of this hell. Noise and blood and earth rain down and the air flies with metal. He sees an elbow poking out, a chin, a leg, a foot. He and Irish cross another trench, drop to their knees, duck, crawl forward themselves when they can no longer stand. And then, back up again, and this time it is sandbags that fly through the air. They cross Zillebeke Road and head for Zillebeke Bund where new dugouts have been cleared and where horse and motor ambulance are to meet them. They take the wounded there and to a farm nearby, and from these points the injured men are moved back to the cellars of the Asylum.

They help load, and turn back for more. The route is pocked with craters, and almost impassable. They walk past dead horses, night bulks of flesh; they run alongside soldiers who are carrying supplies and empty stretchers and rations and blankets up to the Front. Someone shouts that two hundred more stretcher bearers are being brought up; they must keep on, relief is coming. But the Germans have broken through; they have taken some positions and are well inside Sanctuary Wood. In the distance, behind the Canadians, Ypres is heavy with smoke and fire from constant shelling, though more damage to that city could hardly be done, so thoroughly was it destroyed a year ago.

The designated stations continue to change. When the road is blocked, the men are redirected across country to Menin Mill, where cellars have been cleared and packed with new supplies. A hut has been set up beside the mill, and those who have a bit of luck arrive just as others set up spirit stoves and get to work serving hot cocoa and bread. Jim and Irish grab a tobacco tin of cocoa and gulp it down, and back they go because there are still more wounded to carry back. Finally, it is almost daylight and just as the two are lifting a soldier, a shell explodes so close, bricks and shrapnel hit their skulls and backs and they are knocked to the ground. They get up, and they are breathing hard, and they are alive, and Irish yells, "We have to beat it!" and they manoeuvre the stretcher out of that place as quickly as they can. They assist the medical officers and they continue to transport to the Mill, to Hell Fire Corner, to meeting places where ambulances pull up quickly; and so the injured go from Advanced Dressing Station to Main Dressing Station to Casualty Clearing Station. It is while Jim and Irish are offloading patients that they learn that Major-General Mercer, who commands the Third Division, is missing and thought to be dead. The news is met with shock and disbelief but it only makes them more determined to keep moving, keep trying, keep doing what has to be done.

After two full days without rest, after a counterattack on the third, Jim and Irish are told to find a place to catch some sleep and they crouch together, close and low, in the remains of a shelter that is far enough back to be deemed safe—as safe as they might be anywhere while still in range of Fritz's guns. The shelter is partly dug from the earth, partly blown away; they shift and move and share the little water they have left between them. They are out of food and too tired to look for any, and Jim is grateful for the spelling off, grateful for the fatigue of his body. But his mind is filled with what he has left behind and he doubts that he will ever sleep again. "This is the land of hell," he says, "the true Valley of the Shadow." The sky lights up with exploding stars as he speaks.

Even this far back he is rolled up inside a roar so constant he crouches and squints, as if crouching and squinting will protect his body and close his ears. He wonders what it would be like to shut his ears to sound—knowing that sound will enter him anyway, through his body. He is bloody and dirty and his eyelids are encased with soot and he forces them to close, and a silence—perhaps it is Grania's silence, having searched and found—encompasses, creates a different sort of shelter, one that fits the contours of his lean young body and makes it safe. For a moment, a fraction of a moment, the entire world on both sides of the ocean is still. And Jim sleeps. And curled at his side, his friend Irish, who can command his body to rest anywhere, also sleeps.

*

Grania rubbed her eyes. She stared at her hands and arms and felt her body sink into heaviness. She pulled away from the face of the clock and turned to leave but as she did so, she found herself reaching to steady herself against the corner beam as she had always done. Beneath her fingertips she felt the forgotten column of dates scratched into wood. Heading the column were two words she could barely see but which she knew to be there: *Ice out*. The scratchings of Uncle Am, part of the history of the town, each date recorded the day the ice broke up every year and left the bay. Ever since he had come to live in the tower apartment, he had added to the beam, satisfied—perhaps even comforted—by the continuity. Grania strained to see through the dusk: *April 12, March 29, March 21, April 4, April 17*. The columns marched through the years until they reached the present, this year's date written not two months ago.

She held tightly to the ladder and lowered herself rung by rung. She pulled the trap door shut and continued to descend until her feet touched the floor. The parlour was dark. Neither Aunt Maggie nor Uncle Am had returned. From below, a rising glow had begun to spread along Main Street as electric lights came on in house and business, here and there. Grania stood at the open curtains and watched an invisible breeze bend the tips of the trees and bow them to the town. Clouds were rushing across the sky, but the horizon remained darkly neutral. The early night sky was so like the colour of the bay, it was impossible to see the line between.

A light flickered across the water—perhaps a lantern from a point of land. The southern arm of the bay blurred to darkness. Grania stayed at the window until bright light was cast behind her from the hall. She was not startled, but she turned. Aunt Maggie opened the parlour door and switched on the corner lamp, illuminating her own face.

"I saw your coat in the hall," her lips said in the lamplight. She did not ask how long Grania had been standing there alone in the dark.

Chapter 11

We know that our soldiers will bear themselves bravely and that where danger threatens they will always be there to do their part, battling for the Empire in this great world war. Should any fall, as fall indeed some must, in such terrific fighting, there will be mourning . . . but it will be a great consolation to the relatives to know that their loved ones will have suffered in a great and glorious cause.

The Canadian

He woke with his cheek and hand and wrist resting against cool earth. He had been dreaming of Grania. He was disoriented and, feeling dirt beneath him, wondered for a moment if he were in a grave. *Stop, Grania told him. I stop, and focus. I try to make sense of the situation, and then I let in the extra cues.* He looked up to a sky that was murky, stirred up, as if the battle below had churned it. He turned his head to glance at Irish who was still sleeping, chin tucked to chest, arms pulled in tightly, as if he'd been forced to make himself small to fit the space. His big hands were tucked into his armpits.

Jim raised his own right arm to check his wristwatch. He looked at the dirt that was caked to his fingers and under his nails. Three days earlier, he had been asked to check off a list of supplies that were being unloaded from a service wagon, but he could scarcely force his hand to hold the pencil. He'd worried momentarily, and passed it off as fatigue. He turned his hand over now, as if asking it to explain what had gone wrong. Instead, he thought of Grania again, her small hand inside his own. Her fingertips had explored his palm the night they'd sat below the beam of the old pier after the performance at Naylor's. He shouldn't think of her. Not here. But he needed the thought of her.

What did you expect? he asked himself, and he answered, *Not this.*

If Grania were here beside him he would be able to tell her about the hands. If only he did not have to look at the hands. In death they told more than the face; he knew that now. It was the hands that revealed the final argument: clenched in anger, relaxed in acquiescence, seized in a posture of surprise or forgiveness, or taken unawares. Clawing at a chest, or raised unnaturally in a pleading attitude. *How can this be? My life, pulling away?*

He thought of the still-living boy he had been ordered to set down in the yard of the dead during his first night's work. How could that have been only weeks ago? Old sandbags and straw had been thrown over the faces of the dead boys, but that did not keep their hands from being on display. He'd mentioned this to Irish, but Irish didn't notice the hands and told him not to look if it bothered him. Jim never mentioned it again. There was silent agreement about what was talked about and what was not, even between the two of them. Jim did not tell Irish that sometimes he felt the irrational desire to kneel on the earth beside one of the dead boys outside an aid post, or beside someone who had been rolled aside in a trench. To kneel on the earth and break the boy's fingers if he had to. Just to put the clenched and angry hands to rest.

Irish jolted awake.

"When I think of it," he said. "The confounded drill always comes back." He spoke from behind, coming out of his few hours' sleep as if he were continuing some other conversation and not waking in a dirt hole, pressed together, cramped and stiff from the cold. "I hate how it kicks in. Sure enough, the two of us work like clockwork, Jimmy boy. But watch, if we ever get out of here, they'll put us back at the drill again as if we haven't a notion of what to do."

"I hate it, too," said Jim. But he knew that long after the brain fatigued, the drill kept them moving. A sort of memory machine installed in the body: sturdy coordinated parts, well-oiled arms and hands and legs and feet. Two men or four to a stretcher, it was all the same. Without a stretcher, it was the three-handed seat. *Bearer grasps own left wrist with right hand, other bearer's right wrist with left hand, bearer to left grasps first bearer's wrist with right hand, leaving left hand free to support.* Elaborate words of the drill spilled from one area of the brain to another, whether the brain was worthy of the information or not.

Jim stretched his legs and tried to force sensation down to his calves and feet. In the last two days there had been times when he'd moved so quickly, so hunched over with back muscles clenched, his heart had raced wildly.

The body remembered the wild heart. The body remembered slick and treacherous footing, shallow trenches, the danger of Blighty Bridge, mats and duckboards laid over the worst places, ooze seeping through the cracks. The body remembered the lurch and roll of the dead. Feet and legs had memories of their own. In Belleville, he had learned from Dr. Whalen that nerve messages from the legs were sent to the spine and up to the brain. Now, he knew that brain was solid greyish matter that came out of split heads like chunks of dirty sponge. It came out of nostrils and mouths blown open from inside and out. He knew, too, that the knowledge would be kept inside the matter of his own brain—forever.

But he wanted to tell Grania about the hands. She would under-stand. He would lie close beside her, and they would speak with their own hands. If it were dark, she would place her fingertips over his lips and she would gather his words into the place of their shared understanding.

He wanted to tell her how sorry he was that he'd left. He had been so hopeful, so filled with desire to help in the war. He wanted to do his bit like everyone else. But no one at home could have any idea of what this stretch of earth in the Salient now contained: scar, and death, and the memory of impossible acts. The terrible thing was that no one at home would ever know. Because what was happening was impossible to be told. Young faces, set and worried as the boys marched forward—soon to receive the ration of rum that would brace them before they went over the top—were seized in pale grimace only hours later, when regimental bearers and field ambulance bearers tried to clear the battlefields. Many of the dead were never brought in.

Jim shook himself and tried to force images that were more hopeful than leaking brains. A few weeks ago, on a trip to the line, it had been dark when he and his squad were led to a small treed area and told to catch a few hours' sleep. At sunrise, he had wakened in a shaft of light shining through the leaves. The warmth on his eyelids had been an unexpected gift. He'd opened his eyes inside a network of sandbagged structure and zigzagged tunnel with corrugated-iron roof, and dugout underground. The trees had not yet been blasted to pieces, although the remains of one shattered stump pointed to the sky, not a foot away from the place his head had been resting. It was easy to see that only the day before, the stump had been part of a living tree.

Birds were singing in that copse. He'd heard their songs, and extended the moment as long as he could. With eyes closed, it had been possible to listen to the singing and believe that war did not exist. He had opened his eyes, and squinted. Narrowed the opening between his lids and narrowed it again and found that he could look straight up to a soft warm sky without letting in hurt or damaged branches, or pock-marked trunks of trees. But stray bullets had begun to whiz overhead and a branch in open leaf fell beside him. He stayed flat to the ground and, with the others behind, crawled to safety.

There were images of Ypres, too. He had stored those after his memorable first trip by horse ambulance through the City of the Dead. All the boys wanted to see the place, even though anyone who'd been there spoke of it with sadness. He had listened to words like grandeur, splendour, magnificence, but those words referred to its former state. In its present state, the city was in ruins.

Bricks and rubble were heaped as they'd fallen. A road had been cleared over broken cobblestones and debris. A middle-aged man in ragtag uniform was sitting by himself beneath a jagged arch, staring blankly. Much of the population had left or had been removed but, astonishingly, people emerged from holes and underground basements as the horse ambulance rattled past. Columns inside destroyed churches stretched up into Belgian sky. Between columns, rows of misaligned chairs in the open air were coated with powdered stone and debris. It was as if civilization had one day been caught off-guard and frozen in a single moment of destruction. He thought of the tableaus he and Grania had seen at Naylor's Theatre. "They all fall down," he muttered under his breath, as the horses' hooves clattered over the improvised road. "Husha, husha, they all fall down." For hours, he could not get the chant out of his mind.

The Conciergerie was no more than a chimney reigning over a hill of brick and crushed stone. Irregular-shaped metal and twisted gears of a giant clock lay beneath a tower, and he remembered his hands oiling the gears of the giant clock in Deseronto. He had climbed the ladder behind Grania, up into the tower, and she had shown him the scraped-away portion of the clock face, and they had peered through and looked out over the bay. He'd stood behind her and put his arms around her, resting his palms against the front panel of her skirt and over the softness of her belly. They had stayed like that, and all had been peaceful there, above the town.

In Ypres, he saw the former hospital, easy to recognize, now an upright front wall with no building behind. Two statues had survived in their niches but a bell lay dented on the ground. In the main square, the majestic Cloth Hall and the once beautiful cathedral were in ruins from direct hits, or destroyed by fire. As proof that at least two more inhabitants had refused to leave and were still in hiding, a woman came out from behind a shattered building. She was pushing an elderly man in a makeshift sling that had been painstakingly attached to two wheelbarrows. The woman was young, dressed in black from head to toe, including a kerchief that came down over her forehead and was tied under her chin. The old man, thin and frail, was bundled in blankets and lying inside a hammock-like arrangement that had been strung between the strapped-together barrows. The hammock was tightly suspended over the top of the front wheel. Bundles of belongings were resting between the handles of the first barrow, the one the woman had lifted and was pushing along. The entire makeshift carrier had only two wheels, and though it was long and awkward and obviously heavy, the woman was able to propel it forward as a sort of hammock-barrow-cart. To Jim, the fact that she could push it at all was a sight of amazement. She did not look up as the horse ambulance clattered past in the opposite direction but she kept on determinedly, staying out of the way, heading towards the western outskirts of town. She seemed to know her direction with surety, and was trying to leave by pathways that had been cleared through rubble along the edge of the road. The main road was used by troops moving in and out of the line at night.

It was that picture, the one of the young woman gripping wooden handles and pushing the roped-together barrows, that stayed with Jim now. She had been wheeling her father, or grandfather, or maybe a sick and elderly neighbour, out of the destroyed City of the Dead.

Irish and I carried sandbags all day. I tried to exhaust myself so that I could drop off to sleep. We reinforced huts with sandbags and even scraps of iron. Day runs to night and back to day again. In the night, everything moves: horse, mule, watercart, motorcycles, guns, soldiers, ammunition, jars of rum. Stash and Evan are working with us, and this makes things easier. Between carries last night, the four of us sat in a close circle on the ground with a boy from Number 8 Field Ambulance whose name is Christie, and we ate bully beef and bread—five to the loaf. We had honey that Irish scrounged and shared out and squeezed onto the bread. We are always hungry. Everyone I know tries to put his hands on extra grub. But having someone to share it with is more important than having the food itself— there isn't a man who doesn't know that. Irish reminded us of how he found nine dozen tins of marmalade when he whipped open the oven door of the old mill the day we were sent to clean up. Tins galore were lined up inside the oven, row after row—someone had taken the time to be neat. Irish pulled them out four at a time with his big hands, and found more tins stacked on the floor behind boards leaning into a corner. Someone had left in a hurry. Or forgot the hoard and moved on. We pocketed two each and opened two more and ate the marmalade out of the tins, with our fingers.

After the five of us finished our bread and honey, we were on our way again and that is when three shells burst around us in rapid succession. It was the closest call yet. Evan and Stash were a slight distance behind, and Evan hit the ground in a hurry. We all did. But Evan is nervous and there is a worrying tic in his cheek. He rolls his fingers when he's upset or afraid. He says that what will be, is written. It is what the boys here say and believe, but I am not so certain. What Irish and I know is that when we are carrying the wounded, if one of us gets it, we both will. We work closely together and that is the way it will be.

In the evening I was sent out after dark to get rations from a truck but machine guns started up and I had to lie on the ground. I hate the sound, the pecking away. When it was safe, I moved again but my boots made a loud sucking noise in the mud and I was certain that I could be heard by everyone on both sides. There is a terrible whispering in the night that never goes away. Sound is always worse in the dark.

At night I helped a CMR man who told me his name was Oak. We put him in a motor ambulance that was headed back to the Asylum. He had been buried by falling earth and had shrapnel injuries, and I bucked him up with spirits of ammonia. A corporal with a splinter in his eye had brought him as far as the dressing station. We heard later that the ambulance driver had a finger shot off during the trip. A colonel who was in the same vehicle as young Oak died before arriving at the Clearing Station. The colonel was badly cut up.

When we hear about the dead, Irish and I nod. There is nothing to say, no energy to say it. One moment a boy is alive, the next moment he is dead. We've heard the news now, too, of Lord Kitchener drowning. The ship he was on was sunk by a mine off the Orkneys, and he went down with it. Death is surely everywhere and all around.

*

The last night before being relieved, Jim and Irish were called up to the aid post. There were few men around, and the M.O. sent them out to try to bring in a boy who had been reported injured. Regimental bearers were in another location, picking up wounded. A soldier who had crawled in by himself had given the boy's location. The boy, they were told, was propped against a low mound of mud, a long piece of metal embedded in his body.

It was dark, and shooting had settled down and things were quiet enough, though the lull might not last. There were no stars, no moon. Jim and Irish were given explicit directions and went out as silently as they could, avoiding unspeakable entrapments. Boots were everywhere, and tin lids embedded in the mud. Jim tried not to ask himself if they were attached to the living or the dead. They quickly found the boy and they stooped, one at each side. The boy was breathing rapidly, barely responding. Jim saw at a glance that they had no choice about how to do the carry. A projectile had passed through him, a long jagged piece that entered near his collarbone and protruded at an angle midway down his back, on the same side. The metal object—they did not know what it was—had been hit itself and then somehow propelled through his body. Jim groped for telltale dampness, but if the boy had lost blood, it had already seeped into the earth. They did not dare to lay him down—the metal could shift and penetrate a vessel or a major organ. Judging from his breathing, it might have passed through one lung. They abandoned the stretcher, and the drill kicked in.

Throw the patient's arm over your head.

The boy's arm was tucked like a stranglehold in the neck of Irish's tunic. His hands were soft; Jim had felt them, the fingers unclenched.

Patient sits on bearers' hands.

He and Irish looked at each other across the boy's shoulders. They could scarcely see the whites of each other's eyes.

Bearers rise together and step off: right-hand bearer with right foot; left-hand bearer with left foot.

Jim signalled and they pushed off, up quickly, from stooped position to standing. The soldier's head flopped sideways and knocked against Jim's helmet. Jim had to stay tilted to support the head, his own neck protesting as they started out. An explosion erupted to the right. Fritz was angry, retaliating. The explosion had been some distance away, but it forced them down more quickly than they had come up. Their knees hit the ground but the soldier between them stayed upright, just as he was. Jim caught the look on Irish's face when a Verey light lit up the sky in the distance.

"We've done this before, Irish."

The order is given by bearer No. 2. Ready! Kneel! Lift! March, taking short paces.

As they rose, Jim heard a crack, a whip snapping behind him. His legs gave out and he found himself on his knees again—one knee; his other leg was twisted behind. Irish was down, too. Miraculously, they had refused to drop their patient. It struck Jim how they must look out here, not knowing where to set a foot, ignoring the scurry of interrupted feeding rats under a starless sky.

"We'll have a good rat hunt," he'd heard a boy say one morning before dawn. Jim had been standing outside a dressing station as the men moved forward. "After the battle. See what they've been feeding on over on Fritzie's side." Shortly after that, the rum ration had been poured. Jim saw the empty jars being carried back down the line. The boy had not returned. Few of the boys had returned that day.

Another Verey light, closer this time, and then another, illuminated the horizon as if a town fair was beckoning across the countryside.

Half up, half down, Jim counted under his breath. They rose together, but the same split-second found them down for the third time. They sank to the rotting earth. Jim could hardly believe what had happened. He saw himself and Irish, both on their knees, the half-conscious boy between them still upright, the arm tangled in the neck of Irish's tunic. Jim felt a sudden surge of laughter—nothing could suppress this. He began to shake as if a low howl inside him was working its way out. There was a rapid response of gunfire. Knowing that his laughter had been silent, he wondered if it had been aimed at him.

"What the hell?" Irish whispered. "Keep quiet."

Maybe he'd made a noise after all. But now he heard laughter coming from Irish. The two began to shake uncontrollably and they stayed on their knees for what seemed like a long time, until they were wheezed out, muscles heaving in their chests. Through the darkness, Jim could see the gap between the whiteness of his friend's front teeth.

The human chair. The body between. The firing stopped. Jim realized, with relief, that it had not been aimed at them at all. *When flashes come, when flares and fireworks are all around, you see sudden silhouettes, men walking, both sides, out here in No Man's Land. Working parties. Some carrying rolls of wire. The figures freeze until the blanket of darkness falls again. And then, movement starts up once more.*

Unwiped tears rolled down Jim's cheeks and he prayed that the boy did not understand what was happening. He whispered, "Lift, Irish, for God's sake, when I give the word."

This time the boy's body did not threaten to topple. They had the balance of it from the start and they stood on four legs like a single machine. If they were shot at, Jim did not know, because he stopped hearing. Nor did he think of the weight of the carry. He concentrated only on placing one foot, the other foot, one foot, the other foot. They stumbled, corrected, moved forward. Left, right, left.

Avoid lifting over ditches or walls.

The training line brought him close to hysteria; he might start laughing again. *Don't think. If you do, God knows, you'll give permission for something else to break loose.* Instead, he started his chant, *Infirtaris . . .*

He and Irish got their patient down and into the trench, and suddenly Jim felt more exposed here than he had out in the open. Arms and legs, backs and hands, were numb when they brought in their man. It had taken them forty minutes. The M.O., sleeves rolled up, arms and shirt splattered with blood, looked at the two of them, looked into their faces and nodded. His glance took in the projectile sticking out of the soldier's collarbone and back, and he sucked air between his teeth and called for assistance. He reached for the morphine and the carbolic acid and he went to work.

*

My Love

I am sending this letter from our new location. After breakfast and without warning, our section was told to pack up and get ready to march. Irish and I did not march, as it turned out, and travelled by motor ambulance all the way. We camped in a large field and now we are billeted in barns and lofts and tents. I am in a tent. I am not permitted to name the nearby town. Censor's strokes may already be through this letter. One of my first jobs was to sort through a hill of equipment that belonged to wounded men who were sent back to Blighty. Whenever possible, the kit follows along behind. It was a mess of a job but I managed to get things straightened out. It is queer to see the keepsakes the boys squirrel away: a rabbit's foot; a ball-bearing; a tiny pocket light; a length of coloured cord; a calendar diary no more than an inch square; a spent bullet casing with a pencil cleverly stuck into its end; a photo—everyone has a photo.

The boys we look after here are in a room crowded with three rows of beds. It is somewhat of a hospital and rest station, and both Irish and I will be here for CENSORED. The injuries are not severe enough for Blighty, and once the boys are healed, they are sent back up the line. Some have infections; many have joints swollen from arthritis. Every ailment you can think of. I am learning the meaning of things I did not know when I worked for Dr. Whalen. DAH means disorderly action of the heart. PUO means pyrexia of unknown origin, a fancy way of saying fever. But you probably know these things from your work at the school hospital.

Irish and I cart water and serve breakfast and stock supplies and help the medical staff, and generally do what we are assigned to do. It is more or less like the work of the orderlies. I am now on the night shift and hope to finish this letter with no interruptions. I had a bath yesterday, the first in three weeks. I heard from one of our boys who returned from hospital in Étaples that they have a bathhouse there that can take 70 men at a time. He said that cigarettes arrive from Canada in unending supply. The boys in hospital are given oranges and chocolates and cigarettes to bring with them when they're sent back up the line. Some of the wounded in hospital send word to their friends to open parcels that come while they're away, and the eats are shared out among the men. The treats are appreciated far more in the trenches than in the hospitals, where everyone is well looked after.

I am being called this minute to heat some Oxo. I have to close. All my love, Chim

He did not tell Grania in the letter that when he first walked through the town, he met up with two men from Number 10 Field Ambulance and learned that one of the boys he had met during training in England had been killed by a shell. There had been nothing left of him to scoop into a sandbag, they said.

Jim remembered him as a red-haired intelligent boy named Egan, who looked no more than seventeen. He was so eager, he quickly became known as Eagern. He had left school to join up and had lied about his age. Some of the underage boys served in the line for months before they were found out and sent home. Some were sent back to England to fill in time until their next birthday. When they were deemed to be of fighting age, they returned to the line again, often to their old units. It was not easy to think of Egan not existing. According to the men from Number 10, he'd had no burial.

Several weeks back, at a time when things were quiet, Jim and Irish had been sent forward on a night working party to help reinforce a dugout that had been used as a dressing station and that would be used for the same purpose again. The sides and walls were eroded and had fallen in because of recent rains. The small party left after dark and arrived at the location a half hour later and the men started to dig. But the stench was impossible; the more they dug, the more terrible it became. It was all Jim could do to keep from running away from the job. He cleared a shovelful of earth and, through the dark, saw a pair of knees embedded in the dugout wall. And then, all around him, men were digging up body parts of French soldiers. Mud and slime were alive with skulls and arms and hands. They were told to give up and abandon the site, and they were glad to get out of there before daylight.

While he had been in the town near their new billets, Jim had passed a small church and he'd retraced his steps and entered the building. It was damp but peaceful, and there had been no one else inside. He sat in a pew and propped his feet on a low wooden rack that had been laid over the floor. He stayed there as long as he could, resting and thinking. Thinking how hopeless had been the life of the red-haired boy named Egan, whose flesh no longer existed.

I have begun to talk to myself at night. I try to be careful not to keep anyone awake, but Irish, never far off, has noticed. I should be exhausted; there is so much outside work to do. We have been put in charge of building latrines and incinerators. Stash is our best mason; he seemed to know something of the job when we were told to build a fireplace. Stash has always managed to attract stray dogs and cats; this time he adopted a white kitten and shoved it inside his shirt as he worked. Wherever the strays are, they will find him.

On Sunday, we attended Divine Service, and after that I had guard duty. Tonight I'll be working the night shift. Stretcher bearers are a versatile lot behind the lines; we are used for many duties. I saw close up a severe shell shock case. Two friends from the 8th brought him in. The boy's body was shaking; his head was twitching and his eyes rolling around without focus. His arms and hands and legs and feet were twitching, too. He was unable to stand and had to be propped between the boys before they could drag him to a bed. This is a terrible sight and affects everyone. It is like watching a convulsion that never ends. He was nineteen years old and the only word he could get out was Mother. He called out, again and again. A chaplain came in and told us not to worry, that the boy had only lost his nerve. But it was more than that; it was a serious and disturbing case.

We've heard that counterattacks by our Canadians near Hooge on the thirteenth have been successful in taking back trenches. This news revives everyone, after the terrible losses. Stories circulate, as always. One of the bearers I met from the 10th told me that a badly wounded man crawled all the way to the aid post in the dugout and when he got there, he tumbled down the steps, unconscious. They treated his wounds and got

him back to the Clearing Station, and now he is happily on his
way to Blighty.

I wrote about the bath but not the how and where of it. I did
not mention the lice in our clothing. These are soundless, laying eggs in our seams and feeding on our blood. When we
have a chance to sit around, we pick them out one by one and
crush them. The boys call them crumbs. If there is a fire, or a
stove, they burn them on top to hear each separate pop. Some
of the boys scrub at their seams with toothbrushes drenched
in creosote. But even if we rid ourselves of the creatures for a
day or even an hour, as soon as we are back to work, looking
after the boys, or in dugouts or barns or billets, we are lousy
again ourselves.

We were marched to a bathhouse in town that had been set
up by four Jocks who were assigned to build the apparatus.
Four local women stood by—it was an open warehouse sort of
room—while we were naked. Some of the boys joked and
laughed about the women's presence, but I did not. We were
told to strip down and pass our dirty clothes to one woman,
and then we were doused with cold water. We had two minutes
to soap down and then out again, and a dip into the vat. It was
only slightly warmer, but better than the cold-water dousing,
and then we were out for good and another woman handed us
a clean set of underwear and new socks.

Irish was in front of me in the line, Evan in front of him.
Stripped down, a dirty-looking bunch we were. In the midst of
all, Evan began to hop from one foot to the other, complaining
in a tumble of oaths that came out in rapid succession. "For
mercy sake," Stash told him, "be still and quit jumping
around." But Evan shouted out that he was infested. Others
shouted back, "Do you have something new to tell us?" His
clothes had been collected so I didn't know why he was carrying on, scratching and scraping. When I looked, I swear—Irish
said later he couldn't believe his eyes, nor could anyone else—

fleas had taken over and covered Evan's two legs from the knees down. He looked as if he had pulled up a pair of high socks knitted from black moving bodies. When the boys realized what was up, they scattered to all sides so the fleas couldn't hop over onto them.

We still try to find food during every spare moment we have. Irish managed a trade for extra bread and milk and cakes tonight, so we had a good feed. There was meat for our supper but it was smelly and tasted rotten. Occasionally one of the boys will catch a rabbit and pass it on to someone who can make a stew. We are all thankful for the scroungers.

Chapter 12

A Palate Sound

K   Kiss   Kill

"Place the hand in front of the throat. As sound is uttered, push
   hand forward.

Explode the aspiration.

A good supply of breath is necessary for this sound."

                                                    Illustrated Phonics

Stories continued to circle. The squad was to attend gas school, and
weeping shells would be thrown at them; a man in the 49th commit-
ted suicide; the squad was going up to the old graveyard to fill sandbags all night; one of the self-inflicteds had held an empty bully beef
tin and shot through the can and his own hand so that no powder
burns would show; the major was to give a lecture on bandaging
techniques and attendance would be mandatory; the road back of
the main communication trench needed repairs to allow the use of
wheeled stretchers. And there were persistent rumours that Number 9 Field Ambulance would be following 7th Brigade, about to
leave for the Somme.

   When they had the chance, Jim and Irish, Evan and Stash managed to get some time off together and walked to a nearby village in
the evening to look around for a place to eat. They had heard of a
small *estaminet* that was said to be better than others, and after
walking a mile to get to the village, they traced their way in and out
of narrow streets, trying to find the establishment. Evan insisted

that he knew the way; he'd been given instructions. After disputing, and giving up, and following Evan again, the four came upon it suddenly, near the end of a street that narrowed to a short alley and then a path.

It was, in fact, a small house, not a restaurant or tavern at all. The front room had been converted and there were square tables and chairs, so many squeezed into the one room that it was difficult to stand, once seated. From the entrance, Jim caught a glimpse of a tiny kitchen that held not much more than a counter and a tile stove and two deep stone sinks—one filled with dirty dishes and jars, the other with unpeeled potatoes. Two long sausages hung from hooks beside a planked door on the far side of the airless room.

The main room, only twice the size of the kitchen, was dim and crowded and choked with smoke. Sound bounced from one wall to another. Candles of the type sent in packages from home were jammed into bottles and stood upright on saucers, stuck into melting wax. The flicker and glow of flames threw shadows around the room as men waved their arms about. Everyone was talking at once, and there was laughter. Several voices called out a greeting as the four friends entered and pushed their way through to the only empty table in the place.

Jim sat, and thought how good it was to hear laughter. He asked for the same as the others were eating—eggs and sausage and *frites*—and Madame Camillone, a thin-faced woman in her forties who ran the business with her plump sister Marie—disappeared into the hallway beside the entrance and returned seven or eight minutes later with the food. The red wine was homemade. A *verre* was served to each of the boys, a *verre* that was a small jar. There were no glasses to be had.

Off-key voices had begun to sing in a back corner while the four were eating, and right away Jim recognized the song. He had seen the outlines of a battered piano when he'd come in, but it was shoved against the end wall and chairs were pushed against it; there was no room for anyone to sit at the keyboard and play. The song the boys were singing was "The Aba Daba Honeymoon," and many voices were sputtering hilariously over its speeded-up lyrics. Several tables provided different versions, one set of lyrics flying into another. The result was a staccato-like pelting of words colliding in mid-air over the boys' heads.

Irish, first to finish his meal, shouted in Jim's ear. "Why don't you sing for us, Jimmy boy. Show them what you can do at the piano."

Jim shook his head. Apart from Irish and the other two, he preferred to stick to his own company. Few of the boys in the 9th knew about his ability to play. In any case, for now he was content to sit on the hard chair in the warm and noisy room and feel the wine as it tilted over the rough rim of the jar and onto his tongue and into his gullet.

Madame Camillone and Marie were making signs to each other over the heads of the boys, and Jim saw Marie's plump hands signal that she was going to the back to start cleaning up.

Irish was pointing at Jim now, and the other boys picked up the call and began to clap and hoot for him to go to the keys and sing.

There was no way out. He took the last gulp from the jar that had warmed in his palms and he stood, feeling hands on his back as he was pushed and propelled towards the wall. Chairs were scraped back to make room. The piano, he saw, was missing its top panel. An empty seat quickly appeared before the keyboard. The boys waited while Jim sat down, and he stared at his hands, now resting on the keys. He had the Lloyd hands. Everyone from his island family had been musical. After his grandmother had died he'd left the only home he'd known and travelled a thousand miles from the Atlantic coast to Ontario, and now he had a job as a stretcher bearer and that was good enough for him. He and Irish and Evan and Stash knew what to do and how to do it.

He thought of Grandfather Lloyd holding the fiddle with tenderness, as if it were a living thing, and he had the old feeling he'd once had when the older man had stood at his back. His fingers came down on grubby keys, the ivories more grey than white. The piano needed tuning, but he carried on as if Grandfather were right there behind him. He did not know who was responsible for keeping time; they'd always passed the rhythm back and forth. Loose piano wires did not bother the two of them; nor did a flat note here and there—though on this piano, many notes were flat.

To start, his fingers raced through "Alexander's Ragtime Band," and the boys in the room clapped wildly. He chorded in between, as if accompanying an island reel, and then he played "Our Boys in Brown." After that he slowed the pace and sang "I Wonder Who's Kissing Her Now," and the boys joined in. Madame Camillone and Marie had stopped their work and were squeezed together in the doorway, their aprons brown with dirt and splattered with spills of wine.

It was after Jim stood up, ready to return to his table, that he reconsidered and decided to play one more tune. He sank to the chair and, this time when he sang, the other voices fell away so that his was the only voice, and it filled the room. He had learned the song in Deseronto during the short time he'd lived in the tower with Grania. They'd been lying on the blue blanket, and he had sung the song for her, every verse, and she had shown him the spot between diaphragm and abdomen—the place that she said was the origin of song.

> "On life's fitful ocean 'mid glamour and strife,
> As I wander afar among men
> O, my heart often sighs for fond tho'ts will arise
> O a hame hid awa' in the glen."

He sang three stanzas in his strong clear voice, his eyes raised unseeing to the wall in front of him. When he finished, three Jocks in the room stood and held their jars high in praise. Except for Jim's chair scraping away from the piano, there wasn't another sound in the room as he returned to his table. His friends were looking up at him, and he paused to see their faces before he sat down. Evan was relaxed; for once the tic in his cheek could not be seen. Stash looked fierce but could not keep from smiling. He met Jim's eyes and nodded. And Irish—a low appreciative whistle came from the gap between his teeth. And then, suddenly, hooting and laughter surrounded, and everyone in the room began to talk at once.

Irish slapped him on the shoulder with his big hand. "Good for you, Jimmy boy. It wasn't an Irish song but it did just fine and was loved by all. But you'll have to get that wife of yours to make an honest man of you. And next time, sing us an Irish tune."

The four stood amid shouts and entreaties to return, and after paying the two sisters, they pushed and manoeuvred their way between crammed-in tables, and stepped outside onto the uneven cobbles of the darkened street.

*

All day Thursday, the four friends fumigated blankets. By nine in the evening they had handled and stacked an even eight hundred. After that, when the tents were taken down, they were advised to sleep in the local schoolhouse. Thursday night after dark, Stash left camp and walked back to the village they had visited, and deposited the white kitten in the care of Madame Camillone and Marie, at the *estaminet*. He returned with four precious eggs, which the boys— though they'd had their supper—cooked up immediately and ate with a loaf of bread scrounged by Evan. The sisters had sent fond wishes to "Jeem," who had played the piano.

By Friday at two in the morning, September the eighth, after an eleven-hour march, they were sitting in the third-class car of a slow train. When they stopped, it was to eat canned beans and hardtack and drink lukewarm tea. Their fatigue was so great, not one of the Ambulance men had the energy to grumble.

Jim stared out the window at the dawn and wondered if sleep was a mythical part of his past. Everyone else had crashed out moments after boarding. Snores and odours filled the car. The train pulled past woods of dark and eerie shades of green. Travellers and woods seemed joined in a world that was moody and undersea. At seven in the morning the train passed through Calais; later, Boulogne and Étaples, where Jim saw M.O.s and nursing sisters walking near the rails and between tents and buildings. It was said that in the grave-yards close to the hospitals, there were separate sections for officers and men. He thought of the friend he'd met during training, who worked here now. Wullie had sent a letter in August telling him that the King had made an unannounced visit to Number 1 Cana-dian General Hospital. The following day there had been a service in the cemetery, the second anniversary of the Declaration of War. *Every grave was decorated with flags and flowers*, Wullie wrote. *It was a mournful and dignified occasion, and there was a strange and solemn beauty to the affair.*

Jim looked out to a grey sea and thought of Grania, how she wanted to be taken to the ocean, his ocean, on the east coast, directly across the water from where he now found himself. He had spent his childhood on rolling field and red soil that faced out over the north shore and the Gulf of St. Lawrence where it widened into the Atlantic. He tried to pull that scene inside himself now, and thought of the house and parlour where he had grown up. From the time he was a young child, after his parents died and he'd been taken in by his father's parents, he had been aware of the world of music. His own ears had listened to Grandfather's bow moving with grace over the strings of his instrument. The older man had the same long, slender fingers that Jim had inherited from generations of Lloyd men who had lived before them both. Jim had been present to see Grandfather Lloyd step-dance two weeks before his unexpected death, when his heart had stopped abruptly.

Jim remembered the old cookhouse on the cliff—once a part of a now-abandoned lobster cannery; the changing attitude of the dunes as sand heaped against the slopes or washed away in winter storms. He thought of waves crashing into shore and licking up the sides of those same dunes, every year displacing the red sand. He thought of the thick mush of the red roads and the mess while trying to get through them; the pack ice in the Gulf when red soil streaked through spring-dirty chunks that broke up beneath the cliffs. One of Grandmother's hounds had disappeared over the cliff the same winter Grandfather died. The hound had been Grandfather's favourite. Jim followed the tracks through the snow right to the edge of the cliff, and neither he nor his grandmother could account for the dog's behaviour. Grandmother's geese had not fared any better. In early summer, the dozen she'd raised and cared for were found dead by the pond one morning, close to the farmhouse.

In the fall, the days were sunny and the evenings cool, and wild geese called overhead as flocks followed the coastline in resolute Vs. The island took on mellow tones, giving no sign that the season would be followed by wind and stormy weather.

Jim's Uncle Alex, his father's younger brother, had stayed with farming, but in Ontario, having left the island as a young man. As there was no other Lloyd relation on the island after Grandmother's death, the farm was sold. Part of the money had come to Jim, and was now in the Bank of Montreal—a start for him and Grania when he returned home.

Home. Wife. They had joined their lives together. He tried to conjure Grania's face: the way her eyes watched his lips, her intense focus and alertness, her always-questioning gaze. He thought of the touch of her fingertips and he was sorry, deeply sorry, that no ship was waiting on this French coast to take him home across the Atlantic. Instead, he and the boys were on a train that, with rhythmic click and side-to-side sway, was transporting them towards the Somme.

*

Entire camp cities had sprung up behind the lines—cities of never-ending noise and activity. The effort expended to transport food and water alone was astonishing. And there was endless activity related to water treatment, garbage disposal, movement of guns—it was impressive to see the line-up of big guns—ammunition, horses, mules, service wagons, relief parties, ambulance, medical supplies, blankets, tents and stores. The whole machine was bigger than one imagination could dream up. While they were on the move, the boys began to hear stories of the Australians' fighting spirit at Pozières. The Aussies, known for their stubborn courage, had fought during July and August and had captured from the Germans, at colossal cost, the crest of the Pozières ridge. Stories of their bravery and endurance made the rounds.

Irish had had a chill since the men of the 9th had begun their march. They crossed rolling open plains of French countryside, interspersed by woods, where they rested for their breaks. Before and after the march, officers stood over them to ensure that they rubbed their feet with whale oil and changed their socks. By the time they stopped overnight in an orchard, Irish had a low-grade fever. He accepted bread and cheese and beans brought to him by Jim, grinned weakly, and fell into an immediate and deep sleep. Jim and Evan propped him between them and half-dragged him to the barn. They bunched together some straw, pulled his blanket over him, and left him like that while they went back out to the orchard.

Mail had caught up to the Ambulance while Jim was in the barn: there were three letters from Grania, and a package of fudge. He shared out the fudge, kept four pieces for himself and Irish, and walked down to the brook where some of the boys had been washing. Rinsed-out socks and underwear lined the bank, all sizes, ragged and ridden with holes—and lice, too, Jim reckoned, as he glanced at the motley display. Long benches had been set up, where some of the men were shaving. Stash was sitting at the end of one of these, one hand holding a letter from home, his free hand stroking the back of his newest pet, a mongrel pup with outsized ears that stuck straight up and gave its tiny face a permanent comical expression. Jim met the new stray, who had been named Tock. He walked farther along the bank until he was alone, and took the letters out of his tunic and spread them on the ground, arranging them by date. He flattened the creases and placed his photo of Grania beside the letters and read slowly, as slowly as he could, and tried to draw her into himself as he read.

In the morning, he had a hard time rousing his friend. Irish lay on his side, one big hand flopped open, the tiny photo of Clare resting in his wide palm. After a breakfast of cheese and porridge, they put on their packs and marched until twelve-thirty. The extra socks that had been rinsed out the night before hung from the outside of packs to dry while the men marched. Irish was feeling no better. By Wednesday, during the march towards the damaged town of Albert, he had a high fever and was urged to report sick.

"I hate to desert you just as we're going up the line, Jimmy boy," he said, and it was true. They worked as a pair, and everyone knew it.

But Irish was too sick to work or to make jokes. It was raining and he was soaked through. His legs and puttees were coated with mud, and he was having difficulty lifting one foot before the other. The only thing that cheered him was the sight of the Virgin statue in Albert, tilted almost upside down from the church steeple and ready to fall. For days, the boys had been hearing about the famed statue of the leaning Virgin.

*

The recently won German dugouts were a wonder, a deep labyrinth of rooms reinforced with planed boards, and even having electric lights. One of the dugouts had become an Advanced Dressing Station. Because of the surrounding chalk country, trench lines, with their piles of white chalk along the sides, could easily be seen during the day. Irish had been left in Albert, lying in a back room of the Main Dressing Station, on one of several low cots lined up along the brick floor. The windows had been darkened and the insistent smell of acetylene gas was ever present in the building. His temperature had been 104 degrees when he'd finally seen the M.O. As the nights were colder now, he had become worse by trying to stick it out. He had been chilled over and over again.

Finner, his replacement, walked beside Jim as four squads followed their sergeant, leaving the Chalk Cliffs at five in the morning and heading for the crossroads. Jim thought of the German prisoners behind wire cages whom he'd seen farther back the night before. He had stared hard as he passed, wondering again what kind of man was the enemy. Some of the German soldiers were sitting on the ground, tearing up old sandbags to make replacement puttees for themselves, wrapping the brown rags in circles round and round their lower legs. The Germans were talking amongst themselves and paid no attention when the Ambulance boys went past.

Evan was more nervous than ever; the tic in his cheek was pulsing and he was rolling his fingers again. As they walked Jim kept an eye on him, ahead and to the right of Stash. They moved forward by twos, with spaces between each pair. Beside Jim, Finner was talking in a low continuous monotone that filled any silence there was to fill between the noise of the guns. His voice was getting on Jim's nerves, but Jim knew that Finner was nervous. He looked young, barely of age to be here. Perhaps, Jim thought, it was because the rest of them were looking and feeling so old. Finner had been with them only a few days; he'd been sent up a day before they marched towards the Brick Fields. In any case, he would not, or could not, shut up.

Jim tried to keep Finner's voice on the outside rim of his consciousness. He pulled into himself and kept walking, being careful of his footing. There were shell holes and craters everywhere, and the men passed a huge pit where a mine had been exploded. The desolate land around them had been stripped of every blade of grass, every bush and shrub and tree. What lay before them now was churned to a scene of utter waste. By the time they reached the trenches and found the aid post, an unspeakable bombardment was in progress. The ground throbbed and the air ricocheted around Jim's head. The gathered sound seemed to enter him through his mouth instead of through his ears. The dead were buried and half-buried; the wounded lying or sitting, staring out in pain.

Jim went to work in the trench, kneeling as he applied a dressing.

He reached for his stretcher and motioned to Finner. Evan and Stash had walked farther along and were now out of sight.

They loaded a soldier whose arm had been splinted to his side and who had shrapnel in his knee. As they stood to start the carry, a lieutenant ran up to them. A Canadian they'd never seen before.

"Beat it!" he yelled. "Get the hell out of here. The boys are over the top just ahead."

Jim was in the lead and tried to get the injured man away, but he was slowed by trying to manoeuvre the stretcher and by the uneven sludge underfoot. He and Finner got themselves into a communication trench and then onto a track, and though the shelling was heavy and coming at them from all sides, they were able to get through the open unprotected area. They carried their patient as far as the cemetery tramline where the wounded were being cleared out on trucks to the next point.

On the way back, they passed Evan and Stash coming out, and Jim caught a glimpse of their faces. Stash, intense, as always. Evan, pale, the tic in his cheek more marked. More and more stretcher bearers were going up and down the line. Jim felt his stomach cramp. He had a vague memory of having eaten hours ago. He and Finner were sent farther forward this time. The dead and dying were inside and outside trenches, lying in water and mud. The clearing went on and on as they carried the wounded back, one by one by one, so that they could be moved again, eventually reaching the Dressing Station at the Brick Fields. New bearers who arrived told Jim and Finner that twelve surgeons were working non-stop over the operating tables set up in the dressing station in Albert. In his mind, Jim saw the unthinkable—blood spilling out of the boys onto the floor and tables, on the hands and arms and white aprons of the surgeons as they went about their work. Many of the boys died of shock before they could be attended to, their bodies out of equilibrium.

They tried to help a young soldier from the PPCLIs, a boy who looked no older than Egan had been. He must be older, surely, Jim thought. He kneeled to see what he could do. The upper part of the boy's forehead had been staved in, but not his eyes—a skull case. Jim had heard the M.O.s referring to the boys as "skulls" when pieces of missile or shrapnel were lodged in the head or when the plates of the head were crushed in. The boy's round eyes were fixed directly on him as he and Finner did the lift. All the boys feared mutilation. They would rather take a single bullet, and told him this all the time. A single bullet was merciful because there was less chance of a septic wound and gangrene—if they survived. The boy with the injury to his forehead did not survive a hundred yards of the carry; they laid him in the mud alongside swollen and distorted bodies that had been there for some time.

They worked all day and all night. The following day, Jim realized that Finner had finally shut up. He had no recall of when this had happened—this day, or the day before, or in the night. He thought of Irish and how his friend was well out of this. Irish had often said, "These are the sights the mind gorges on in horror forever, Jimmy," and Jim knew that he was right.

It had been raining for some time now, and the yellowish-grey mud attached itself to boots and clothing, slowing them, adding weight to the carries and to their own legs and feet. Blankets that covered the wounded were filthy. Jim and Finner had long been out of rations. A shell burst near them and they fell to the ground, momentarily shocked. Jim landed in a hole half-filled with water, and his empty stretcher flew in the opposite direction. He crawled out, soaked through—though it didn't matter anyway, because of the rain. He looked around for Finner and saw him lying on his side in the mud, but Finner moved and pulled himself to his knees.

The next time they were at the clearing point, Evan and Stash caught up to them. They were all told to go forward again to meet up with another group of bearers who had been sent ahead. They followed one another single file, Stash in the lead, and found themselves slipping and sliding over boards that had been laid down to help with the footing. Boxes of ammunition were being delivered on the backs of a half dozen mules ahead, and just as the bearers began to pass, the mule in the rear slipped off the boards and into the layers of muck. The animal floundered in panic and instinctively they reached towards it, but they had to stand by and watch its crazed eyes sink lower and lower, almost directly at their feet. Stash looked as if he would jump in after it, but the mule was up to its neck and disappearing. It sank completely under and a voice inside Jim said, *No head*, and he considered the normality of the thought.

"It's a little mule, for God's sake," Stash was shouting into the air. "It's a living thing. There must be something we can do."

But there was nothing they could do. A voice from behind was shouting angrily, "Keep moving! Go on past." The voice in Jim's head said, *Mules don't panic, horses do. They're used here because it's easier to cure them of colic.* But the waste of both was terrible. It was one of the horrors of the war—the terrible waste of living creatures. Thousands upon thousands of horses and mules were buried and unburied across the scarred landscape in these corners of Belgium and France.

Stash was still angry when they joined the other squads. Earth was spouting around them, and smoke wafted through the air. This was followed by a stillness that seemed unreasonable. The clouds were low, the late-afternoon sky as grey as the earth. There was a zigzag cut in a trench to Jim's right and beyond that a jagged piece of corrugated iron used as a partial shelter. The place was crowded and smelled of unwashed men. Jim did not want to be in such a place. So many bodies together invited trouble. He stood unmoving, trying to sink into the quiet that had fallen on all sides.

The officer in charge was giving orders to the bearers who had arrived before them. While he was organizing, he was tying long strips of white bandage to the ends of sticks. A whine was heard, and there was an explosion to Jim's left. Scarcely anyone ducked. But they all watched as some fifteen feet away, Stash reached up with a hand towards his throat. He made a hissing sound and folded forward like a jackknife, and slumped to the ground. Evan, who was closest, kneeled instantly beside his friend. A piece of stray metal had struck Stash in the neck and he had died instantly.

Jim felt his legs running the short distance between them. He collapsed on his knees beside Evan, who had already turned Stash's body face up. There was little blood. The two men dragged their friend aside and Jim stood looking at him in disbelief, vowing that he would be properly buried. He realized that the officer was shouting at him, "Get out there with the others!" Finner was behind the officer, ashen-faced. A stick had been thrust in his hand. Some of the other bearers raised their own sticks, which were tied with bandages, up and over their heads. Jim felt a wrenching pain in his gut and he thought he would vomit. Evan looked as though he were in shock, but his feet had already begun to move away from Stash's body and towards the officer. In groups of four, three in Jim's group—each group with a stretcher—they worked their way up and out and began to pick their way across No Man's Land.

They dipped into craters, stepped over wire, circled obstacles and sank, at times, knee-deep. They were surrounded by a silence more eerie than the one that had settled over them before they left the trench. Even as he moved, Jim was thinking what a sight they were, a sight not seen before. Each group held high its white banner, nothing more than a rain-soaked bandage drooping from the end of a stick, to keep them safe.

They did not have much searching to do. All around the area, bearers were ducking down, checking bodies, leaving the dead and loading the wounded. Jim and Evan and Finner kept walking forward, Evan rolling his fingers, Finner holding the stick high. But the going was bad; they had to slog their way through. Up ahead, five hundred feet or more, Jim saw two new bearers rise out of the mist and gloom. Two more followed, and two more, and the realization came to him that he was watching his enemy stand up and out of the German line. Like the Canadians, each group of Germans carried a stick tied with a length of bandage. With caution, the men of both sides made their way towards one another, step by step, step by step. *Be sharp,* Jim told himself. *Still the mind.* A German soldier raised his arm and pointed a finger at Jim and then at the mud beside him. The German was unarmed. He kneeled, then stood and pointed again, this time using sign language to beckon Jim to come ahead with the stretcher. When Jim and Evan and Finner reached the lip of the crater where the German was point-ing, they saw that the German's partner was down inside the crater and had already applied one of his own dressings to a soldier from the 42nd. The boy was conscious, slumped back against a sloping wall of mud. He looked as though he had been there for some time. His shoulder was bare and had taken a wound through to the other side, and Jim knew that he was in shock because he did not cry out when he was touched. The boy's body began to shake uncontrol-lably. Finner dropped the stick with the white bandage and jumped down into the crater. The German who had applied the dressing helped lift until they could get the boy at a level with the others' feet and onto the stretcher. Jim stood up, gripping the handles, and looked eye-to-eye into the face of the German who had beckoned him to this spot.

The face of his enemy stared back. The eyes were expressionless inside the distinctive curve of helmet. He was large, taller than Jim, and heavier, but about the same age. His eyes were grey-blue. There was a horizontal streak of mud on his chin, as if he had wiped it straight across with his hand. His uniform was as filthy and mud-caked as the uniforms worn by the Canadians.

Neither Jim nor the German spoke. Jim thought of Stash's body, how it had jackknifed as it slumped. He tried to hate the man who stood before him. But there was only coldness, no other feeling. Coldness, and the hatred of war.

He turned his back and started for his own line and, as he did so, across the desolate and injured landscape, he saw pairs of men, German and Canadian, binding their wounded, raising the injured on stretchers, carrying them back to their own lines.

*

After carrying out three other men, Jim and Evan tenderly laid their friend's body on a stretcher and carried it as far back as they could, to ensure that he would have a burial. Jim and Finner were told by one of the Ambulance corporals to go to a dugout and rest until they were called for. Evan was sent back to the Chalk Cliffs.

The dugout was in ruins, the roof imploded, but there was enough space at one edge to provide shelter for the two men. They crawled into the place gratefully, their bodies exhausted. Jim grabbed at a ground sheet that was partly buried in the wall of mud. He cleared it off as well as he could and wrapped it around the two of them. He spent some moments trying to funnel rain down and away from their already soaked boots. Both he and Finner had long ago given up their puttees. Like every other bearer during the past days, they had used them as outer bandages for the wounded.

He sank back against the soft mud and tried to force his body to relax, even knowing that this was a place where he would never sleep. He became sharply aware of the odour of decay, and behind Finner's shoulder he saw what looked like hair. In disbelief, he found himself staring at a large eye embedded in the dirt wall. Detached of orbit and skull that had once housed it, it could have been planted there. Jim closed his own eyes, rejecting what he had seen. Finner reached back at that moment to push away a lump behind his shoulder, and his hand went through part of the carcass of a mule. There was a rush of foul-smelling liquid and gas. They both leaped up and Finner frantically scraped his hands and arms and clothes in the mud, trying to clean them. Without uttering a word, they found another shelter and crawled into it, this time without a ground sheet.

Jim lay there with his eyes open. He thought of the surprise on

Stash's face, the way his friend's hand had reached up to his throat as if to catch Death before Death could catch him. Jim turned his back to Finner, making sure that their bodies were still pressed together for warmth. Silently, his lips moved: *The Lord is my shepherd; I shall not want. He maketh me to lie down* . . . Just as silently, tears streamed down his cheeks. Finner's body heat began to seep into him. The two men, moulded together, sank deeper, and settled into the stinking mud.

*

"Have you ever been in pain?"

From his chair, Jim looked at the soldier in the narrow bed. The young man seemed surprised to hear the shrill sound that was his own voice. Without waiting for Jim to reply, he went on.

"I keep telling myself I should be able to bear this." His voice lowered. "But the pain isn't bearable at all. It won't go away. It has a life of its own. I understand this now but I don't know what to do."

"Tell me where the pain is." Jim kept his own voice to a whisper, hoping the patients in the adjacent beds would not wake; they slept fitfully as it was. "Maybe there's something to be done."

"There's nothing to be done. It's through my whole body. I thought the bottom half of me was shot off. But it can't be, you see, because my hand can reach down and feel the skin on my legs." He paused, and sucked in a long breath. "On the way here, bumping up and down in the ambulance, I tried to concentrate. I tried to think of ways to get the pain off me, to get it out of me. The way we flick lice into the fire. For the crumbs, at least, the pain is over fast."

"What's your name?" Jim knew this full well; he could see it on the chart from where he sat.

"Thompson. The boys call me Tommy. Strange, isn't it, that my family never shortened my name. I never had a nickname until I came here. You know— What's your name?"

"Jim."

"You know, Jim, you always think—when you have to get out

there, across No Man's Land and fight—you think, well, *I can't*. And then you tell yourself, *I can, I have to, I have no choice. Other boys have done it and are out there now.* You hear machine-gun bullets rattling inches over your head, but you know you have to go over the top. You hear Number One blow his whistle and you tell yourself, *I can't stay here. Get up. Step up on the level and go.* The worst sound of all is the silence before the whistle blows. And after doing that, after going over the top, here I am alive and in hospital and now you would think I could handle the pain."

Jim wished the boy would quiet down. He'd had morphine, the nursing sister told Jim, but it didn't seem to be working. Only the severe abdominal cases were brought here. The M.O. had worked non-stop for fifty hours and was asleep on a stretcher on the floor of the storage room on the other side of the hall. He had warned everyone not to wake him—*real* emergencies only.

Jim was assigned the night shift and had reported at one in the morning. Irish had almost recovered now. His fever was gone and he had rejoined the squad before the route march out, when they'd headed for Warloy. Irish was still on light duties and was working during the day. Their billets were in a marquee tent and all the boys had had a bath and a shave. The caked mud had been scraped off, and new puttees had been issued. Everyone had clean socks and under-wear. For the moment, the boys of the Ambulance were clean again.

After the last stretch of duty, Jim had turned down a promotion. He and Irish were staying together, no matter what. Finner was now Evan's partner, having replaced Stash.

The beds were crowded in rows, and it was Jim's job to keep an eye on this end of the ward while the two nursing sisters changed dressings—they had started at the far end of the room. A mixed odour of disinfectant and cleaning solution thickened the air and swelled his nostrils. If more patients arrived, he would go outside to help carry them in, and while he was out he would take some good deep breaths. For now, he had to sit here, in one spot. In the early morning, half past four, he would go to the tiny kitchen to prepare the liquid diets. In the meantime, he had to listen to the boy who refused to stop talking.

"None of it makes sense," said Tommy. "Going over the top into machine-gun fire doesn't make sense. Joining up doesn't make sense, not any more. I used to work in a newspaper office. I couldn't wait to quit my job to get here."

Jim thought of the expressionless face of the German stretcher bearer with the grey-blue eyes. No, none of it made sense. War ground on like the headless, thoughtless monster that could not be stopped. The bad fairy tale that refused to end.

"Maybe you should try for a bit of rest," Jim whispered. "I could get a cup of Oxo. I can go and look."

At the end of the ward, a boy cried out as if from far away. The boys held conversations inside their own nightmares. Jim had known for a long time that the wounded talked incessantly in their sleep.

"If I *could* sleep, I'd *be* asleep. There are strategies, aren't there?" Tommy whispered, as if he and Jim were in this together. "How about a strategy to defeat pain? If I think about my breathing, the pain throbs along with my breath. But if I could get into a position to portion it out, or get behind it, I might have something left to meet it."

He rambled on. He was not looking at Jim now, but staring up at the low ceiling overhead.

War made the boys old. Some of the boys who were twenty, or twenty-one, or twenty-three, looked ninety-three. If Grania were here to see his own face, she might look past; she might not recognize him. He had left the training camp in England only five months before and already he was an old-timer. Many of the boys he'd trained with were gone. Gone west.

"Pain has a colour," Tommy said loudly. One of the nursing sisters at the end of the room looked in Jim's direction and frowned. Tommy closed his eyes as if he were staring inwardly, right into the colour of pain. "Green is what I hope for. Black is bottomless. If I can get to red or orange, I'll be able to hover somewhere between."

The living burrowed like cliff swallows into holes in the trench walls. Two of the infantry boys Jim had heard about had crawled into shallow funkholes scooped out side by side, their legs sticking out. When a shell hit, their four legs had been sheared off at the knees.

"If I die, let me die cleanly, with my boots on and fighting to the last," a boy in the 49th said to Jim one night. That boy was still alive; Jim had seen him come out of the line.

Each of the boys, if he had to stay in the line any time at all, tried to protect his head, scratched out a space of his own. Some of the boys strung up canvas sheets and dove under them when they heard a shell go over—knowing that the sheets would do nothing to protect them. They all knew that cover was an illusion. It was what one created in the mind that enabled one to keep walking and breathing. Many of the boys *never* sought cover—except from gale or sleet— and walked around unharmed. The boys who dove for protection every time they heard a noise were often the ones who were blown to bits. The ones who survived the odds again and again were called lucky—by some. If their luck continued, others stuck near them, especially new boys coming in, hoping to be safe in their company. Others stayed as far away as they could get, believing that because immunity had gone on so long, their number would be coming up. Irish never said much about any of this. But one day he grinned, and pointed to his own front teeth. "See this gap, Jimmy boy," he said. "This is the mark of luck."

Jim wished his friend had never said that.

"Pain is a trickster," Tommy said. This time, Jim was startled by his voice. He thought Tommy had drifted off to sleep.

Had Stash felt pain? His hand had reached up and at the same moment there had been a hissing noise. Jim thought of the expression on the face of Irish when he'd been told about their friend. Irish had not made a sound; he had turned away and had not spoken of Stash again. Evan, too, never talked about his former partner. He'd adopted the mongrel Tock, and carried him out the day they marched, and gave him to a small boy at the edge of a village where they stopped to rest.

In the days before their march away from the battlefield where Stash had died, Evan and Jim had gone to see the new machine of war—thankfully on their own side. It was called by some a land boat and by others a tank. It was huge and heavy, but at least one of the machines had not protected the soldiers inside. Their charred remains had been removed for burial, and the burned-out tank had come to rest uselessly against a clump of trees. Many of the boys visited, to touch and wonder, but a few were killed themselves; the Germans purposely fired at the site. Evan and Jim went to see, but stayed back at a safe distance.

Jim thought of Grania now: the way she leaned her head against him when he sang, the way she watched his lips for words he was about to say. Sometimes he felt as if she knew what he was going to say before he did. A letter had been waiting for him when he walked the long walk back from the Chalk Cliffs. He had smoothed out the sheet of paper and stared as if it were a missive from an unknown place. He had searched for Grania in the words; he had searched for face, eyes, lips, body, self. *Wife.*

Grania loved him. Her letter said so. But how could he write to her of love from a place where body parts worked their way through mud; where death dropped from the sky in a blackened Albert that was bombed repeatedly; where a man who had willingly joined up in Barriefield was decapitated while driving an ambulance in France; where a bullet missed Jim's temple by inches, lodging between sandbags in a place he had lain, wide awake, trying to get through another sleepless night?

"One thing I do know," said Tommy, whose voice sounded suddenly thin and weak.

But Jim did not want to hear what Tommy knew. He wanted to shout: *Stop! Stop talking like this about your own pain. Have some decency!*

But even thinking this—he who was in absolute health, who

dared to move, eat, urinate, shit, speak with undamaged mouth and tongue—even thinking this, surely he was the one who should be accused of the cruellest kind of indecency. He was here, sitting upright in a ward, surrounded by wounded boys. And he had not been hit.

He was the one who had better muster some decency.

IIII

1917–1918

Chapter 13

Three biplanes visited Belleville from Deseronto, and alighted in a field. Each was carrying an officer and an observer. When they came near, the cattle and horses at work were greatly frightened and ran around the fields.

When the machines landed, a large number of citizens rushed to the place, and some from school ran to see the biplanes. For many, this was their first close view of a flying machine.

The Canadian

Cora had seen them, Grania was sure, but she'd already disappeared into the hall on Mill Street as Grania and Mamo and Tress reached the outer door. It was not a cold day but a fall wind was blowing straight up from the bay. Mamo walked slowly because of her arthritis. At home, it was difficult for her to get out of the rocker after she'd been sitting for long periods, and her back was sometimes in pain, but she managed to climb the stairs to get to her room every night, and she made her way through the passageway to breakfast every morning, where she lingered over her cup of Pekoe tea. "I keep going," she said. "If I keep moving, I'm fine."

Most of the women in the Red Cross work room had taken their places. Some were sitting, or stood around the long centre table, ready to pack boxes and make up standard kit bags; others sat on chairs arranged in a circle and were sewing, or knitting scarves or cuffs or socks (*socks must not have a ridge under the heel nor at the end of the toe*) for the coming months of winter.

Grania saw her friend Kay and gave her a wave across the room. Kay was still dressed in mourning—black hat, black dress—though her husband had been killed two and a half years earlier, in April of 1915. Grania had still been working at the school then. Kay, struck by grief, volunteered at the Red Cross every Friday afternoon and knitted for the boys at the Front. She had given up her house after her husband's death, but instead of returning to her parents' home, she had moved in with her grandmother, a widow who had a small house on Thomas Street, two streets back from Main. Her grandmother, known as Granny to the town, had been looking after Kay's two-year-old son while Kay worked every morning at the glass factory. But Granny was having problems of her own: she was forgetful, and had begun to wander. Grania seldom saw Kay's secretive smile any more, but what would there be to smile about?

In the work room, supplies were stacked in corners, and on a desk shoved against the wall, and on open cabinet shelves. Cora had tacked a notice, eye-level, near the door so that no one would miss the latest news from Dominion Headquarters. The new instructions contained a list of items that were to take the place of the earlier "Comfort Bags." Vermin shirts and cholera belts were no longer required. Cora, self-appointed woman in charge, had taken it upon herself to see that orders were carried out to the letter. There was a Dominion-wide knitting competition, too, and Cora had announcements to make concerning that.

In the sewing circle, eyes looked down as the women followed their stitches. Grania watched conversation ripple from one pair of lips to another. As always, in a group, words jumped the circle quickly and could not be read. When Mamo and Tress were with her, Grania was included. She had only to cast a sideways glance at either to follow their familiar lips—lips that formed words without creating so much as a whisper, lips that supplied silent commentary as they had been doing since she was five years old. Keeping her inside the circle of information.

Cora was reading aloud, her face tilted towards a sheet of paper. Tress went quickly to the doorway, untacked the copy of the same sheet and brought it to Grania so that she could follow along. The knitters looked up in unison, their hands never pausing while they listened to Cora's voice. Grania wondered, idly, what Cora's voice was like. She nodded to Tress and was reminded that looking into her sister's dark eyes was like looking directly into Mother's. She checked the sheet while Cora read.

Handkerchiefs will be of unhemmed cheesecloth, 18 × 18 inches, laundered, tied up in dozens. No shaving brushes will be placed in kit bags on account of serious danger of anthrax poisoning. Trench candles of newspaper and wax are not satisfactory and are not to be sent to warehouses, as they can no longer be shipped overseas. Bed pads, 17 × 17 inches, 6 layers of newspaper, 1 layer of non-absorbent cotton, are to be covered with cheap gauze—not cheese cloth. Use pattern from Dominion HQ.

For an hour and a half, Grania sorted and layered and packed. Each item that passed through her hands was carefully tucked into its own space: facecloth, toothpaste, toothbrush, writing pad, pencil, shaving soap, razor, small comb, chocolate, tinned fruit, chewing gum, cocoa, curry powder, matches, tinder lighter, pen nibs, toilet paper and, finally, a mouth organ.

She hoped that a mouth organ would reach Jim. She thought of his long fingers creased over the stubby metal, his palms hiding the double row of shadowed gaps as he held the instrument to his mouth, his right hand cupping rhythmically. It was almost two years since Jim had held a mouth organ to his lips while the last of the guests listened outside on the veranda at Bompa Jack's—hours after the wedding ceremony, after the feast had been praised and enjoyed, after the kitchen furniture had been put back in its proper place because the dancing was over, after the wedding guests who weren't dancing had had a chance to sit in the parlour on high-backed chairs, to exchange news and have a visit.

Bompa Jack had worn the same old bow tie to the wedding, along with the one good pair of trousers that he owned, and a truly new shirt that Great-Aunt Martha had ordered from Mr. Eaton's catalogue. By the time the dancing had ended, he had changed back into his comfortable farm clothes. Grania thought of how content she had been to sit on the veranda beside Mamo as dusk settled over the milk house and the barn and turned their shapes to silhouettes. The remaining relatives moved in and out of the farm house. Father and Mother, Tress and Mamo had stayed overnight. Bernard and Patrick had left early, to return to town to look after things at the hotel.

And then, fatigue had set in—from the excitement of the day's events, from reading lips of well-wishers for hours. It had been a relief when darkness had fallen and she could no longer follow conversations. She'd thought she might collapse into a deep long sleep. And then Jim had come to the rescue and they'd left in the automobile that had been lent to them by Uncle Alex.

Dulcie, rescued by her new husband, waved goodbye to the wedding guests and the couple drove away.

Now, Great-Aunt Martha was dead; she had died of a stroke in the spring, and Bompa Jack was alone again. Father went back to the Ninth Concession every two weeks to visit his father, taking supplies Bompa Jack might need from town, and staying overnight. Grania had gone with him at the end of August, and Father had surprised her during the supper meal at Bompa's table. He talked more than he ever did at home, telling her about the days when he had been a boy growing up at the farm in that very house. "We did our chores, and once they were done we were allowed to play cards—except Sundays," he said. He waved his hand over the table at which they were sitting. "The boys against the girls. Brother Am and I were great players in those days. We played forty-five, and in the fall when the geese were fat we twice won a goose, playing partners.

Rummy 500—that was another game we liked. On Saturday nights there was sometimes a party in someone's home; in winter we went with a team on the sleigh. There was always a violin, someone fiddling. Sometimes a man brought a banjo. If there were enough people, there was square dancing in the kitchen. One year the teacher boarded with us and she helped my mother make soap on Saturday mornings. But the summers were hard. We all put in time picking stone. Back-breaking work. And we cleared hardwood to burn, to make potash that was taken to Kingston to be sold."

Bompa Jack loved the old stories. It was all Grania could do to keep up with the two of them, when one added details to a reminiscence of the other. Late in the evening, Father went outside to fetch a bottle of whisky—though Grania had not seen him bring one to the farm—and that was when she had gone upstairs to bed.

Grania's hands selected and tucked and dipped into the box, the positioning of each item determined by its shape. She had fallen back into her old cocoon, no longer looking to Mamo and Tress to see what was going on. She thought of the latest package of tinned chicken and cake that she had sent to Jim. Last year in the fall, Bompa Jack had asked her to send apples from the farm. He would want her to send more again this year. The first time was an experiment; she'd wrapped eight, each one separate in a layer of newspaper, all sent with the hope that they would be edible on arrival. Jim had received them weeks later and reported that they hadn't rotted at all. He'd been grateful to have them. This year, if she could keep the parcel a reasonable size, she would send more—a dozen, perhaps.

But when she carried parcels to the post office, she still felt as if she were dropping them into an abyss that might or might not lead to *over there*. Each time she left the building, she felt as if she had given up something dear. The sending was an act of both belief and disbelief. Anything sent in the direction of the ocean might be swallowed by darkness and waves. Even after the trouble and care that went into the preparation, only a tiny part of her believed that what she had gathered and wrapped with her own hands would cross the wide ocean and be unpacked by the hands of the man she loved. As if to encourage this lack of faith, the sender was asked to write a second name on the outside—in the event that it could not be delivered to the first. She had begun to print Orryn's name as the alternate address, in case Jim was on the move and the parcel did not catch up to him.

Many times, Grania had imagined Jim reaching out, the tearing of paper, the careful folding of string—tucked into Jim's pocket for future use—the lifting and examining of contents, one item at a time. Sometimes, months after she sent a parcel, a letter arrived thanking her for khaki handkerchiefs, for Oxo, for candy, for the navy blue scarf, for knee caps. But the acknowledgements were so long coming, they were by then unconnected to the earlier act of mailing.

She thought of the *Empress of Ireland*, which had sunk in 1914, a few months before the war began. She'd been working at the school—it was the end of May, a Saturday morning. She had been invited to the sewing room to see the girls' train dresses, the ones they designed and cut out and sewed for travel home in June. It had taken a full day for the news of the *Empress* to filter into the school and into the room where the students were finishing their fittings. Miss Marks walked past the doorway and saw Grania with the girls, and came in out of the hall to say—with lips and hands and serious face—that a ship had gone down in the St. Lawrence River, on its way to England. It had been rammed by the Norwegian collier *Storstad*—the teacher held the newspaper in one hand and finger spelled the name of the collier with the other. Many people had drowned. Grania remembered Miss Marks shaking out the *P* sign with her hand, to show the passengers going down and down and down.

It was much later—in the fall when they were at school again and Grania was back at work in the hospital—when the second story of the *Empress* came in. Rosaleen, an Irish woman, a hearing woman on the domestic staff at the hospital, came running down the stone steps from outside, one of her thick heels missing from a shoe. She had lost it on her way across the grounds and the loss of it meant that she entered the bandage room at a running limp. She was waving an envelope, a letter she had mailed four months earlier to an aunt in England. The same letter—everyone present was allowed to look and wonder and touch—had come back that morning, stamped with the miraculous words: *Recovered by divers from the Empress of Ireland.*

It was Cedric who uncovered the story for the school paper. The Canadian Pacific had hired divers to go down and blast a hole in the hull of the sunken ship. Not only had the divers retrieved silver ingots and cash and jewels from the ship's safe, they had also brought up four boxcar loads of mail, and all of this had been dried and sorted and delivered back to the senders. Cedric was so taken by this, he published the details. "Rosaleen's letter has been reposing on the bed of the mighty St. Lawrence River, ever since the sinking." That was Cedric's word, *reposing.* "The stamp was washed off, but the writing was perfectly distinct when the envelope was returned to sender."

How they had marvelled at that one letter surviving inside a mailbag deep under water. Under water with bodies. Grania had not forgotten that part of the story. More than a thousand people drowned when the ship went down. No one tried to blame that on the Germans. But when the *Lusitania* was torpedoed and took its place in the news, the *Empress* was forgotten because so many horrible events in Belgium had by then intervened. Now, both ships were in watery graves—one at sea, and one in the mud of the St. Lawrence.

Grania thought of Grandfather O'Shaughnessy, the sheet twined round and round him before he was buried at sea. She thought of Mamo, living without him all these years. Grania had not considered adult loneliness when she was a child.

She looked over at Mamo now. Instead, she saw Cora's lips moving and Cora's gaze directed at *her*. Cora was telling everyone about her daughter, Jewel, arriving this very day from Ottawa, by train. She would be waiting at home and they would have a visit—a good visit, Cora said, once her duties at the Red Cross were finished for the day. Jewel loved living in the capital. She had even been close to the Parliament Building when it was on fire last year, and she was able to report in some detail the tragedy of the event. One boy who witnessed the fire, Cora said, had never been right in the head since.

Grania pretended not to understand what Cora was saying. She looked down at her hands and methodically packed the box. Sometimes the easiest way to deal with Cora was to pretend. At least Jim's name had not been shaped on Cora's lips. Some days, she came right up to Grania and said, "Have you had a letter from Jim today?" If Grania had not, it was difficult not to feel badly. Mail was the event of the day for most people in town—mail and papers. But not for Cora, who had no family member overseas.

Grania remembered the first wet winter of the war when Orryn was training in England and sent a letter to Kenan from Salisbury Plain. *We've had another fierce storm here, and the mail tent blew down. Most of the letters were sucked up into the sky and have never been seen again.*

She imagined thousands of envelopes drawn up into a funnel of darkness hovering over the land. Not like Rosaleen's letter, which had gone straight down. Rosaleen's had *reposed* on the bed of the St. Lawrence and had risen again to be *returned to sender*.

Cora was beaming now; she was on to another topic—Vernon Castle. She had been honoured to meet him, she said. She had shaken hands with him and his wife, Irene, and they had promised to dance at a benefit in Deseronto. Now that he was teaching flying here at Camp Mohawk, the town would be seeing more of the famous dancing couple.

"Moving picture stars," said Cora's lips. "Imagine. In our little town. And he has an expensive automobile."

Tress and Grania exchanged glances, but Mamo did not look up.

Vernon Castle had visited the hotel. He had stopped in at the dining room for a meal because he'd been told about Mother's cooking. He wore his uniform and silver wings; he had a delicate fine-featured face, with a broad forehead and seagull hairline. He'd chatted with the whole family. Father came out of his office to meet him. Patrick wanted to know about his pet monkey, and was told that it was back at the camp. Tress and Grania shook his hand. The Flight Commander told the family that his squadron would have to move to Texas in November, because of the winter flying conditions around Deseronto. Patrick, still in high school, had been thrilled to meet the famous flyer; Castle was his hero. Grania knew that her younger brother was itching to go off to war himself, despite being under age. On the weekends, he often ran out of the house and stood on the street or in the yard at the back, and looked up to the sky. When Grania asked, he told her he'd heard the buzz of an aeroplane. He had already visited both training camps, Rathbun and Mohawk, to have a look around, and he had talked to the men who were learning to be flyers. One of them permitted him to sit in the front pit of his machine while it was parked in a row between other aeroplanes.

Grania glanced Cora's way again.

"We were talking about fears," Cora's lips said. The sentence seemed to be directed at Grania.

Grania stopped daydreaming. She'd been left behind in the last conversation. But this time she couldn't ignore Cora because the woman was right beside her, peering into the box Grania had just finished packing.

"I was saying how fearful it must be to know that someone could approach you from behind in the dark and you wouldn't even know." She was facing Grania, her lips articulating firmly. Without giving her a chance to answer, she snapped up the instruction page from Dominion Headquarters that Tress had taken down, and moved away to tack it up again, by the door.

"No," Grania said, and saw at once that her voice had Cora's attention. Cora's back had tightened.

The raised voice of the deaf, this is what it sounds like when we don't keep it close.

The knitters looked up from their stitches, hands unfaltering in their rhythm. Mamo and Tress were staring.

"No," said Grania again. She made her voice bigger. This was not the sweet little voice that Cora described. "I never, ever, think about what is behind."

Cora's back relaxed but she did not turn around.

Behind doesn't exist, Grania muttered to herself. *The dark, now that is another matter. Not one that I would discuss with you.*

On the way home, Grania put the old question to Mamo again. "Why is Cora like this? Why does she seem to be angry? Why is she always angry with me?" Her fingers were tapping the side of her skirt. Her very existence seemed to offend Cora.

But Mamo could only shake her head. "It's a long road without a turn," her lips said. She had a firm grip of Grania's arm and they took their time stepping up to the boardwalk and walking back to the house. Tress had left them and had hurried ahead to Meagher's store to see the newly arrived bolts of winter cloth that had been advertised in the paper.

Mamo caught Grania's attention and stopped to speak. "Cora has a narrow way of looking at the world," she said. "But if someone's heart is small, you can be sure that the person always lives with the knowledge of it."

*

While the women had been indoors, packing boxes for the Red Cross, Bernard, out walking, had been pinned with a white feather by Jewel, Cora's visiting daughter.

Grania wanted to march right out to speak to Jewel.

"She doesn't know anything about my lung, Grainy. There is no point explaining to her or anyone else."

But Bernard had been humiliated. Grania saw it in his face as he left the house to go through the passageway. She thought about him through supper and again when she went upstairs later and paced around her room. She looked at Jim's photograph—he was squinting as he leaned back against the split-rail fence at the end of the path in the woods. She remembered how he had pulled the leaves from the strands of her hair. She ran her fingers over the surface of the photo, and then she stared out at the darkness of the bay. She closed the curtains, and sipped at the cup of tea she had carried up from the kitchen. She could not settle down. When Tress came upstairs, Grania left the room to go down.

She paused on the landing and looked through the porthole at the back of the house. She sometimes thought of the scene outside the glass circle as her own dark ocean—her ocean of land. She pressed her forehead to the thickness of glass. Another season was drifting by. Her husband had been gone for two years. She was at loose ends. Mamo had taught her long ago about *loose ends*. "Fidgety," Mamo had explained. "When you don't know what to do with yourself. That's what it means to be at loose ends."

Grania wanted to talk to Bernard.

She would wait until things were quiet. She would persuade him to stop what he was doing—cleaning up, or polishing glasses in the beverage room. He'd be working at something. His breathing was fine as long as he stayed away from stairs inside, or hills outside. As long as he moved at a measured pace.

Grania wanted to coax him to the lobby to sit beside her. They would behave as if they were guests—the way she and Grew sometimes sat across from each other during the late afternoons, reading war news in the papers. She and Bernard would sink into two of the grand leather chairs. They would converse non-stop. She would use voice, and he would pay close attention; he would speak softly and she would read his lips. He knew the single-hand alphabet, even if he had never learned as much of the sign language as Tress knew.

But Bernard kept his thoughts to himself. Still, Grania wanted him to be angry about Jewel pinning him on the street. She wanted him to know how valuable he was to her. She wanted to tell him, too, that she had seen him early in the week, on the stoop behind the house on Thomas Street where Kay lived with her Granny. He'd been fitting storm windows at the back, helping to prepare the house for winter. She wanted to say, *Invite Kay for tea, Bernard. She's lonely, too. She has been alone for a long time. I'll invite her, if you like.*

Grania knew that it was becoming more and more difficult for Kay to leave Granny alone. Some people in town called her Runaway Granny now. Granny had made her way up to Aunt Maggie's unlocked apartment one day, and climbed the ladder to the clock tower. Another morning, she had been found in her nightgown on Mrs. McClelland's stoop. Kay was looking for a woman to help with her son, during the hours she worked at the glass factory. It was becoming impossible to leave Granny and the child alone.

Grania wanted to talk to Bernard about all of this. And after Bernard would speak, she would tell him— *What* would she tell him? That on Friday the twenty-first of September, 1917, she was filled with a desperate longing. A loneliness so brittle, she believed that she would break in two.

*

It was nine in the evening when she went through the passageway and over to the hotel. Bernard, as if he had known she was coming, was walking towards her across the lobby. He held an envelope in his left hand and before she could touch it, he rotated his closed right hand over his heart. *Sign language.* His lips were saying, "Sorry, Grainy, sorry," before he reached her. She saw Jim's letter coming towards her. It was the feather, the damnable white feather that had upset Bernard. Otherwise, he'd never have forgotten. He had stuffed the letter into his jacket pocket and there it had stayed. He'd meant to give it to her when she got home from the Red Cross. He was writing S-o-r-r-y in the air, in careful, even script. She stopped him. She was full of smiles.

"When I was out in the afternoon," he said, "Jack Conlin asked me to give it to you. He was making a special trip from the post office because he wanted you to have it right away. A second mailbag came in. He met me on the street, and then Cora's daughter . . ." Bernard looked past Grania's shoulder but not before he placed the envelope in her extended hand.

Grania hugged him and looked around the room. She and Bernard had the place to themselves. She headed for a large armchair in the corner and sank into it.

The envelope was wrinkled, but untorn. The handwriting was small but recognizably Jim's. The envelope had an English stamp and an English postmark, and there was a thickening beneath the paper. Grania held her breath. She looked up to see Bernard, watching.

"Go ahead," his lips said. "Open."

She slit the envelope carefully. Every envelope, every letter, was stored in the biscuit tin in the house, upstairs.

She pulled out a picture postcard in sepia tones. Printed in the lower front corner in white lettering were the words, *The Leas Bandstand, Folkestone.*

Jim was on leave.

The picture showed a circular bandstand on the left, a wide terrace in the middle. Below that, were a grassy slope and a narrow boardwalk above the sea. A row of lampposts stretched off into the distance. Some people in the picture wore capes over their shoulders; others were being pushed in wicker wheelchairs. Men in more wheelchairs were lined up near the terrace. Taking the air. A scene, perhaps, of a Sunday afternoon. On the grounds were folding chairs made of wood and canvas, each with a high back and its own small awning. In the open-air bandstand, uniformed bandsmen were either playing their instruments or preparing to play.

Grania turned the card to see three words, handwritten: *On the Terrace.* Inside the envelope, Jim had tucked a thin sheet of paper. His once generous handwriting was tightly scrunched.

My Love

I have ten days' leave. The bandstand you see on the card is on the Upper Leas. After every eight songs and marches, they play "Nearer My God to Thee." It must be what the people want. There are some who have nothing more to do during daytime hours than stroll through the streets and walkways. In Radnor Park I watched model yacht races. Some sails are as tall as I am. The water is cold but there is a beach and enough hardy people to swim and play around shore. Sometimes I walk to the pier and watch the small turbine steamers as they prepare to leave. The water does not have a big sound. I sat on the pier and thought of you. I met a New Zealand boy who is also on leave. His name is Kirkpatrick and he's from a place called Palmerston North. He was with the ANZACs in Gallipoli and has interesting stories to tell. His unit is now in France.

I'll mail this at the local Post. Enclosed is a souvenir. I think of you always.

Believe me, I will be coming home.

All my love, Chim

That was all.

Grania removed a second sheet of paper from the envelope and unfolded it to find a square of white silk, its edges expertly sewn in matching thread. Two stemmed flowers in shades of pink and mauve were embroidered into the lower corner. These were surrounded by pale green leaves, and tied with a silk knot. The stitching along the inside border was a continuous beaded pattern. In and around the flowers were the hand-embroidered words: "With All My Love."

She held the handkerchief and thought of Jim's hands, his long fingers touching the silk before he made his purchase. She looked again at the picture on the card and tried to imagine this place where he had taken his leave. If she had been with him, she could have seen what he had seen. She could have tucked in against his side as they walked arm in arm, inhaled the grainy air of Folkestone, watched as he described the sound of the dark waves.

But the envelope had been sent weeks ago. Jim would not be safe in England at all. Not now. He would have returned to France before the envelope was even on board the ship that carried it across the ocean.

She raised the silk and pressed it to the soft spot below her ribcage, the spot at the centre. The place of the onset of breath before it becomes song. She held it there and did not move.

She looked up suddenly, self-consciously, remembering that she was not alone. But Bernard had slipped away and was in his tiny office behind the desk. Her body was still. She sat there for a long time, until two guests came down the stairs, men who tipped their hats in her direction and greeted her before they went out the main door and into the street.

*

The letter Jim did not send was written in his head while he lay staring at the ceiling from his bed in Folkestone. His photo of Grania was on the bedside table. He lay between clean sheets. When he'd first felt them against his skin, it was as if old memory had touched his body from a forgotten place. There was an eerie darkness in the room and in the town. No lights showed in the streets outside. Images took turns showing themselves to his mind while he lay there, as if a lantern show were in progress, projecting one picture after another, with no one at the controls.

> There is a feeling, without my partner, of being unprotected, even here in England. So far, Irish and I have been untouched, though we've had our share of close calls. Some of the new boys try to stay near us when they hear how long we've been out, especially the ones sent up as replacements. Irish and I know that it is not a matter of luck. Evan always says, "If it is written," and I am beginning to believe this myself.

Irish will be next for leave, when I return. He is worried that
Fritz will interfere before he can gather his belongings. It's the
way I felt the last few days before I got away. It is natural to
expect something to interfere, to see ourselves pinned there
forever.

Things have been difficult, but no one seems to question the
higher-ups. When Fritz lets loose the mustard gas it saturates
everything it touches. The boys suffer terribly. We try to help
but can do nothing but stand by. The skin bubbles up and some
boys go blind or drown in their own froth and secretions—
slow strangulating deaths, no place left for air. We try our best
to get the boys out of danger. We are compelled to wear masks
ourselves and there is a good deal of stumbling as we go. There
is constant worry that the patients' masks will slip or be pulled
off during a carry. To be inside the mask is suffocating. You
feel a tightness in the chest, as if there is no breath to take.
Some of the boys rip off the mask when they think they are
out of danger, but they end up suffering more for doing so.

The day before I left I carried a boy from Belleville, though I
didn't know his name. He recognized me when we did the lift
and lowered him to the stretcher—there were four of us. "You
used to work with Dr. Whalen," he said, "in Belleville. Will
you get a message to my mother? Will you look her up when
this is over and tell her I tried my best to play the game well?"
Irish cut in. "You'll be home to tell her yourself, lad. No more
about that." We started out, a shoulder lift, and walked back, a
mile and a half. Just before we got him to the dressing station I
thought rain had begun and then I realized that only my collar
and one shoulder were wet. The boy's blood had seeped right
through the canvas. He might have died shortly after we
started out, or along the way. We'll never know. I spoke to him
and he didn't answer; we stopped to check and had to leave him
by the roadside so we could go back for the living. A burial
party picked him up the next day. I made inquiries and found

out who he was; I'll write to his mother. At least he'll have a
known grave—unlike the boys who are out there rotting on
top of the soil, their entrails filled with gas, their faces gnawed
by rats.

A few days before that, a number of wounded boys Irish
and I carried to safety—after terrible exertion—were killed by
shells at the very place we'd set them down. The loading place.
Two shells landed, one after the other, both direct hits. The
injured boys had been so hopeful of getting to Blighty. One of
the boys wept, knowing his war was over. He was in much
pain but was not even concerned about losing his leg. Another
boy we carried wanted out so badly, he injected gasoline into
his own knee. We took him to the collecting point but because
he was removed to the separate place for Self-Inflicteds, he
survived.

I crossed to England by hospital ship—I should not have
done so, but my friend Wullie in Étaples somehow arranged it.
I spent a night with him and was able to avoid the leave camp
in Boulogne. The day after my visit, Number 1 General was
preparing to evacuate large numbers of wounded. All activity
took place in the dark. The ship's deck was covered with
stretchers. A boy moaned pitifully through the night. I don't
know why but that one boy's pain bothered me more than
dozens of wounded lying on the battlefield, crying out. The
nursing sisters changed dressings the entire way across the
Channel, going from one boy to the next. I offered to help, to
hold supplies, to give sips of water, and they were glad of the
extra hands. One of the lads working the hospital ship told me
with satisfaction that during last year's steady flow of injured
from the Somme, a mile of surgical gauze was used every day
at Number 1 Hospital alone. The boys who kept track, he said,
were rolling gauze in their sleep.

The Channel was quiet; more than one ship made its way
across in the dark. Wullie told me that there have been months

when Number 1 General has sent three thousand casualties to England. After Vimy, more than five thousand. Sometimes the wounded are held at the coast near Le Havre for days because Fritz lies in wait in the Channel.

In the little time I was at the coast, I was taken around and shown parts of the hospital. There are many buildings and huts and tents, and a bugler on duty for fire call. Gasoline drums are painted black and red, and are placed outside the tents for rubbish. Wullie gave me a new razor and a bar of soap for my kit, and took me to the canteen as his guest. Everyone was good to me. I had deloused before leaving my own billet and had my certificates and passes tucked away, but I had another bath in Étaples at a bathhouse along the road. I even managed another change of underwear—the second since starting out.

The quiet in Folkestone is disturbing. I had my pass stamped, and obtained permission to alter my plans. I do not wish to go to London. It would not be possible to walk into a theatre, to witness a lighthearted show.

At night I hear the guns across the water. It's as if only the guns give permission to drop off to sleep. One day you told me—we were sitting on the blue blanket—you told me about the way understanding for you is sometimes delayed. I know more about that now. More about the gap between what happens and what is understood. What is there and what is not. So much tries to make entry; so much is determined to invade. Sound knocks us over, blocks all thought, seeps into the body like deadly gas, seeps into everything around until there is no rift or fissure left unfilled.

It is difficult to be here, wondering about my friends.

The first thing I did in the hotel was draw a bath and sit in it for hours, adding hot water as I soaked. I must have dropped off to sleep; I woke, talking to myself. Most of the boys go directly to London to take in the shows, but they, too, return to empty rooms. Sometimes they meet a girl and she will go back to the hotel with them, if the hotel allows it. I have heard them joking. But the diseases add up. We have sent thousands of boys for treatment to the place they laughingly call Pecker Hill. They laugh, but the gonorrhea and the syphilis are not laughable diseases.

This town is hilly and steep. There are shelters above shore, and narrow wooden steps that bring one down to walkways beside the sea. I strode out of town at a fast pace for thirty minutes, and back again at the same pace. Towns are close together all along the coast. My fourth day here, I met a boy from New Zealand. I wrote to you about him. We go round together during the day, and he tells me about where he has been. He was injured, a gunshot wound above the knee, during the Gallipoli campaign but recovered after months in hospital and is back at the job again. He lost many close friends in that campaign.

Soldiers from training camps nearby take a turn on the promenade, and we do the same. Today in a restaurant I picked up a knife and fork and stared at my hands and wondered what to do. I asked myself why people did not shout when I put the fork to my mouth. No one made a grab for food. Every day, afternoon tea is served on the terrace, another life. Kirkpatrick and I walked to the six-and-a-half shop, but our tea cost more than six and a half. It makes no difference. I see now that no civilized person would understand how we live. It would be pointless to try to explain. No one would believe. *Over there* is a life invented by and known only to ourselves.

Chapter 14

In after days when a mother says of a son, a wife of a husband, a sister of a brother, a daughter of a father, that he fell in the Great War, what feeling will be aroused in the hearer? Sympathy? Not so much, perhaps, but rather a sense of being in the presence of one who has had a great honour conferred upon her—the honour of having had a dear one brave enough to go forth to fight for his country. It is just as pleasant and grand a thing to die for Canada and the British Empire today as it was for Rome in the brave days of old.

The Canadian

Was she the only one who was angry?

She stood in the laundry at the back of the house, in the midst of steam and swirling odours of ammonia and soap. The laundry was a room of square tubs and mangles, of puddles on the uneven floor. Old cake tins were turned upside down over irons on the stove. Above the laundry tubs, Mother's *Receipt for Clean Clothes* was tacked to the wall. Mother made the soap and bottled it herself, trusting the job to no one.

Grania gathered up an armful of linens. Sheets and pillowcases were to be changed in the bedrooms of the house today, and she had promised to start the job. She noticed movement in her peripheral vision and looked out the back window into the eyes of Carlow. His hind legs were on the stoop, his front paws scrabbling at the glass and the outer sill. He was letting her know that she was alone in the house; he always knew when everyone but Grania was next door at the hotel. It was the only time he put his paws up to the window, instead of barking, to be let in.

She opened the laundry door. "Smart old dog," she said as he passed. He moved stiffly, his back end waddling side to side as he walked away from the hall and towards the passageway. She called after him, "YEW," and smiled to herself, and watched one ear perk up as he kept on.

Carlow wasn't angry.

Mother was always tired these days. But the more everyone pitched in to lighten the work load, the harder she worked. There were days—with everyone moving about inside—when the house seemed to shrink, as if it could not possibly contain the entire family. At other times it was large and empty—as it was now, with Grania there alone.

Father was staying in his office more and more at the hotel. Sometimes, in the evening, he had a supper tray brought from the kitchen, and he ate alone. Bernard was gradually taking over the day-to-day affairs of the hotel, working in his own tiny office. Grania knew that Father was concerned about the business, especially after the passing of the Temperance Act the year before. There had been problems ever since, and many hotels in the province had had to close or had been auctioned off. At first, the ones that did stay open had to obey strict controls to keep their licences—hours were shortened, regulations tightened. Sometimes men from the town came to the hotel late at night, looking for liquor or beer, but they were turned away. Bernard had told Grania about that. Father had begun to go out at night, too, sometimes several nights a week. If Mother knew where he went, she didn't say. Grania had walked into the parlour one afternoon and had seen angry words between her parents, but they stopped speaking when they saw her, and Father turned and went back through the passageway. There could be a huge fight one room away and Grania would have no way of knowing.

She asked Tress if she had noticed anything between their parents, but Tress—ever Grania's source of family information—replied that she knew nothing about that. Still, Grania wondered. She realized that she rarely saw her parents in the same room together any more. Not that they had ever been outwardly demonstrative. She remembered them only as hard-working. But they never seemed to reach for each other, or touch. Not in front of anyone. Surely, she thought, surely at night. But she had been away at school many years, and when she'd returned for the summer holidays, she had been wrapped up in her own excitement at coming home. Perhaps there had been more changes than she'd ever thought about, during the years she'd been away.

There were changes in the town, too. Camps Rathbun and Mohawk, on the outskirts, were busy and thriving in the good-weather months because flyers continued to be trained. That brought business to the town. But the big mill had closed and its employees had gone elsewhere to look for work. Married employees moved their families out of town. The population was shrinking. The nearby lumber supply had dried up; the Rathbuns had not floated logs down the Moira for a decade. Many of the smaller industries had shut down, too.

Sometimes the hotel rooms were full, sometimes there were no guests for several days at a time. But Mother's cooking kept the dining room busy, especially at midday and for weekend meals.

Tress worked in the dining room along with the rest of the family, but she didn't want to hear news of the war and did her best to ignore the papers. She worked for the Red Cross twice a week, saw her friends, and looked forward only to the day when Kenan would be home. Mail from Kenan came as often as mail from Jim.

Grania carried the linen upstairs and stripped the beds, one after another, wondering if there would be mail this afternoon. At the breakfast table, she had accidentally knocked a spoon to the floor and Mamo had looked up straightaway. "Drop a spoon, receive a letter," her lips said, and they'd all laughed. Grania had plucked up three more spoons and dropped those, too. The crash didn't bother *her*. Mamo shook her head and said, "That won't work, Grania. It can't be intentional."

They were all waiting. Waiting for mail, waiting for the temperance laws to change, waiting for the fighting to end. Everyone had been hopeful in April, when the Americans entered the war. But the war still wasn't over and now American lives were being lost, too. It was difficult to think of the war in any other way except loss. Aunt Annie had sent a letter from Rochester to tell the family that her eldest son had joined up and had left with the 1st Infantry Division. He'd arrived in France before July but she did not know his whereabouts now.

We live inside a feeling of terrible necessity, Grania thought. The war marches on and no one speaks of it ending. The Kaiser refuses to stop the flow of blood until his army is defeated. Until, until. She went to the hall to get linen from the table where she had dumped it, and carried sheets to her room and dropped them on her bed, and she pressed her hands to her ears as if, by doing so, she would silence the flow of her own thoughts.

She allowed herself to think of Jim's departure. He had climbed into the coach and looked for her in the crowd and leaned over the backs of the others in a train that overflowed with grinning, cheering boys, some so young they were barely out of school. They, and the trainloads of boys that followed, came from towns and cities and hamlets and villages all over Ontario, from western Canada and from the north. Long after they reached England, weeks later—shipping dates were kept secret for security reasons—there were photographs in the papers of boys pressed against ships' railings as they began their journey across the sea to replace the boys who had preceded them. Sometimes, Grania cut out and saved newspaper clippings or photos, and stored them in the drawer of her closet where her catalogue family had once lived. Unlike Tress, Grania read the papers. She read every word she could find.

In the late afternoons and evenings, when things were quiet between hotel kitchen and dining room, she still sat in the lobby near Bernard while he went about his work. Bernard's presence was comforting, even though the two of them looked up only now and again to exchange glances. Grew still came by, too, after working in the barbershop, knowing that Father had so many papers delivered to the hotel—Toronto papers, the *Intelligencer* from Belleville, the *Citizen* from Ottawa, community papers from town and from Napanee. At times, especially when there were few overnight guests, Grania and Grew were the only two in the lobby, sitting across the room from each other, reading about the war.

Occasionally, hotel guests left magazines behind. If these were British, they contained more photographs of the war. Men leaning into walls of sandbags; muddy holes in the ground labelled *dugouts*; rows of crates ready to be moved from one location to another. These and the machinery of war, added up to Grania's picture of *over there*. There were horse-drawn wagons at a standstill in front of crumbled buildings, and mules with heavy loads slung across their backs. There were carts and canvassed wagons and motor ambulances—Grania's attention was always attracted to the cross, painted on wood or canvas, or sewn to an arm band. In one magazine, two wounded men posed for the camera, each with an arm in a sling and a cigarette between his lips. The men were grinning widely, faces and uniforms covered with mud. Sometimes there were stretchers in the photographs and the men lying on these were bandaged—heads or arms or legs. She examined part of a neck, an eye, a darkened chin, a narrow line of face. Jim had told her in one of his letters that the first question the men asked when he carried them back was, "Is it good enough for a Blighty?" The ones who did get a good Blighty were returned to England. Some were sent home.

But, always, headlines of promise and victory were lined up side by side with obituaries and photographs of uniformed men who had died. There were times when, after a battle, the lists of the dead occupied eight columns of a newspaper page. Casualty lists took up as many as three pages. This month she had cut out one clipping that declared that, since the beginning of the war, 331,578 men had left Canada to go overseas. She had stared at the number. Jim was one of those. If he hadn't signed up, there would be 331,577.

Grania hated the silent proclamations, hated the rows and rows of names of silenced young men. And the poems, the endless poems by patriotic citizens, many of them women. Occasionally, there was a poem by Rudyard Kipling. She had read Kipling when she was at school. But Kipling himself had lost his only son, at Loos, the September before Jim left Canada. Shortly after Grania finished her work at the school hospital, she had read about Kipling's grief, and about his son John's body, which had never been found after the battle. John Kipling had been with the Irish Guards.

Maybe Kipling was sorry his son had gone to war. Maybe, like Grania, Kipling was angry, too.

*

When she entered the dining room for the midday meal, the first thing she saw was that Tress's chair had been pushed back from the family table in the corner. The second thing she noticed was that food had not yet been brought out from the kitchen. Mamo was not in her usual place but in Grania's seat, beside Tress, an arm over Tress's shoulder. The fingers of Mamo's right hand were tapping against the table. Mother was standing behind both chairs, her lips tightly sealed. In that moment, Grania saw again how alike Tress and Mother were. The same high forehead, the same hairline. She saw, too, that Tress had pushed her hair back behind her ears.

But her glance had also taken in the telegram stretched between Tress's hands. Even from the doorway she could see the words in bold print across the top: TELEGRAPH COMPANY. Tress was crying; her chest was heaving up and down.

Panic, sudden and terrible. This is how the news comes.

Mother looked up. Seeing Grania, her lips formed the words, "Kenan, wounded." Her right hand fluttered awkwardly in the air and she spelled A-L-I-V-E with her fingers. She wanted to be certain that Grania understood. Bernard came in, out of breath, his hand pressed to his chest. Patrick was at the high school and had not yet arrived for his dinner. Father had been sent for and came in from his office. They all sat down around the table, Grania with them, as if they were about to start the meal, but no one got up to get the food. Tress continued to heave and sob, and Grania, putting the picture together, felt a word pound like a heartbeat inside her, *JIM, JIM, JIM.*

But it wasn't Jim. It was Kenan, her childhood friend, her protector, her bully. Relief washed away in the guilt of knowing that it was Tress's husband and not hers who had been named in the telegram.

But Kenan had not been killed. Surely this would mean he would be coming home.

How badly? How badly injured?

All of this went through her thoughts within seconds. It was later, much later in the night, when she was lying wide awake in her bed across the room from Tress, that she was able to put fragments of the scene back together.

It had been Grania who'd stayed with Tress the rest of the day, and who took her upstairs in the evening, and made tea, and sat with her on the edge of the bed, and rubbed her sister's shoulders to relax her, and covered her with blankets, and held her hand tightly until, finally, Tress was able to sleep. Only then, after Tress was settled and as Grania lay awake in the dark, only then did the picture of what Mother had done in the dining room explode in Grania's mind.

Mother had spelled the message about Kenan with her fingers. A-L-I-V-E. Not by air writing, not by printing. Mother, who had refused to acknowledge the sign language these many years, had used the single hand alphabet of the deaf and had finger spelled the word.

Mother had sent a word to Grania in the language of hands.

*

In the morning, after breakfast and after Tress had gone out, Grania went back up to the bedroom and closed the door and pulled down the biscuit tin from the closet shelf.

She sat on the edge of her bed and set out her letters from Jim on the ribbed spread. Beside the letters, she laid the photograph of Jim leaning into the split-rail fence. The letters represented more than two years of separation and all of the communication she had received. There were three bundles, each tied with a shoelace.

The first bundle, 1915, was from England, where Jim had completed his training. The second contained letters from *Somewhere in France*, written to the end of 1916. Letters in the third bundle had been written this year, 1917, and were also from *Somewhere in France*. But Grania knew that Jim was not always in France; he'd been in Belgium, too.

Cedric had written about Belgium in the school paper, especially at the beginning of the war. In the fall of 1914, the students returned to school full of news and excitement about older brothers and fathers and uncles joining up, all to help poor brave Belgium, a country none of them had given a thought to before. In the first newspaper of the term, Cedric wrote: "The father of King Albert of Belgium, who has been leading his brave little army with conspicuous skill and gallantry, was a deaf man. He was known as the Deaf Duke of Flanders."

Older and younger students passed the news from class to class that day. They claimed the Deaf Duke as one of their own, as if he'd been a grand uncle to them all. Later, one of the children showed off a letter from home, relating the news that the factory in her town had held a bee and made a stack of blankets from overcoat cloth for the Belgian refugees. Grania often thought of the *poor Belgian children*, asleep under thick blankets made from Ontario cloth. And the Dominion Salt Company in Sarnia sent a thousand bags of salt. Cedric had written about that, and Grania had created a picture in her mind of salt being poured into the outstretched hands of Belgian refugees.

She untied the third bundle of letters now, and spread them out and picked them up, one after the other. Jim's handwriting, once broad and generous, had become smaller and smaller as the war progressed. She leafed through, reading a phrase here and there. It did not surprise her to find that she knew most of the contents by heart.

Fritz's long-range guns are aiming for our horse lines. The waste of horses, the loss, is truly terrible.

Our helmets were inspected this morning before CEN-SORED. *My clothes were soaked, covered in dew. There is a stream nearby, its waters swollen. Branches tip over the edge, and a few copper-coloured leaves hang on.*

One afternoon, we watched Fritz's aeroplane do stunts at low altitude. We are safe where we are. We are out for a rest and will be, for some time. Evan found a turnip at the side of the road and picked it up and ate it, but complained of stomach pains an hour later. There are no men to be seen in the villages except the very old. Occasionally, a young man returns on leave, rolls up his sleeves to help his family for a few days, and goes off again.

I worked until midnight, and four hours after that. I have never seen mud as deep as in this place. On the way up the line, we walked single file, dodging shell holes, the fellow before me shouting, "Hole in front." I shouted the same for Irish, who was behind, but I was the one who fell into the hole. The mud was runny and thin and I was up to my armpits. When we returned to our billets, Irish had another story to tell.

Roll call was followed by bath parade in pouring rain. We stood for hours with no shelter. Every time we step, there is a squishing sound from below. We went up the line and carried for the next ten hours. That was yesterday. Today I am shovelling mud.

Canadian mail follows us wherever we are. If you only knew how your letters save me.

I dream of being clean. I dream of coming home. I dream of standing in one spot and believing you are there.

Grania tied the letters together again and replaced the biscuit tin on the shelf. Tress had not returned; she had gone to see Jack Conlin about renting a place before Kenan arrived home. Jack owned a small house at the far end of Main Street, the eastern end past Naylor's, not more than a ten-minute walk from the hotel. He also owned a large house that was divided into two dwellings. He and his family lived on one side. All three places were occupied now, but Tress wanted to let him know that she was looking.

Grania lay back on top of the bedspread and glanced around the room—at the oval mirror, at Mother's sampler, at the framed daffodils, the zigzag tear in the blind. Nothing much had changed. But Tress's life had changed. It had been altered suddenly. If Grania had been the one to receive the telegram, what would she be doing now?

She got up and put on Jim's brown jacket, the one he'd left with her before his departure. She went downstairs and out, heading for the shore and the woods.

If Jim had made it this far through the war, he could manage to its end.

But the war might never end. Three years ago, everyone had been certain that the boys would be home for Christmas. After that, the prediction was changed to the following Christmas. And then, predictions stopped. War churned on as the earth circled the sun. Reliable and grim, it continued to swallow hundreds, thousands, hundreds of thousands of young men.

She put one foot in front of the other and she walked and walked. Walking did not bring the men home but, for the moment, it made her feel better.

*

Somewhere in France:
My Love
   I have had word of Kenan. My friend Wullie from Number
1 General wrote to me after he learned that Kenan was from
Deseronto. He remembered me mentioning Kenan's name,
and recalled that he was married to your sister. By chance,
Kenan was admitted during an evening when Wullie was on
orderly duty. He said that Kenan was sent to England some
time ago, and that when he starts to speak, he'll be first rate. It
happens that the boys stop speaking for a time—I have seen
that here, too. There are always CENSORED. *And some of*
the boys stop hearing. They become deaf, even when there has
been no injury. Kenan's Blighty is bad enough, Wullie said,
and one arm won't be useful again. But the arm was not taken
off. The injuries to his face are severe. But Tress will know this
already. In the last letter you sent, you told me she had heard
from the hospital. Tell her what you can from this letter.
   All my love, Chim

*

For two weeks Grania helped Tress in her new place. They polished mirrors, mixed vinegar with water, scrubbed the inset windows of the parlour doors. She teased her sister. "You're so grand, having drawing-room doors!" They mopped and swept, upstairs and down, sewed and ironed curtains, carried in two armloads of wood to place beside the small fireplace in the parlour, and stacked the rest under the overhang of the shed in the backyard. There had already been snow; the coal scuttle was full and set inside the back veranda. A late order of coal had been delivered to the shed and flew down the chute, its black dust rising in a cloud. Grania stood with Tress at the back of the house and watched and felt the shimmer through her body.

Kenan was to sail to Halifax and there he would board a special train, but he would not be home by Christmas. He and other wounded soldiers were to be in the care of medical personnel during the journey. He would be with "walking cases," accompanied as far as Belleville, where Tress was to meet him. No longer did he require daily medical care. A follow-up message would provide the exact date and time of arrival—possibly towards the end of January 1918, after the New Year.

Ever since official notification had come, Tress's every word, every glance, every bodily posture had been attuned to Kenan's arrival. He was on his way. Grania, watching her sister, noticed that she often looked up from what she was doing and glanced eastward as if Kenan might appear at the end of Main Street. Or with his long-legged stride, emerge from the woods near the edge of town.

After the first telegram was received, four letters had followed, each describing Kenan's condition in a different way. The first was from Number 1 General Hospital, which had treated Kenan before he was evacuated from France.

His eye and facial wounds, severe as they are, are luckily confined to one half of the face. As there are no present signs of infection, closure of the wound will take place in due course. The left eye will never see again but our Doctors are thankful that the right is undamaged. The left arm, though not amputated, will no longer be useful. We have no reason to believe that a prosthesis will improve matters in his particular circumstance.

The second letter was from a "special ward for facial wounds" and had been written by a nursing sister in England.

Kenan has not yet spoken, but speech will come and he understands all that we say. We are greatly encouraged that he is sitting up. He dresses every day with only a little help, and walks as he would normally.

A terse message after that, from the Canadian Red Cross in London.

I beg to inform you that your husband was seen by our authorised visitor, who found him going on well and certainly improving in every way. A further report will be sent as regards his condition from this Society.

But a further report had not been needed. The last letter Tress received was from another nursing sister.

Our Kenan is making excellent progress all in all. It is with pleasure that I tell you he is a great favourite of the staff. We are hopeful that in another few weeks he will be permitted to start the long journey back to Canada. We are certain to miss him when he leaves, much as we know he is wanted home.

Jack Conlin had kept his word about letting Tress know when he had a place and she had moved to the end of Main Street as soon as the house was ready. Tress had been saving every dollar she could from her pay assignment and separation allowance. Over Jack's objections, she paid two months' rent in advance. She had to be certain it was hers; she wanted a place of her own.

Once the cleaning was done, the entire family helped to furnish the house. Father delivered several pieces of furniture from the hotel—an iron bed, a seagrass mattress, four chairs, a chest of drawers. Tress ordered a kitchen table from Mr. Eaton's catalogue and, for the veranda, a small square-topped table and two wicker chairs. As soon as the roads were hard-packed with snow, Bompa Jack brought in a screen for the fireplace and two parlour chairs, delivered by sleigh from the farm on the Ninth.

Mother sorted through linens and gave Tress the extras. Mamo stitched and crocheted. Bernard and Patrick arrived with Father's tools and added pantry shelves, repaired window sashes and checked the fitting of the storm door, late in the season as it was. Even Kay sewed a mattress pad for Tress and took it to her as a gift.

When Grania first walked with Tress through the narrow, two-storey house, what she saw were rooms that reminded her of their childish creations when they'd furnished rooms from pages of the catalogue. The kitchen was the only large room; it stretched across the entire width of the house at the back. Behind the kitchen, there was a windowed veranda with a rough-tiled floor. Flat stones outside led to a slope that tilted narrowly towards the bay. Everything else, inside and out, seemed to have been created in miniature.

There were two rooms upstairs, one on each side of the peak of the house: the main bedroom, now furnished, and an empty room for a child. Grania knew of Tress's disappointment both before and after Kenan's departure, when she'd learned that she had not conceived. It was impossible not to remember the plans Tress had made for babies, the ones she would name Pritchett and Jane. Grania thought of the ledger in the school hospital, the *Nurses' Central Registration*. At some time during the stay of every young girl at the Ontario School for the Deaf, a date was written beside her name, along with one other word: "Indisposed." Indisposed meant that blood had appeared, blood in the underpants or on the sheets. Blood that was to be reported.

Blood had appeared in Grania's bed, too, after Jim had left. But that event was met with silence and went unreported, and she had kept her disappointment to herself.

Tress has a house, Grania thought, and Kenan is safe. He is coming home and he will never have to go back to war. He may be damaged, but he is coming home. We have not lost Kenan.

Chapter 15

*It was only yesterday, coming down the road to our billets, I
happened to meet one of his sergeants who told me about his
death. He was the best friend I ever had.*

Letter from the Front

All day, the town had been preparing for the heavy March storm.
The afternoon train arrived, even though the temperature was
dropping and snow covered the tracks. Snow had begun to fall
steadily, and swirled around the back of the hotel until drifts
blocked the rear entrance and the stable doors. The family was
locked in. Tress and Kenan were in their own house at the other end
of Main.

From the porthole window, Grania watched the formation of
peaks and troughs and rippled waves. Her ocean field was now
entirely white. At four in the afternoon a cutter went by on the
road in front, and after that there was no activity at all. The mail
managed to get through in the late morning and had been fetched
by Patrick. The storm had swooped in from the northwest and
down the length of the bay. After supper, no sooner had the snow
stopped falling than it was followed by freezing rain, a layer of
bluish-white that locked on to doorsteps and encrusted the verandas of the town.

Was it possible that Jim lived outside in weather like this? It was.
Sometimes he slept in lofts or huts, or on shelves in barns, or in
billets, or on beds of straw. There hadn't been much news since

Passchendaele in the fall, but the papers now boasted that Canadians were bravely holding parts of the line. Grania had no idea of Jim's location. The last letter she received—stamped with the censor's stamp—had been written five weeks earlier, at the end of January, and said only that the Ambulance boys were rotated in and out of the line and that she was not to worry.

Rest periods, he wrote, *mean continuous parades and inspections. They are determined to keep us busy, but there is a more relaxed atmosphere behind the lines, and some evenings there are even concerts and entertainments. Last night there were skits, and a kazoo band.*

One night, he wrote from a French village where he slept on a chicken-wire mattress, nine men to a tiny room of three-tiered bunks. He had to sit on the floor to write the letter, he said, the page propped against his knees. He'd spent Christmas behind the lines at a small farm. He and Irish and seven others pooled their money to buy sausages and pork and gave them to the woman of the farm, who cooked up the meat for their Christmas dinner.

All the boys call her Mother because she is so good to everyone. At Christmas we were given cigarettes and tobacco, an orange each, and some filberts. We shared these with the woman's family. Some of the boys had no trouble getting their hands on a bit of rum for our celebration.

Grania thought of her own Christmas. There had been no guests at the hotel for four days, which meant that everyone had a rest from work. Tress, still living at home then, had hung a wreath outside the front door. In early December, Bernard and Patrick decorated a small tree in the lobby. Mother wanted a tree in the house, too, and it was put up later, Christmas week, in the far corner of the parlour. In the town, celebrations were subdued; it was the fourth Christmas of the war. Grania sent homemade chocolates to Kay and her young son, and asked Bernard to deliver them. She was sure she did not imagine Bernard's quick agreement to have an excuse to visit Kay.

On the twenty-fifth, the family sat down to Christmas goose, and everyone joined hands around the table for grace. Mother said a prayer that Kenan would soon be home from England and another special prayer that Jim would be kept safe.

Father brought out a bottle of brandy and added some to the carrot and raisin pudding, and everyone drank a small toast at the end of the meal. Mamo had knitted gifts for everyone: for Grania, a woollen hat with a turned-up rim, in cornflower blue; for Tress a shawl in her favourite rose colour. Patrick had *La Grippe* during the holidays, and coughed continuously. Grania tried to stay out of his way because she was still vulnerable to infections, especially at this time of year.

Fry and Colin had stayed in Belleville to help out at the school because more members of the staff had left to join up. Fry wrote that they'd taken the children to Griffins Theatre to see a moving picture that starred Charlie Chaplin, and the children laughed throughout the entire picture. Colin had helped the students to decorate the chapel blackboards with Christmas scenes.

Cedric wrote his usual pre-Christmas notes in the December newspapers, and Grania read these in her room.

PARENTS: Read This!

Do you want your child to have a merry and happy Christmas? If so, make sure that your presents are sent in good time for the distribution of boxes on Christmas morning. It would save us a great deal of trouble and anxiety if they all arrived before the 20th. If sent later, they are apt not to get out here in time. We will do all we can to make your child happy on that day. If he does not share in the joys of the occasion it will be your fault.

Among presents for girls, don't fail to include plenty of hair ribbons. These are always in demand, as are also handkerchiefs. Other useful presents are kimonos, bedroom slippers, rubbers, over-stockings, mittens, toques, aprons, scarves and collars of lace. Both boys and girls are always anxious to have skates, so don't overlook these if your child has not already got a pair. Don't send jam, fruit or catsup in glass bottles. Every year we get one box or more in which such things have been sent, but which got broken on the way, often to the ruin or injury of other things. The children get as much of such things here as is good for them.

Grania had spent every Christmas of her childhood at the Belleville school, from the time she was nine years old. In some ways, she missed those frantic days filled with expectation. So much excitement in the morning when the children were wakened at five-thirty and taken to the main sitting room of each residence to see the tall trees decorated with strung popcorn, and ropes of silver tinsel, and crocheted cone baskets, and tiny angels with cheesecloth wings. Then, after breakfast, no matter if the weather was disagreeable, the Roman Catholic and Anglican pupils were walked to church in the city, escorted by several of their teachers. Everyone bundled up and followed one another in a long line. At the churches, the deaf children were brought to the front. Sometimes they signed a carol or a prayer for the rest of the congregation, and sometimes they watched the congregation sing. After church, they were marched back to the school and into the chapel to see the Christmas address given by their superintendent, and then, finally, restlessly, they sat on benches before a platform that had been erected in the large sewing room of the main building. Every year, the platform was piled high with presents sent from the children's homes. Every year, too, Father had sent a box of toques and mittens to the school—especially for the poorer children.

Some of the girls and boys brought their own hand sleighs—an easy way to carry parcels back to the dormitories for opening. It was only after she had become a senior that Grania understood that every box sent from home had been opened *before* Christmas. She had been called upon to help the assistant matron fumigate all clothing that had been sent, and each item had to be put back in its rightful place in its Christmas box.

This year, in the January paper, Cedric followed up in his usual style: "We are sorry that the parents were not here to take a walk through the dormitories after the boxes were opened. Such sights are not often seen. The beds were littered with every kind of goody, while mechanical toys of all kinds were running over the floors. These did not last long, most of them being junk before the day was out."

At home, all during the season, Tress had been preoccupied with the thought of Kenan returning. Now, she was gone. Although she was only ten minutes away, Grania missed her. She missed her the way she had when she first went away to school. She tried to shake the old feeling of loss but it slipped easily back into place. She was glad for her sister, glad that Kenan was home, glad they had a home to live in. Tress walked back three times a week to work during the midday meal in the dining room, but Grania, standing alone at the window in the upstairs room of their parents' home, felt as if she had been snagged by a net.

Locked in the compound. Tell Dulcie to run for help.

Was the house more silent now, with Tress gone? Was there more silence between their parents? Grania did not have to hear silence to know about it. Father had let Bernard take over more responsibility for the business of the hotel, but he himself was remote, staying in his office most of the time. He frequently went out in the evenings, and Grania had several times smelled alcohol when he returned.

As for Mother, Grania wondered if she felt alone, the way Grania did, without her husband. It would not be possible to talk to Mother about this.

At least Mamo was here. Mamo was always here. Sometimes, after dinner, she and Grania sat in the parlour and Grania read short items to her from the town paper. Mamo now had what she called "old eyes."

Before Kenan arrived home at the end of January, Grania had stayed overnight with Tress a few times in the small house, sleeping in the bed with her upstairs. But Grania was needed early in the morning to help; it was easier for Mother if she remained home. And now, Tress and Kenan needed privacy. The family had been so happy to see him, to welcome him back. But Kenan had not spoken. He could use one arm and both legs. For the past five weeks he had not left the narrow house at the far end of the street. Not once.

Grania had not gone to Belleville with Tress to meet him, but Mother and Father had. They had been at the station to greet him and to bring him the rest of the way. When Grania first saw him after he arrived in Deseronto, she was ashamed of her reaction. Except for the fact that he was sitting beside Tress, she would not have recognized him. The young man who sat before her was smaller than the Kenan who had left in 1915. Diminished. His face was partially bandaged when he first came home, but now the bandages were off. The rest of his face, the undamaged half, was terribly pale. His dead arm hung from the shoulder, a loose limb. Grania did not know if she had made a sound when she first saw him. She did not know if Tress had either, or what Tress had said. Now, Tress and Kenan were at home, working things out.

As Grania considered this, she wondered if she had made up her own part about being a married woman. A woman who had once lived with a man for a short time. Had she not, since her husband had left, gone right back to her old home, her old room, only to sleep in her old childhood bed?

When Jim comes home, she said to herself . . . but that was where things became vague. She had no idea when that might be or where they might go. Some future time connected to events unseen and far away. Others were in charge of determining outcomes that affected her life and Jim's. *Chim.* Thinking his name made her feel alone and unconnected. Everyone has lost something in this war, she thought. We have waited so long, and we have all lost something.

She stood at her bedroom window and peered out. In all of the winter whiteness, perhaps silence was everywhere. She would ask Mamo. Beneath the window she saw undisturbed snow in the street, and a glistening over the new layer of ice. When snow covered the earth, did it also absorb sound? She felt safe during snowstorms, although this was something she could not have explained. Perhaps hearing and deaf people were joined in the same way for a brief time in a silent world. But logic told her that movement, even in snow, must surely make sound; that the layer of ice would alter the silence. And this year there was much snow and ice—there'd been no January thaw, no February melt. Fry had written from Belleville to say that the city was worried about the possibility of spring flooding and that ice was dangerously jammed in the Moira River.

But it had been a good winter for skating—at the school rinks in Belleville, and on the rink cleared on the Bay of Quinte here in Deseronto as well. Grania had been out skating several afternoons. One Saturday, she persuaded Kay to join her. To her surprise, Kay had agreed to come, and had even permitted herself to laugh. They had both laughed, and enjoyed themselves. For a fleeting moment, Kay's eyes and cheeks had taken on the old secretive glow.

Grania smelled a new fire downstairs. This meant that Father was back from his office, a rare evening when he would be in the house. He continued to receive updated notices about what alcohol he was permitted to stock and how he was permitted to serve it, but business had been slow since Christmas. A worker he had recently hired had left for the war. The woman who worked part time doing ironing in the laundry had left, too; she moved to a factory because it paid higher wages.

The smell of burning wood was stronger now. Father would have turned on the lamp in the parlour so he could read in his corner chair. If he wanted company, the door would be open.

Grania decided to go downstairs to join him. When her hand touched the bedroom door, she felt the vibration, the *hit-hit* of the broken shutter clattering against the outside of the house. The wind had shifted and was blowing from land instead of from the bay.

Many nights, she had fallen asleep to the hit of the shutter, the pattern of her breathing taking up the whim and rhythm of the wind. Just as she reached the bottom stair and pushed aside the curtain, Mother came out of the kitchen, leafing through a cookbook as she, too, walked towards the parlour. Grania recognized the picture of the schooner on the brownish cover. Inside the cover were the words, "Eat fresh fish. Save the meat for our Fighting Men."

Everything was war, even the cookbooks. This one had been sent a year ago by the Naval Service in Ottawa and had been used in the hotel kitchen ever since. A year ago, Mother could buy round steak for eighteen cents a pound. Tonight they'd eaten creamed canned salmon. Tomorrow, there might be salmon fritters or salmon loaf. Some hotel visitors did not like fish, though it had always been served on Fridays—several other days in the week now, too. She thought of the food at school: *fresh bread, fish on Fridays, as much milk as a child desires at every meal, no tea or coffee to pupils under twelve.*

Before she went to the parlour, Grania stopped to peek around the kitchen door. Patrick was at the table doing his homework, and she gave him a quick wave. Stay in school, she thought. Don't run away to Kingston to sign up. If you go, you'll break our hearts.

The paper train had arrived, as if to spite the storm. Father had carried some of the papers over from the hotel and was reading *The Mail and Empire,* his eyelid drooping so that he looked half-asleep as he read. Grania sat in an armchair across from Mother and began to sift through pages of the *Intelligencer* and the *Deseronto Post.* The "War in Review" was a regular feature she scanned every evening. She looked through the current list of complaints: the shortage of paper; the gasless Sunday; the meatless weekday; war flour; war bread; sugarless candy; more fish; at times, no coal. She was sick of war. Sick of papers filled with rumour, speculation, opinion, every word written by people who were themselves safe. War was a nightmare they were trapped inside. Yet some people in town—some who had no one in the war—managed to turn their backs and carry on.

She, too, wanted to turn her back, if only to get through each day. One recent letter she'd had from Jim had been like a document of dark history that had no connection with her at all; reading it made her realize more than ever how her own life was suspended. He had been gone for two and a half years, and the war showed no sign of being over. Every event reported was worse than the last—except Vimy Ridge, almost a year ago. That had been good news. A great Canadian victory. But rejoicing was bittersweet when thousands of boys went down. No one who lost a husband or son, a brother or father, was jumping for joy after Vimy—despite what was written in the papers.

Jim had been at Vimy. He had written about the mixed mood after the victory. The burial parties and stretcher bearers had followed the advancing troops and there was a good deal of sorrow, as well as elation, during those heady days.

The one flicker of spontaneity Grania had detected in the recent dark letter of Jim's had been about finding a can of green beans. *Not like brown beans we always have,* he wrote, as if that had been the most exciting event of the week. In the same letter, he described the winter sky. When she read the letter, she felt that she could be sitting on a plank beside him in a farmer's yard, looking up at sullen clouds and leaden light. But she would not have heard the sound.

At times, the ground shudders beneath our boots. The air vibrates. Sometimes there is a whistling noise before an explosion. And then, all is silent.

Those sentences had not been censored.

Mamo came in and adjusted her rocker near the fireplace. Her eyes looked tired—her old eyes. She wore spectacles ordered from Mr. Eaton, but she was not able to read as much as she used to. Grania could not remember the last time the four of them had sat together like this in the parlour. And Carlow, too, was present, asleep near Father's chair.

Some people never used their parlours—not Aunt Maggie and Uncle Am, except when her uncle climbed the ladder to oil the tower clock or adjust its hands. Not Bompa Jack, at the farm. Bompa Jack's parlour had two doors, but the doors were kept curtained and closed. The last time they were open was for Great-Aunt Martha's wake. Here at home, the parlour was used all the time. Often by Mamo, sometimes by Mother, sometimes by Grania. When Father was in the house, it meant that Bernard was looking after things next door.

If only Bernard would speak to Kay. If *he* didn't, someone else would. Bernard was kind-hearted. The home-stayer. And Father was pleased that Bernard liked the hotel business and planned to stick with it. The temperance laws were not going to last forever.

The only person missing from home this evening was Tress. Grania tried to think of what Tress and Kenan might be doing on a snowy evening like this in their tiny house. Tress had revealed little about how they were managing. Kenan was adjusting, the family said to one another. He did not go out. He and Tress were getting used to *the changes*.

Mamo visited every Sunday when the weather and the footing allowed, walking slowly because of her arthritis, sitting with Kenan for an hour in the afternoon, talking to him about family news. But Kenan never replied. Kenan's uncle had come once, but stood awkwardly beside Kenan's chair and left shortly afterwards, telling Tress to send for him if she needed help. When Grania visited, she and Tress spoke and signed. If Kenan was in the room, he watched and listened, but he did not join in.

The only thing Tress had told Grania was something Grania had not expected to hear—nor could she have imagined. When she was told, she wanted to take Tress in her arms and protect her. But Tress had told her in a controlled way, watching her face to see her reaction. Kenan must not be blamed.

"His arm swings like a missile," Tress said. "The dead arm hits. He has no control over it."

Grania saw the bruise the day Tress told her this, an ugly swelling on Tress's side. She had put her hand on Tress's skin. She thought of Kenan rolling over in their bed, the iron weight of the arm that was left behind. Or when he tried to lie down, the arm swinging forward. Kenan, who wouldn't hurt anyone.

It had become apparent, too, that he suffered terrible pain, especially in his hand. The pain in the dead hand seemed, at times, to be unbearable. During the day, the hand was shoved deep into his pocket to keep the arm from swinging uselessly as he walked from room to room in the house.

But the worst thing of all was that he remained silent. Dr. Clark visited and revisited and said that in spite of the severe injuries to his face, Kenan's throat was undamaged. Vocal cords, tongue, larynx, pharynx—all were intact. "Give him time," Dr. Clark advised. "Gradually, he'll resume a normal life." Kenan accepted the Veronal prescribed by Dr. Clark, but he refused all visitors except the family. His silence had spread like a fog through the small house, and now the fog had encompassed Tress.

Grania had found herself saying to Tress, during one of her visits, "Let me try. I'll come and talk to him alone." But she had no idea how she would do this. She had studied home nursing; she had worked at the school hospital. But she had never dealt with anything like this. She was relieved when Tress's lips replied, somewhat pinched, somewhat forced, "What can you do that I haven't tried?" Tress was practised at pushing things out of her mind; Grania knew that very well. *I tell my brain to stop thinking,* she used to say when they were children. *And then I go to sleep.* But Tress did not look rested now. Tress looked as if she were not sleeping these days, at all.

*

A shadow slid across the parlour and Grania looked up. Grew, the barber, had somehow come into the room without her seeing him and now he stood beside her chair, his presence breaking into her thoughts. He must have entered from the hall. Who had let him in out of the storm when they were all here? Patrick? No, she saw surprise on the faces around her. The door was never locked. Grew had known this and, unannounced, had walked in.

He was wearing a long wool coat, a cap and a dark green scarf. His overshoes must have been left at the door; his shoes were dry. An odour of whisky wafted from his clothes. He has a private supply, Grania thought. Never mind the Temperance Act. She thought of Father then, going out in the evenings. Father and Grew together. Now it made sense. Was that why Grew had come?

Grew took off the heavy coat, removed the cap, held the coat over one arm and the cap in his opposite hand. His face looked a hundred years old.

Father made a sudden move, an attempt to intercept, as if he had done this countless times before. Carlow pushed himself up from his front paws and watched. Grew staggered and then straightened, and made himself rigidly tall. He seemed to be using every one of his muscles to hold himself upright. He leaned forward, tried to place the coat on an empty chair, missed his footing and ran four or five steps across the room. *Things that move* . . . He was so drunk, Grania wasn't sure he had seen Father, who, startled, had taken a few running steps alongside. Grew couldn't see any of them; Grew was looking inside. She sat upright in her chair, tensed—as were Mother and Mamo in theirs.

"Come on, Grew." She read her father's lips. "I'll take you home."

"No," said Grew. "No."

It was at this moment that he seemed to notice, with some surprise, that the cap was still in his hand and the green scarf around his neck. One hand plucked at the scarf until it slid off and dropped where he stood. The cap fell on top of it. Father bent forward to pick these up and Grew took advantage of the moment to hurry towards the corner, where he slumped quickly onto the round stool in front of the piano. Because the stool had been wound low, Grew's knees popped up, and this made his height seem ridiculous.

His upper body began to sway. He tilted forward over the key-board and then, far back; for a moment it looked as if he might fall off the stool. His hands were stretched in both directions; the notes must be falling out of his fingers. Mother and Mamo were staring as if he were a home invader they had never known or met. Grania did not know what he was playing, but his right foot pumped one of the pedals and the music crossed the hardwood floor and entered her feet. The sound that entered her was ragged, like the shaking down of coals. It vibrated against her arms as she gripped the wooden panels of her chair. *There is something amiss, something amiss.*

Mamo stared hard at the scarf over Father's arm. Grew's hands were rising and falling against the keys and Grania wanted to slam her own hands into something to make him stop. But she sat frozen like the others, as if the four—five now, Patrick was in the door-way—had been handed tickets and must see the performance to its terrible end.

Only Grania's eyes had seen the descent of the folded strip of paper as it had fluttered from Grew's bony hand when he first bumped down on the stool. The paper was resting now, almost hidden, on one knee; it jiggled precariously while his foot continued to pump the pedal. The paper was narrow. TELEGRAM. She didn't have to see the words to know its message: *Deeply regret inform you Pte Richard Grew officially reported killed in action.*

Only son of.

Now they all knew. Mother's mouth was open—was she wailing? Carlow was scrambling back and forth to the doorway in the hall. Grew's hands were propped unmoving on the keys and then he stood to full height. Father, still holding the cap and scarf, was say-ing, "I am sorry, Grew. I am truly sorry." And then he swore. "Damn," he said. "Goddamn the war."

Grania's legs were trembling, her arms too. She pressed one hand into the other to force them both to stillness. *Richard is coming home to be a barber like his father.* No, Richard won't be coming home. She forced herself to look at Grew's face and then she stood and walked to his side. Unbidden, unwanted in the midst of the terrible grief that now filled the room, a line from her *Sunday* book erupted inside her head.

He rushed to the woodshed and wept as though his heart would break.

She knew the whites of her eyes were as red as if miniature blood vessels had burst without warning around her pupils. She had no tears. She felt Grew's sagging shoulder beneath her hand. At least, she thought, angrily, he won't have to stand in that anxious cluster of people outside the windows of the newspaper office after every battle. He won't have to do that any more.

When dispatches came in, the lists were posted on boards outside: *Missing, Wounded, Prisoners of War, Burials, Gas Burns, Transferred to hospital, Removed to England, Died, Killed in action.*

How could one keep going, when all the news was bad?

There'll be no one left, she thought. Soon, there will be no one left.

*

When she first saw Patrick in uniform—after he ran away and signed up in Barriefield, and after Mother marched him right back and unsigned him because he was underage and still in school, and after he ran away a second time and signed up in Belleville, right after the backed-up ice let go in the Moira River and tossed the footbridge aside and caused violent flooding, and after a third time in Napanee, after Mother gave up and knew, as everyone did, that Patrick was leaving at four o'clock this spring day and was here to say goodbye—after all of this, Grania asked: "What did Grew play on the piano that night, the night of the big storm? What was the name of the song?"

Patrick was facing the lens while Grania stared intently down and into the tiny window, shaded by her hand. She was trying to keep her hands steady, and pressed the camera to her waist. Behind her young brother, as she centred him in the scene, she could see the backyard of the house on Edmon Street that faced the side of their own drive sheds behind the hotel. A corner of slatted roof sloped low over the neighbour's turkey run. No one would ever know from the front that there was a turkey run a half block behind Main Street. She had been told for years about the gobbling.

Father was behind Grania, slumped tiredly against the back stoop. Mother was inside, upstairs, lying on top of her tightly made bed. Tress had come from the other end of Main to say goodbye and was standing inside with Mamo at the laundry window, waiting for Grania's camera work to be finished.

Patrick, now posed in the camera window, had an unlit cigarette dangling from his lips. Grania had never seen him smoke. His arms hung loosely at his sides; the sleeves of his tunic were an inch too long. His puttees were tightly wrapped, the knees of his trousers baggy above them. His boots were narrow and slickly polished. His hair was short, his neck too small for his collar. One ear stuck out beneath his cap. On his face was a half grin. He was a boy who was heading across the sea to have an adventure. The family knew that he had lied about his age and invented a new name for himself. His name—he had finger spelled it for Grania—was now Vince. She did not know how or why he had chosen this name over any other. The only thing she could think of was that it began with the letter *V* after Patrick's hero Vernon Castle. Castle had died in February, in an aeroplane crash during training in Texas, while he'd been teaching a young man to fly. The papers had been filled with local memories about him. Grania could scarcely bear to think of the handsome flyer who had moved with such grace, his slender dancer's body falling hard out of the sky.

"Tell me the name of the song," Grania said again. "The one Grew played that night."

She had been shown the letter written by Richard's platoon lieutenant. Grew received it exactly one month after the arrival of the telegram.

I must tell you that I have known your son from the time he enlisted. In losing him I have lost one of the best men from my platoon, and I am very sorry. Both officers and men desire me to say how much we miss him. You may be extremely proud of the fact that he was always ready to do his duty and that he was willing to sacrifice his all for the cause. He died nobly and in service of the Empire and his King. I am able to say positively, from witness reports, that he was killed by a sniper's bullet while on night patrol in No Man's Land, and that he died instantly. I know it will relieve your worries to learn that he did not suffer at the end. You should also know that one of our Canadian boys managed to kill the sniper almost immediately. It is most unfortunate that we were unable to recover your son's body. Shortly after that episode, the area came under heavy fire and we were forced to remove ourselves to another location.

Grew had come to the house with the letter. He'd stood unmoving while the single page was passed hand to hand. He refused to sit down during the visit. Grania remembered, too, that every member of the family had remained standing until he turned abruptly and left.

"It was the one about the Irish Laddies," Patrick's lips said now. He was forming the words with care and she looked up quickly from the window of her camera so she wouldn't miss the title of the song.

"The one Grew was playing was 'The Irish Laddies to the War Have Gone.'"

Chapter 16

Shrapnel shells were so named from the inventor, Col. Shrapnel,
a British officer who fought in the Peninsular war. It was in this
war that they were first used and so effective were they that the
Duke of Wellington wrote to Col. Shrapnel a letter of thanks
and congratulations on his great invention. The first shells were
round and were not, of course, so destructive as the finished arti-
cle of the present war.

The Canadian

The first thing she noticed as she entered the room was that it was in
shadow. The summer sun was bright enough outside, but the curtains in every room of the house except the kitchen were tightly
closed. Her glance took in the outline of Kenan, sitting in darkness
on the curly-birch chair that used to be in an upstairs hall of the
hotel. At least he was out of bed, where he often stayed now. Tress
must have persuaded him to come down to the parlour.

Grania detected a shiver of movement on the other side of the
room, a shiver that seemed to happen without Kenan's consent.
Things that move . . . She felt a tiny rush of fear, gone in an instant.
This is Kenan, she told herself. We played under the pier. He was
my bully. We played hide-and-seek.

> Hide-and-go-seek
> Your mother's a leek

We didn't know how a mother could be a leak but we found that so funny we fell down laughing. It wasn't until my third year in Belleville that I learned there are two words for the same sound. That a leek does not come out of a water pipe. Where the rhyme comes from, no one seems to know.

When Kenan left for the Front he stood on the veranda with Grania and Tress and did a little tap dance in his boots. *Charlie Chaplin went to France, To teach the ladies how to dance.* Curly-haired, long-legged Kenan. Now, before her, sat Kenan of one dead arm and a scarred half face.

She glanced over to Tress, who stood in the middle of the room looking like sorrow itself. Her dark hair had been pulled back severely, exaggerating her high forehead. Grania wanted to grab her sister's wrist and make for the door. *Let us run for it, said Dulcie.* Every caption she knew, Tress knew, too. Had she not shouted them into Grania's ears? Grania looked back at Kenan. In the elapsed seconds, he'd managed to shrink inside Tress's palpable gloom.

What about me? Grania thought. What does Kenan see in my face? *Blend in, try to look normal.* Something I've always been good at; deaf people are. We are so well trained.

But this is not about me. This is Kenan, my friend, my bully, my brother-in-law. At the very least I could walk from room to room and throw open the curtains, prop the windows with sticks, arc back the sashes, let air swirl around walls and doorways and floors. That's what is wrong. There is no fresh air to breathe here.

Instead, doing none of these, Grania walked over to Kenan and kissed him on the right side of his face, the side where he had a cheek. His curls were flopped over part of his forehead, on the left. The hand of his dead arm was shoved into his dead-arm pocket. She thought of Colin, who had always tried to draw attention away from his deafness by shoving his hands deep down into his pockets, but who succeeded only in looking as if he were trying to make himself disappear.

Grania looked up at her sister. Tress was talking and signing, not to Kenan but to her. In a glance she saw that Tress, without realizing, had slipped into their childhood language of hands, the one they'd invented many years ago. The body memory was there, everything understood. While Tress's hands and arms fluttered, Grania's peripheral vision caught a twitch and flutter of Kenan's one seeing eye.

O Kenan, Kenan.

Tress seemed suddenly relieved to have an excuse to get out of the room. "I'll leave you two to visit," she said. Grania watched the words spill into the air. As Tress turned and shut the drawing room doors tightly behind her, Grania said to herself, *We cleaned those windows, we hung those curtains, I teased her about being grand, I teased her about having drawing-room doors.*

She sat down and faced Kenan. The ceiling was low and the weight of it diminished them both; it held in and magnified the stale air. Although there was no need to light the fireplace, an odour of old smoke hung in the room. Whatever she and Kenan might have to say to each other, nothing would be said in here.

The boy was punished and locked in. A tearful boy, locked in a tower room, stood on a stone bench and peered out through the bars of a narrow window. The boy was still locked in the room on the page—a page Grania had not turned for a long time.

Kenan had not moved. He seemed to be waiting for nothing and no one. She had to get them both out of this room. She thought of the glassed-in veranda at the back of the house. They could sit there and look out over the narrow width of yard that sloped to the bay. She motioned with her hand.

"Come," she said aloud, but she knew her voice had betrayed her and escaped high. *Control the voice,* said the inner voice that was always there.

Kenan stood and followed, nonetheless. They went through the door at the far end of the room, crossed the kitchen and entered the back veranda. Sunny, not much used, Grania saw. Not now. No one could stand sunny.

She bumped the small square table along the tile floor and dragged the wicker chairs to face the row of windows. Kenan's body tensed and she understood again that she had made more noise than she'd intended.

"Here," she said, but in her uncertainty, she left out the *r*. Part of the word stuck in her throat. "He-e."

Now the chairs were side by side and they sat down. Grania pointed to the rocks on shore, the grey waters below. The sun had lifted itself high in the sky. There were small pleasure boats on the bay—a small white boat, a larger one with a fringed canopy under which two people idly sat. Grania's hands made the sign for *peace*, for *quiet*, crossing in an X shape and arcing down.

Kenan's right hand made half the same sign, half the X, and she glanced over, surprised.

There was no expression on his face.

Both afraid. In a flood, she thought of the calf and the girl, herself and Mamo. Pages turned in her head. Mamo in the rocker and Grania at her side in her own small chair. Mamo's lips shaping BOTH AFRAID BOTH AFRAID.

Everyone was afraid of something. Tress was afraid of what had happened to her husband and her marriage. Kenan was sitting beside Grania, a reminder that Jim, too, could be blown up. Or, like Grew's son, he could be killed and disappear. Her breath quickened. She was afraid she would break down here beside Kenan, whom she had come to help.

"Both afraid." The words blurted out. She had not intended this. At the same time, her hand shook out the sign for *both* in the space between them. How could she have hoped to be of any help?

Kenan's right hand lifted and again he mimicked her sign, this time the sign for *both*. She looked directly at him. His lips moved, though he had never seen the picture of the calf and the girl facing each other on the page. His head nodded slightly, just barely.

Yes. He *was* afraid.

"Poom," she said.

Out of the depths of childhood.

Out of the dugout they'd cleared beneath the pier.

Out of the complicated and uncomplicated past. Out of the smell of damp and rotting wood, the odour of a child's fart released into the already dank space that held four playmates and no confession, so they never knew or cared who did it. But they all remembered Grania's refusal to learn the forbidden word when they tried to teach her, and they roared with laughter when she replaced it with a word of her own. "Poom."

"She probably thinks it's like poo," Tress had said, and they all laughed again, even Grania.

"Poom." This was Kenan.

One eye watching. Fixed on Grania's face the way she imagined it fixed on Tress when Tress could not move towards *him*, when he could not move towards *her*. When he would not permit his young wife to help. *Both afraid.* But now, he was not afraid.

And neither, any more, was Grania.

Had he spoken aloud? Or was she imagining?

His lips moved again. "Poom."

The muscles of his body quivered, his dead arm tucked to his dead-arm pocket. Grania's inward laughter floated, high-pitched and gasping, out into the air. And this was how Tress found them when she ran to the veranda. Grania, who could not stop laughing, her eyes dotted with red, her inward sigh moving out.

Kenan's face, for the first time since he had come home, crumpled in a half smile.

*

She reviewed every exercise she could haul out of memory. For weeks, they went through the rote, one word at a time. An hour

Tuesday, an hour Thursday, all through the summer. Some days, during the lessons, Tress stayed in the house; other days, she went out. When Kenan could tolerate an extra lesson, Grania visited Fridays as well, leaving Tress and Mamo to go without her to the Red Cross work room.

They can tell Cora whatever they like, said Dulcie.

Kenan watched Grania's lips with interest. He listened with his head tilted, her soft melding voice as familiar as his own childhood.

> an
> ab
> art
> An abrupt departure.
> Absolution of sin.

> ock
> ick
> The clock ticks.

But not for Grania. The clock pulsed for Grania. Thinking about it, she could feel the pulse against the palm of her hand.

> mis
> Met with mishap.
> Mistakes will happen.
> A great misfortune.

The drills she thought she'd forgotten, the ones she had recited for Miss Amos and Miss Marks, flew into her fingertips and into her head, came off her lips like childhood rhymes. Kenan tried to say *que* and *qui* and *qua*—and his mouth remained open. They worked with *sp* and *sm*—sounds that looked so nearly alike.

And she remembered sitting at the child-size table in front of the tilting mirror at school, specially designed furniture for little deaf

mutes; staring at her own lips until they became so distorted she
had to turn away.

bre
Breathe.
Breathe through your nose.

Kenan made sounds. In three weeks he was rhyming nonsense
syllables.

mafasa
safama

Grania watched *s* follow *p*, pulled down by the scar of his lower
lip. She watched forward and backward movement of the muscles of
his unscarred cheek. She checked his profile, his good side, the way
she'd been trained, yes, trained, to grasp meaning, even sideways,
from the speaker's lips and face.

pro
Proceed with care.
Proclaim the good tidings.

Words tumbled from Kenan's mouth.
Lesson over for the week.
They joined their right hands, and squeezed.

*

Before walking back up Main Street to return home, there were
days when Grania stayed and had tea with Tress. But Tress was
pulling away; Grania felt this, even as Kenan was coming back. One
day, she asked what was wrong, but, in response, Tress moved
sharply about the kitchen, her arms and hands abrupt and quick, her
elbows pointed out. She did not want to talk.

On the way home, Grania went over and over Tress's reaction. She could not clear her mind; she could not take a step without seeing Tress's face. Tress was angry and the anger settled over Grania like a cloud.

At home, she looked for Mamo, but Mamo was busy. Mamo had begun to stay in her room more and more, in what was almost a secretive way. And she was always tired when she walked through the passageway to join the family for meals in the dining room.

*

By the end of August, there was no longer any need for exercises, but Grania continued to stop in, to sit with Kenan and visit. Kenan was speaking well, but he had not walked out of his own house. Women from town occasionally brought berry pies, molasses bread, jars of currant jelly. Tress accepted each gift at the front door, along with messages for her husband, but Kenan never came to the door himself, never allowed himself to be seen.

Tress had become more remote, and Grania began to wonder if she should visit at all. She resolved to speak with Tress today, ask if she no longer wanted her to come. She glanced up the stairs as she entered—she had not been up there since before Kenan came home. She thought of the empty room across the hall from the main bedroom. And the pain on Tress's face. There was always pain, mixed with anger.

Tress was wearing her summer jacket when Grania arrived; she quickly signed that she had to go out. There was no opportunity to speak.

Kenan was in the glassed-in veranda, seated in one of the wicker chairs. The other chair had been arranged to face him, and Grania sat down. She was weary and her limbs felt heavy. A gloomy sky streaked with grey hung over the bay. She had nothing to say, nothing to tell. She looked out at the water. This was their bay; this was their town; these were their lives. They had all been children together, their futures before them: Tress and Grania and Kenan and their friend Orryn, who was still alive in France. And then, at nine years of age, Grania had been sent away and her life had become separate. But her life had been separate before that, too. She began to talk. Face to face, this is what she told Kenan. Unplanned, it all spilled out.

Those years they were growing up as children together in a company town. A Rathbun town with an exploding population. Early years, after her deafness but before she was sent to the Belleville school. Everything Kenan had been hearing with his ears, she had been stowing in pictures in her memory. Different childhoods, same town. They might have been on different planets. Had she missed things? She didn't know what she'd missed. She had constructed her world in her own way—without background conversation, without overheard information, hearsay or noise. Protected by Mother and Father, extras added by Mamo and Tress, later by Patrick, and whatever could be picked up from Bernard, who was older than the others and most often at work in the hotel.

She'd learned that she had to have an extra eye. *Dulcie dreams her own third eye.* She needed it when she was a child and she needed it now.

"Tell me," said Kenan. His careful lips. "I want to know."

Tell.

"The names of people, the people you could hear," she told him. "I learned them from the way I could see and from what I could put into pictures. Mr. Dow had no teeth on one side, the left. His first and second wives died. The third was young but she had an old face. Tress and I called her the old child bride.

"Father O'Leary had a birthmark behind his right ear. It was shaped like the pipe he clamped between his teeth. When he died, it was a hot summer—do you remember? I was home from Belleville. He was laid out in the coolest room of the house beside the church, a downstairs bedroom. The window was open and the wet cloths were kept in a basin of cool water on the bureau. Two women took turns wringing out the cloths and changing them, putting them over his face so it wouldn't turn black before visitation. Mamo took me with her. She told me not to be afraid, that life and death went together. Just before the mourners arrived, the basin of water was shoved under the bed.

"Mrs. Grimes was so large her body moved side to side even though her feet walked forward. She looked as if she would never make any progress. Anton, her husband, owned the store. When I see his name printed, I still think, *The man with the beautiful name*, and I say to myself, *An-ton*.

"Frenchie, who used to work at the mill, had wavy hair. I trusted him but not Meryl, his wife. She had sneaky eyes. The family moved away, remember?"

"More," said Kenan, the years of his own childhood washing over him in pictures.

"Kay—every minute of the day, held her cheeks as if she'd swallowed a secret. She still does. She's the best knitter in town. We saw how good she was when she started coming to the Red Cross. She still comes, even though her husband . . ."

Months after Kay's husband, Lawrence, had been killed, and after Grania had moved home again, she still had not gone to Kay's house. She knew that Lawrence had been sent out one night to a listening post in No Man's Land, and that the post had suffered a direct hit. The shell could have killed anyone but it had chosen Lawrence.

By visiting Kay, she would have to admit that one more young man from the town was dead. Mother tried to make her go; Mamo urged her to visit. But Grania could not. Not because she didn't care, but because she cared so much. And Jim had only recently left.

She had seen Kay with Lawrence before he left for the war; their love was visible. Kay's baby was born after Lawrence marched away. Lawrence never saw his son except in the one photograph Kay sent across the ocean. The boy was now three.

When Grania was able to release some of her own selfish fear, she went, by herself, to visit. The two women hugged each other in the doorway, and sat at the kitchen table across from each other. Grania could easily follow the words on Kay's lips; she had known her all her life. She wanted to ask how Kay was managing. How the days were bearable. But she did not.

She did read the word *barren* on Kay's lips. "The house is barren, an empty shell. It isn't a home." Kay hated everything about it except her child, whom she loved fiercely. But she did not want to return to live under her parents' roof. Shortly after that, she moved in with Runaway Granny. Though her grandmother was known only as Granny then.

But Kay had found ways of supporting herself. She was hired to do etching at the Clapperton glass factory. She worked in the basement alongside twelve other girls from the town. And she took in sewing. She had six paying customers. She could knit anything and she was good with a crochet hook. Kay had skated with Grania the past winter, when the ice was thick on the bay.

Had Grania been speaking aloud about Kay? From Kenan's face, she saw that she might have been, though she wasn't sure.

"Go on," he said. "I want to hear."

It was true; he did want to hear. She could tell from his one eye. He wanted to hear what she could see.

"Mr. McClelland, the baker, has a stern face and a pucker at the side of his mouth. He holds his wife's hand in the summer. They sit on the stoop at the side of their house on Main Street, and he doesn't look stern at all when he's with her. Cora's daughter, Jewel, pinned Bernard with a white feather and I hated her for that, though Mamo told me I should never hate. Jewel used to love to dress up in fancy clothes. Remember the borrowed jewellery and the fancy lace-up boots? She moved to Ottawa after she married. It was when she came back for a visit that she pinned Bernard.

"Billy Needles looks like the youngest in the family but he's the eldest. He's still alive—at the war."

She bit her lip. This wasn't meant to be about who was alive and who was not.

Keep going.

"Marguerite has a twin brother who moved to Montreal. I could never say her name correctly after I saw it printed. The spelling confused me. When she talks about her twin, she looks to the left as if he's invisibly attached to her side. Mr. Whyte, the butcher, moves his head right and left when he speaks, and his wife, Doree, talks so quickly I've never been able to lip read a word she says. Do they understand each other? Mr. Felix has a moustache that hangs over both lips; he's hopeless.

"Mrs. Martinez has a Spanish accent that takes me by surprise every time I meet her. Any word she says that contains an *r* and I'm in trouble. Her daughter has a lisp. There's a space between her front teeth and the way she shapes the letter *s* is different from the way everyone else does. I understand her. I just have to remind myself to adjust when we have a conversation.

"Minnie's hair is as straight as a yard of pump water—that's what Mamo says. Minnie makes me laugh. Every time we meet, she has a happy thing to say. Her husband has a thin nose and a beard that interferes. He and I have never had a conversation, but he has the most beautiful hands of any man in town."

Except my Jim, but he's not from the town.

"The Jamieson twins go to the side windows of the glass factory on their way to school because they know the seconds are placed on the inside sills to cool. They ask the girls for them and then they sell them door to door for a few coppers.

"Jack Conlin chews tobacco. When he's not chewing I understand what he says. And Cora—she's the easiest person of all to lip read and the one I wish I couldn't. She used to tell me what a sweet little voice I have. But not any more."

Cora, who had said to Tress in disbelief when she'd first learned about Grania's marriage: "She married a hearing boy? Your sister. A hearing boy."

Grania stopped. She was running on and on. Blurting it out. Soon she would be telling him that she used to see words in twisted yellow rope.

"All of this." Kenan was speaking softly, to himself. "You see all of this."

What Grania was seeing was that Kenan's face was beautiful, as it had always been. Only now it was beautiful and terrible at the same time. He did not flinch under her inspection, and she *was* inspecting, looking into the ripple of scars, the obliterated eye, the deep folds on a surface that had once been smooth skin. *No one else looks at his face,* she thought. *He doesn't give anyone a chance.*

"Do you know what I said, Grania? When the sentry challenged me? I came close to being shot because of it."

Her body went cold. Had she read his lips correctly? *Who* challenged? What had Kenan said? She knew he had not once spoken about the war since coming home. Not even to Tress. Grania knew she must pay attention. She had to see every word. She had to read past and through the scars.

"What do you mean? Say slowly."

Tell.

"The sentry, the guard." Kenan was speaking carefully, slowly, directly to her. "He gave the challenge and I was supposed to give the counter-challenge, the password. I approached from the side. We'd been sent out on a trench raid. But shells started bursting around us and we scattered and I was hit. I lost my way and came back at the wrong point, and I stumbled into the post . . . it was after midnight . . . it was so dark. So much noise. There was no silence in that place. The boys went mad from the sound. Some tried to dig their own graves.

"I had to prove I was not the enemy—not Fritz. I had to do it in a split second. The sentry was crouched at a corner—sandbags were piled high, at an angle. I had lost my direction. I saw a glimmer of bayonet in the dark. I knew he was nervous, I could tell from his voice. I thought sound was coming from his rifle, off the blade. My arm wouldn't move. I was holding my other hand to my face. I had no rifle. I didn't know how badly my cheek was blown apart. I could barely see. I said, 'Don't shoot me,' but I couldn't think what I was supposed to say. I knew then that I was going to pass out. I couldn't think of anything except, *Get past this man, Get past this stranger*. And then a word popped out of my head. I heard my throat make— my mouth was full of blood—I heard my throat make the sound *Wooms*. Your sound, Grania. Our old password. The only sound I ever made that gained me entry to anything."

Grania did not move.

"It saved my life. He could have shot me but he didn't. He must have caught a glimpse, must have seen something of my uniform at the same moment. Who knows what he saw? It was so dark, it was impossible to see the fingers of our own hands."

Grania looked down. "Tell Tress," she said softly.

Kenan ignored her.

"The sentry said 'What the hell did you say?' 'Wooms,' I said again. He started to laugh, not loudly, a low rumble. I can see him laughing now. Even though I was seeing him with one eye, I'll never forget his face. Then he saw *my* face and he said, 'Oh, Christ,' and that's when I fell forward and down. My hand couldn't hold my face together any more. He shouted. And the stretcher bearers came running to carry me back."

"Tell her," Grania said. "She needs you to tell her things. She wants to help."

"I don't need her help."

She thought of Tress knotting together the belts, the stockings, the ties. Tress had thrown her a lifeline. Tress had pulled her to shore and tugged her out of the floating dark.

"Tress was in our fort," she said. "She knows the password, too." She thought of Tress shouting down and into the deadened tunnels of her ears, *"Give the password was the next demand!"*

"Yes," Kenan's lips said, but his one eye was looking past Grania now. "Tress was in the fort. She knows the password, too."

Chapter 17

Toronto Exhibition:
In the glass case I saw the blood on the Prussian soldier's over-
coat, and on the British soldier's cap which had been struck by
shrapnel. I saw a pair of Belgian trousers which were torn away
by a shell. I think the Belgian who wore them lost his leg. I liked
to see the wonderful things from the great war.

                                                    The Canadian

She loves the train. The feel of it, the largeness, its strength and its might. She and Tress travel first to Belleville, where they wait outside the station to change again, for Toronto. She loves the smell of cinder around the tracks, the odours from the cattle yards beyond, the activity as men haul the express wagons loaded with freight, pulling the wagons by their long handles along the platform. Beyond the men, she sees in the distance the coal chutes and the conical cinder piles where the engines dump their fire, and the water tower with the long dangling chain. She loves the way the men stand. Patient, waiting, shifting their caps to the back of their heads while they speak into the air and stare down the empty track, ready to go into action, set to offload and then load the baggage cars. She loves the anticipation as puffs of black smoke rise beyond the vanishing point in the tracks. Moments later, the train rumbles and shakes into sight. It slows as it approaches, and the engineer and the fireman glide past, smiling down over the iron wheels. She loves how the engineer, his arm leaning on the open sill, manages to stop the passenger cars directly at the spot where she and Tress are standing, just feet away from the moving train; and how the brakeman swings down and the conductor hauls out the step and places it before the open door. Tress climbs aboard and Grania puts up a hand to steady her hat, and she follows her sister. They turn left past the water cooler and choose a double seat three rows from the end. Grania sits by the window and leans back, and now she is swallowed by the tunnel shape of the coach; she is suspended between the life she left behind this morning, where all is familiar, and the sudden faces of strangers and the possibility of adventure that might open up before her.

Mamo has helped her and Tress to pack. "Two dresses that won't crease too much. Enough underwear for three days. And keep your hat on at all times except when you're in bed." She has arranged for them to stay in Toronto with Mother's brother Uncle James and his wife, Aunt Minna, and it is she who has bought the tickets. Grania now knows that the secret hours Mamo stayed in her room were spent sewing a suit for Dr. Clark's wife, Mildred. Her arthritic hands remembered the old skills and created a splendid tailored suit of fine English broadcloth with a calf-length skirt, and a long jacket with sleeves that narrowed at the wrists. The money she received has funded the trip to Toronto. It is Mamo who has noticed the coolness between the sisters and who has insisted that it is time for the two of them to get away.

"The mail will be here when you return," she told Grania. It is Mamo, too, who dreamed up the idea that she herself would move into the little house with Kenan while Tress has three days away on her own. A change. Neither of the sisters has considered taking a trip or thought about "a change," but now they find themselves side by side, leaning into the velour of the seats, each seat with its rectangle of laundered cloth fastened over the headrest. Excitedly, they shift and settle and focus silently and self-consciously, and they stare out the window.

Grania stares at the freight train that slides past and makes it seem as if she herself is moving, though their own train hasn't left the station. She glimpses the backs and noses of cattle between slats of the moving freight cars, chunks of straw sticking out beneath the boards, dirty water—or is it cow pee?—dripping onto the tracks. And then her own coach gives a tug and pulls away from the platform. The train gathers momentum as it crosses the narrow Moira River, passes the houses, the fields, the ponds. Ducks fly up in startled pairs from marshy areas near the tracks, and the city is left behind.

They face forward, and because of the newness of the journey it is ten or fifteen minutes before they begin a soft conversation of lips— not hands; they don't want busybodies staring. Tress does not have to speak aloud—what reason would there be to do so?—but shapes words with her lips, and Grania watches and replies in low tones, keeping a close eye on Tress's expression so she'll be sure to see the signal if her own voice begins to rise.

The peach-basket lady is on board, riding backwards in an end seat that faces them, and, while the train sways side to side, constantly correcting its own balance, the peach-basket lady looks out the window and back to the aisle and keeps up a whispered conversation with herself. She is wearing a long dress, and wisps of hair stick straight out from under a navy straw hat. Everyone on the train seems to know her. Grania and Tress have seen her during the past few years, riding the trains between Belleville and Deseronto and Napanee. She simply appeared one day, and since then she has been sighted as far as Queensboro, travelling to the pyrite mine and back. She may or may not have a ticket or a pass, buried under the heap of clothing at the bottom of her basket; if she does, the conductors never ask to see it. There is a wide rack above her, stretching the length of the coach, but she does not place the basket up there, preferring to keep it beside her or on her lap. There are never peaches inside, only her clothes and always a quart sealer of maple syrup poking up. If this is consumed and replenished from time to time, no one knows for sure. Her husband, it is said, was once a brakeman with the Bay of Quinte Railway and was killed by a moving engine moments after checking the switching on his section of track. And then, years after the accident, with her few belongings in the basket with the half-hoop wooden handle, the peach-basket lady began to ride the trains. She whispers silently and continuously to herself, and Grania lip reads the words from her own seat. When Grania smiles, Tress's lips shape the silent question, "What did she say?" and Grania replies, in a low breath, "She says her fat is jiggling because it's a jerky ride today." Tress smiles and settles back. If they were children, they might have made the crazy sign beside their ears, but now they just wonder about how she gets her food and if she washes in the train lavatory or at the stations, or if people give her money, or if she has relatives in some town along the way. No one knows anything about her except that she has no children and that she is always riding the trains.

In Toronto, Grania plans to buy presents for Christmas with the money she has been saving from Jim's assigned pay. She receives fifty dollars a month now; when Jim first left, her allowance was forty-five. She has made a list of what she wants to buy: a Windsor tie for Father, almond-scented hand lotion for Mother and, as a surprise for Patrick when he comes home—in hopes that he will go back to school—a dictionary with 763 words. She saw it advertised for nineteen cents in the Toronto paper. She has already sent an early Christmas parcel of chocolate and pound cake to Patrick, and eight separately wrapped apples from Bompa Jack's farm. Patrick is still training in England, and Grania prays that he will stay there until the war is over. People are saying it really will be over soon, after the August push began a new momentum against the German lines. But this has all been said before.

For Mamo, she will buy an extra bottle of Canada Bouquet. For Bernard, a Tipperary collar. She is not certain, but Bernard disappears several times a week when he is off work, and he has been seen going into Runaway Granny's house. One day, he was there to oversee the delivery of coal. He says nothing about this to anyone, and Grania is hopeful that he and Kay will find a place for each other in their lonely lives. She has not breathed a word of this to Tress because Tress is preoccupied with her own troubles. Besides, Grania knows that Bernard likes to be private. If anyone speaks to him about Kay now, he might run in the opposite direction. She mentioned this to Mamo, and was not surprised to know that Mamo has noticed and is keeping quiet, too. Grania looks over at Tress and wonders if there are things that they won't be able to talk about now. But Tress's eyes are closed; she is resting.

The Exhibition is on in Toronto, and Grania and Tress plan to attend during their visit. Last year a Toronto cousin wrote to tell them that the grandstand show included a mock night attack on the dugouts of the Hun. Grania does not want to see such a spectacle this year, not while Jim is *over there*, not while the headlines are shouting about the big push. Nor does she want to see blood-stained trousers that reveal the exact place a man's leg was torn off. She has imagination enough to fill the picture gaps, and does not need artifacts to point the way. Instead, she will go to see the livestock, and the food exhibits, and the midway, and she will take in the outdoor sights at the fair.

Their first venture out, the day after arrival, they treat themselves to a ride on the streetcar and a trip to Mr. Eaton's store. For three hours they browse through women's clothing, coats and collars, serge skirts and kid gloves. They go up to the Grill Room on the fifth floor and indulge in the 25 cent Afternoon Special, and they order what they would never find in the hotel dining room at home: lobster salad with mayonnaise dressing; fancy pastry with whipped cream to go with a shared pot of tea. "Aren't we grand?" Grania says. Her words can scarcely be heard, but Tress knows exactly what she says and shapes her own words back. Again, they avoid the use of the sign language in public, though they use it animatedly enough in front of their cousins and Aunt Minna and Uncle James. If Grania misses a reference to someone's name, or if everyone is talking at once, Tress scrolls out the words for her into the air. Tress is relaxed here; Grania has noticed that she smiles more and joins the shared laughter with the cousins. She is more like the old Tress, but Grania still detects the anger.

On their last afternoon in the city, they hurry through crowded streets and find the moving picture theatre where Lillian and Dorothy Gish and the handsome, moustached Robert Harron are starring in *Hearts of the World*. They arrive just before the moving picture begins; the screen is the largest Grania has ever seen. The lights dim and she sits, rigid and straight, and focuses her attention so she won't miss a single thing. Tress sits close beside her. Grania frowns when she sees how rapidly the scenes change. She squints, trying to follow the multitude of detail, trying to get into the rhythm of the changing pictures. She strains to read the actors' lips on the silent screen, and sees two French words, *libre* and *merci*— words she knows because when the war began these travelled from lip to lip at the Belleville school. Tress nudges, not knowing the French words, not being able to lip read the way Grania can, and Grania whispers their meaning into her sister's ear.

But there is action in this picture; so much happens, Grania can hardly bear to watch. Earth erupts like a volcano spewing high. Young men in trenches grimace at one another; men go over the top and fall down. More men are running running towards the enemy, and jumping down into trenches and stabbing with bayonets. There are flame throwers and explosives with long handles and mud, and more mud, and water, and marching men, fighting men, battle after staged battle. She almost believes that one of the uniformed men who wears a cross on his sleeve will turn his face to the audience in Toronto, in the dark, and that the face will be Jim's.

Tress reaches over and clenches Grania's hand. She won't let go; she nearly wrings it off. There is so much sadness in the film: a mother dies, a father dies, another mother from the village. There are caved-in buildings, and bodies buried under rubble. The youngest boy, the brother with the angelic face, makes Tress cry, but Grania's favourite is the Disturber, the young woman who is full of life and up to mischief. The Disturber even helps to save the young lovers, in the end. Grania lip reads the wedding ceremony performed by the lovers themselves as they prepare to die in each other's arms. Again and again, Tress, with no warning, wrenches Grania's hand and, finally, when they are out on the street and standing in the fall sunlight again, Grania stops and faces her sister and, not sure of what she has missed, asks why the movie upset her so much at some times and not at others. And Tress says, "The music. The music was so intense, so rapid, my heart started to pound and I thought I would have to get up out of my seat and run out."

They go to a restaurant and have tea again and they both look as if they have come through the war themselves.

On their way to Aunt Minna's they buy postcards for Jim and Fry and everyone at home, even though they'll be back in Deseronto before the cards arrive. They stop at the post office to buy stamps and a woman at the front of the line becomes agitated while they are waiting their turn. Grania watches the lips of the clerk behind the counter; he is speaking in anger to the woman. He makes a half-turn away and gestures rudely. The woman rushes out of the building.

"What is it?" Grania whispers. "What happened?"

"German," Tress's lips say.

"The woman?"

"He said so. She said she wasn't but he wouldn't believe her."

"I read his lips when she turned to go out," Grania says. "He said, 'I hate the Germans.'"

That night, their last in Toronto, the sisters lie in bed, side by side, in the room that one of their cousins has vacated during their stay. So much has been seen in the big city, Grania goes over the wash of pictures in her mind. She is wide awake, and stares at the shadows in the unfamiliar room.

Tress is still; she must be asleep. But she feels Tress's foot press against her own. It happens again. She is uncertain at first, and then she realizes. Two taps. She waits, and taps back. She is one tap, Tress is two. They begin to tap foolish, meaningless messages with their feet and toes, and suddenly the mattress is shaking beneath their laughter. They carry on, tapping and laughing, and finally they stop, and go to sleep.

The next day, they say goodbye to Aunt Minna and Uncle James and their cousins, and they travel home, and when they reach Belleville and climb down, ready to change trains, there is the peach-basket lady, waiting to climb up. The jar of maple syrup sticks up above the clothing; the contents of the basket look the same as they did a few days before.

Grania reminds herself that a letter from Jim might have arrived while she was away. But she is glad there has been a diversion, glad that for a short time she and Tress were able to think of something other than Jim at the war and Kenan's slow recovery.

They stand on Main Street in front of the house and hotel, and they look at each other.

"We've become serious," Grania says, and they hug goodbye. "We hardly ever laugh any more."

But Tress is anxious to get home. She places a palm on Grania's cheek and gives a half smile. She hugs her again and then she turns and hurries towards Kenan and her own house at the end of Main.

We've missed each other, Grania thinks as she watches her sister go. But maybe things will be better now. We've missed each other and we seldom have a chance to laugh or have fun. All we do is wait out the war.

Chapter 18

If there is a sudden onset of what appears like a hard cold, one should go to bed, wrap warm, take a hot mustard foot-bath and drink copiously of hot lemonade. It is universally agreed that it is possible to perfect the powers of resistance of the human system so that it can throw off almost any infection, not excepting Spanish Influenza.

The Napanee Express

In the dream it was winter. Jim was outside, shaving from a tin cup partly filled with ice and partly with melted water. He was humming. There was snow all around, and he wore a thick jacket and a close-fitting knitted cap. When he finished shaving—he had no mirror—he turned and told her he was going to make a perfect angel in the snow. He fell hard, straight back. She was shocked when his arms did not reach out to break his fall and by the violence of the way he went down. He looked up at her and flailed his arms and legs to make wings. Then he stood. He moved his feet a few inches to change direction, and fell again. Another hard fall, another perfect angel. No jagged edges, no footsteps between. "I'm coming back," his lips said while he lay there in the snow. "I told you before, Grania, I am coming back."

She had left the blind up the night before, and when she woke Saturday morning she could tell by the outside light that Mother must have slept in. Mother never slept in; she always came to Grania's room to wake her. Every morning they were first up and walked through the passageway together to start breakfast at the hotel.

Father was at Bompa's farm. He had stayed away five days but would return today to take delivery of a new horse. The horse breaker was to arrive at noon, and that meant there would be plenty of men outside, around the back of the house. It would be busy at the hotel, too, with weekend steamer excursions stopping at the wharf. Bernard had said he would help out in the dining room at midday. Mrs. Brant had said she would come in, even though it was her day off. Grania thought of Mrs. Brant passing raisin cookies to her when she was a child. Now, she passed small paper-wrapped parcels to Mamo to store in the O'Shaughnessy trunk. But only when no one was around.

Grania's head and throat were aching, but she rose quickly and opened the door of her parents' room. She went to her mother's side, bent over her and put a hand on her shoulder.

"Mother," she said quietly. "Mother. We've slept in."

Mother opened her eyes, startled. She raised her head to look at the alarm clock, and sank back. "I forgot," she said. "I forgot to wind it." She reached up as if barely seeing Grania, and squeezed her hand.

Grania was shocked to look down at her mother's face like this and see her looking so vulnerable. Mother seemed to have shrunk since Patrick had left. The soft lines around her eyes and mouth tightened as soon as she pushed herself up and sat on the side of the bed.

They had both gone to bed late. The night before, just after Grania had finished setting the tables for morning, she was leaving the dining room when a woman came running into the hotel, through the main entrance. She had a wide and ugly bruise across her left cheek and she kept looking back as if someone was about to come in behind her. Bernard came out of his office and spoke to her. Grania stood, waiting, wondering what she should do. She tried to read the woman's lips, but it was difficult because the woman kept her head down and she was crying. Bernard was trying to make sense of what had happened. He had a hand on the woman's arm and was looking past her, out into the darkness of the street. He left her, and went to the door, and stood on the veranda outside and then came back in. He noticed Grania for the first time.

"Tea, Grainy. Can you make some tea? Let's bring her to the dining room. There's no one in there."

The woman was perhaps forty, forty-five. Her hair was partly grey, partly black, and pinned back severely. Her cheek had begun to swell, and Grania went to the kitchen to get a sliver of ice from the ice box. She thought of something Mother had said not long ago, while speaking about a family in the town. "The husband," she said, "does not treat his wife well."

Grania knew what that meant. Words couched the actions, even though everyone knew what went on behind the family's closed doors. And now, here was another woman, discouraged, defeated, her glance darting back to the doorway. She had stopped crying but she hadn't stopped being afraid.

Mamo had already gone to bed, but Mother came through the passageway and talked to the woman, whom she knew slightly. An hour later, Bernard walked her to her brother's home, where she insisted on going.

They had all been upset by this, and Grania and Mother had gone to bed very late. Now they would have to move quickly to make up time.

Grania left her bed unmade, and washed and dressed quickly, coughing several times, trying to clear her throat. Before going to see if Mother was dressed and ready, she paused to glance out the window. There seemed to be a high wind. She looked up to the sky, and a V of geese crossed her vision, a ragged, uncertain formation overhead. The flock was followed by a second, more orderly V. If she hadn't looked up, she'd have missed both. One more season coming to an end. The day before, Mamo had announced that the birds would be heading south early; her bones could tell. Grania thought again of the woman with the bruised cheek the night before, and of the fear—not only that the woman had felt but that

Grania and Mother had felt, too. Before they'd finally gone to bed, Mother had stopped Grania outside her room, speaking carefully so that Grania could read her lips.

"In all the years your father and I have been together," she said, "he never raised a hand to me in anger." And then she added, "But I've lost his attention, and it is partly my own fault." Grania, taken by surprise, had nothing to answer, but Mother turned abruptly anyway and went into her room, alone. Grania thought for a long time about what Mother had said.

Grania now looked at her reflection in the oval mirror and tried to steady herself. There were shadows under the eyes that stared back. Her skin was pale, and she wondered why she hadn't noticed this the day before. Had she looked like this when she was in Toronto? Tress hadn't said anything. She hurried out of the room. Mother was on her way downstairs and Grania caught up, and they quickened their steps. Mother took her arm, leaning a little. They turned on the lights in the hotel kitchen and set to work.

By the time Grania was free again, it was twenty minutes before noon. She had not told Mother about her sore throat, but there had been no need. Mother had noticed her paleness right away. But there had been only a quick comment; they'd worked hard all morning, passing each other in the kitchen and dining room. Now, Mother wanted her to write up new menus, complaining that the old ones were stained and spattered, that the job had been put off too many times. It was Grania's careful printing she wanted on the new ones. "Do something while you're sitting," she said. "Take one of the old menus with you." When Grania nodded and was about to leave the room, Mother stopped her and put both hands on her shoulders. "You look as if you need more sleep," she said. "Maybe you're coming down with something."

But Grania wanted to go out; she wanted to get away from the stifling air that was constricting her throat. She would do the menus later in the afternoon, when she went to sit near Bernard in the lobby. She knew the menu by heart and would not need an old one beside her to start anew: Fried Eggs and Back Bacon; Hot Porridge and Currant Scones; Aggie's Special Soup; Hot Pot and Irish Soda Bread; Chicken Pie; Upside-Down Cake. On Thursdays, Custard, or Raisin and Apple Pie. On Fridays, Panned Fish—Pickerel or Trout. Canned fish, too—Salmon Loaf. On Sundays, Roast Beef with Pan Roast Potatoes.

She returned to the house and looked out the back window. Father was outside now, speaking with Jack Conlin, who was chewing tobacco. The horse breaker was there, too. He was holding fittings in one hand and a whip in the other, although, by reputation, he rarely used the whip. Grania had her first look at Father's new horse. It was nervous in the paddock, as if it knew that some outrage or defeat was about to take place.

Funnels of dust were whirling near the doors of the shed. Older boys from town leaned into the fence in a semicircle, waiting. Two younger boys were sitting on the top rail, their caps tilted in the attitudes of the older men. Other friends of Father came in from the Mill Street side and fastened the gate behind them. They stood back, a few feet away from the inside paddock.

Grania knew that if Mother looked out a window and saw her leaving, she would be sure to try to stop her. Still, there was so much hullabaloo in the backyard, she didn't concern herself with Mother. The noon steamer would be docking shortly and Mother would be attending to dinner and the first course. Grania would not be missed.

She wasn't sure where Mother kept her ruby salve, so she went to the small pantry, took an opened jar of beets from the shelf and dabbed a drop of purple juice onto each cheekbone. That would fix the paleness. She rubbed the drops vigorously into her skin. Mother could easily see through deception; she always did. She could see through shadow and beet juice and pallor—but Mother was not in the house.

Grania looked towards the back window as she left the pantry and saw moving paws—Carlow, scrabbling to get in. She was alone, then. Mamo must be next door, and Bernard, too. She let Carlow in and he settled on the floor and watched her. She leaned over to pat him, feeling dizzy as she did. She went to get Jim's brown jacket, and left by the side door, shutting it carefully behind her. She wondered if she would be too warm, but the wind gave a quick reply in gusts off the bay. Her legs wobbled as she moved in the direction of shore, heading west towards the woods where she and Mamo had always walked. She glanced at the station and the wharf on the left, and passed the coal shed farther on. A rawness scraped at her throat, and pain dug into her chest like a spade. She began to unbutton the jacket but, just as suddenly, she became cold again and tightened its folds around her. She walked past the Jamieson twins and watched the motion of their arms as they threw a ball between them. *Things that move* . . . The ball swerved wildly in the wind and veered in a wayward arc. It blurred out of sight just as Grania's legs almost gave out. She believed, momentarily, that she had been struck. But that could not be—there was the ball in mid-air, between the twins again.

She thought of the letter she had received from Fry the day before. Fry had received her postcard from Toronto. She wrote that the new epidemic had struck hard at the school. They were doing their best to keep it out, and most children had been given the vaccine. Several had become ill on Monday. By Tuesday, four dormitories were filled with sick children. At the time she was writing, six. There'd been no point in moving children over to the school hospital—except for the serious cases.

> *Most have mild form of that influenza, but one girl has pneumonia. Everyone is tired, this is just beginning. It must run the course, Dr. Whalen says. I think school will stop mail coming and going. No parcels allowed from home. Children are not permitted to leave grounds and teachers are asked not to receive visitors at home. Picture shows and schools in city close one by one. Some people on streets of Belleville are wearing masks.*

But some good things happen. Apples are growing. Nothing keeps the trees—four thousand this year—from being loaded with fruit! Yesterday evening, I was tired but walked through orchard with Colin and picked a bushel myself. Colin helps farm boys when he can.

Other news at school—naming of cows occupies the children. So far they have chosen Molly, Roos, Mrs. Gordon and Snow Queen. And—no surprise—there are more rumours that the sign language will be phased out. We predicted, remember? Soon there will be no positions for deaf teachers. Superintendent says Oral Method is the future—now we copy United States. Some teachers already discourage use of sign. Who can believe that deaf children will stop creating language with their hands? It's as natural as air we breathe. If children are not permitted—in dorms, in classrooms, when they are out to play—they will be dull children and we will all be sorry. Already, we hear of children being punished for using sign.

Grania had read the letter twice. She stood still now as she thought of what her friend had written, and she steadied herself again. Her hand was tapping against her skirt. Leaves were falling as if they were weighted, but just before they touched the ground the wind caught them and tossed them up again. The air was spinning with reds and golds and browns. In a few weeks every tree would be bare. Invisible gusts off the bay rattled at her clothing, and grains of dirt pelted her face. She choked as she inhaled. In a moment of panic, she thought she might fall to her knees.

There is something amiss.

She faltered, but as she reached the edge of the woods, her legs were steady again. Her vision blurred. Just before she entered the path that was partly hidden by trees, she looked over the water and saw the noon steamer moving up through the bay. In a soundless world, black clouds puffed out of the smokestack and were grabbed by a wind that thinned them to wisps of grey. In five minutes, a crowd would tumble onto the wharf—sightseers out for a fall excursion, visiting both sides of the bay. They would disembark and cross the road and pack the dining room where Bernard would at this moment be moving between tables as swiftly as his body would allow without breaking into a run. Mrs. Brant would be sagging into a kitchen chair, reaching for a saving cup of tea now that the main work was done. Mother would be calling out commands, making a last check. Pulling her apron over her head and folding it across the step stool. She would stride to the desk in the lobby and her hand would lift the bell. Not that the overnight guests needed prompting. Most of them returned because of the cooking. In the evenings they hovered at the bottom of the stairs, a restless clump, awaiting the signal for supper. Every one of them knew the story of Sir Wilfrid Laurier who had once left his campaign train, crossed the street and entered the hotel to have a bowl of Mother's soup. Every one of the guests knew that Sir Wilfrid had paid high compliment as he left.

Grania could not remember what she was doing here. She was on the path but had no recollection of entering the woods. She tilted her head to look up to the tip of the highest tree and saw that it was bent in the direction of the town. A good fall wind.

The wind howls, but not the leaves.

She imagined the sound of wind around her. *It all depends,* Jim had told her.

She searched the sky as if there might be howling to see. Would Tress say she was silly? Would she make the crazy sign because Grania was trying to see the sound of the wind? No, Tress would not do that. But Tress had played; Tress had entered the old night-time language, with no rope between.

Grania stepped forward again and this time she went down, holding the half crouch that caught her, surprised by her legs crumpling so completely. She tried to push herself up from the earth with both hands but she couldn't rise. It was easier to stay crouched in the leaf-filled hollow between criss-crossed roots. She had a momentary thought that no one but Carlow knew she had gone out.

She closed her eyes and pictured Jim. Each time a letter was placed in her hands there was a belief in the merging of their lives. But after each letter had been read and added to its bundle—a fourth bundle now, for 1918—she had to fight the fading of that belief. She knew how small she was in world events, how small her town, how small her country. And how big the war. The Kaiser punished everyone by continuing to fight. Jim had been gone for three years. Every day, when she opened the papers, she could not keep her body from lurching towards the lists of wounded and dead. So many boys from surrounding farms and towns and cities were gone forever.

At the time of his last letter, Jim had been behind the lines. But the day he wrote the letter, he was preparing his kit: *We've been ordered to turn in one blanket.* That meant the unit was moving again. Now the papers were filled with more news of the push forward. "The Hun is on the Run," one headline had stated.

Of course there might be no letters at all. It was what everyone feared but no one said. One of Uncle Am's friends who'd worked at the sash and door factory had received a telegram *and* letters. Even after being notified of his son's death, he received two more letters—one written the evening the boy was to go up the line, the other written the morning he died. It was a horror, Uncle Am said. His friend wanted the letters but dreaded the missives from his dead son as much as he had dreaded the imaginary telegram before it arrived. *Deeply regret inform you . . .* To make matters worse, letters sent overseas by the boys' parents had begun to come back, "Killed in action" stamped across each envelope. These arrived weeks after the boy was in his grave. "At least he has a grave," Uncle Am had said. "Not like Grew's son, lost and buried in clay and mud. At least the boy had a decent Christian burial."

Grania's vision blurred and she pressed her hands to her cheeks as if contact with her own skin might affirm her presence. She thought of Mother's beet juice as she sank—this time she went all the way down. She thought, *My skirt will be filthy*. She thought, *I'm cold*. A pain shot through her ribcage and for a moment she could not take a breath. She rolled, feeling the leaves shift beneath her. She tried to sit upright, knowing that if she could not get up she would choke. She struggled with the button on the collar of Jim's jacket and tried to force it open. She pushed herself up on her hands and knees and began to crawl, her skirt and stockings scraping dirt. In her urgency to reach the clearing she kept her mind focussed so that she could stay on the path. She felt a gurgling sensation on one side of her chest, and in disbelief she lifted a hand and pressed it beneath her left breast. At the same time, she said, *Bubbles. How can there be bubbles in my chest?* Fluid tilted up and over her tongue and spilled onto her hand, which was now bright red. She tried to pull forward the last few feet but sank to the earth, face down. Air moved in and out, past the gurgling in her mouth.

Chapter 19

If we could decapitate a singer in the midst of a song ... the beauty of the voice would be gone, and you would simply have a reed-like effect.

Alexander Graham Bell

"Do you ever wonder about your breaking point?" said Irish. "What it might be?"

They were off for a few hours and were leaning back against the wall, their cups filled with tea. They were in a tiny shack they had built from salvage, behind a tile factory in Bourlon that had been battered to pieces. In the past few days they'd been in Cagnicourt, Queant, Inchy, across the canal bank to the old German front line, and then ordered back to the Inchy side again. They were badly shelled Friday night, and relocated again on Saturday. Everything was speeded up, moving fast, the Canadians fighting alongside the British. Irish had heard that the French and Americans had taken eighteen thousand prisoners. The Hindenburg line was gradually being cleared. The positions won reached the outskirts of Cambrai, an important road and railroad centre. Between shifts, Jim had gone to the top of Bourlon Ridge to get a view of Cambrai and the surrounding towns.

During the fighting, every road leading to the front had been crammed with guns, tanks, motor machine-gun units, infantry, cavalry, engineering supplies, cooks' wagons, water carts. All night Saturday, at the Advanced Dressing Station, stretcher bearers had transferred cases from horse ambulance to motor ambulance. Two hundred stretcher cases came in, and one hundred walking. The men were fighting hard. More than fifteen thousand casualties had been evacuated in six days. As wounded men were loaded onto trains, empty cars returned carrying dressings, blankets, more and more stretchers. Flat cars and French boxcars with layered stretchers inserted into their sides were used constantly. The Red Cross was right on the heels of the army, making daily deliveries and supplying comforts for the wounded.

Despite the high number of casualties, the advance was continuing. The clearing of the battlefields and the treatment and evacuation of the wounded were taking place as if every man was an essential unit of a massive, oiled machine that was beyond the reckoning of any one part of it. *Regimental Aid Post, Advanced Dressing Station, Collecting Point, Main Dressing Station, Clearing Station, Depot.* Everyone knew his place, where to collect, where to carry, where to report. The locations changed as divisions rolled forward or replaced one another. The wounded were moved back by stretcher, by strong arms and shoulders, by wheeled stretcher if the roads allowed, by wide-gauge rail, truck, horse-drawn wagon and motor ambulance.

Jim was staring at Irish. They had talked about everything else, but not about breaking points. Irish had Clare's picture out of his pocket and was running his thumb over its surface. Jim patted his own pocket over Grania's photo.

"Every man thinks about his breaking point," Jim said, after a silence. *Time lag,* he thought. *The moment between utterance and understanding. Or between understanding and utterance.*

Irish did not interrupt. He was waiting. He tucked Clare's picture back into his tunic.

"You've seen the boys leave their senses, Irish. Gone over the edge."

"But do you feel it lurking?" Irish was insistent. "In the air beside you, or creeping up behind? Especially here. Things are moving so fast we can scarcely keep up."

"It keeps us off balance," said Jim. "So much movement, the speed of things."

"That's what I mean. Things are off balance."

"Off balance might be a good thing, who knows? I don't trust a fellow who believes he has everything under control. For me, off balance is real, a companion that travels close. I might be surprised by something, I might not."

"You're canny, Jimmy boy. Canny will get you through."

"Canny? I don't think so. But I do things. I take measures—to hold things at bay." He hadn't intended to say this.

"Measures? What measures?" Irish was pushing, laughing a little, the gap showing between his teeth. They'd been together for three years and he hadn't heard this.

"You know. A chant under the breath, a line from a song."

"Tell me."

Tell. Jim thought of Grania.

"Sometimes I say—fast—to myself:

Infirtaris,
Inoaknonis,
Inmudeelsis,
Inclaynonis."

Irish laughed so hard he could scarcely speak. "Tell me again."

Jim repeated the verse, faster this time. "It's supposed to sound like Latin. My grandmother taught me. She said it came from the time of Henry VI. It's nonsense. But it helps if I say it in the noise of the guns, when we're trying to get a carry out of a tight spot." Another pause. "Something else, too."

"What might that be?" This time, Irish looked as if he did not plan to be surprised.

"The boys," Jim said. "The ones who are terrified. They've never accepted war. What war is. The ones who do, it seems to me, know they're prepared to die. That doesn't mean they think about death, or dwell on it. You know how they hate talking about this stuff. They accept. But some just can't. You've seen them, Irish, crying for their mothers, holding their hands over their ears."

"More than I care to think of."

"I can't be the only one who notices that the ones preoccupied with dying are the first to be killed. Always looking over their shoulder. It's better to carry on. Know our tiny job in the order of things, and get it done. That way, we'll all get home sooner."

He thought of the boys he'd taken back to the Self-Inflicteds. They were kept together in one spot as if they had measles or some other communicable disease. Some died for it.

They had finished their tea, but Irish reached for the last mouthful in the cold cup.

"Don't, Irish, it's bad luck to leave it sit and then drink the last bit." He tried to take the tin cup from his friend's hand, but it was too late. Irish gulped it down, laughing. Jim was sorry he'd spoken.

Evan came into the shack with Finner. Ahead, Cambrai was burning. And anything else Fritz could put a flame to. The two men had carried in boards to fix up the place. Evan had also brought a scarred tabletop—a slab of wood two feet by two—and propped it low on heaps of fractured tiles until it rested evenly. They all sat on the floor, one on each side of the square, admiring; it gave them immense pleasure. Evan laid some bacon on top of the slab, for morning. He'd been scrounging. Evan was harder now. The tic in his cheek was there, but he was harder. And he was never still. Jim thought of him as the most restless man he'd ever known.

Finner threw an extra blanket into the already cramped corner of the shack. They had done everything they could to make the place comfortable, even though they'd probably be leaving in the morning.

Finner was upset about the cook. He lined up his complaints. The meat at supper had turned, and had a bad taste. There was to be no hot breakfast in the morning—rations only. The food gave him stomach pains. He went on and on about the cook.

"Never mind the grousing," said Irish. "It's no use. There's probably nothing else the man can do. He'll make us a good porridge when he can. We're off for the evening, so let's try to enjoy ourselves. Anyway, Finner, when you point a finger at someone, remember that three fingers are pointing back at you."

Finner looked down at his hand, pointed a finger at Irish, and laughed.

*

As it turned out, they were roused in the early hours of the night, long before morning. They grabbed up their belongings, took the bacon with them, abandoned their lean-to shack and their tabletop and headed into the woods. They had just settled themselves into a former German trench—recently evacuated—when severe bombing started up, all around the area they'd just left. Fritz had not finished fighting yet.

It was pitch dark but the sky was alive with explosions. No one spoke; they wouldn't be heard anyway. They wrapped blankets around themselves and leaned back. Irish was asleep in an instant. But in the first lull, the sergeant came to find them and told them that several men had been caught out and were wounded. He needed a few of the boys to go out and see if there was anyone they could bring in. Another bearer party would be coming up behind. Jim grabbed a stretcher and woke Irish. But now Irish was grumbling.

Evan and Finner were behind, and veered to the left to search a separate area. Jim and Irish split off to the right. The ground rumbled underfoot and then everything was still. Jim saw two bodies close together, far ahead, in front of the ruins of a shattered building. He pointed, but Irish had already seen. They headed there directly, stumbling over uneven ground. When they reached the two men, they saw right away that the one on his back was dead. The dead man's right arm was bent at the elbow, hand open, as if waiting for a ball to drop from the sky. The other soldier had a deep injury to his thigh, but he couldn't move by himself. Irish tore open a dressing; Jim watched his friend's big hand lay it gently over the wound. Irish looked up then and gave the signal. They lifted the boy onto the stretcher and started off in the direction of the newly designated dressing station.

"This will get you a Blighty, lad." Irish told the boy. "Don't worry about a thing. We'll have you with the doctor in minutes."

Jim was in the lead. His body assumed the old rhythm. With Irish in step behind, the weight of the soldier was even between them. They had done this so often, so many thousands of times, the added burden was like part of their own body weight. *We've turned down promotions*, Jim told himself. *So we can keep doing this, get the boys to safety, stay together as a team.* He thought he saw something move, up close, and he came to a halt, feeling Irish make the adjustment behind. *Things that move . . .* There was a shout. It was Irish. And a sudden sound that forced Jim to close his eyes—only for an instant—and then there was a whoosh, a rushing sound, and something louder, an explosion that rocked him forward and sent him flying off both feet. He took a step in the air, even as his hands released the grips of the stretcher. He shouted, and reached behind himself to regrip the handles that had been harshly yanked away as he was hurled forward.

He tried to get up; his body was in tremors; his spine was hunched and would not or could not straighten. The shock had entered him as a physical blow, and it vibrated his chest until he believed his heart would explode. Debris had cascaded upward and was now falling back to earth in slow motion, as if taking time to rearrange itself. He looked behind him. The sky lit up and he could see all around the circle of undulating land, as if he were standing in an open field on his grandfather's farm.

"Irish!" he shouted. "Irish! Where the hell are you?"

He straightened, all the way up, and fell again to his hands and knees. Fragments of wood from the stretcher entered his night vision: a triangular piece of torn canvas, flesh, soft pieces of something scattered in a perfect circle like the sky overhead.

"Where?" he shouted.

But there was nothing. Irish and the boy had disappeared.

There was nothing to put into his hands.

The noise started up again. Or maybe it hadn't stopped and was only now re-entering his ears. His hands groped a three-foot radius on the ground around him, his palms connecting. "Bone," his voice said, slowly and deliberately, and he began to name each object that his hand felt and his eyes could see. "Strap, sleeve, button, finger." For his right hand had clamped around a wide and thick finger.

He stared at it, unbelieving, through the dark. He shouted, and shook out his hands and jumped up, staggering back. He rubbed his hands against his trousers, scrubbing, scrubbing, and shook them out again. The sky lit up briefly. He looked down at his own feet and willed them to move. Boots, legs and arms were studded with dirt and blood. He saw out of his peripheral vision another stretcher, one that had been propped against a broken wall, abandoned, he didn't know why. Why would anyone abandon a stretcher here? It seemed odd, out of place. A furrow in the ground tripped him but he regained his balance. "Stretcher," he said. "Casing, lantern, rifle." For there in front of him was a signaller's lantern on the ground, and beside it an upside-down rifle, its bayonet stuck in the dirt. Someone wounded must have been picked up here, the rifle left behind.

He had no plan. He kept his body tall, ramrod straight. He kept walking and walking and tripped over a German sandbag that had burst and he entered a trench to the right of the one he and Irish had recently left. He walked past two men he did not recognize, tripped over one of Fritz's fire steps that now faced the wrong direction, kept going, turned a sharp angle to the left, and continued. The trench seemed unusually low. Instinctively, he ducked, head down, his training kicking in, though there was no danger here. He did not pause as he passed another soldier and a voice said, "You all right, mate?" Something about his face must have jarred the man because the soldier looked at him and then quickly away.

Jim did not alter his pace; he looked past the man and kept on. A two-foot remnant of earth, a crest more solid than its surrounds, rose in front of his feet and he stepped around it and headed towards the place in the woods from which he and Irish had come. Stumps were pointing to the sky in silhouette; he noted these as he kept on, always heading back. He heard another voice, his own voice, reciting, singing now, at the top of his lungs in body-racking sobs: "*IN FIR TAR IS IN OAK NON IS IN MUD EELS IS IN CLAY NON IS . . .*"

An officer stopped him. Clamped a hand firmly on one shoulder. Forced him to stand face to face.

"Hold on," he said. "Hold on a minute. What's your name?"

Jim looked at him. *Lieutenant, vertical scar, right cheek, old wound. Someone he knows?*

"My name?"

"Name." *Gently now. The man's voice.*

Jim's mind scrabbling. *Hold on. Hold on tight.*

Chim. Better. Better now.

"My name is Chim, sir. Jim."

"All right, Jim. Get yourself back to the dressing station. They'll take care of you there. You can get back to your unit from there, too."

Chapter 20

The Influenza epidemic continues unabated. Its ravages are not confined to this city or Province or even to Canada, and cable reports indicate that it is rapidly spreading over the civilized world. It has baffled medical skill to an unusual extent and has claimed more victims perhaps than any other epidemic in a score of years.

How to Fight: Avoid crowds, coughs and cowards but fear neither germs nor Germans. Keep the system in good order, take plenty of exercise in the fresh air and practice cleanliness. Remember, a clean mouth, a clean skin, and clean bowels are a protecting armour against disease. To keep the liver and bowels regular and to carry away the poisons within, it is best to take a vegetable pill every other day, sugar-coated, made up of May-apple, aloes, jalap, to be had at most drug stores, known as Dr. Pierce's Pleasant Pellets.

The Napanee Express

Thunder, in her body. The way the shadows moved across the curtain, the storm must be far off. A half-light morning. If she could somehow raise herself, push away the bedclothes. She looked at the walls and tried to attach her gaze to a familiar object: bureau, wardrobe, washstand, jug. No framed daffodils. The mirror with the reed trim was gone, leaving a faded oval shadow. In place of the mirror, a small wooden cross, hanging from a nail. One of the hall tables was at the end of the bed. Why? And why enamel plates on its surface? She tried to answer her own questions but words scattered in her head as if they had never been joined in thought. She tried to move one foot but the foot was heavy. Legs were heavy, too, ankle to knee. There was a bucket on the floor beside her. A slight turn of her head and she saw what was inside: a ragged cloth spattered with red. The smell—menthol, garlic, onion—what? The odour was coming from her.

At the side window, shadow and light. The blind was pulled down as far as the sash but the zigzag crack let in a jagged glow. She thought of Tress. They had spied on the travelling ladies who'd sat on the upper veranda next door. She forced herself to focus. The bed across the room was empty. She remembered, then. Tress moved out before Kenan came home. She closed her eyes and sent a silent message. Maybe Tress would come back and take the stench away, open the window wide, help her. *Help.*

She moved her hands over the cloth that covered her chest and realized what she had not known before. She was weighted with poultice—wet and stinking. The door opened just as she scraped the soggy layer from her chest and dropped it into the bucket. Mildred, wife of Dr. Clark, with her frayed nurse's bag and her wide, knowing smile, entered the room. Stepping out from behind her, Tress rushed past and kneeled at the side of the bed. Mother, her grey hair pulled back in a bun, stood in the doorway. Her expression was anxious, uncertain. As if forbidden, she moved neither forward nor back.

Tress's lips were the first to move. "You've been in and out of sleep." She dragged her fingertips up the length of the opposite arm. *Long time.* She lifted Grania's hand, held it gently, began to rub her wrist, her dry dry skin.

"Fever," she said. "High. Very high. For nine days. I was not allowed to come to the room. You've been sick for three weeks."

Mildred opened the brown leather bag and lifted out thermometer, drinking tube, green soap, two thick masks—one of which she tied on. She handed the other to Tress and told her to wear it. Mother, who had stayed back until now, crossed the room to the front window. She raised the inside pane and propped it with the stick that rested on the sill. The blind got away from her and flapped upward, and Grania winced in pain as light shot into and behind her eyes. The blind was tugged down again. Mother left the room, pulling the door shut behind her. She tried to smile at Grania as she went out but her face was taut. Grania saw the attempt at the smile and thought, *Sorrow.* But Mother was gone. Replaced by shadow and light.

Mildred and Tress were speaking behind lumpy masks that smelled like turpentine and disinfectant. They looked as if they were chewing behind the cloth, chins bobbing. A faraway part of Grania wanted to laugh but she could not laugh. Glances were exchanged above her. *What?* They did not seem to understand that she wanted to rest her eyes and her aching chest and her weary weary head.

Tress reached for Grania's hand once more and rubbed with the same soft pressure. Her fingers seemed to be saying, *Don't slip back. Stay with us.*

Mildred pointed to the bucket, pulled down the bedclothes, peeled off the remaining layers of poultice under Grania's back. Thermometer under the tongue. Mildred's blue eyes, close and calm. Grania had known these eyes, the face behind the mask, since she was a child.

The thermometer was withdrawn and examined while Tress accepted a jug of hot water from arms at the door. The blankets were removed from the bed and Grania was covered with a large flannel before she was rolled and turned and washed, Tress propping her from behind. The odours were taken from her, peeled like layers of old skin. She'd been soaking in foul oils, herbs, onion, she didn't know what. She coughed, and her lungs filled with a heaviness so terrible she laboured to get one breath in, one breath out. Mildred's chin moved behind the mask and she and Tress exchanged glances again. Mildred rubbed a wet cloth over Grania's temples. Tress nodded and made the sign for sit, for chair. Grania felt Mildred's strong arms pull her forward. The room swayed, circled, swayed again. She knew that if she were moved she would lose consciousness. But she felt Mildred's will steady her on the edge of the bed.

A fresh gown was slipped over her head, and as it was tugged down over her nose she tried to inhale, to pull the clean scent of it inside her. Then, both feet were on the floor. Tress and Mildred were on either side and Grania was lifted, half dragged, to a chair by the window. This puzzled her for a moment because it was Mamo's rocker, her heavy arm rocker, brought up from the veranda. There was confusion over seasons. One season or another, Grania had no recollection of it being carried into the room. Someone had been sitting, rocking, maybe sleeping in Tress's empty bed, watching over her at night. *Mamo?*

Grania looked towards the window, eyes squinting. She wanted to banish the heaviness, to have her body somehow drift outside. She wanted to feel the padding of leaves underfoot. If she could walk the shore, enter the woods—*had she fallen?* A flicker of memory. *The shoe pushes into the leaves, shoosh shoosh.* First, she would have to know what was going on. It was difficult to keep her eyes open. She tried to think things through, but her head was in a muddle and she was too tired to ask.

Tress's eyes stared above the mask that pouched over her cheekbones. Grania watched Mildred strip the bed, roll the pillow cloths into a ball and remove a strip of rubber sheeting. Mildred had begun to hurry—or did it only seem that way because Grania's vision had slowed? Mildred must have other patients to visit.

Tress stirred a teaspoon of aspirin powder until it dissolved in water, and she waited while Grania gargled and rinsed the back of her throat. The two women lifted her into the newly made bed and tucked the blankets under her chin. Grania closed her eyes. *Jim,* she thought, for the first time since she'd been awake. *Chim.*

She remembered nothing more until she woke and saw that darkness had slipped behind the blind. Once more the stench slid into the room and lay beside her. She wondered if this might be

Death, if Death were in her bed. She'd been harshly wakened from the most wonderful dream about an orange, its juice squeezed onto her tongue. Every drop made her stronger. She looked around her and saw a jagged crack of light but did not know if time had elapsed or if anyone had come into the room for twelve hours, or twenty-four, or forty-eight. Sometimes a shadow sat in Mamo's chair; sometimes the chair was empty. Someone rocked, or the chair tipped back and forth by itself. There was a faint scent of Canada Bouquet. She opened her eyes and saw Father. Another time, Bompa Jack stood over her. *There's still a good leg on the cook. He would find a new husband for his sister Martha. Everyone was laughing.* But no, Great-Aunt Martha was gone. Died in the spring. A year ago? Two? Bompa Jack walked to the door, paused, looked back. Was the bedroom door open or closed? Grania saw a flash of metal before he disappeared.

What she could not know was that, downstairs, a fourteen-inch Quarantine card had been fastened to the parlour window for the past three weeks. Nor could she know that the hotel had been closed and that passengers had not been allowed to detrain or disembark in the town. From her bed Grania could not see the black crêpe nailed to the front door below. Nor could she read in the town paper: "*All that was mortal of this beloved mother, mother-in-law and grandmother was laid to rest in Deseronto cemetery. The attendance at the funeral as well as the floral offerings indicate the esteem of a large number of citizens.*"

Mamo's illness and death had been swift. *Unfortunate victim of the Influenza epidemic.* Her grave had been dug through brown and brittle grass and hardening earth. The surrounding trees were bare of leaves. "Loved and loved us dearly" had been carved on a dull flat stone that had been erected only two days before. The grave, as she requested, was on the side of the hill, high above the grey-green waters of the bay that for half her lifetime had reminded her of a soft shore in the beautiful land called Ireland.

*

Grania woke with no more energy than she'd had the day before. Day? Week? She could smell kerosene that had been poured into the drains of the house and though the odour made her gag, she recognized what it was. She tried to pull herself to a sitting position but ended up rolling onto her side, looking helplessly towards the door. One arm hung over the mattress.

Someone will come.

She stared at the door as if her will alone could force a body to enter. She looked at her dangling hand, which, of its own accord, flipped over, palm up, and made the sign for *die*. Well, then, there it was. Her hand had done this without any help from her.

Fragments of a dream burst through her consciousness. She and Jim had been standing together on the ice of a pond. Death was with them, but was waiting in dark water below. Jim tried to help Grania to shore, but each time they moved, the ice cracked underfoot. She managed a step but the ice shivered and dissolved and she felt herself slip under. She opened her eyes to darkness and held her breath, and stayed down where it was deep. The water pressed on her from above.

Someone was reaching for her, pulling her up, and she clung to the bank, half in and half out of water. When she looked back she saw that Jim's legs, body and shoulders had disappeared. His face, above water, showed confusion, helplessness. He scrambled to get a finger-hold in drifting ice and pulled himself forward and tried to flip his body up and over the edge. He tried again. Grania, now safe on the bank, willed him to her side. She willed him to safety.

*

The family believed that she was out of danger. She read this on their faces when they came to the room. They no longer wore masks. Mother, Mildred, Tress came and went, holding fluid to her lips and changing her sheets and gown. She barely saw who was there. She knew that no one else saw Death, that she was the only one aware of its presence, lurking close.

Death was waiting for her to break, she knew that. Beneath the covers, one of her fists snapped downward and made half the sign for *break*, for *broken*. A picture of Bridie, at school, came into her head. Young Bridie with the heart-shaped face, the irrepressible grin. The rapid hands that refused to be interrupted. *Don't break my talk*, she used to say to the other girls. *When I make story, don't break my talk.*

Tress walked into the room and Grania lurched into the present, distancing herself from the figure that hovered boldly at the end of the bed. Tress looked as if she had just faced punishing cold; her cheeks were red from the walk along Main. She rubbed her hands together and warmed them before helping Grania to wash and change into a clean gown. She handed Grania a cup of juice. While her sister's back was turned, Grania looked at the cup and then over to Death. Memory bubbled up, the *Sunday* book close to the surface. *Here, said the Mexican. Drink this.* Grania could kill Death. She could put poison in her cup and offer to share.

Tress faced her again. *Sorrows of her own.* Everyone who came into the room carried sorrow. Tress's cupped hands pulled down through air, the sign for *now*. Her lips said, "I want you to walk to the chair."

Grania turned her head away and refused to read Tress's hands or her lips. She did not want to be encompassed by Tress's energy or her sorrow.

But Tress would not be put off. She fluttered her hand in front of Grania's face to get her attention. "Mildred said you have to get up every day from now on. Dr. Clark said so, too." She added this as if to give weight to the order. She pointed to the empty rocker.

Grania's legs trembled as she leaned into her sister and took uncertain steps. Death turned a shoulder in disdain as they passed. She dropped into the chair and tried to catch her breath. Surely her breathing was loud enough to be heard. If so, Tress was not letting on.

Grania cast a sideways glance and shuddered. If Tress would stay in the room, she might not sink back. But Kenan needed Tress at home. She couldn't ask. She deliberately turned her attention to her sister, forcing herself to speak. Her voice was jagged in her throat.

"Tell me what month it is."

Tress nodded. Her lips and one hand formed *November*. She flicked a finger from the back of her wrist to show time. "I was up before five. Kenan still has trouble sleeping. When he gets up, I get up too." Two fingers popped off the opposite palm—*get up*. She slipped a strip of sheeting under Grania's arms and knotted it behind the chair to keep her upright while she made the bed. Even so, Grania slumped uncomfortably.

"Kenan?"

But Tress did not want to talk about Kenan. Was there still anger inside her sorrow? Grania saw no trace of it. Well, then, what about Bompa Jack? She wanted to ask if he'd been in the room.

What is real and what is not? asked Dulcie.

"Bompa Jack," she said. "Was he here? When I was sick?"

Unexpectedly, a quick grin across Tress's face. "You saw him? You saw the gun?"

Had she misunderstood? Had she missed a word? No, she couldn't have, because Tress was miming a rifle held, a trigger pulled.

"Gun?"

"He came to town when he learned how sick you were. He brought the rifle from the farm—the one he used when he shot the wolf. He laid the rifle on the floor under your bed—it had to be lengthwise." Tress drew a finger up the length of one arm. "He insisted that the steel of the barrel would draw out the fever. No one was allowed to argue. He brought eggs, too. He wanted to mix them raw with homemade whisky for you to drink, but Father said no. Mother shouted when he came with the gun. Maybe she thought he would shoot you."

Grania laughed for the first time since before she had sunk to her knees in the woods. At the sound, Death recoiled in the corner.

"What else?"

"Uncle Am sneaked up one afternoon and stuck an ace of diamonds in your shoe. Left shoe. He said it wouldn't work in the right."

"Shoe?" Thumbs rose and fell. Arms weak. *Which?*

"Black, two-strap. From the closet. He put the shoe under your bed, beside the gun."

Grania nodded and glanced towards the closet door. She was creating pictures.

"The enamel plates? Did I dream those?"

"They were brought up from the warming oven in the kitchen when you were clapped—chest and back. Mamo did that . . ." *A flicker. Something. Tress's face.* She continued. "Everyone had a remedy."

"Mamo?"

A pause. "Has a cold. Won't come to the room while you're recovering." Tress stepped behind her quickly, to adjust the sheeting.

"The mirror. Why is it gone?" Grania pointed to the oval shadow on the wall, the cross that hung in its place. Someone had prayed.

Tress, in front of her again.

Something to hide, something to tell. Once more, Tress turned away.

"Tell." The childhood demand. *Tell me at once, said Dulcie.*

"Your hair, Graw." Tress came back, and leaned over her.

Grania raised a hand to her scalp.

So much effort to lift an arm.

How could she not have known? Her scalp was soft and bare. There was no hair, none at all. Her fingers ran back and forth over her head until her arm tired, and she lowered her hand to her lap.

"Bring the mirror. The one you gave me when I went to school. It's in the top drawer."

She was too weak to hold it, but Tress propped it up while Grania stared at a thin face and bloodshot eyes and the bony outlines of a scalp.

"It will grow back." Tress's lips were insistent. "Everyone says so. Mildred. Even Dr. Clark."

*

Grania lay back against the pillows and stared at the rectangle of window above Tress's old bed. The curtains had been fastened back now that she was able to bear the light. Except for Death at its post, Grania was completely alone.

She remembered Mother coming in and sitting on the bed and telling her she'd been talking to herself and could be heard through the wall at night. Although Grania was surprised, she didn't care. I hardly ever sleep, she thought. I lie in bed and dead men march through my dreams. Dead men who will never come back. I think of Grew, and Kay, and wives and babies and fathers and mothers who are left to grieve. I think of all of these.

She dared to think of Jim. She had forbidden the family to write to him to say that she'd been ill. He must not know. She did not want him to worry. He had to stay focussed and keep himself alive. She brazenly brought the picture of him into her mind. His leanness, his earnest face under the brown hair, his muscular back, his long arms, his slender fingers and hands. During her illness she had not had to fight off the daily fear that the boy from the telegraph office might come to the front door. Before that, every time she walked through the hall she tried not to look in the direction of the street in case a silhouette could be seen on the other side of the glass. When the boy did come, she hadn't been there to see. Tress had received the telegram about Kenan and had read it before Grania even knew it had been delivered.

She thought about the nights she had lain in the dormitory at school during her first year away from home. The countless times her lips raced through the chants: *Don't let me live here forever. Don't let me be an orphan. Let me go home again.* Father told her to name her fears boldly in the dark.

Don't let Chim die.

She had not seen her husband for three years. If he were here now, she would have something new to tell him about being deaf. Something she had not known before. That when she had been so sick, her body had been deaf all over. He would want to know about that.

Through the upper part of the window she looked at the flat line of sky, more white than blue. She was sorry that from here she could not see the bay. The branches of the single tree outside were bare and motionless. She had forgotten what month it was; she would have to ask again. As she lay in her bed and stared at the tree, a hawk dropped like a miracle from the sky and rested on the branch closest to the window. She held her breath. The long tail, the grey markings were inches away from the glass. For a moment, she and the hawk were still. Then, in a flick, it was gone.

She turned her head and made an attempt to pull in deep breaths. She coughed and tried to exercise her lungs. Orders from Mildred. *Expand your lungs. This is the most important thing to do.* She thought of Jim and vowed to gather, bargain, summon whatever was needed to get well. She did not glance in Death's direction. She willed herself to cough again. She expanded her lungs, and expanded them again. She tried to cough some more.

Chapter 21

I am lost without him. I sincerely hope it ends soon for me . . . I feel I would just as soon be pushing up daisies as living like a gopher in this place, with all my dear friends gone.

Letter from the Front

Never before had he talked to the dead. Now, the only real conversations he had were with Irish. With the living, he was silent. The replacement had arrived, his new partner, a decent boy who'd come directly from training in England. His name was Hirtle, and he was from Nova Scotia. He tried to tell Jim about his girl in England, his friends who had joined up and where they were and what had happened to them all. But Jim did not want these bursts of intimacy. He did not want to be unfriendly; he did not want to get to know anyone new, exchange stories or backgrounds. The promotion was offered again and, this time, Jim accepted.

"Do you remember cracking hickory nuts?" he said to Irish. "Do you remember how plentiful they were? That first fall I stayed with Uncle Alex, we had a sackful to bury. We collected the blackened husks after the frost, and if they didn't come down on their own, we climbed the tree and tapped the branches to help them along. There were trees all along the fenceline. If the husks didn't crack open then, they did after another good frost, once they were in the ground. Before winter, we dug them up and put them in the root cellar. Uncle Alex asked me to take some to Dr. Whalen, and I did.

"In the winter, we spilled out a heap of them on the floor in front of the stove. Placed them one by one on a two-foot section of rail someone had given Uncle Alex—a railroad man—and we cracked them with the shaker. Aunt Jean placed a piece of oilcloth under the rail to catch the shells, but no matter how careful we were, bits and pieces scattered around the kitchen floor."

He paused, thinking of the nutmeats inside each cool brown shell.

"There was a hickory tree on every farm, Irish. You must have grown up with them all around." He stared at nothing, tried to keep the conversation going.

"Cambrai was taken on the ninth. The Canadians, the Royal Naval Division to the south, everyone was so strong. The Australian infantry fought their last; they captured Montbrehain on the fifth, before they handed over to the Americans. Cases poured into the dressing stations in our area on the eleventh—Canadians and Imperials—so many, we had to call other sections to help. By the twentieth I was in a truck, driving through Douai.

"Fritz has not treated the civilians well, Irish. As we move forward we see people who are horribly undernourished and thin. The young men were taken away. I saw two girls who might have been twelve and thirteen, digging a grave. A man's body was on the ground beside them. I heard the shovels hitting earth, grating against rock. A stray dog ran down a path, its ribs showing. Stash would have whistled for it, made it his pet. I passed the scene in a moment, but the sound of the shovels stayed in my ears all day. And the look in the girls' eyes—I knew they would not stop until they'd dug the space they needed.

"We receive great welcomes in the villages and towns. But Fritz has been looting as he retreats. Even roadside niches are bereft of statues. The engineers are busiest of all; every bridge has been blown up along the way. There are booby traps, too, and warnings of poisoned wells. But the billets get better and better as we move forward. Our dressing stations are treating civilians now—I was embarrassed at first, because most who come in are women. I'm no longer embarrassed—they are only needy and hungry and in want of medicine and care."

Jim did not say aloud what he was also thinking. How one night after a fourteen-hour shift he lay on a stretcher and tried to sleep and realized only then that he had not thought of Irish the entire day. He had forgotten his friend in the midst of chaos and responsibility and fatigue. He had lain there, staring into the dark, feeling a uselessness that was mixed with betrayal and shame for being alive.

"Next stop for the Canadians and the Imperials may be Mons, Irish. The end of the fighting is near. Five weeks. If you could have managed five more weeks. I have already written to Clare. I sent the letter to the address you gave me. I'll visit your parents, and I'll visit Clare, too, if I ever get home."

Chapter 22

11/11/18: France: Canadian Corps 0645 aaa Hostilities will cease at 11 hours on November 11th aaa Troops will stand fast on the line reached at that hour which will be reported to Corps HQ aaa Defensive precautions will be maintained aaa There will be no intercourse of any Description with the enemy aaa Further instructions follow.

Grania was pulling herself to a sitting position when Tress, pale and excited, and waving a newspaper, burst through the door. "Come to the window, Graw. You must," she said. "I'll help." She ran to the bedside, but Grania insisted on getting up by herself.

A crowd had gathered on the steps of the hotel. Men and women were on the veranda and even more were walking down the middle of the road. Everyone was waving and laughing. Children at the edges of the crowd were striking pots and pans with sticks and wooden spoons. Grania watched rhythmic hands rise and fall. Some of the arms were shaking handbells. Automobiles draped in flags were driven up and down the road. Occupants waved their hats in their hands and people jumped out of the way. Two figures in an open car were dressed like Charlie Chaplin, each with a brush moustache. They waved their Charlie Chaplin sticks and pointed them to the sky. Grania recognized Mr. McClelland, the town baker, his stern face opened in laughter. And she saw Cora, watching everything, her lips moving non-stop. A man on a splendid white horse rode up the edge of the street, just below the boardwalk. He turned and rode back. Was this the horse of one of her Irish great-uncles, ridden in the July parade? ..

Bernard was downstairs on their own veranda, talking to several people. Men were shaking hands and hugging the women in the street. There was a glimpse of Mother in a black dress below, and then she was gone.

Grania's heart was beating quickly. "What?"

"The war. It's over. News started to come in by wire at three this morning. The Kaiser has run away. The noise is unbearable outside. I came as soon as I could. Kenan is at home, trying to see from an upstairs window."

Grania looked down at the Ottawa paper that Tress had thrust at her and which she had dropped to the floor. An oversized headline read "PEACE!" and below that: "WORLD WAR ENDS; ARMISTICE SIGNED; KAISER IS OUT; REVOLUTION GROWS."

"Father?"

"Out there somewhere, in the street. Jack Conlin closed the post office and rushed here to get him. Bernard said he would stay at the hotel to keep an eye on things."

"Mamo?"

Tress's face. As if she's been struck.

"We couldn't." She clenched her teeth hard, and breathed out, and then she looked directly at Grania. "We couldn't tell you, Graw, not when you were so sick."

It was certain, then. What she'd been afraid to ask. Grania's legs gave out without warning. She felt Tress's arms tighten around her. Tress half dragged her back to the bed. They sat on the edge.

"The orange," Grania said. "I dreamed the juice, squeezed onto my tongue. It was Mamo who looked after me."

Tress nodded.

The empty chair, rocking.

"The flu?"

Tress nodded again.

"When?"

Watch the lips. Tell.

"Just as you began to get better, when the fever came down. It was so quick, Graw. The funeral was three weeks ago but Dr. Clark said you couldn't be told until you were strong and well."

She has no recollection of October. It is gone, lost to her. And she is not strong and well. She has only tried to come back for Jim. But she has not thought of Mamo. Somehow she kept believing that Mamo was there. Mamo has always been there, to help her live. Mamo, who wiggled her fingers to show the love moving back and forth between them moments after Grania was born. Now there was nothing but emptiness. Nothing at all.

Mamo removed every trace of yellow from the room because yellow was the colour of death.

Mamo was in the rocker all those nights. The scent of Canada Bouquet.

Mamo nursed her back.

They held each other, the two sisters. They were so, so tired. They held each other, and though Grania's body was shaking, and the whites of her eyes were streaked with red, it was Tress who cried and cried and cried.

Chapter 23

Resolution: The Deseronto Town Council requests that the Prime Minister, Sir Robert Borden, demand that the Kaiser, his sons, and members of his staff—civil and military—be brought to the bar of justice in the same manner as any other notorious criminals. And further, that all those of the German people or their allies who may have been in any way responsible for such atrocities as have scandalized the world, be similarly dealt with so that none may escape.

Minutes of the Regular Meeting

Jim was safe. Patrick was safe and still in England. Dr. Whalen's son and Aunt Annie's son were safe. Letters and papers were scattered about the floor as Grania sat in the rocker and read. She was up more hours in the day now.

One morning when she was alone in the house, she made her way to Mamo's room, pausing to lean against the wall to rest along the way. The blinds were pulled. She sat on Mamo's bed and looked around her in partial darkness, her breath quickening, the old feeling of tightness constricting her chest. She held it in, pressed it close, remembered Mamo telling her that some grief was so big it had to be kept inside. Understanding this was no solace. There was no energy to fight bleakness or despair. Mamo was not there to love or be loved. She was not downstairs, reading in the parlour, or rolling out dough in the hotel kitchen, or sitting at the family table drinking P-Ko tea. Grania could not turn to see her coming through the doorway, to take her arm as she walked back along the hall. Mamo had become ill, and she was gone from Grania's life, and now there was only emptiness where she had been.

Grania stood, but before she returned to her own room, she went to the bureau and lifted the stopper of Mamo's Canada Bouquet. She had to steady herself. She held the small bottle to her nose and breathed in the scent, and tried to keep it with her all the rest of the day. And for days after that, she went back to the room, and inhaled the scent, and sat on the edge of Mamo's bed.

*

During the weeks that followed the November eleventh celebrations, the newspapers had much to say about the end of the war. Picton had held a torchlight parade. Belleville celebrated with fireworks and bonfires and a long torchlight procession. The deaf children at the school wrote about seeing crowds of people who were ringing bells and about men and woman dressed up in funny costumes, parading through the streets. Confetti was thrown, and talcum powder, and children blew whistles, and flags were waved. Men had put the figure of the Kaiser on a wagon and horses had pulled the wagon around the city.

There was speculation about how and when to get the boys home, and everyone had an opinion. The cowardly Kaiser had run away and the Dutch had let him in. Uncle Am came to tell the family that eight days after the Armistice, the town council passed a resolution that was to be sent to the prime minister, in Ottawa. A thousand copies had been printed. Some ended up in the hotel lobby, and Uncle Am dropped one off in the parlour downstairs.

The aviation camps, Rathbun and Mohawk, were closing, and the authorities were wasting no time. The engines had been taken out of the aeroplanes, coated with Vaseline, and were stored away.

Grania thought of Patrick. She wondered if, when he came home, he would miss the buzz and manoeuvre of aeroplanes around Deseronto's skies.

After the Armistice, too, the school paper arrived in the mail. The superintendent had put in a notice about the Spanish influenza being almost eliminated from the school. "All restrictions, all indulgences that resulted from its prevalence, are now removed." The embargo on the receipt of mail and parcels had also been lifted.

Of all the papers that came to house and hotel, it was this one, from the Ontario School for the Deaf, *The Canadian*, that Grania decided to save for Jim. Because this was the one that described the Armistice celebrations in words of sound.

She thought of Fry. She thought of Colin who had tried so many times to join up but who had never got to the war. She thought of the hundreds of children at the school and how they would have learned about the Armistice from hands and fingers and lips. She thought of the hearing superintendent and the hearing staff at the hospital and the hearing matron and hearing teachers and hearing dorm supervisors, and she thought of Cedric, the hearing editor, who had printed in his paper, for all of the deaf community scattered about the province, the country and the continent to read:

In the wee sma' hours the bells in the city of Belleville began to ring, and every work shop, factory or yard that possessed a steam-whistle blew that whistle; and every person that owned a bell rang it; and every train that passed through the city wasted the company's steam in blowing a continuous shrill whistle that wakened the heaviest sleeper and made every old cow grazing peacefully near the tracks lift her head in wondering surprise. There were church bells, fire bells and dinner bells; steam whistles, horns, bugles, trumpets, fiddles and tin cans; milk pails, tin trays, enamel dishes, old kettles and biscuit boxes. There was noise enough to reach to the furthest planet in the heavens. But who cared? Din? It was music, grandest music, and the very sound of it was life-giving, hope-inspiring, the very best noise we ever expected to hear.

V

1919

Chapter 24

Princess Hair Tonic
We do not guarantee that our tonic will grow hair on the back
fence, or make long flowing hair with two or three weeks' use, or
cover a bald head with a two-inch growth of hair with a week's
use of our remedy. No, all we claim is that our tonic is the best
hair tonic and hair grower ever produced, and if used as directed,
will do all any hair tonic can do.

Wednesday afternoon. The hands showed ten minutes before one
on the O'Shaughnessy clock. In the morning, Grania had done
nothing more than stand at the porthole on the back landing and
watch the birds as they flew in hungrily to pick at seeds and crushed
corn she had set out below. Bernard came through the passageway
from the hotel, and she met him in the downstairs hall.

"Grainy? Do you still want to go?"

She nodded. "Stop worrying. I'm all right." The last words
melded together like a song; she could feel them. She slipped into
her coat and covered her bare head with the blue hat Mamo had
knitted two winters before, and she wrapped her scarf tightly
around her neck. Soft snow was puffed along the veranda railing.
The tree branches, too, were pocked with snow. She was well buttoned up when she crossed the street and walked the short distance
to the barbershop, holding tightly to Bernard's arm. It was no

longer snowing, but the clouds were low and heavy and allowed only scant light, even in the middle of the day.

Grew watched from his window as they stomped the snow from their boots. During the epidemic in the fall, he had closed his shop for two weeks. Aunt Maggie said that other public buildings had been forced to shut for a short time: Naylor's, the library, their own hotel with the Quarantine card in the window. Some of the people in town wore masks while they went about their business. Grania tried to imagine the town coiled in upon itself while Death swept through. Death had taken its place in her room, but it was Mamo and not she who had been swept away. She tried to imagine Mamo's grave. She had not been taken to visit and would not see it now until spring. She had asked Tress and Bernard, separately, to describe it. When she thought of Mamo, she hated the part of herself that was so well trained she could not cry.

The bench outside the barbershop was piled high with snow. Bernard picked up the broom that leaned into it, banged out the snow and did a last sweep of the bottom of his own and Grania's boots. He swept the bench with a few flourishes for good measure. Grew was still watching from the window, finishing his lunch where he stood. He swallowed a chunk of bread and bolted the last of his tea as they came through the door.

He's thinner than ever before, Grania thought. All because of the news that Death brings. *Grew had staggered across the parlour floor and his hands had pounded the keys of the piano. His bony knees popped up because the piano stool was wound low. Finally, he'd permitted Father to take him home.*

He wiped his hands down the front of his drill coat and greeted them by raising a finger in the air as if he were about to conduct a secret meeting. It was as if the three of them had formed a prior conspiracy and now found themselves face to face in the same room. He reached towards the top of the window and tugged down the blind. He turned the Closed sign outward, and lowered the blind on the glass door as well.

A single light hung from the ceiling and created a central glow in the room as if it, too, were part of the secret. *Thumb to the lips— private.* Grew's finger touched his lips, as if to say *Shhh.*

Light from outside seeped in around the edge of the pulled blinds. Grania's glance darted at the shadows thrown across the walls, and then back to Grew's yellow-toned skin. She looked at the skin of her own hands and saw that it too was yellowed by the light. She removed her hat and handed it to Bernard. Under Grew's inspection, she felt the blood rush to her cheeks.

He shook his head, slowly, deliberately. She could see his tongue. "*Tst tst.* The red hair," his lips said. "The lovely red hair. Eyebrows, too."

Bernard had already sat in an empty chair by the window, and now he grinned encouragement. "Go ahead, Grainy." He pointed to the leather chair. "Sit up there."

The tray to the side of the chair was lined with clippers, razor, a thin pair of shears. Her fingers grazed the strop hooked under the armrest, and she settled back. Grew pumped the chair and adjusted it so that Grania was facing him. Bottles and jars were stacked close together on the mirror shelf, and sent out odours of pine tar and alcohol. She had already seen the soaps and shaving cakes on a shelf of their own by the sink.

"This is what we do," said Grew. He exaggerated the words on his lips the way he had always done, believing this helped her to understand. He covered her from the neck down with a weighted apron, and wrapped a warm towel around her throat. The odour of alcohol, she now realized, was coming from him.

He lifted the caps from two small blue bottles. Mamo had taught her the colour. They'd practised the word together the afternoon of her eighth birthday, IN-DEE-GO. Grania had been given an indigo scarf and wrapped it around her neck and paraded around the house, trying to look grown up. *Dulcie's mother declared that the scarf made her look too old.*

"Glycerine," Grew's lips said. "Jaborandi."

Grania looked over to Bernard, who shrugged and tried, unsuccessfully, to spell the last word with his fingers. Grew watched and waited and smiled as if he'd been permitted to witness communication between members of an exotic tribe.

He held one of the uncapped bottles under her nose, something unidentifiable. Not entirely pleasant.

He turned the chair to face the mirror, and tilted it back before she was able to get a long look at herself. The mixture dripped onto her scalp—she felt the wet pool of it—and Grew's fingers began to draw circles along her temples and the top of her head. His fingers moved with such pressure and firmness she was forced to relax, and she sank back and closed her eyes. He massaged the contours of her scalp until her head was throbbing, and he applied a small amount to the area where her eyebrows had been, taking care that the mixture did not drip down over her lids. After what seemed a long time, he positioned the chair upright and pushed the towel farther down and massaged the back of her head and the base of her neck. When she checked the wall clock she saw that she had been in the chair only twenty minutes. *Dulcie sat on the barber's stool surrounded by swirls of hair scattered in a circle about the floor. Never had there been so good a barber.*

"Good?" Grew said. "The circulation—better?"

She smiled for the first time since she'd entered the shop. "Better than goose grease." It was her voice that had spoken. Her hands moved and the sign flicked off her fingers before she could stop them.

"Ah," said Grew, "poultice."

"Not poultice," said Bernard. "They rubbed goose grease and turpentine on her skin when she was sick. That was only one of the remedies."

"I heard about the rifle," said Grew. He tried to smile but the attempt only forced a grimace between his gaunt cheeks.

He took up a second cloth now, and wiped away all traces of oil so that none would come in contact with Grania's clothing. He removed the apron that covered her and unwrapped the towel from her neck. She felt lighter, bare. But calm.

"Next Wednesday?" He wrote a note to himself on a jagged scrap of paper and nodded to Bernard. "I'll add a dash of sage for scent. I'll make up the mixture ahead. Same time?" This to Grania, the last two words exaggerated.

Grania thanked Grew softly and slipped down and out of the chair. She was still buttoning her coat when Grew walked to the end of the room and reached up to the wall cupboard. He stood by the open door, tilted his head back and drank from a bottle. Tress had told her that Grew was taking Veronal now, along with his drink. Now that the production *and* sale of alcohol were forbidden, no one knew his source. Not Father. Since Mamo's death, Father had been staying home.

Grania followed Bernard outside, her scalp tingling under the hat. She looked back, but the blinds were tightly pulled and she could not see so much as a shadow inside. Grew had made himself invisible the moment they left.

They crossed the street and passed Cora of the prying eyes, and Grania managed to muster a smile. They passed Meagher's store, and she looked in and saw Aunt Maggie standing by the counter. She tapped the window and waved, and Aunt Maggie turned and saw her and blew a kiss. Grania allowed herself, in the chill air, to receive it, along with the faintest wisp of hope.

Chapter 25

Someone has sprung the question: "Can the deaf think?"
Why not ask a few more: "Can the deaf eat?" "Can the deaf
sleep?" "Can the deaf breathe?" It strikes us that the fool-killer
misses a good many possible swats with his club.

The Canadian

Saturday morning, she kept going to the window to watch for the horse and cutter that would bring Fry. The road from Belleville was still hard-packed with snow. The thaw had not fully begun though the days were warmer. Most of the day, sunlight streamed through the south-facing windows. Soon, the cutters would be put away in the barns until next winter. This was the season when Patrick, as a boy, had taken an axe and a pick to chop and shape channels through the ice and snow, front and back, to drain water away from the house as the snow melted. Mamo had once leaned out of the upstairs windows with a hoe, poking at and detaching the fattening, dripping icicles that hung from the roof.

Mamo's rocker had been brought down to the parlour. Grania noticed that no one else used it these days, except herself. While she sat, she felt as if she did not have a plan in her head for the future. There were days when she had the energy to do nothing more than sit in Mamo's chair and wait for Jim to come home. Sometimes, upstairs, she stared out at the icy waters of the bay. Jim was in England, maybe Wales, she was not sure which. Patrick, too, though they had not met up with each other.

She had just received a letter from her brother. Along with tens of thousands of others, he was waiting for a ship to bring him home. The letter arrived in Canada quickly; it must have gone directly into a mailbag that was put on a departing ship. He wrote that the locals had declared it to be the coldest winter for years. He was in North Wales, a place called Kinmel Park, and there weren't enough blankets to go around. The men were restless, and anxious to get home. Many had been ill with the deadly influenza when it swept through.

The next stage will be to Liverpool, across the bay, but so far, on the camp bulletin boards, we see no postings for ships about to sail. There was a time when we weren't getting much food and one of my friends—his name is Victor—and I found our way into a Red Cross hut and sat on the floor in the dark and ate the only thing we could find—plum puddings from Canada that weren't given out when they should have been, at Christmas. There were hundreds of them on the shelves. I must have eaten a dozen, myself. I lost count. But I paid for my appetite a few hours later, and couldn't keep a thing in my stomach for two days. It was same with Victor. A week after that, all hell broke loose in the camp. The boys were restless and tired of waiting, and the situation became bad. There were riots, but we stayed clear. We are lying low, staying out of trouble, and plan to do nothing more than sit tight, do what we're told, and wait for our ship.

A horse and cutter came into view and there was Fry, next to Colin, who held the reins. Grania quickly pulled on Jim's jacket and ran outside. Fry waved and had already begun to sign before the cutter stopped. Two women, hotel guests, stepped out and crossed the hotel veranda next door just as Fry jumped down.

Grania hugged her friend and held her close. She had not missed the shock on Fry's face when Fry saw her thinness and her short short hair. She detected a faint scent of lavender now, and remembered how her friend had placed crumbled bits of the dried stalks in her bureau drawer at school. The two friends were signing rapidly, Colin too. It was only after a few moments that Grania sensed the two women watching and looked up to see that they had stepped down to the cleared boardwalk and were staring as if the three friends were performing a sideshow. *Dulcie frowned when she saw that the travelling ladies disapproved.*

Fry's hands spoke. "Never mind." Her hands fell to her sides, hands that were trying to hide. "We'll talk in the house," her lips said.

Where no one will see.

But Grania's hands were burning to speak. It had been months since they'd conversed, their bodies leaning towards each other, their hands and fingers bringing forth the news.

Colin led the horse around the back to the drive shed, and Grania and Fry followed him part way and stood by the side door. Fry was perfectly still, her head tilted down a little, while she waited to go in.

Grania looked at the face of patience on her beloved friend.

She has become more tolerant, and I less, she thought. She remembered Fry's visible frustration when they'd been students, when sign language was being used less and less. "As long as we permit hearing teachers to disapprove of our language," Fry had once signed—her hands moving rapidly—"we will always be made to feel ashamed."

But Fry would not respond to Grania now. She would wait until they were in the house. In private.

Tress came to the side door and greeted Fry with a hug. "Where's Colin?"

"The horse," Grania replied. With voice. Why did she feel she was betraying Fry by speaking aloud? "The horse had to be taken back." She pointed in the direction of the drive sheds.

And fell into the dark pool. The pool that was always there, waiting for the slip between sign and voice. She sank into the memory that had brought her to its edge. Words, always words that weighed like stones. *The horse had to be taken back.*

From lips around her when she was a child she had seen and read, *taken back, taken aback*. Sometimes one, sometimes the other. For a long time she had thought they were the same.

"I was quite taken aback," Aunt Maggie had once said to Mother, when Grania was in the room. She had looked offended at the time. Grania, eavesdropping the lips, did not know what the conversation was about.

Taken aback where? Where had she been taken?

Grania had never asked. It was one more mystery to add to the others she carried inside her. Years later at school, when the words finally tumbled out, it was Miss Marks who intercepted and explained.

"Put an *a* before *back* and the meaning changes," she said. "To be taken aback is to be surprised—by something unexpected."

One more complication. The language of the hearing was never simple. Language is our battleground, Grania thought. The one over which we fight, but with no desire to be part of the conflict.

The news brought by Fry and Colin was about Colin's job. Once again, he had been offered work in a printing office in Toronto, and this time he had decided to accept. He would finish out the school term and Fry, too, would stay at her job until June. But there was bigger news. Fry would not be looking for work in Toronto. They were starting a family. Fry had not wanted to tell Grania by letter, but she signed excitedly to her now. The baby was due in October.

When it was time for her friends to leave, Grania stood at the door while Colin went back to the drive shed. Before putting on her gloves, Fry cupped a hand and smoothed it down over Grania's skull and the hair that was slowly growing back. They hugged, and Fry batted away her tears, and Grania stood in the doorway, looking down the street, a long time after the cutter disappeared.

Chapter 26

Tramp, tramp, tramp, the boys are marching,
I spy Kaiser at the door.
We'll get a lemon pie and we'll squish him in the eye,
And there won't be any Kaiser any more.

Children's chant

She expected word of Jim's arrival any day. Already, it was April. Was she still talking in her sleep? She would ask Mother. If so, it would not be a surprise. Her body was jittery. Every day by three o'clock she wanted to lie down. Instead, she walked through the passageway and helped out in the kitchen or dining room, changing linens or setting tables. Never before had she experienced this kind of fatigue. If Mamo were alive she would say that Grania's blood was low, and would reach for the blackstrap molasses. But Grania had gagged over it at school, a spoonful every day, and knew she could not stomach it now.

Grew no longer came to the hotel lobby to read papers across the room, but Grania wished he would. Lately, she had been reading about the after-effects of the Spanish flu. Many people had become deaf after recovering from the illness. The doctor who wrote one article said that most cases would likely be permanent. For people who have lost their hearing, he wrote, it will be like starting their lives over again.

The way Grania had relearned the language when she was five? And Nola? And Bridie? And Fry, who would always rely on the language of hands? Some children managed voice and some did not. Every one of the deaf children at school had been sent there by parents who hoped that some miracle would prepare them—for what? For a new life that would miraculously be found?

Grania's losses were different.

Mamo.

But she could not cry.

Mother came into the room, waving a telegram. Grania had no way of knowing that the boy from the telegraph office had delivered it to the front door. Mother smiled when she put it in her hands and stood beside her for a moment, before she went back to her work.

Jim would be home the following Friday. He would take the train from Halifax. Grania immediately wrote to Fry and arranged travel to Belleville on the Thursday. She wanted to stay with her friend the night before, but she would meet Jim at the station alone. She would insist on being alone.

I told you, Grania, I'm coming back.

I've told you all along.

*

Early Thursday afternoon, she sat in the parlour and tried to read. She put the paper down; news did not interest her today. She walked to the window and looked out. An auto drove by slowly in the rutted road and turned up Mill Street. There were two men inside. She walked to the hall and checked the clock, but the minute hand hadn't changed since the last time she looked. She laid her palm on the polished wood and thought of Mamo.

She had four hours to fill before she could board the train. Her case was packed. Fry would meet her at the station in Belleville. She went through to the back and shoved her feet into a pair of Father's old boots at the door, and stepped outside. She hugged her arms and stood on the slippery stoop behind the laundry. Although it was windy at the front, here she was in perfect shelter. She looked up to the windows of the hotel, where Bernard had reserved the largest room at the back for her and Jim. She had moved her clothes over the day before. The bed was made—she had changed the linen herself. Unlike Tress and Kenan, she and Jim had no house of their own, and could stay at the hotel as long as they liked. Until they decided what they would do and where they would go. One place they were sure to go was to the sea. In Jim's letters since the end of the war, he had promised to take her to the coast during the summer. He wanted to show her the island where he had lived and grown up. *It's important for us to go there*, he wrote. *Soon you will be able to stand on a cliff and face the sea, and feel sand on your bare feet. And I will tell you about the ocean's roar.*

She turned her face to a spring sky of hazy blues. Unless clouds moved in, there would be a worthy sunset in the evening. She felt a hand on her shoulder and almost slipped as Mother hauled her back. Mother shook her head, concerned about her being out without a jacket, and Grania didn't argue.

But she was still restless.

Just as she started out to look for Bernard, wondering if he had gone to visit Kay, he came looking for her to say that she was wanted at the door. She was handed a note from Tress, delivered from one end of the street to the other by the Jamieson twins. They were dressed in tweed trousers and knitted sweaters and identical caps, and seemed to merge momentarily in their efforts to become a single messenger. With self-importance, the two thrust the envelope at her and watched her face as she read. The message was grim.

I can't pace here another second. Tell Mother you're coming for tea. I know you're leaving in a few hours but if you are ready and packed, do you have time to stop in? Kenan has been lying in bed all morning and refuses to get up. He turns away from the window, and won't even look at the light.

Back towards the light. Grania thought of Miss Marks at school: *To lip read, you must sit with your back towards the light. The light should fall on the speaker's face.* But Miss Marks had never seen Kenan's half face. Or Tress's face since Kenan had come home.

Maybe the time had come to walk out with the O'Shaughnessy bag, Mamo's old clock bag with the shoulder strap. *When things get bad.*

*

She crossed the street and tried to hurry, but a sudden weakness in her left leg took her by surprise. Every time she was feeling fit and strong, her body let her know that it would not be hurried in its healing. Her limbs moved, but at a pace of their own. The weight of the burlap bag over her shoulder did not help. She thought of the *Sunday* book. *Toiling through the woods.* A boy carried a load of sticks on his shoulder, his knees buckling under the weight. A dog, one paw lifted, seemed to be offering help—or at least encouragement.

She glanced to the right. Despite the railway tracks and the buildings between the street and the water's edge, most back alleys afforded a glimpse of the bay. In the afternoon sun, light bounced off its partly frozen, shrinking surface. Uncle Am would soon be scratching a new date into the beam of the tower: *Ice out.* The boardwalk was damp, the road a mess of spring mud.

But there was a wildness, an energy in the street. The wind had picked up and was gusting into her face. Though she was slowed by the force of it and by the weight of the bag, she kept on. She gave the strap a little hitch and the contents shifted against her hip and thigh. If Cora were to pass by, her nosiness would get the better of her. But Grania would not tell. "Potatoes," or "apples," she might say. Or "It's a bag full of the red hair that fell out of my head. I've saved every strand since fall."

She was still going to Grew every Wednesday, escorted by Bernard. Every second week, the first thing Grew did—after pulling down the blinds—was to measure what he declared to be the longest hair on her head. He did this against a piece of string, which he held to her scalp with his thumb and then knotted. He stretched the string alongside a spring tape measure that was kept in a small brass-bound case. He held up the knotted string, and though it seemed to her that there was no new length to measure, the hair always measured an extra eighth of an inch. Grania did not know if the treatments were helping or if the hair would have grown back anyway. "You see," Grew told her, offering his sad smile, "the treatments are working." The string was hooked over its own nail beside the mirror. Except for Grania, Bernard, and Grew, no one else knew what it was for. The knot farthest from the end measured more than three inches now. But the hair that had grown back was darker—not as thick as it used to be, and it was a deep auburn instead of the bright red it had once been. But it was growing back. And soft. Softer than it had ever been. When she was alone at home, she sometimes sat on the edge of the bed and rubbed her palms over her skull. When she pushed her hand forward, the hair was smooth; when she pushed it back, it was like sliding her fingers the wrong way through velvet. The growth was uneven, the hair slightly longer behind her ears.

"There is a nerve there somewhere," Grew had explained, exaggerating his words. "That is why the hair grows faster in those spots." Around the crown, growth was slow. No matter how much Grew massaged, the hair in that one place balked at coming in.

After each treatment, Grew still headed for the cupboard the moment she and Bernard were about to go out the door. He was never able to wait. He did not seem intent on being secretive, but he was partly concealed when his head tilted back behind the cupboard door while he drank straight from the bottle. He never looked them in the eye as they stepped out. Grania was passing Grew's shop now, and she looked in at the photograph of Richard in uniform, still leaning against the window.

She was wearing her knitted hat and she was warm under her spring jacket, but part of her welcomed the wind knocking against her as she continued towards the far end of Main. If only she had as much energy as the wind. She would shout into it. The wind could scoop up her voice. Unknown to her own ears, her words would disappear into the sky.

She would shout for Mamo and Mamo's life.

She would shout for Grew's son, Richard
  and Kenan and his wounds
  and Kay's husband, Lawrence, and their fatherless son
  and Orryn, who marched proudly into Bonn after the cowardly Kaiser fled; and who shot away the helmet-spike, nose and ears from the statue of the Kaiser; and who wrote in a letter to Kenan that a German bystander implored him to blow the head off, too.

She would shout for Jim's friend Irish, whom she would never meet.

And for all of the boys who had died; and for all the people who were sorrowing.

The wind could have all of that.

She thought of the soldiers returning, the ones who had been deafened during the war. There were so many in this area of Ontario, classes were being held in the Belleville school, in the same rooms in which she had studied as a child. A lip-reading system had been adapted for them; she did not know who was doing the teaching. Fry wrote that a teacher had been sent to Boston to take the course so that she could come back to teach the soldiers.

War and flu. Separate causes, similar losses. Deafness, even baldness. On the home front it was clear that hundreds, even thousands of men and women had become bald because of the Spanish flu. Until she read about the search for remedies, she had believed that she was the only one. The only one she knew of in Deseronto—unless others were in hiding. Extreme high fever caused the hair to fall out, or so the experts said. So many bold claims were made for new hair restorers, it had become an embarrassment to read the advertisements. Blend in, that was what the newly bald persons were advised to do. But blending in was something she was already good at. Every deaf person was an expert.

Except when your hair falls out. What then? Doesn't that make you rather conspicuous?

Jim might not recognize me. Jim doesn't even know I've been ill.

Tress was at the front window of her narrow house, looking out. From the sidewalk, Grania could see the puffiness around her sister's eyes. She might have splashed cold water over her face but she had not managed to hide her sorrow.

Grania stepped inside the enclosed porch and set down the burlap bag. She had not been here for several weeks. She slipped out of her shoes and into the slippers she always left here. Tress led her to the parlour, pointed upstairs, pointed to the clock and looked away. Kenan might be listening. Kenan, who had left here dancing. His days of soldiering over. Kenan, who had taken several steps forward but, stuck inside the same nightmare, kept slipping back.

Grania tried to picture him upstairs in the bedroom. She thought of what Tress called the "dead arm" that had bruised her skin, the arm that lay between them like a corpse in their bed. It wasn't the arm; it wasn't even the half face. It was the terror inside him that wouldn't let go.

"Put on a jacket," she said. She didn't give Tress a chance to blurt out what she had stored up to tell. "Bundle up. There's a wind."

She returned to the porch and gathered up her outdoor shoes and the bag. She carried them through the house to the back door that faced the bay.

She put on her shoes again and stepped out to the yard. Tress followed. Grania ignored the sign *Why?* that flicked off the side of her sister's temple.

They were in shelter and could not be seen from houses left or right because of the trees and the shed. Grania had spotted a suitable place, and she pointed to it now. Near the bottom edge of the yard, a striated boulder was perched where the sloping ground descended to the rocky shore. The boulder was three feet high; Grania and Tress had sat there together last spring, their feet tucked under their skirts while they looked out at pleasure boats in the bay. Now, bundled up, they stood in the wind, fifteen feet from the same rock.

Grania opened the O'Shaughnessy bag and reached in. She probed gingerly and lifted out a pale green cup and handed it to Tress. A chip was missing from the rim.

"Throw," she said. She pointed to the rock.

"Throw? Are you crazy?" Tress made the old crazy sign beside her ear, fingers bent, wrist waggling.

"No. Not crazy. Mamo and I, we did this sometimes."

Dulcie throws a cracked cup against the fence.

"You and Mamo? Where?"

"Near the woods. By the bay. Past the old coal shed. Next time we walk there, I'll show you. When we were finished, we covered the pieces with rocks. Now throw."

Grania had a milk-white saucer in her hand. A deep crack was forked across its surface. She positioned it between forefinger and thumb, tilted her body at a slant and let go. She saw but did not hear the saucer hit, and watched the shards fly high. She gave a whoop and flicked out both palms and signed, *Wonderful!* She reached back into the bag.

Tress was watching, her mouth open, her jaw dropped.

"Close your mouth," Grania said. "It's rude. Throw."

Tress looked at her own hand as if the green cup were attached. She pulled back her arm, pitched hard, and exploded into laughter as the cup smashed. The wind blew furiously as if catching the mood. Green and white fragments lay at the base of the rock. *More,* Tress signed. Fingertips touched fingertips. *More.*

Each of them threw a monogrammed hotel bread plate with Y-shaped cracks. They let them fly together and the plates spun through the air and dropped.

"Where did you get these?" Tress was laughing so hard she was doubled over. She had to repeat so that Grania could understand.

Grania read her lips and grinned. "I have a supplier. We saved them until they were needed."

"We?"

"Mamo and I. We threw them before I left for school in the fall and when I came home every June. Other times, too." *When things get bad.* "There will be more. Mrs. Brant keeps the cracked ones. She's my supplier."

At this piece of information, Tress looked astonished.

"Mother?"

"She never knew. Still doesn't. Mamo stored the dishes in the clock bag. In the O'Shaughnessy trunk."

"All those times you and Mamo said you were collecting rocks . . ."

"We were smashing dishes. But we brought rocks back, too."

It was Grania's turn to laugh. She pulled out a glass and tossed it underhand. It shattered on top of the boulder and the pieces sat in the hollow like an archaeological find. "That was for Chim," she said. She wasn't laughing now. "For missing Chim. For all the danger."

"This is for Kenan!"

Grania saw the shout on Tress's face. Tress whammed a gravy boat into the side of the rock and followed it with a sugar dish lid. "For the dead arm. The swinging arm." She yelled again into the howling air. "For his beautiful face." She sank to the damp tufts of old grass where the last bit of snow was clumped, and she began to cry. The wind whipped the tears until they were streaked across her temples.

"Stand up," Grania said. "Stand up and finish. This won't work if you give up. Can't you see that Kenan will walk out of the house when he's ready?"

But Tress stayed where she was.

Grania flung a vinegar stopper, which twirled clumsily and crashed. "That was for Cora. The last time she talked to me she said, 'You poor little thing. It must be hard to be alone without your husband.' Do you know what I said? I said, 'Alone is easy. It's being *with* people that is hard.'"

She dug into the near-empty bag. "This is for Mother. Who tries to hold things together, I know. But she has never given up the guilt

and, because of that, we might never get past it." It was a small plat-
ter but it was the heaviest dish, the hardest to throw. It connected
with the boulder, and its jagged pieces sagged to earth.

Grania slumped to the ground and put her arms around Tress.

*Everyone was afraid of something. Grania had been afraid that
Jim would not come home from the war. Kenan was terrorized by
what he had been through. Tress, of what she and Kenan had to
deal with. Bernard was afraid to make a move towards Kay, but
now that he had begun a slow courtship, he might have the courage
to go on. Mother was afraid when Patrick became Vince and ran
away to war. Father, afraid he couldn't keep the hotel going to support the family. And now, Mother and Father, both, feared the
loneliness they'd created between themselves.*

*Had Mamo been afraid? She had rocked in the chair at Grania's
side every night because she'd worried that Grania might die. She
had kept everyone away from the room until the fever passed, so
that no one but herself would be in danger. Other hands had
pushed trays of food, fresh linens, fluid in bottles through the doorway.*

*Grania had not hung the picture of daffodils back on the wall,
and she never would.*

Grania had not said goodbye.

"You're crying," Tress said. "Graw, you're crying." Tress pulled
herself up off the ground and now she reached for Grania's hand
and pulled her up, too.

Grania felt the struggle, the column of air pushing up. She began
to sob, her chest heaving in and out in rapid breaths. She tasted salt.
Her tears were salt. She could not see through the crying. She tried
to look into the darkness of the clock bag. Her hand groped and
pulled out two china saucers. *For Mamo's P-Ko tea.*

"These are the last," she said. Her face was wet, her cheeks
unwiped. "These are for Mamo."

Help me. Help.

She gripped one saucer and handed the other to Tress. As she did, she glanced up to the bedroom window. The two of them stared up. Kenan had pulled back the curtain and was at the window, watching. They didn't know how long he'd been there.

Grania waved, and Kenan raised his good arm and made a throwing motion through the air. She and Tress turned to the rock and pitched the saucers with all the strength they had.

They faced the bay then, both silent. Grania reached up with a palm and wiped her tears.

"Now," she said, "we'll go inside. We'll tell Kenan to come down for his tea." Her thumb and index finger stirred into her left hand, *tea*. "After that, I'll catch the train. And we'll clean up the pieces when the rest of the snow melts."

Chapter 27

The train shook the platform and rattled Grania's insides. She was close to the crowd but alone, and separate, and behind. A band was playing to the left of the station, back a little. Her body was aware of the rhythmic beat of the drums. Ahead of her, beyond the train, the sky was the clearest blue.

She saw him the moment before he stepped down. Eyes that were earnest, but old. *Old eyes.* The train loomed behind him. He was in uniform, and she thought of the creases she'd pressed down the sides of the last pair of civilian trousers he'd worn.

His face was fuller. He looked taller, as if he'd grown.

From her first glance, she understood. She knew now that it was like returning from the land called *School.* Only this time, Jim was returning from the land called *War.*

She would never know where he had been. Nor would he know where she had been.

He looked at her. Eyes intent, alert, searching his own.

"Wife," he said aloud.

She was wearing her long spring coat and a hat he had not seen before. It was blue and had a turned-up rim and was pulled low over her forehead. He could not see the red hair that must be tucked up inside. Her eyes were round and large under the brim of the hat.

Eyes and nose and lips and face. Face pale, thinner than he remembered. How was he to believe that he was home?

Tears flowed down her cheeks for the second time. She watched as he made his way between men and women on the platform. His eyes never left her face.

"Wife," he said again. And then, "*My* wife." He could not stop the sob.

"Sorrow," his lips said then. His body lurched forward. The peach-basket lady was standing on the platform, watching. The troops hung out the train windows, shouting and laughing. Most were travelling on to Toronto and points beyond.

Grania caught the edge of Jim's last word, caught it sideways as she circled the crowd. She felt his hands, the weight of them as they pressed down upon her thin shoulders. He pulled her towards him. Hands and arms held her gently, tightly, against the rough wool of his tunic. She leaned forward. He felt her stillness, her strength.

Sorrow, she said to herself, and she thought of Kenan at the upstairs window of the narrow house, of Mamo's grave that she had not yet seen, of herself and Tress throwing the last of the saucers from the O'Shaughnessy bag. *Sorrow can be borne.*

She shaped the *C* and the *H* and she said aloud, "Chim." She pulled back, to see him, and her hand reached up to his face. She ran her palm over its wholeness, one cheek, and then the other.

He is different, she said to herself. But some things are the same. For now, we will live in the present. That will have to be enough. Until we are better.

She looked at his lips; she touched them.

"Grania," he said. "Say my name. Again."

He heard the soft laughter. The sound of her.

The sight of her.

His arms tugged her to him again. The train was moving off, sliding out on its cross-country journey to a distant ocean. This time, she did not pull away to see if he wanted to speak.

Acknowledgements

My sincere thanks to staff members of Sir James Whitney School (former Ontario School for the Deaf), Belleville, Ontario, for welcoming me and permitting archival access to school newspapers of the period 1900–1919. Excerpts from *The Canadian* are, by and large, as I found them. Special thanks to Keith Dorschner, Archival Coordinator, and his wife, Christina, who responded to my many questions and arranged to meet me each time I travelled to the school; also to Cheryl Manning and former Superintendent Paul Bartu.

I acknowledge the generosity of Louise Ford, Executive Director of the Ottawa Deaf Centre, who arranged for me to work within the volunteer program and directed me to important resources; and Jon Kidd, President of ODC, and head of Sign Lines Canada, a skilled and insightful teacher of American Sign Language. Many others tolerated my barrage of questions as I struggled to learn ASL. Among these, Bonet Hebert, Les Sicoli, Maria Bossio and Carol Fowler. Warm thanks to Sherri Cranston for sharing her many insights during our weekly interviews; and to Oliver Sacks, whose *Seeing Voices* was helpful for its extensive bibliography.

Some of my accomplices as I researched Irish settlement in Tyendinaga Township: Bernard and Annie Freeman, octogenarians who responded to my ad in the *Napanee Beaver* and welcomed me to sessions around the kitchen table at their farm. Bernard's amazing memory filled in gaps about the history of pioneer farms along the Ninth Concession and my great-grandfather's Deseronto hotel. For help with Irish names, thanks to Dr. Mary Comerton, Barbara Lunney, Maura Strevens and Ronan Murphy. In Deseronto, Ontario, a big thanks to Bev Reid at the Town Hall for help at every turn. Thank you, Dennis Vick, Floyd Marlin, Stan Marek, Ken Brown (Archives Coordinator), and Irene and Tom Usher at the Town's Edge B&B.

For First World War research I am indebted to many friends for sending or lending documents, among them Margery Dexter and Wendy Scott, and Karen Fee for permitting me to read the war diary of her grandfather, William George Oak. Michel Gravel and I swapped books, letters and information. Carol Reid offered her considerable expertise and goodwill at the Archives of the Canadian War Museum; documents read include "A History of No. 10 Canadian Field Ambulance." I am especially thankful for permission to track the footsteps of Joseph H. Macfarlane of No. 9 Canadian Field Ambulance (Ref. 19800281) while I created my own fictional character Jim. Thanks to Jack Granatstein for permitting me to sit in his office and turn over my questions like slow stones, and Dennis Fletcher for his enthusiasm in locating war photographs at Vimy House. Thanks to Barbara Norman, Music Division, National Library of Canada, for her personal interest and remarkable expertise in First World War music. Lyrics from "Dear Hame hid awa' in the Glen" are by A. D. MacIntyre, 1904. A special thanks to Norm Christie in Ottawa, publisher of CEF Books. Of the many helpful CEF books, I acknowledge *Letters of Agar Adamson*, *The Canadians at Mount Sorrel*, and *The Great War As I Saw It* by Canon Frederick G. Scott.

Thanks to Bruce Cherry of Back-Roads Touring, in London, England, who toured me through the battlefields of France and Belgium; Susan Zettell, Jane Anderson, Terry Gronbeck-Jones, Rita Donovan, Joel Oliver, Jean Van Loon, Merna Summers, Fran Cherry and Larry Scanlan for sending or suggesting materials. Jackie Kaiser, my agent, was first to read the manuscript, and her support and enthusiasm are appreciated more than she will ever know. Thanks to Nicole Winstanley, agent, for her energy and goodwill on the international front. I am very grateful to my American editor, Elisabeth Schmitz at Grove/Atlantic, and British editor, Carolyn Mays, at Hodder & Stoughton, for their helpful comments.

Important among the many books read and for quotations used, I acknowledge Alexander Graham Bell, *The Mechanism of Speech* (1916); E. B. Nitchie, *Lessons in Lip-Reading* (1905); M. I. Ives, *Illustrated Phonics* (1909); Martha Bruhn, *The Müller-Walle Method of Lip-Reading for The Deaf* (1915); and *Sunday 1894*, a children's book published in London by Wells Gardner, Darton & Co. I acknowledge Clifton F. Carbin's *Deaf Heritage in Canada*; J. Schuyler Long's *1910 Manual of Signs*; the Champlain Society's *Ontario and the First World War*. Books about the Spanish flu by Richard Collier and Lynette Iezzoni were helpful, as were *Whisky and Ice* by C. W. Hunt, Kenneth Cameron's *History of No. 1 Canadian General Hospital Canadian Expeditionary Force 1914–1919*, Donald M. Wilson's work on the Rathbun enterprises, and D. W. Griffith's film *Hearts of the World* (1918). The children's chant in Chapter 26 is a variation of "Tramp! Tramp! Tramp!," an American Civil War song by G. F. Root (1820–1895). Jim's chant, "Infirtaris . . ." dates from circa 1450; this 1842 version was collected by Iona and Peter Opie in *The Oxford Dictionary of Nursery Rhymes* (1980). Every effort has been made to track original sources, but additional information about copyright is most welcome.

I acknowledge and thank The Canada Council for the Arts, Millennium Fund, and the former Regional Municipality of Ottawa-Carleton for grants awarded during the writing of this book.

Loving thanks to my Mother and my Aunts and Uncles, the eleven hearing children of my late deaf Grandmother. Love to my husband, Ted, my daughter, Sam, and my son, Russell, for encouragement during the long, exhilarating and often sad journey; and to Aileen Jane Bramhall, soprano, for her expert explanations about voice and song. To Russell, thank you for sharing your extraordinary knowledge of music, sound and silence. To Sam, thanks for the careful proofreading of the final manuscript.

Last but not least, a huge thanks to Phyllis Bruce, my Canadian editor and publisher, who checked in along the way, who found and sent garage-sale books and First World War sheet music and who waited patiently for me to finish at my own pace. Thank you, Phyllis, for your steady belief in the book and for your editorial expertise.